RUNNING AND JUMPING

Steven Kedie

RED DOG
UK

Published by RED DOG PRESS 2022

Second Edition

Paperback ISBN 978-1-915433-22-0

Ebook ISBN 978-1-915433-23-7

www.reddogpress.co.uk

For Lou Lou.
This book exists because you gave me a love of sport. I think you would've liked the story, but you would've phoned me about all the swear words.

And

For Matt Hulyer and Jo Cook.
For all the time spent and memories shared. I hope I did your words justice.

PROLOGUE

I AM SIX years old, sat next to my grandma on the floral couch, dressed in Spider-Man pyjamas, watching the Barcelona 1992 Olympic Games on TV.

Linford Christie is on the screen, the last few seconds before the Men's 100 Metre Final. That thousand-yard stare down his lane. No emotion. No tricks to put off his competitors. Full on focus. The runners line up. Best of the best. One of eight to be crowned King.

Marks.

I'm transfixed.

Set.

The runners are up from their blocks and moving, everyone coming to a stop a few metres in.

'False start,' my grandma confirms. I'm on edge, my feet bouncing on the floor, legs twitching.

Back to the line. Back in their blocks. Refocused.

Marks.

A long moment of pause.

Set.

The silence of expectation. Every second feels like months to me as I wait for the sound of the... Gun.

They're running.

Linford pulls away and wins. I'm off the couch, on my knees, like I've scored a goal at Wembley. I stand and look at my grandma. She's smiling. Happy for Linford, happier for me.

'I'm going to do that when I'm older.'

'Do what, Adam?'

'Win a gold medal at the Olympics.'

My dream is born.

PART ONE

1

Beijing, August 2008
The Olympic Games

I KNOW IT'S big. The smoothness of my approach, the speed into the board, the take-off, the height I get. I hang for what feels like hours. I land, pushing forward out of the pit. I look at the flag – white – and the marker boards, my imprint in the sand. The official measures the distance.

I bounce on the balls of my feet, trying to control the adrenaline pumping through my body, waiting for the confirmation of what I already know.

It's announced: 8.36 metres.

I have just jumped a new Personal Best, a new British Record.

I lead the Olympic long jump final.

I react with a shake of the fist to the camera, a short smile to everyone watching back at home, allowing myself a brief moment of celebration before I walk back to the seating area, to try to be cool and act calm, to convince my fellow competitors this is exactly how it's supposed to be, despite the fact there are fireworks going off inside my head.

We can't touch each other in this sport. During our jumps we can't push each other, lean on each other, hit, or kick each other. As a competitor speeds down the runway or pushes off from the board, all we have is how we act before, during, and after our jumps. That's how we crank up pressure, how we impact and influence those here to beat us.

I put my tracksuit back on and sit, surrounded by thousands in the Birdcage Stadium, alone with my thoughts. I allow myself a moment of flashback to Linford Christie, Spider-Man pyjamas, and my grandma's smiling face.

I'm in the gold medal position; living my dream.

Then I breathe and pull myself back to reality. This is the Olympics. The pinnacle. The best in the world are here and the fact is, 8.36 metres won't be enough to win. To leave here with the gold medal, I'm going to have to dig deep inside me and find more height, more distance, and improve my new Personal Best.

My third jump is a foul, but no one goes further than 8.36 metres, so now I'm three rounds away from gold.

From turning a dream into a reality.

At the end of the Third Round, twelve competitors become eight, and the jumping order changes. I'm leading, so I'll jump last. Second, will jump seventh and so on. Dan Hall, whose British Record I've just taken, is still there, hanging on for his last shot. We catch each other's eye and I wonder what it must feel like to know you've only got three jumps of your career left.

I wait to jump in the Fourth Round as Roberto Lopez nails 8.49 metres, pushing me from first to second, from gold to silver. I try to respond, concentrating on the basics, a smooth approach and take-off, but only manage 7.89 metres.

I fume at my lack of reaction to Lopez's jump. I sit, angry and tense as the Fifth Round starts, trying to control my breathing and focus on the fact I'm still in the silver position and one good jump can change everything. But, with the fourth jump of the Fifth, Chris Madison jumps 8.38 metres, moving me into the bronze position. Then, as I stand at the top of the runway watching Toby Williams jump and get measured at 8.43 metres, I take in the fact that in one round I've slid from second to fourth and out of the medals.

Now is the time to react, I think. Now is the time to show them all.

My run up isn't perfect, and I stretch into the board, somehow hitting 8.01 metres. I look at Len, my coach, in the stand and shake my head. He makes a gesture with his hand, encouraging me to calm down, to relax. I should go and talk to him, but we've been doing this long enough and I know what he's going to say. The simple fact is, I need to jump further.

Round Six. We're all thinking the same thing: one more chance. Everyone is tense and tired. Our legs and minds ache. I try to focus, but it's hard not to listen to the voice telling me I've got to nail this one. So, I watch Dan as he steps to the line. His whole career chasing Olympic Gold condensed into this one final jump.

Come on, mate, I think, one big one for a medal. Silver, though. Gold is mine. He starts clapping a rhythm and the crowd join in. The clock moves down: 0.47... 0.46... 0.45... He lowers his head and drives forwards, desperate for his last attempt to go over 8.49 metres and win gold, adding to his bronze from Athens. He's moving well. His turnover increases into the board and he's up...

Red flag.

I see it before he does and I bow my head, knowing what's coming.

Dan screams, 'Fuck!' to the Beijing sky and smacks the sand with his fist before slowly lifting himself up. He gives the crowd a dejected wave and walks away from the pit for the last time.

I switch my focus to the remaining competitors. The men in the medal positions jump their last jumps but there is no change to their order. Bronze: Chris Madison. Silver: Toby Williams. Gold: Roberto Lopez.

I've known since the jumping order changed that the last jump of the Olympic Final would be mine. I try to treat it like any other jump, like all the thousands I've done before, to not think that improving my Personal Best by fourteen centimetres means an Olympic Gold medal. I move down the runway and hit the board well, but as I'm in the air, I know it's not enough. My body wells with disappointment as I realise there'll be no medal.

I've failed.

IN THE MEDIA Mix Zone, I'm with David from the BBC.

'Adam, how do you feel having finished fourth in your first Olympics? A new British Record. You must be over the moon.'

'I feel pretty shit to be honest. Fourth is such a crap place to finish.' I see David's face drop and I realise I've just sworn on live television.

'Sorry,' I say. Before quickly adding, 'I'm disappointed I didn't improve on the Second Round. Everyone else got stronger as the competition went on. Three more centimetres and I'd have been in the medals. It's frustrating. That said, it's been a great experience and a real learning curve about what it takes to win medals at this level. I wasn't good enough today.'

I.

Wasn't.

Good.

Enough.

Words I know will haunt me tonight.

'Today aside, how has your Games experience been?'

'I've tried to take as much knowledge as I can from the whole thing. Hopefully, that can help me in the future.'

'And finally, just a quick word about Dan Hall. Retiring today. You finished ahead of him. Is this a passing of the baton between generations?'

'Not in my mind. Dan Hall is a great long jumper and has helped me a lot, especially in the last few days. He's been working hard to medal here yet was always happy to give me advice. The man is a legend in my eyes. I can't speak highly enough of him.'

'Will you buy him a retirement drink tonight?'

'If he gets me a birthday one.'

David laughs and asks, 'Is it your birthday today?'

'Yeah.'

'How old?'

'Twenty-three.'

'Well, something to celebrate there for you at least,' he says, 'Thanks for your time, Adam. Have a great night.'

'No problem,' I say, before adding with a smile, 'I'd just like to say sorry to all the license payers for my language.'

At the Village, I wait impatiently as we go through the motions of the security checks. Once through, I race to my room and sit on top of the single, standard issue, multicoloured, Olympics themed duvet, and unplug my phone from the charger on the small bedside table. I ignore all the messages and missed calls and dial her number.

It rings twice before, 'Hello.'

'I'm sorry, Grandma,' I say.

'Oh, Adam,' she says. 'You've nothing to be sorry about. I've heard you say worse than that in the back garden. Not that it's OK. But you said sorry. I thought you handled it really well. It's not easy when they interview you straight after a competition.'

'I meant for not winning a medal. I told you I'd win one.'

My grandma who, despite her desperation to, didn't feel up to travelling to Beijing, says, with a force I wasn't expecting, 'Well, you certainly don't have to be sorry about that. You make sure you get me tickets for when you win in London.'

'I will,' I say.

'I've recorded your final. When you get back, we can have a day in a few weeks, and we'll watch it together. You can talk me through all the details I missed on the tele.'

'That'd be good,' I say.

'Adam,' she says, her voice calmer. 'I'm very proud of you. You're chasing a dream. That's a special thing to do in life. And this is just the beginning. Not the end.'

'Thanks,' I say, my words barely audible. A tear rolls down my cheek and onto my tracksuit bottoms. I wipe it away, but another replaces it.

'Disappointment is OK. But don't let it ruin what you've achieved so far.'

She's right, as always.

I adjust my position and lean back against the bright white pillow. 'Are you OK?' I ask.

'I am. I called in on Margaret next door this morning and we had a nice cup of coffee. She's doing better since her fall.'

'That's good,' I say.

Fifteen minutes pass with me listening to updates from her life. I'm amazed at how she fills her days, especially since my grandad died. Always busy, always helping people, checking on, and looking out for them. She laughs as she tells me something one of my younger cousins did, then, almost abruptly, says, 'Right, that's enough from me. Now, listen to me, Adam. It's your birthday and you've just competed in an Olympic Final, so, I want you to promise me something.'

'What's that?'

'That you'll stop feeling... how did you put it so eloquently?' She pauses, searching for the right phrasing, then says, 'Oh yes, that's it, stop feeling so shit and go out and enjoy yourself tonight. Relax. Have some fun. Celebrate your birthday and your achievement. Do you promise me?'

I smile. 'Yes, Grandma.'

CLUB BUD. THE place to fulfil my promise.

Our group is a mix of swimmers, rowers, and a couple of sprinters whose games have already finished. Some wear medals around their necks, proud smiles on their faces. We stop on the red carpet outside the club and pose for the cameras.

Inside, at the bar, my senses adjust to the dark surroundings. This place has been the talk of the Village. I watch athletes, dressed casually in T-shirts that advertise the country they represent, dancing and drinking, mixing with former competitors. Our drinks arrive and we toast Dan's retirement and my birthday. Dan downs his first bottle and orders another.

As it arrives, I ask, 'How do you feel?'

'Strange,' he admits. 'I'm disappointed in my performance, but pretty sure I'll look back in ten years and feel I had a good career. That might change in the next few days, though.'

'At least you've got the wedding to keep your mind focused.'

'Yeah.' Dan pauses and, after a few seconds, says, 'Tonight's about not worrying about tomorrow.' Another pause. 'You pleased with a PB in your first Olympic Final?'

'Not really. I came for a medal.'

'Don't worry, your time will come.' He takes a drink then says, 'I'm gutted about that record. Would've been nice to retire holding that.'

I start to apologise, but don't. That's the nature of the game. Dan wouldn't have cared less if roles were reversed.

We move from the bar to go out to the terrace, passing through the dance floor. The room has large TV screens on every wall and another behind a booth where two DJs are playing dance music in front of a huge Budweiser sign. Chinese dancers, on raised platforms, move their bodies to the beat.

Outside on the terrace, under rows of red lanterns, more athletes and people associated with the Games and its sponsors drink free Budweiser. A TV crew film people who have jumped, fully clothed, into the swimming pool in the middle of the terrace. We find a place to stand near some large circular white sofas with half domed roofs and assess the scene.

'This place is crazy,' I say.

'Welcome to the Olympics,' Dan says. 'Once athletes have finished their events, they're like teenagers on their first parent free holiday.'

Our group swells and contracts as people see faces they recognise and start new conversations. Talking to people is simple here. There is a common denominator between us all. It's easy to smile at someone and say, 'Where you from? What's your sport? How did you get on?' Everyone has a story to share. The highs of unexpected medals to the lows of injury hit performances.

Henning Rudman, a German long jumper, sees me through the crowd. He leaves his group and walks slowly towards me, shifting his weight to his right side with each step. His hamstring snapped on his second jump of the Qualifying Round.

We shake hands and hug. We've known each other a long time through competition, and there's a genuine friendship between us. I ask about his injury and he shrugs.

'Nothing on the board in Round One. I was trying too hard. You did brilliantly. I watched you leading.'

'I wanted to be leading at the end.'

'You have something to celebrate. Your new PB.'

'It feels like a PB means nothing without a medal.'

Henning nods his understanding as a female athlete appears at his side and says something in German. Henning responds and then introduces us.

'Mia, this is Adam. Adam, Mia.'

She smiles as I reach out my hand and shake hers.

Dan appears and Henning turns to congratulate him on his career.

I look at Mia and say, 'What's your event?'

'Triathlon. I raced today.'

'How did you get on?'

'I was fourth.'

'Me too. My event was this afternoon.'

We laugh at the matching detail.

I ask about her race, and she tells me how poor transitions let her down.

'It was nice to meet you, Adam,' she says minutes later, when Henning indicates he's returning to their group. I smile and say, 'You too.'

The alcohol takes hold, and we move back inside to the now full dance floor. People are exaggerating moves, pulling poses. The speakers blast out 'I Love Rock n Roll' at one point and we raise our fists and loudly sing along. I'm unsure how much time passes, but I leave the circle and move through to the bar.

Mia appears beside me as I'm ordering shots. I offer her one.

The drinks arrive, and I slide a glass over to her. 'To finishing fourth. The worst position.'

'To London.'

We clink our glasses together and she tips her head right back as she downs the shot. Her face automatically screws up into a funny shape, and then she exhales a 'woo' sound. I take in the full view of her. She's attractive. Her body, as expected, is perfectly toned; formed from hours and hours of hard work in the pool, in the gym, on the road. I'm about to say something when she leans forward and kisses me. I move my arm to her back, pulling her closer. After a few seconds, our lips part. She laughs and then moves close to my ear and says over the noise of the music, 'Don't go back to the Village without me,' before disappearing back to her friends.

I stand at the bar, taking in the scene.

A voice cuts through the noise of the club. 'If I'd known you'd get the attention of a woman like that for finishing fourth, I'd have brought my medal out just to see how she reacted.'

I turn and see Chris Madison beside me. The man who beat me to bronze by two centimetres.

He's smiling, indicating he's joking.

I'm not ready to joke about finishing fourth.

I don't think I'll never be ready.

He senses my mood and offers his hand out to shake. 'I guess you and I are going to be spending a lot of time together.'

I stiffly shake his hand, realising that today is the first day we've competed against each other, despite being similar ages and at the top end of the same sport for a couple of years.

'What do you mean?' I ask.

'You and I are the future. The next four years will be all about us.'

I try to assess if he's joking or drunk. He holds a half-finished beer, but his eyes are clear and he's not stumbling over his words.

'That's a bold statement.'

We're both leaning on the bar, and I turn to watch the people in front of us enjoying the end of an Olympic cycle. He does the same.

'Not really. Think about it. Lopez, the new Olympic Champion. He's thirty-three. He might do another year for the Worlds, maybe two, as the Europeans are in his home country. But London? He'll be thirty-seven. Too old. Toby Williams is too injury prone. He's my teammate and all, but his hamstrings are fucked. Hate to say it, but he can't do the work required. Breaks down every couple of months. His silver jump was a lucky hit. Nothing more. Luka Cooke is thirty. Fifth in the Olympics is the best he's ever done. Personal best jump and still didn't medal. You honestly think at thirty-four he's going to improve that much? No way. Not in my time. Dan Hall has retired but you and I both know he hasn't been a threat since 2004.'

I turn to face him and say with a hardness to my voice, 'Careful, Dan's a friend of mine.'

'Doesn't make it any less true,' he says with a shrug.

I pause and take in his arguments. 'You're dismissing a lot of talented guys.'

'Like who?'

'Henning.'

'Talented, but not gold medal talented.'

'What about Luis?'

'If Luis finishes above us in London, you can fuck my sister.'

'Can I see a picture first?' I ask, allowing myself a smile.

He ignores me. 'I'm telling you. I got a bronze medal at the Worlds last year. Bronze again here. The next four years I'll be hitting my peak. My plan is to dominate. Way I see it, only you can stop me.'

Madison walks away, leaving me stood alone at the bar.

Beijing 2008 is over.

London 2012 has just begun.

Rival: *n* **1.** a person or group that competes with another for the same object or in the same field. **2.** a person or thing that is considered the equal of another: she is without rival in the field of physics.

Rivalry: *n, pl* –ries active competition between people or groups.

Source: Collins Essential English Dictionary

2

I WAKE ALONE, unsure what time Mia returned to her room. I lie still, allowing my eyes to adjust to the light that comes in through the curtains.

My body aches with the combination of post competition pains and a hangover. My brain is a cocktail of emotion and thought. The high of leading, the hollow feeling of others eroding my medal chances with better performances, the enormous frustration at feeling like I had nothing left to compete in the final rounds. There's pride in there at the thought that I'm the British Record holder, mixed with an anger when Madison comes into the picture inside my mind.

All of it, including Mia: the flirting, the dancing, the kissing, the awful late-night version of 'Happy Birthday', and finally, the drunken sex, race through my mind like a film being fast forwarded. I let it all play and finally it stops, Chris Madison the sole focus of my thought: *Only you can stop me.*

One drunken night wasn't going to erase the failure. Defeat often clings to me, especially when I know I could've been better.

I SHOWER AND dress, then walk to the Food Hall where I stand alone in the breakfast queue, knowing when I take my first mouthful everything in my mind should adjust. That's Len's rule, the system we've been following for years. Anger at losing is OK. Feel the pain all night, no problem. Hurt is good. Makes you never want to feel it again. But once you've taken that first bite of breakfast, focus must shift to what comes next. A training session or competition, anything in the future. That first mouthful is the reminder that work continues and the defeat can't be changed. It's not a perfect system, but it's helped me not lose some of my energy after events in week-long rages.

I find a spot in a quiet corner of the hall, pick up my spoon, dip it into my cereal and bring the food towards my mouth. My taste buds react, and I swallow the mouthful and think about London.

'I WANT TO be the Olympic Champion.'

Len, framed in the entrance to his room, says, 'Things are going to have to change.'

'Be brutal.'

He invites me in, and we stand: face to face, coach to athlete, man to man.

Len looks me in the eye and delivers his words in a slow, precise way. 'The first session I ever coached you in, you told me you wanted to be the Olympic Champion. And when I watched you jump, I knew you had the ability to be one of the best. But the problem is, sometimes you think your natural talent is enough. It's not. I've tried to tell you that talent will only take you so far. Frankly, I don't think that message has ever really sunk in with you. Your ability has taken you further than most. Fourth in the Olympics. Now you're in a tough position. Some people would think that by continuing to work in the same manner, naturally you will improve to higher achievements. I can assure you that will not happen. You will stall in your progress. To be fair, the fact we're having this conversation suggests a shift in your attitude.'

'So, what needs to change?'

'Application, work rate, and overall lifestyle.'

'And I thought you we were going to talk about the big stuff.'

His face hardens. 'This is what I'm talking about. If you want a serious conversation, have one. No jokes.'

I raise my hand to indicate I accept his point.

'If you want to improve, you have to give me total dedication. Every set of every session, every day, needs to be taken seriously. Currently, that's not happening.'

'OK.'

I fold my arms across my chest and listen.

'That said, you're not unprofessional. When you want to focus and listen, you're capable of working hard. But it's clear your level of work only really picks up as summer approaches. You make no secret of your love of competition, so I understand that change. That love is going to be crucial to achieving your goal. But this is not the UK Championships, Adam. If you want to be the best, you've got to act like the best. All the time.'

'I will give you everything.'

Len nods again. 'Training begins again on the last Monday in September. Come back focused and ready to work.'

'Only you can stop me…'

3

ON MY FIRST night back in the non-Olympic world I drive to Didsbury to meet Johnny and Pete in a pub. I order the drinks at the bar. Nodding to my glass of fresh orange, Johnny says, 'I thought you'd be having a couple of beers to relax before training starts?'

'I've given up drinking.'

'How come?'

'To win gold in London.'

I hand them their drinks and we move across the pub. It's Wednesday, a quiet night with couples on dates huddled across tables and small groups of women sharing bottles of red. We sit on low leather chairs in the corner by a small bookshelf filled with old leather-bound books.

The conversation is dominated by the inner workings of the Games and I confess my devastation at finishing fourth. They tell me how they got together to watch it with our other friend, Mike, and how they couldn't believe Madison beat me by two centimetres. I don't reveal my conversation with Madison, despite thinking about it a thousand times since it happened.

I've known these guys since I was eleven. They quickly settle into piss taking about me swearing on television. I steer the conversation away from Beijing and towards their lives. I ask about Pete's girlfriend, Laura, and how her trainee solicitor job is going, about Johnny's new flat, and Mike's hospital rotation.

My phone beeps, a text message appearing.

I thought you'd have called by now.

I type a response: *Been busy seeing family and stuff. How are you? Good. Do you want to meet up? I'm off at the moment. Tomorrow? I'll call you.*

Great x x

'You back in the room now?' Pete asks.

'Sorry.' I laugh. 'The busy love life of a nearly medal winning Olympian.'

Pete asks, 'Who is she?'

'It's that teacher from our school.'

Johnny looks at me. 'You're seeing one of our teachers? Is it Mrs Grant?' Pete laughs at the reference to our old art teacher who we used to joke was so old she was actually a ghost who haunted the school.

'No. She, Abbie, is a teacher at our old school, not one of our old teachers. I told you about her at the time. Santa,' I say, referring to one of the nicknames we had for our old headmaster, 'rang me and asked me to go in and talk about the build-up to the Olympics. An ex-pupil success story sort of thing. We're inspirations don't you know?'

Pete and Johnny laugh.

'Anyway, Abbie's a history teacher there. Started a couple of years ago. At the end of the day, I was in the staff room and she gave me her number.'

'What's she like?'

'She's all right,' I say, before sipping my drink.

'Wow. A romance for the ages. Just like Shakespeare wrote,' Johnny says, sarcastically. 'She's all right,' he repeats, his fingers forming quotation marks in the air.

I shrug. 'What do you want me to say? She seems nice. We had a bit of a flirt when I was at the school. She's attractive. I'm happy to see where it goes. She just got a bit intense with the texts and stuff before I went away, and I had to say I needed to concentrate on Beijing, and I'd contact her when I got back.'

The pair looks at me. Johnny says, 'You poor little Olympian with the girls texting you.'

'Piss off,' I say. 'It's not like that. I just didn't want any distractions. She's nice. I'm going to meet up with her after Dan's wedding.' My tone has become defensive.

'I'm going to need to see a picture of her,' says Pete.

'Why?'

'To prove she's not Mrs Grant.'

We all laugh.

Later, I drive them both home, dropping Pete off last. He opens the car door, gets out and, before closing it, leans down and says, 'We're proud of you, mate.'

I CAN'T SLEEP. I keep thinking about goals and focus, dedication and performance, Beijing and London.

I get up and go downstairs, and quietly open the door to my dad's office. I switch on the light and shut the door. I look at the framed photos on the wall. Mixed in with family portraits and a photo of my sister dressed as Dorothy from the *Wizard of Oz* are images, both colour and black and white, of me in action. In one photo the sixteen-year-old me is frozen mid-jump, legs stretched out high above the pit, face straining with the effort. Another shows me posing with my dad after winning gold at the UK schools' competition.

There's a new picture, showing me in my Team GB tracksuit weeks earlier, before leaving for Beijing.

I sit at my dad's desk. I take a writing pad out of his drawer and a pen from the pot and write: *I, Adam Lowe, will be the 2012 Olympic Long Jump Champion.*

I sign it, fold the paper, and put it in an envelope. I leave the office, walk to the front room, flick on a lamp, and stand in front of the bookshelf. I look at the dictionary and thesaurus, side by side. The books are packed tightly together, unused and unmoved in years. I slide the dictionary forward. As the book comes loose, another envelope falls to the floor. In its place I put the new envelope and put the dictionary back. I pick the other one up, sit in a chair, open it, and take out the contents. I read the words the nineteen-year-old me committed to paper. The words that have been the focus of my last four-year cycle: *I, Adam Lowe, will win a medal in the long jump final of Beijing 2008.*

I read the words, knowing I've failed.

My failure is in two parts. One, I didn't win a medal. And two, four years ago I should've written that I would win gold at Beijing, not just a medal. My dream is to be the Olympic

Champion, and I should've gone to China with the mindset that only winning gold was good enough.

I think about Chris Madison, the man who finished two centimetres ahead of me. The man who won bronze when I won nothing. The man who thinks the next four years will only be about me and him.

In the dark of the early morning hours, I swear to myself London will be different.

What some see as a life of sacrifice, others view as a life of dedication.

4

'LADIES AND GENTLEMEN, the bride and groom.'

We, the assembled guests, applaud as the newlyweds enter the room hand in hand, wearing huge smiles. They wave at people as they walk through their friends and families to the top table. Dan looks smart in his dark suit: the red tie, red handkerchief sticking out of his pocket, the three-quarter length jacket. His blond hair is styled with gel, a rare sight. He has looked relaxed all day, which is the first time since before Beijing I've been able to say that about him.

I'm seated at a table called *The Sopranos*, after one of Dan and Michelle's favourite TV shows, with a group of guests that include some of Dan's childhood friends and their partners, along with his sister, Hannah, and her boyfriend, Simon Lewis, a swimmer who I know.

Gareth, one of Dan's school friends, introduces himself and his wife and then asks, 'How do you know Dan?'

'I used to train and compete with him,' I say.

He says, 'You took his British Record.'

I shrug.

'I'm surprised he didn't pull your wedding invite,' Simon says, laughing.

I smile and say, 'I think he did and Michelle wouldn't let him.'

Gareth looks at me and Simon. 'So, you've both been to the Olympics?'

'Yeah,' we both say.

'This table is not going to do anything for myself self-esteem, is it?' Gareth says. 'Two Olympians. I can barely run a mile.'

Drinks are poured from the complementary wine in the middle of the table. I decline and pour myself some water from a jug.

During the starter, Gareth asks Simon, 'Are you going to London?'

'That's the plan,' Simon says, glancing at Hannah who is talking to Gareth's wife. 'Although we've not had the full chat about it.' He smiles. 'I'll work towards getting there.'

'How old will you be?' Gareth says.

'In London? Twenty-eight.'

'Bit old for a swimmer, isn't it?' I ask.

'Honestly, if it wasn't London, I'd retire in a couple of years.'

'What would you do instead?'

'What any self-respecting athlete should do.'

'What's that?'

'Reality TV.'

My phone buzzes with an incoming text message. I take it out of my pocket. On screen, there's a message from Abbie: *Are you still on for next week?*

I quickly type a response: *Yeah.*

Her reply comes through before I've put my phone away. *Great. Looking forward to it x*

A waiter removes my empty plate as I decide whether to respond again.

'Everything OK, sir?'

'Yeah, fine,' I say before putting my phone away.

OUR MEAL PASSES with a lot of conversation and laughter, with Gareth entertaining us with stories of Dan as a teenager. We finish dessert and then the serving staff pour coffees and fill champagne glasses with a toast drink. Again, I wave away the offer of alcohol.

'I'll have it,' Simon says. I nod to the waiter who fills the glass.

Simon lifts the drink towards me and says, 'I toast your new-found dedication.'

We listen to Michelle's dad as he gives a moving speech about his daughter. As his speech ends, we clap as he kisses her, then we sip our coffees as he shakes Dan's hand and passes him the microphone.

Dan stands in front of his friends and family, Michelle, seated to his left. Her face seems to be fixed in a constant smile.

'My wife and I…'

He milks the reaction, letting the applause run for a few seconds longer, then raises his hand, gesturing for it to stop.

'…would like to thank you for coming.'

The room is quiet again, every eye fixed on him.

'It takes a special kind of woman to be with an athlete.' He looks at his new bride. She looks embarrassed by his words yet smiles a shy smile that makes her look more beautiful.

'It's true,' he says. 'Being in a relationship with an athlete means you need to be patient, understanding, and independent. You need to be prepared to sacrifice parts of your life to allow the person you've chosen to be with to chase their dream. At times, you need to be selfless, because the person you've chosen to be with will be selfish. There are times when you won't be the most important thing in your partner's life. You won't be their focus. They will take you for granted. They will be irrational, grumpy, and arrogant. And horrible to live with.'

Dan stops and forces himself not to cry. Michelle is crying.

'To be in a relationship with an athlete, dare I say, an *elite athlete*' – a few cheers come from another table – 'takes hard work.'

Another pause. A deep breath.

'When I met Michelle, I got incredibly lucky. Not only was she beautiful and funny and didn't always mind staying in on Saturday nights, but she also bought into my dreams. She did so with a selflessness that I still cannot believe. She took me for what I am. She supported my dream. She supported me, not only as a partner, but as a fan.'

He breaks. Tears pour out of him. He takes the red handkerchief from his jacket pocket and wipes his eyes.

Michelle says, 'I love you,' softly.

He pulls his hand away and drinks some water. His head remains bowed slightly, and he doesn't make eye contact with anyone.

'I didn't achieve my dream of Olympic Gold. I don't think I have the words to describe how much I love the fact I've shared chasing that dream with Michelle. She means everything to me.' He sniffs, wipes his eyes again. 'Today marks the start of a new journey. A journey that will be more equal, fairer. One we can plan together, with new goals and dreams. A journey we can take as man and wife.'

He faces Michelle again.

'Ladies and gentlemen, will you please raise your glasses to the new Mrs Hall.'

'Mrs Hall,' we repeat, glasses in the air.

The bride and groom kiss as we clap.

Tony, Dan's best man, stands and takes the microphone. The room goes quiet in expectation of his speech.

'How am I supposed to follow that?' he says.

As everyone laughs, I think about Abbie.

THE ROOM IS transformed. Dining tables are pushed to the sides, a dance floor revealed from behind a partition. The band set up, the odd burst of music coming through the speakers as they check their instruments one last time. The noise levels have increased, with the day's alcohol intake making people more friendly. Dan and Michelle are moving from group to group, hugging and kissing people, smiling, Michelle turning on several occasions to show off her dress.

I'm stood with Gareth at the bar as Dan leaves Michelle with her bridesmaids and joins us.

'Get us a beer mate,' he says to me just as I'm about to be served.

I add his drink to my order. I hear Gareth say to Dan, 'Did you make a job decision yet?'

I hand Dan his drink and he takes a long drink.

'What's this?' I ask.

'I was just asking Dan if he'd decided about the job offers he's had.'

'What offers?'

Dan lowers the bottle. 'There're a couple of potential jobs. A guy I know runs a coaching company. He's mentioned going in as a partner. I'd just have to put some money in. He's been running it about a year. It's coaching kids, mainly. Another is a project management company. That's a trainee position. So, I'd be in with the fresh from uni lot.'

'Didn't you mention writing a book?' I ask.

'There was an offer. The company kept talking about it after medalling in Beijing. Don't know if that's still on after I fucked up the final.'

There's a pause, feedback from a speaker as the guitarist tunes up.

'I don't know what I'm going to do,' Dan says.

LATER, THE ROOM is darker, and the band is in full flow, smashing through all the standard wedding hits. Floor fillers. The front man giving it everything, encouraging the ring of bridesmaids to keep Michelle dancing. I'm stood just off the dance floor with Gareth and Simon, laughing about a little dance spin Simon had just done. The conversation takes a slight pause and Gareth says, 'I'm a bit drunk, so can I ask you something I've always wanted to ask Dan but it never felt right because he was missing out on them.'

'Go for it,' Simon says, placing a large hand on Gareth's shoulder. 'I'm drunk, so ask away. I won't remember in the morning.'

Gareth asks, 'I've always assumed athletes have a preferred option. So, would you rather have an Olympic Gold medal or a World Record?'

'Gold medal,' Simon says without hesitation.

'What about you, Adam?'

'Both.'

They laugh. I don't.

I'M IN THE middle of dance floor now, fist in the air, singing along to 'Living on a Prayer', out of time with all the other people around me doing the same.

It's one of those brilliant wedding moments where the guests are all relaxed and comfortable with the people they've known for a grand total for eight hours.

Michelle and Dan are smiling, living the moments that will be memories they look back on for years.

Dan makes his way across the floor and swings his arm around my shoulder.

'Adam,' he shouts, a slight slur to the word.

'What?'

'I can't believe you beat me.'

I don't respond, unsure what the right answer is.

'I'll get you next time,' he says before kissing my cheek and laughing to himself.

Former, the worst prefix in sport. Former, as in previously. As in used to be, once was.

As in Dan Hall.

Former British Record holder, former Olympian, former athlete.

Former, as in no longer relevant.

5

WE MEET IN a coffee shop on Thomas Street in Manchester's Northern Quarter. It's an independent place, bare brick walls housing local artists' work. Abbie's waiting when I arrive. She stands and waves me over to a table in the corner.

There's an awkward moment when we're unsure how to greet each other. I lean to hug her as she tries to kiss my cheek.

A man in a retro Subbuteo football T-shirt comes over and takes our orders.

'So, how was competing at the Olympics?' she asks, before adding, 'There's a sentence I never thought I'd say on a date.'

'Is this a date?' I ask. Her eyes widen in surprise at my question. I look down at my T-shirt and jeans, saying, 'I would've dressed up for the occasion.'

She laughs and I start to tell her about my experience. Our drinks arrive. I blow on my coffee and take small sips and change the conversation away from the story that ends with me losing out on a medal by two centimetres.

'How was your holiday?'

'Amazing,' she says, stretching out the word, before telling me how she and two friends went island hopping around Greece for three weeks; lying on beautiful beaches, sleeping in, and lots of laughs. She looks more relaxed, more rested than when we met two months ago. Then, she was at the end of a long teaching year, worn down by the endless hours.

Our coffees are finished. The waiter comes back and asks, 'Can I get you anything else?'

We look at each other and nervously Abbie says, 'I could have another drink, unless you don't want to?'

'No, I'd like another one.' She smiles. 'I'm having fun,' I add reassuringly.

The man repeats our earlier order from memory and leaves.

There's a short window of silence.

'I've got to go shopping for my friend's birthday present later. Would you like to come with me? I won't be long. We could get something to eat afterwards or something.'

'Yeah,' I say. 'That'd be nice.'

We drink our second coffees a bit quicker. I tell her about my plans to relax before training starts again. Time passes quickly. I pay and we leave. We walk down a slope in the road towards the Arndale Centre. Inside, under bright, artificial light, we go from shop to shop while Abbie waits for inspiration.

It's getting towards late afternoon and we're both hungry, so we stop at a pizza chain and eat.

Abbie looks at the wine list as a waitress stands looking bored, tapping her notepad on her other hand.

'Should we get a bottle?' Abbie asks me.

For half a second I think of saying yes, that one glass won't hurt. One glass, four years before London, won't kill my chances. I'm not back in training yet, it's a date, I'm on holiday. But I know it's a mindset. Strength of mind will see me through tough winter training sessions, through hard-fought long jump competitions, through the dark moments when it's not going to plan. I know strength of mind can be learnt. I know if I accept one small glass of red wine less than a week after deciding to not drink anymore, I'll break in those winter sessions or in the dark days.

'I don't drink,' I say.

'Oh. Sorry. I didn't realise.'

'It's OK,' I say. 'It's a recent decision.'

'I feel bad now.'

'Don't feel bad. You can still get one.'

The waitress waits, making me feel awkward, so I order a fresh orange and my meal.

Abbie orders wine and her food.

'Why did you give up drinking?' she asks as we wait for our meals. 'You said before you went to China that you were looking forward to a massive blow out afterwards.'

'Because, when I was in Beijing, I realised that to win the Olympics I need to change a few things about myself to improve my performance. Some things are easily controlled. Not drinking is one of those. I didn't drink that much, anyway. Two training sessions a day with a hangover don't mix. But I was prone to the odd Saturday night out that ended a bit later than it should've. Only every couple of months or so. So, to improve, I stopped.'

'You make it sound so easy.'

'It's just a practical decision. Like making sure I go to bed earlier.'

'Why not wait until you start training again?'

'It's easy to say, I'll start tomorrow. The moment I left Beijing, I started preparing for London. Not drinking is part of that.'

'I couldn't do it.'

'You don't have to.'

After our meal has finished, I walk with her to the tram station at Piccadilly. We stand on the platform and wait. The tram arrives and there's a rushed goodbye where she says, 'This has been fun.'

'It has.' I agree.

'Would you like to do it again?'

'Yeah. That'd be good.'

WE MEET UP a couple more times, including at her place, where we spend a couple of afternoons together enjoying doing nothing before she goes back to work, and I begin training again.

On the days we don't see each other, she sends me regular text messages and, once she returns to teaching, she calls me every night for at least an hour, telling me about her day: the kids, the teachers, the gossip, and politics of a normal workplace. I struggle to identify with her stories, as my job isn't like a proper job.

A FRIDAY NIGHT in mid-September. Abbie's tired from a long week and we spend the night hanging out with her housemate, Lisa, watching forgettable TV. Abbie and Lisa work their way through a couple of bottles of wine.

Later, in Abbie's bed, she says, 'My boss was singing your praises today. You were brought up as an agenda item in the staff meeting. He can't believe the school has an Olympic hero. His words, not mine.'

'He's invited me back to the school to talk about Beijing.'

'He was telling us all. He was very proud.'

'Does he know about us?'

'No.' She shifts her body weight slightly then says, 'Does it matter if he does?'

'No, course it doesn't matter if Santa knows about us.'

She hits my arm softly and says, 'Don't call him that.'

'Why not? I've always called him that. You can't deny he looks like Santa. He used to joke about it himself at Christmas. I remember him saying he was glad the school closed a few days before Christmas to prepare the reindeer.'

'Well, I don't want it stuck in my head next time I have a meeting with him.'

I laugh and say, 'Fair enough. I don't mind him knowing, I just thought the rule was that teachers are only allowed to go out with other teachers? I thought the rule was your boyfriend would have to be some geeky science teacher.'

'I had the rule taken out of my contract.'

'Just in case you met a handsome long jumper?'

She ignores my question and says, 'Is that what you are?'

'What?'

'My boyfriend.'

WE SPEND SATURDAY together, acting as couples do. She is relaxed, which is notably different from when I've seen her on days she's been working. It's like the stress of the week disappears when she wakes up on Saturday morning.

After lunch in her local café, we go in a bookshop and she slowly browses the shelves. She buys a couple of thrillers and we leave.

Her hand slips into mine as we walk back to hers. She's still holding it when we get back to her flat, and she leads me to her bedroom.

Later, with the low glow of the evening sun coming through the window, she asks, 'What are you doing tomorrow? Do you want to do something?'

'I can't. I'm seeing my grandma.'

'Oh.'

'We're watching my final.'

Three seconds, four. No response. Then, 'Maybe I could come. I would be nice to meet her.'

'Not tomorrow,' I say quickly. Maybe too quickly. 'We've had it planned for ages.'

A brief moment of silence passes. Then she says, 'It's a shame. Would've been nice to meet someone in your life.'

'What are you getting at?'

'I'm not getting at anything. It was just a joke.'

'It doesn't feel like a joke,' I say.

I sit up and move away from her slightly.

She sits but stays quiet.

'What's going on?' I ask.

'Nothing,' she says. A clear lie. Abbie moves again in bed, adjusting the duvet, pulling it tighter around her. 'I'm working all week and you're off. Couldn't you see her then?'

'No.'

'Why not?'

'Because we've arranged to watch my final. She's busy. This was the first chance we both had. It's important.'

She looks like she's about to say something, but her jaw tenses and the moment is gone.

'Abbie, don't do this. If you've got something to say, say it. I can't be arsed with games.'

'I'm sorry, I must seem like I'm being weird.' She pauses, contemplating her next words. 'I've not been a hundred per cent honest with you,' she says, before quickly adding, 'Although, I've not kept anything from you to hide anything. That's not what I mean.' Her voice trails off, and she looks across the room like she'll find right words sat on top of the chest-of-drawers.

I feel the atmosphere turn serious. 'Talk to me,' I say as I reach out and touch her arm gently.

'I split up with my ex about three weeks before we met. I found out he was cheating on me. Had been with a girl at his work for about seven months. We'd been together for five years. I was devastated.'

I face her, suddenly conscious I'm only dressed in boxer shorts.

'I was really low when we met. It'd been a horrible few weeks. When we, you and me,' she clarifies, 'met at school and I thought there was a spark there, it took me by surprise. I didn't feel ready to see anyone again so soon after what happened with Josh, but I got this really strong feeling that I wanted to see you again.'

I can see her fighting back tears.

'It's OK,' I say.

'So, when you actually text me after I gave you my number, I was really happy. I felt a bit like a kid again, sort of waiting for your texts and trying to think about how to word the ones I sent to you. And then, all of a sudden, before you went away, you sent me a message saying that you wanted to stop talking until after the Olympics and I felt really stupid. Like I'd come on too strong or I was this mad woman who just kept texting you.'

'It wasn't like that,' I say. 'I just needed to go to Beijing fully focused. I liked the messages as well. I just knew if something went wrong in Beijing, I'd blame you as a distraction. I get that's not the normal start to a new relationship, but it's just how I had to be.'

'When I was on holiday,' she says. 'It was really strange because I was having loads of fun, I honestly was, but then I'd get these really dark moments of feelings where all this stuff with my ex would just come up.'

'That's understandable, isn't it? Given what he did.'

'I know. But then also, I found myself not caring because of what was happening with us. I felt like a bit of a mess. I still do some days.' Her voice is low, her words raw. I realise it's probably the first time I've seen the real her. Full, honest emotion.

She continues, 'And now I'm wondering what we are.'

'What do you mean?'

'You're going to hang out with your grandma when you could be spending the day with me.'

'That's not fair. I told you, it's important. My grandma is the reason I'm where I am today.'

'I've not met your friends, or your parents. You've only met Lisa because she lives with me.'

'Abbie,' I say, tension in my voice. 'It's not like that. I'm really enjoying this. I'm having fun. I thought you were having fun, too. I've just come out of four years of pressure. Granted, I put most of that on myself, but in a few weeks training for London starts and that pressure will start again. It'll be worse this time. So, I'm just enjoying hanging out and seeing where this is going. I really want to see where we go.'

'Me too,' she says.

'I like you,' I add. 'It was only last night you asked if I was your boyfriend, and we had the *being a couple* conversation. I'm going to meet all your friends next week for this birthday meal for Lisa. So, I'm a bit surprised by this. I know what Josh did to you is horrible, but I can't be judged by his actions. I don't know if you think seeing my grandma tomorrow is some kind of shit excuse for actually meeting someone else or something, but I can assure you it's not. I'm not seeing anyone else. I don't want to be. But I don't want to be accused of it either because you're not invited to meet my grandma when I'm doing something that's really important to me.'

She's quiet then says, 'I'm sorry.'

'You don't have to be sorry.'

I stay the night again. As she sleeps, I lie awake going back over the day, my thoughts punctuated by snippets of Dan's wedding speech.

THE FOLLOWING WEEKEND I drive to a Mexican restaurant in central Manchester on Saturday night where fifteen of Abbie's friends are already seated at one large table. Lisa, the birthday girl, is seated on a chair with a pink birthday balloon tied to it.

As I sit down, someone says, 'You must be the Olympian.'

We order and I fall into an easy conversation about the start of the football season with the guy sitting next to me. There are a lot of laughs, a lot of jokes about previous nights out I wasn't on. Abbie repeatedly asks how I'm doing. I repeatedly say fine.

After the main course, Abbie and another girl disappear. The lights dim and they appear from the kitchen with a waiter who is carrying a birthday cake with candles flickering in the dark. A chorus of 'Happy Birthday' starts, and Lisa laughs and hides her head behind her wine glass. Other diners join in and there's a huge cheer and a round of applause as Lisa blows out the candles.

We move on to a bar the girls go to regularly. It's a place that serves food on wooden boards and charges too much for burgers. At the bar, I order for the group, carefully carrying the drinks on a tray and awkwardly placing them on our low table. I sit next to Abbie on a deep leather couch. We're squeezed together, and I have to adjust my body position a couple of times to get comfortable.

'You OK?' she asks.

'Yeah.'

'Are you not getting a drink?'

'No. I'm OK. There's only so much water I can manage.'

'So, are you just going to sit there?'

'It's no different to sitting here with a drink.'

Time passes. Conversations buzz around me. I join in some, answering questions about Beijing a few times. I check my watch and the time is 10:27. I excuse myself and go to the toilet. I return to the group a few minutes later and catch Abbie's eye.

'I'm going to go,' I say.

'What?' she says, making it clear she can't hear me.

Not wanting to shout, I lean over a couple of people and repeat myself. Abbie checks her phone and says, 'It's only half ten.'

'I know.'

I tell Lisa to have a great night. She thanks me for coming and kisses my cheek. I wave to the group as Abbie climbs over her friend's legs to follow me outside.

We stand on the pavement.

'Why are you going?' she asks.

'Because it's getting late.'

'Are you not staying at mine?'

'No. I told you when you invited me out, I'd have to leave before you.'

'How am I supposed to get home?'

'You live with another person on the night out, so I guess how you normally get home.'

'I didn't expect you to leave this early. This is the first time you've met the majority of my friends and you're embarrassing me by going home without me.'

'I'm embarrassing you?' I say. 'You're the one shouting at me in the street, making a scene out of nothing.'

'Nothing? I've invited you out, and you're going home at half ten.'

'Abbie, stop. This is stupid. I've been very clear about my lifestyle. I told you weeks ago I've made changes to my life. This shouldn't be a surprise. I thought you understood.'

'Is it going to be like this for the next four years? Because where do I fit into that?'

I look at her, her arms folded across her chest, slightly drunk, angry at the thought of me leaving her, and I think of Dan's wedding speech: It takes a special kind of woman to be with an athlete.

'If you're asking me to choose between you and the Olympics, I'm going to choose the Olympics every time,' I say.

I know at that point that we're finished. The hurt in her eyes is too deep, the shock on her face too raw. I'm being selfish, but

I'm following my path. The path to Olympic Gold that she won't walk with me.

'I can't believe you'd say that.'

A taxi pulls up, four women get out; laughing as one nearly falls over.

I lower my voice. 'I don't say it to hurt you. But I have to be honest. I might only get one chance to win gold at an Olympic Games. I can't look back in thirty years' time and think I should've done more. If we have any chance of working out, I need you to understand that.'

'Are you saying I'm not worth giving everything to?'

My silence is all the answer she needs.

'Fuck you,' she says. She turns and runs back into the bar.

I don't follow her.

THERE ARE HUNDREDS of eyes on me, and one pair that can't look at me. I'm stood on my old school stage, dressed in my Team GB tracksuit, ready for the photo shoot Mr Francis has planned for after the question-and-answer session. He stands beside me, microphone in hand. He's just proudly introduced me and now opens the floor to questions. Hands are raised, kids pointed at, questions asked.

'Did you meet Bolt?'

'Yes.'

'Do you get loads of free stuff?'

'Yes.'

'Is it scary jumping in front of all those people?'

'Not as scary as standing here.'

They laugh and I relax.

'What do you do before your event? Do you get to watch other sports?'

'Before the event was quite boring. I tried not to burn too much energy, so I spent a lot of time in my room, watching films. After I jumped, I got to attend lots of events. There's lots of parties.'

Mr Francis points to a blonde girl in the third row. 'Jessica,' he says, inviting her to speak.

'Do you have a girlfriend?' Laughter quickly spreads around the hall.

I look at Abbie.

Abbie, who I haven't heard from since Saturday night.

Abbie, who still looks hurt by what I said.

Abbie, who is only in this room because she has to be.

She looks at me.

The laughter fades away.

'No,' I say. 'I don't have a girlfriend.'

'You're chasing a dream…'

6

THE CYCLE BEGINS again. I drive slowly through the commuter traffic towards central Manchester. I turn onto the Mancunian Way, following the brown signs for Sportcity.

I'm the first athlete from the training group to arrive. I find Len in his office drinking coffee from a faded Sydney 2000 mug.

'Ready?' he asks.

'Ready.'

He puts his mug down and looks at me. 'I have a plan.'

I sit on a swivel chair next to an empty desk and Len lays out his vision for making me a Champion.

Then he repeats his annual mantra: never go into an event unprepared. Never lose knowing you could've done more. He hands me my training plan for the year, a thick, printed pack with every session planned out. Each training phase is noted: meso and micro cycles, accumulation and recovery weeks. I know what I'll be doing day in, day out, month on month, between now and next September.

I go into the changing rooms and set down my old training bag, with its faded colour and worn straps, and take out my old training kit. I've made the decision to not use my Team GB Olympic kit from Beijing. I have to earn the right to wear Team GB kit again.

I step onto the indoor track, feeling the familiar, almost comforting, bounce underneath my feet. The excitement of possibilities races through me. The season starts now. I'm rested and fresh. I've had no bad days or injuries, no sickness or disappointing jumps.

I warm-up and stretch. Barefoot, I do foot work and knee strengthening exercises, focusing on how my body reacts to each move and stretch. I put my trainers back on and line up.

Len instructs, 'Four sixties. Controlled. No heroes. I want you to complete all four.'

I sprint sixty metres. My arms and legs pump and push. Up, down. Forwards. I'm focused on form, not going flat out. I hit the sixty marker and slow up, turn and head back to the start, breathing hard, sucking in air.

I've missed this.

AT DINNER TIME, my parents are eating a curry my mum has prepared. My dad rips some naan bread in half and asks me, 'How was training?'

'Good,' I respond, taking a bite of the baked potato I made for myself.

My mum says, 'You must be getting excited about next week.'

I cut up some chicken. 'I'm not going.'

'What do you mean?'

'What I just said. I'm not going.'

'But you have to go. You've been invited.'

'I've got training.'

We all eat. My mum looks at me as she chews, then says, 'Training?'

'Yes, Mum. Training.'

'But it's the Olympic parade.'

I shrug.

'You'll get to go to the palace. Celebrate what you've achieved.' Her voice quivers a little. I know this voice from previous conversations. She wants to shout at me, tell me I'm doing something wrong. It was the same reaction when I told her I wasn't going to university so I could concentrate on being a full-time athlete.

'I don't have anything to celebrate.'

I hear the front door open and a couple of seconds later slam shut. My mum says, 'This is ridiculous.'

My sister, Jane, walks into the dining room, unzipping her coat to reveal her nurse's uniform. She asks, 'What's ridiculous?'

'Your brother's not going to the Olympic parade.'

'Oh.' Jane looks at me. 'Why not?'

'Because he's got training,' my mum says.

I put my fork down. 'I'm sat in the room for God's sake.'

'Don't take that tone with me.'

I ignore her and turn to Jane. 'I'm not going because I don't want to trek all the way to London to smile at crowds and wave flags and smile for photographs because I finished fourth. I don't see the point of patting myself on the back for a job well done when actually, I don't think I did the job that well.' I pause, then say to Jane, 'How was your day?'

Before she can answer, my mum says to me, 'You set a new British Record.'

'And then slid from first to fourth without jumping any better.' My mum goes to say something, but I interrupt. 'Beijing has gone. I don't want to take a day out of preparing for the next Olympics to go and smile politely while the Queen pretends she knows who I am.'

'Seems fair enough to me,' Jane says. She moves into the kitchen and looks in the oven for her portion of curry.

'How many times do you get invited to Buckingham Palace in your lifetime?' my mum asks.

'Hopefully, she can invite me back in twenty-twelve and I can show her the gold medal I've won. If she says, I missed you four years ago, I'll apologise. OK?'

My mum looks at my dad. 'Haven't you got anything to say?'

'If he doesn't want to go, he doesn't have to go. He's not a child.'

My mum ignores him but changes her tone. 'Your dad and I have spent years watching you become the person you are today. We've done everything we can to make sure you had the opportunity to achieve your dreams. You going to the Olympics is very special to us too. We want you to enjoy it all. I don't want you to regret missing out on the things that come with your career.'

'I understand all that, but what you need to understand is, missing a day's training will be the thing I regret. I might not regret it now, but maybe in Berlin or Barcelona. Because I want my career to be about winning Olympic finals, not just making them.'

I SIT AT home, alone, watching the parade. My teammates are on the TV, moving through London on floats, dressed identically in Team GB tracksuits. It feels like everyone is continuously waving. Gymnasts entertain the crowd with handstands as their floats move along the road.

BBC interviewers speak to random athletes. Footage of their successes is shown as they talk about their experiences. Dan appears on my screen, tanned after his honeymoon in Thailand.

'With me is Dan Hall, now retired long jumper. Dan, what can you say about this reception? Thousands of people, everyone here to say thank you to the most successful British Olympic team in years.'

'It's amazing,' Dan says. 'Beijing was such a wonderful experience. We've all been incredibly privileged to take part in such a successful Games for Britain. This parade is a brilliant way to finish it all.' Dan smiles to hide his feelings, to cover his lies.

'You retired after Beijing. How's life not being an athlete?'

'Strange,' Dan says. Another smile. 'I'm keeping busy. I've just got married and been on my honeymoon, so I'm just spending time with my wife and enjoying not having to be in training every day. Enjoying eating things I've not been allowed to, things like that.'

'Any plans, post athletics?'

'Nothing concrete, yet.'

Dan turns and goes back to robotic waving.

Trafalgar Square is rammed. Thousands of people stand in front of the temporary stage. The camera pans across the crowd, capturing the flicker of red, white, and blue as people wave flags above their heads.

Boris Johnson is at the microphone, bright blond hair flapping, talking about falling leaves and falling share prices. He says, 'There's never a wrong time to celebrate the greatest achievement by an Olympic and Paralympic team since 1908.'

I watch Sue Barker interview Rebecca Adlington, who jokes about her family and talks about how great the support has been. She's smiling and happy. A young girl, dreams achieved. There are others behind her, all showing the same smiles, the same sense of pride. Young, super fit athletes, all basking in glory, all looking back on a job well done.

I can only look forwards.

Later, when my teammates are mixing with royalty at Buckingham Palace, I go into the garage. The room is split into two sections. To the right is a cold, concrete floor where my dad's car is parked at night. Gardening tools and a stepladder hang from hooks drilled into the bare brick wall. To the left is my gym area. Mats cover the floor; weights are stacked in rows. I move my medicine ball to the side and get in position.

My teammates sip champagne. I do an abs circuit.

They smile politely and say, 'Pleased to meet you.' I do murder sit-ups and hand to knees.

They talk about Beijing. I graft.

Two centimetres: less than an inch. The width of two sugar cubes. The difference between winning a medal and not.

7

LEN'S PLAN FOR this winter is to train, train, train. He is open about his desire to keep me away from competition; partly to build a base for the coming months, partly to change my attitude to winter work. And it works. Every day I'm always first in, ready to go. As the days grow dark and short, my mind is consumed with becoming a Champion.

In late November, I walk into Len's office.

'Morning,' a voice says as I open the door.

I'm surprised to see Dan leaning on Len's desk, mug of coffee in hand.

'Hello, mate.'

Dan's smile is wide. 'Len was just telling me how well you've been training.'

I look to Len, who nods.

'My star can shine now you've gone,' I joke.

'Piss off.'

'You missing us?' I ask.

He takes a sip of coffee. 'Not too much.'

'You got a job yet?'

'Don't you worry about me,' Dan says. 'Concentrate on trying to improve yourself.'

I leave, change, and complete my warm-up. Dan stands by the side of the track. It feels weird seeing him dressed in jeans and a shirt, no longer an athlete. He watches the tough sprinting session I complete, his face offering no emotion. As I take a drink following the last set he offers, 'You look good.'

'Thanks.'

'Catch-up soon,' he adds.

'That'd be good.'

I shower and change and head back to Len's office. 'Where's Dan?' I ask.

'He's gone.'

MANCHESTER CHANGES AS November creeps towards an end. Christmas lights appear on buildings and are strung up between lamp posts. Markets open in Albert's Square, with rows and rows of stalls offering handmade Christmas gifts, German food cooked in huge, circular pans, strong European lager. The training group goes in early December, eating pork sandwiches and drinking hot chocolate, surrounded by office workers huddled around mugs of mulled wine. The visit is the closest thing we have to a Christmas do.

During the Christmas Eve weights session, sweat pours down my face. This is the last effort before I get two days off in a row for the first time since October.

'Usual Christmas Eve tonight?' Len asks as I finish the set.

'Yep. Same local pub with school friends. Same conversation about New Year's Eve.'

'You love it.'

I laugh.

'I do. It's nice to switch off for a few hours.'

THE PUB IN Altrincham is packed, everyone in the Christmas spirit. People home from other places, catching up with friends. I see my group gathered at a table at the back: Mike, his girlfriend Emma, Pete, and Johnny. All their coats have been piled in the space next to them.

Pete and I go to the bar.

'Where's Laura?' I ask.

'They're on their way.'

'They?'

'Another trainee, Rachel. She lives this way too. They're on the tram now.'

A barman glances my way and I lean forward to make my order heard over Wham's 'Last Christmas' coming from the speaker above the bar.

I send the first drinks back with Pete, pay, and make my way through the crowd back to the table with the rest of the order. Laura and her friend have now joined us. I pass out the drinks and sit down.

'Adam, this is Rachel. Rachel, Adam.'

'Hi.'

She's pretty: dark hair, blue eyes.

'Hi.'

Johnny says to Laura, 'I see the cutthroat corporate world of solicitors doesn't finish early for Christmas.'

'Hardly. The client wants what the client wants.'

'Even at Christmas?'

'Especially at Christmas.'

'My boss has a bed in his office,' Rachel says. 'I think he only sees his kids once a year, on Christmas Day.'

'Sounds like fun,' Johnny says.

'More fun than recruitment,' Laura says.

Johnny tips his glass to acknowledge her point.

'What do you do?' Rachel asks me.

'I'm an athlete,' I answer.

'Adam is our resident Olympian,' Johnny shouts across the table.

'The Olympics? Really?'

I nod and sip my soft drink.

'Yeah, I'm a long jumper.'

'So, your job is just running and jumping? Your *actual* job?'

Everyone laughs.

'Yes,' I say, smiling. 'My *actual* job.'

'I didn't know that was a thing.'

'You've managed to reduce all the years of sacrificing my body, down to "it's just running and jumping" but yeah, it's a thing.'

'Into a sandpit?'

There's a hint of a smile on her lips as I reply, 'Yes, into a sandpit.'

'Don't you ever just want to play in the sand?'

'Every day,' I say.

Conversation moves on to the subject of New Year's Eve.

'I'm not paying a tenner to get into a pub I could walk into for nothing any other night of the year,' Pete says.

'Always the accountant. What's your plan then?' Johnny says.

'I don't know,' Pete responds.

I say to Rachel, 'These two have this conversation every year. It starts on New Year's Day. Johnny says, "next year we're all going away". Then they talk about all these big plans about where to go. New York, Berlin. They say they'll sort it out. Nothing happens and then every Christmas they sit here arguing about what to do.'

She laughs.

'Mike, any ideas?'

Mike laughs. 'Every year, lads. Every year.'

Rachel looks at me.

'I wouldn't lie to you,' I say.

'We could have a party,' Emma says to Mike. 'You're not working.'

'Party at yours it is then,' Johnny says.

I see the fight drain out of Mike. 'OK. We'll do food. You lot sort out the booze. Adam, I can stretch to providing soft drinks.'

'Thanks, mate.'

The conversation breaks up and we talk in smaller groups. Rachel turns to me and says, 'What are you doing tomorrow?'

'Just a family dinner. Parents and my sister, my grandma. You?'

'The same. Well, two brothers and two drunken granddads, though.'

'No boyfriend?' I ask. I want the answer to be no, but as I ask, I wish I could pull the words back into my mouth, reshape and rephrase them, ask all over again in a less obvious way.

She smiles a smile that manages to make her look embarrassed and more beautiful at the same time. 'No boyfriend,' she says.

I smile now, unsure of what to say. I settle on, 'Oh.'

Johnny interrupts. 'Is he boring you with stories about how he was winning in the Olympic Final? He's always doing that.'

'I'm not,' I say quietly to her.

'No,' she shouts back to Johnny. 'He's not mentioned it at all.'

Later, as I'm leaving toilets, I open the door towards me and she's on the other side, nearly stumbling forwards as she tries to grab the door I've opened.

'Hi.'

'Hi.'

She steps backwards to allow me through.

'You having a nice time?' I ask.

'Yes, thanks. I have to leave soon, though. I've agreed to meet some friends near home.'

I check my watch: 9:45 p.m.

'OK,' I say.

We look at each other. Unsure what to say, whether to carry on to where we were going.

A staff member tries to pass us with a tray of drinks. 'Sorry,' she says as she squeezes around us.

We're alone again.

She smiles.

It's like the gun has gone off in my brain and my thoughts have started a 1500 metre race. They're packed together, fighting for position, nudging each other, elbowing and leaning on each other, desperate to be out in front as they approach the bend: Abbie, and how it didn't work, how she wasn't cut out for the life I lead, followed by me wondering if I should be just focused on training and winning, if wanting to continue this conversation is a bad idea, if being alone at this point in my career is a good thing, overtaken by looking at this beautiful woman in front of me and wanting to listen to her tell every story about herself and wanting her to stop talking for just long enough to kiss her.

Deep breath.
Decision time.
'Can I get your number?' I ask.

It's instinct. Everything about the way your body feels at that exact moment tells you. You just know.

8

I EAT BREAKFAST with my family, lost in a daze about her. She's what I think about when I open presents and hand out the gifts I've bought for my family. I wonder when is too soon to text her. When I go to the garage to do an abs circuit I leave my phone in my bedroom, but she colours my mind as I work out. I decide to text her after my shower. I dry in the bathroom, then I walk to my bedroom with the towel wrapped around my waist and pick up my phone. There's a message from her: *What are you doing tomorrow?*

ON BOXING DAY, we meet in the car park at Dunham Massey, a National Trust place close to home.

I'm early. I watch her walk towards me, dressed in a big coat, her face half hidden by a scarf. She moves it with a gloved hand and smiles that smile.

'Merry Christmas,' she says.

I lean in and kiss her cold cheek.

We walk along the path, through a small tunnel of trees. There are families around us, dog walkers and couples escaping the prisons of family homes.

'How was your Christmas?' I ask.

'It was nice,' she says. 'Although I was a little distracted wondering how much time to leave before I text you.'

The old house appears on our left, across the water. We walk through a double gate, stopping to let a child on a new bike come through.

'Funny you should say that. I was having a similar debate with myself.'

'Don't feel smug because I caved first.'

'What can I say? I'm obviously hard to resist.'

'Not so much.'

We walk through a brick archway into the main cobbled courtyard. The park opens up in front of us. There are several pathways we can walk, and she says, 'Let's take the long route.'

We talk about families and Christmas Day traditions. She tells me about the competitive Pictionary games, the kids versus the parents. 'What am I saying?' she says. 'Your Christmas games must be ridiculously competitive.'

'Why do you say that?'

'Aren't there always the childhood stories of sports people throwing Monopoly boards because of an overbearing desire to win?'

'For some people, I bet it's like that. Not for me. I'm not that competitive at other things. Sport stuff, yes, but not games. I don't see the point. Put me on a long jump runway, then it's different.'

'How so?'

'I can't explain it. I'm good at it. And I know I am. I'm never going to be the best Pictionary player in the world, so I don't really care if I win or not.'

'Are you going to be the best long jumper in the world?'

'Yes.'

A deer bounds across the track in front of us and we watch it disappear behind some trees.

'That probably sounds really arrogant,' I say.

'Not at all. Is that the level you're at? The world's best?'

'I finished fourth in the last Olympics. My plan is to win the next one. That's what my whole life since I was twelve has been about.'

'Is that when you started in athletics?'

'Yeah,' I answer. 'I got into it because of my grandma. When I was a kid, it was my favourite thing to go to her house to watch sport. My granddad liked football and cricket, but when athletics was on, Grandma had control of the TV. I used to sit with her watching all the major championships. She would tell me all these stories from the days when she competed. She was a good club runner. When I was really young, she used to set up cardboard boxes as hurdles in the garden, or relay races for me and the other kids in her street. Long jump was always something we would do, marking where we'd landed with our baseball caps. When I was about twelve, I just asked my mum and dad to take me to the athletics club.'

'Did your grandma go to Beijing?'

I shake my head. 'She said she wasn't up to the travel. I'm not sure that's the truth though. Since my grandad died, she's made it her business to look after all these lonely old people who live near her. She keeps herself busy by looking out for them. I don't think she wanted to leave them for too long. Some of them are in their nineties.'

'She sounds amazing.'

'My grandma is the best person I know,' I say. 'I wouldn't be where I am today without her.'

Rachel slips her hand into mine as if it's the most natural thing in the world to do and says, 'I can't wait to meet her.'

We walk in a comfortable, easy silence.

Rachel breaks it with a question. 'What's your biggest fear?'

'That's not a question I was expecting.'

'I feel like I want to know everything about you.'

I think: fear of infection, fear of illness, fear of injury, fear of losing, fear of being underprepared, fear of not being good enough.

I stand for a few seconds, considering how much to reveal. Fear is weakness in my world, and showing weakness is forbidden. Weakness will beat you before you've jumped.

But this is her. There's something easy about revealing these things to her. Something in the way she listens, the way she assesses the answers.

And it feels right to say it. 'Fear of failure.'

I feel her hand squeeze mine.

'What about you?' I ask.

'My biggest fear?'

'Yeah.'

'Looking back and feeling like I've not given everything to the things that were worth it.'

Ten minutes later, as we're heading back towards the main courtyard, she asks, 'Do you feel like you've missed out on normal things?'

'In what way?'

'Nights out and things.'

'I like a night out, they just never compare to the feeling of winning.'

I continue, 'I don't feel like I missed out. I feel like everyone else has. I have an opportunity to be the best in the world at something. Not many people get that chance. I think it's a shame athletes get judged as missing out. We get so much more back. Do you feel like you miss out when you have to work late because you're a trainee and you've got to prove yourself?'

'No. I want to be in court arguing cases. This is what I need to do to get there. I understand your attitude completely. I think dedication to being the best is important.'

Hungry, we go into the café.

The seating area is busy, but we manage to find a small table tucked away in the corner.

Between spoonfuls of soup I ask, 'Did you always want to be a lawyer?'

'You make it sound like I'm on *Law and Order*.'

'Sorry. Solicitor.' I say the word in a fake posh accent.

She gives me the finger.

'Classy. You should do that in court.'

'I took law at college because I thought it would be interesting. It was, and it sort of grew from there, really. I did well at it and decided to do it at uni.'

We've finished eating and our cups are empty.

'Should we get another one?' I ask.

'Yeah. I'll go,' she says. 'I think I might get one of those chocolate cakes. Do you want one?'

'No thanks,' I say. 'I don't eat cake.'

'This is awkward.'

'Why?'

'Because I love cake. I go to the gym at five in the morning sometimes to allow myself to eat cake. And now I feel guilty.'

'Don't feel guilty. It's my choice.'

'But if we go out for a meal or something, I'm always going to want to eat dessert. And I'm always going to feel guilty. Because you're like Mr Sacrifice to Be the Best In The World.'

I smile and say, 'So we'll be going out for meals together.'

'I hope so,' she says.

TWO DAYS LATER, we're on the phone for the hundredth time.

'I bought you a present.'

'What is it?'

'I'm not telling you.'

'Tell me.'

'No. You'll have to be patient.'

'Why mention it then?'

'To build-up the suspense.'

'This isn't suspense. This is shit.'

'You really want to know?'

'Yes.'

'I've bought you a bucket and spade so you can play in the sandpit.'

WE TURN A few heads when we enter Mike and Emma's rented terraced house, hand in hand.

'You didn't waste any time,' Johnny says.

The party is in the early stages. People are scattered around the living room; the first drinks are being passed out. There are crisps and dips in bowls on the coffee table. Laura comes over and makes a big deal of Rachel, before hitting my arm, saying, 'Well, you better not fuck this up because my work life will be hell if you do.'

'I'll try,' I say.

More people arrive and the music gets louder. We spend most of the night talking to Pete and Laura, who keep saying,

'It's amazing that you two are together. You should come around for dinner.'

Rachel stays close to me, sipping wine, and squeezing my hand. We share a lot of smiles and whispered conversation.

As midnight approaches, Laura says, 'Right, we need to make some promises for 2009. I'll go first. 2009 will be the year I run a half marathon.'

'Really?' Rachel says.

'Yeah. I really want to. We should do it together.'

'OK.'

'Brilliant. Right, Pete, you're next. Go.'

'Erm.'

'Come on.'

'OK. 2009 will be the year I get a new car.'

'Boring.'

Laura turns her attention to Rachel. 'You. Go. Nothing boring like him. And you can't use the half marathon one.'

'2009 will be the year I get to know this guy better.' She turns and kisses my cheek.

Laura holds her drink up and says, 'Points for romance. Although it's a little soppy for my tastes. Adam?'

'2009 will be the year I win a medal at the World Championships in Berlin.'

'Well, that makes our half marathon look pretty shit,' Rachel says.

I stop running and gasp for air. I move to the side of the track and lean over. I heave, but nothing comes out. I drop to one knee. My lungs scream. My legs scream. I heave again. Still nothing.

'Let's go again,' Len shouts. 'Keep your hips high.'

I stand and walk back to the start.

Repeat.

9

A SATURDAY IN early February. I train early, then pick my grandma up and we drive to Birmingham to watch the indoors. As we hit the M6 I say, 'I'm going to America for warm weather training in March.'

'That's good,' she says.

'There's a competition too, at the end. I can't wait to jump again.'

In the arena, a few people in the crowd recognise me and congratulate me on my Beijing performance. My grandma smiles proudly as I thank them.

There's no men's long jump, but I concentrate on the women's competition. I study the things the crowd doesn't: how the competitors prepare before a jump, how they react to poor jumps, how their body language portrays their feelings. I watch how they control their nerves and go about their routines. I'm looking for anything I can learn from, to gain an advantage from.

We leave before the last race, as I need to be back in Manchester for Rachel's brother's twenty-first birthday meal.

As I arrive at Rachel's family home, everyone is standing in the hallway, ready to leave. Derek, her dad, with his suit jacket over his crisp white shirt, is next to her mum, Helen, who is adjusting a broach on her coat.

I've met her parents a few times, but this is the first time I've met Rachel's brothers. The tightness of the hallway makes it awkward, but Will, Rachel's older brother, shakes my hand as we are introduced. Lewis, the birthday boy, is at the back of the group, adjusting his hair in the mirror on the telephone table.

We eat at a restaurant in Hale, owned by a TV chef. Between the starter and the main, I stand to go to the toilet at the same time as Derek. We make awkward conversation as we weave through the tables and go up a spiral staircase to the Gents'.

Washing our hands, Derek uses the tap next to me.

As we sit back at the table he says, 'You should see how he washes his hands. It took him ages. Like a surgeon or something.'

'A surgeon taught me,' I say. 'One came into work before Beijing to teach us how to do it. It's to help avoid infections. Apparently, we're more open to it than the average person.' I pause. 'Which I'm aware makes me sound pretty arrogant.'

There's a small laugh from Will.

'The thought process is so detailed,' Derek says.

Later, in bed at her house, Rachel says, 'Can you teach me how to wash my hands like you?'

'Yeah. Why?'

She turns onto her front and looks at me through the dark. 'Because I work long hours in an office with rubbish air conditioning with a bunch of people who don't eat properly and never take a day off sick. They're constantly coughing and sneezing all over each other. If I can ward off some of the infections I'm likely to get, and more importantly, stop you getting them, I'd like to do that. I don't want you getting sick and then blaming me.'

'OK,' I say. 'I'll show you tomorrow.'

I smile in the dark.

'HOW FAR CAN you jump then?' Will asks as we eat breakfast the next morning.

'My PB is 8.36 metres.'

'But how far is that?' He looks around the dining room. 'I know it's far but is it from here to the window?'

'The window is about five metres,' I say.

'Really?' he says.

Derek laughs from behind his paper. 'Leave the lad alone.'

Will stands up. 'Where's the tape measure?'

'Don't do this,' Rachel says. 'Adam's just having his breakfast.'

'It's fine,' I say.

'Third drawer down in the kitchen, under the toaster,' Derek says, putting down his paper.

Will comes back with a tape measure in hand. He goes through the archway between the dining room and lounge and walks to the end of the room, putting it against the skirting board. 'Rach, come and hold this.'

Rachel sighs and gets up. She bends down and holds the end flush against the skirting board. Will pulls the tape measure towards me, walking metre after metre. The tape runs out at five metres. Will looks around and says, 'Adam, pass me that coaster.'

I hand him the coaster my coffee cup was resting on. He carefully puts the edge of it at the five-metre mark and releases the tape. It shrinks into the casing.

'Rach, come here.'

She moves down the room and holds the tape against the edge of the coaster. Will moves, step by step, metre by metre. He slows at seven and a half metres. Centimetre by centimetre to eight metres. He stops just short of the double doors that open into the garden.

'What did you say?'

'Eight point three six metres.'

He moves the tape again. It's blocked by the window. 'So, you can jump further than the length of our house.'

Derek asks, 'How far is the World Record?'

'Eight point nine five metres. Mike Powell, Japan World Championships. 1991,' I say.

'So, another fifty-nine centimetres.'

'I don't think I ever understood how far it was,' Will says. 'Not from watching it on the TV.'

'Is he more impressive as a boyfriend now?' Rachel asks.

'Yeah. He's a keeper.'

They laugh.

I think about Mike Powell.

I FLY TO America with Len.

The Californian facilities are free of distraction. No arguing with my sister, or friends asking me to go out. No bills to be paid or cars to be cleaned. Only training and coaches, focus and work. Eat, sleep, train. Eat, sleep, train. Repeat.

Even in the years when I jump at indoor winter events, it doesn't feel like the season is really starting until we come here to train.

Len stands in front of me and talks about the goals and expectations of the next three weeks.

And then we train. Every day is the same. Training. Training. Training. The final push before the season starts. The season that ends with Berlin. The World Championships.

And a medal.

A FEW DAYS before the end of training, Len and I sit at a small table in the hotel reception. He taps keys on his laptop, then adjusts the screen so we can both see it. He flicks between graphs and spreadsheets and walks me through data and evidence that tells me I'm running faster and lifting heavier than I was this time last year.

'I'm pleased with you,' he says. 'You've taken on-board what I said about focus. The results of the last few months are good.'

Len shuts his laptop. He leans back in his chair and says, 'Tell me about this girl then.'

'Rachel?' I say, 'I've only been with her since December. Nice of you to take an interest.'

'What does she do?'

'Trainee solicitor.'

'Is she into sport?'

'Not really. She goes to the gym a few times a week. She's started training for a half marathon.'

'She sounds busy.'

'She's driven.'

He takes another drink. 'That's good.' He pauses then adds, 'Not always an easy life this. On the road all the time. You need someone to understand sacrifice.'

'She works more than I do.'

'The things that Dan talked about at his wedding, the need for a partner to understand your goals. He wasn't wrong. Rachel, does she understand?'

'More than some others,' I say.

Abbie, the one who didn't get it.

'Good. Because we have a plan,' he says. 'At times, it will deviate from what we expect. You'll have bad days. You'll need a strong partner.'

AS ALWAYS, I arrive at the competition two hours early. I get familiar with the surroundings. I locate the dressing room and the warm-up area, constantly assess the weather.

I'm changed and ready to warm-up exactly an hour before. I jog a couple of laps of the warm-up track, then go through my routine I don't look at my competitors and assess their movements because I know that if I perform to my best it won't matter if they look relaxed or nervous, strong or weak.

I will jump further because I'm better.

We get the call and make our way through the long jump area to begin. There are twenty of us, all prepped and ready, going through our own rituals. I'm ninth to jump, so I find myself a place by the corner of the track, slightly away from the competition. Despite the weather being warm, I keep my tracksuit bottoms and hoody on because each jump takes four to five minutes to complete once it's measured, and the pit is raked for the next guy. A long time stood around waiting to jump in just my shorts and vest, my body temperature dropping.

I watch the first two jumpers, just to assess if they show any obvious signs of being hindered by the wind, then I switch off. I work out who is three jumps ahead of me and keep an eye on them. My preparation starts when they stand on the runway. I stay active without burning too much energy. I don't want my body to cool down too much from my warm-up. The precise order of the warm-up, the routine I follow, tells my body it's time to go to work.

Jumper Six stands on the runway. I lift my hoody off and place it with my bag. I bend and unzip the bottom of my tracksuit bottoms. A V opens near my ankle and I step out of them. I do a few stretches. I move forward to my position as Jumper Seven goes. I wait, staying active but not too active. Jumper Eight moves to the runway. I move in behind. Waiting, waiting. He's a clapper, trying to get the crowd to create a rhythm. Clap, clap, clap. His time ticks down. Tick, tick, tick. He starts his run up and I move onto the track.

The officials measure and rake his jump. I stand on my marker as the minute clock resets.

I don't clap.

I look down the runway, over the pit, and settle my focus on a black bar at the front section of the seating just after the bend of the track. I don't look at the pit, don't think about the board. Just the bar.

This is what the last six months have been about, the next step to Berlin. To London.

I breathe and mentally block everything out. The immediate world around me goes quieter, the focus softer.

I lean back slightly, then push forwards into my run up. I drive through the first few steps, bringing my body up into my sprinting position. Hips high, straight back. I move quickly down the runway. I hit the board and push up through the air, my legs kicking as I hang. I land in the sand and push forwards. Always forwards. Up and out of the pit.

I check the flag: white. I check the board. I know the jump is OK. Solid not great. It's measured at 7.87 metres.

I head back to my spot, dress again, and move across the track to where Len is sitting. I look to where he's sat and my eye is drawn to his right, two seats up.

He is here.

Len moves to the front of the stand so we can talk.

'What the fuck is he doing here?' I say.

'Who?'

'Him.'

Len turns and sees Chris Madison, leaning slightly forwards, concentrating on the event.

'Forget him,' he says.

Beijing: 'Only you can stop me.'

I look back towards him.

Len snaps me out of it. 'Hey,' he says with force. 'Look at me, not him. Now, listen. That guy is going to be everywhere you jump in the next four years. Every major event you compete in, he's there. And he won't be sat in the stand. He'll be kitted up and ready to roll. Fully prepared, ready for war. So, you better get used to jumping when he's around. Because every jump you jump, he's going to be right behind you trying to beat it. This guy is serious about his work. I've heard the stories. You want to win; you're going to have to beat him. Get used to his face. Because it'll be watching you for more than just today. OK?'

I nod.

'Your hips dropped a little on your first one as you moved into the board. You kept them high second time. Keep that going. Don't let it become a habit. Remember every session we did. High hips. High hips.'

I go back to my place and wait to jump again.

I force myself to not look at him. Force myself to not meet his eyes. I keep warm a bit further away from the runway than on the last two jumps, facing away.

Stripped and ready, back on the runway. I try to focus, to stick to the routine. High hips, high hips repeating in my mind.

I lean back. I run and jump. Hang and kick. I look back: red flag.

I slam the sand and look at Len. He shakes his head, lifts his chin with his hand. Behind Len, I see him. Watching, judging.

Dressed again. I tell myself to focus, remind myself it was all for this. To be better in competition, medal in Berlin, to keep improving until I'm the best in the world.

His face in that Beijing nightclub keeps appearing.

On the runway, breathing to clear my mind. Rachel's words appear: 'Your job is just running and jumping?'

I move into my run up. My hips are high, my speed good. I hit the board and jump, knowing it's good. The flag is white.

It's measured at 8.39 metres. A new Personal Best.

I suppress the instinct to throw my arms in the air and celebrate. I don't want him to think I'm pleased. I want him to think I expected it, to think I've got more.

I look to where he was sitting. His seat is empty.

I don't know if he saw.

RACHEL DOESN'T MEET me at the airport because of work, but she does finish early, promising she'll cook for me. She opens the door and greets me with a huge smile before throwing her arms around me.

'I missed you,' she says.

She leads me through to the kitchen.

I sit, and she asks me question after question about the training camp and the competition. I answer them, but I'm distracted by her. I've been giddy to see her, like a teenager. I watch her cooking and I know I have to tell her now.

'I, erm, I missed you a lot,' I said.

She turns, wooden spoon in hand, and says, 'I know. It was so strange not seeing to you every day.'

'I just...'

Derek walks into the kitchen and spots me. 'Hello, Adam. I didn't realise you were here.'

'Just got here, two minutes ago,' I say.

'Rach says you won your competition and jumped a PB.'

'Yeah. I was very pleased.'

He leans into the fridge and pulls out a bottle of lager. As he clicks the top off it with a bottle opener, he says, 'You look well.'

He's referencing my training tan. 'Nothing like training in the in the California sun,' I say.

'Maybe I should think about doing that,' he says, lifting his bottle and smiling. He taps his stomach and leaves.

'How are your mum and dad?' Rachel asks.

'I don't want to talk about my mum and dad,' I say, standing up and moving towards her.

'Oh.'

I gently slip my arms around her and turn her to face me. 'I missed you a lot,' I repeat. 'And I wanted to tell you.'

'You've told me.'

'Let me finish.'

I'm nervous, my stomach doing flips.

'I wanted to tell you that I realised something while I was away.'

'What?'

'That I love you.'

She smiles and kisses me. Stopping, she says, 'I love you too.'

Citius. Altius. Fortius.
Faster. Higher. Stronger.

10

LIFE ROLLS ON, a cycle of training and preparation, rest and recovery. There's a surprise meal for Pete's birthday and family Sunday dinners. Friends talking about summer holidays, nights at Rachel's cooking late dinners after we've both finish working.

In early June, we manage to spend an afternoon in Manchester shopping for my sister's birthday. Walking out of H&M on Market Street, we almost bump into Michelle.

'Hi,' she says, kissing me. 'I've not seen you in ages.'

'I know.' I turn and introduce Rachel. 'Rachel, this is Michelle, Dan Hall's wife. I used to train with Dan.'

'Nice to meet you,' Rachel says.

'How is Dan?' I ask. 'I've called him a few times, but never get an answer.'

Michelle pauses, just for a brief moment, before saying, 'He's really busy. Did he tell you he's decided to work for that kids coaching company?'

'No.'

'Well, yeah. He's gone in as a partner. So, he's learning all the ropes, getting to grips with running a business. He's had a few speaking gigs too.'

'Good stuff. Keeping busy then, not missing us lot at training.'

'He's still doing bloody abs circuits in front of the breakfast news every morning.'

I laugh at the image.

'You guys should come around for dinner one night,' she suggests. 'It'd be good to see you. Both of you,' she adds, turning to Rachel.

'That'd be good. Get Dan to ring me. I'm in Berlin next week for the Golden League.'

She kisses my cheek again and waves bye to both of us as she disappears into the crowd of shoppers.

I MISS MY sister's birthday to go to Berlin. We planned this meet as it's in the same stadium the Worlds will take place in. Len wants me to experience running down the runway, jumping in the pit, to experience the big crowd in that stadium, prior to the Worlds. He wants everything to feel familiar and comfortable when I go back in nine weeks as part of Team GB.

The stadium is full, people out to watch top level competition in the Sunday sunshine I take in every detail: how far the warm-up track is from the changing rooms, the position of the main track in the stadium, the bright blue running track.

'What's up?' his voice says from behind as I put my bag down in the jumper's area.

I ignore him.

'I saw you jump in California,' he says.

I ignore him.

'You jumped well. Eight point three nine metres. A long fucking way.'

I turn and smile. 'I'm starting to feel like you're stalking me.'

He laughs and shakes my hand. It feels like a friendly gesture.

I don't ignore him as the competition begins. He's jumping three places a head of me, so I'm always watching for him. Always wanting to know where he is so I can start my preparation for each jump. I can't ignore him because he leads from the Second Round with 8.34 metres. All day his name sits on the top of the board, the name to beat.

I hit 8.17 metres in Round Four. My best of the day, but not enough. For the first time all season, I don't win.

He does.

I finish fourth.

'FOURTH'S THE WORST,' Michelle says to Rachel at dinner the following week.

'Why? Surely last is the worst.'

'No, no, no. You and I would think that as normal people. But they' – referring to me and Dan, the only other people around their wooden dining table – 'aren't normal.'

Dan says, 'Fourth is the worst place to finish because it's the closest place to the medals, without getting one. Finishing last, you had no chance. But fourth is so close. Too close. Fourth breaks your heart.'

'Like in Beijing,' I say. 'Two centimetres was the difference between me winning a medal and nothing in Beijing. That's the margins we are talking about. In Berlin I jumped 8.17. Third jumped 8.18. One bloody centimetre.'

'What did last jump?'

'I don't know.'

'And he doesn't care,' Dan says. 'Because it's not about who's behind you, it's about who beat you.' He turns to me and asks, 'Who finished third?'

'Henning,' I say.

'I bet Henning doesn't know what you jumped.'

'I thought you would've known the results. Are you not bothered now?'

Dan looks straight at me and, with no hint of a joke in his voice, says, 'The last thing I want to do at the moment is watch long jumping.'

'Are you coming to Berlin?'

'No.'

He stands and clears away the empty plates from our starters. He moves quickly to the kitchen, Michelle following.

'Is he OK?' Rachel asks.

I shrug.

They return from the kitchen and we are served with our mains. As we eat, I ask Dan about his job and he shrugs and says, 'It's OK.'

We finish and Rachel insists on helping Michelle clear the plates.

Left alone with Dan, I say, 'I'm surprised you're not going to Berlin. I thought you'd want to come and watch. No pressure, enjoy the sport for what it is.'

He looks at me, his eyes cold. 'When you retire,' he says. 'You'll understand that you don't want to spend your time sat watching a bunch of guys do something you love, knowing they're not doing it as well as you could.'

I'm left silent, a silence that's broken by the laughter of our partners returning from the kitchen.

AS SUMMER CONTINUES, our diaries become more important. We sit across from each other at Rachel's parents' dining table one night, comparing our work loads, when and where I'm competing, when I'm due to fly to the Team GB holding camp in Portugal. We write down the days she's at conferences and the days she knows work will be hectic. The number of days we can actually spend together reduces with every page we turn.

'It'd be easier if we lived together,' she says. 'At least then we'd always see each other in the morning and at night.'

We share a look, both breaking out in smiles.

'Really?' I ask.

'Why not?'

'We could rent somewhere in town,' I say. 'I could cycle to work, you can walk.'

'It'd save all this running around, meeting at parents' houses after work.'

'Plus, you love me and can't wait to live with me.'

'The practical side is more important.'

'Thanks for that,' I say, laughing.

A FRIDAY NIGHT in Rome, at the Golden Gala event.

One of those nights where everything works. My run ups are spot on, my take offs are good. I feel strong and quick. The event develops quickly into a battle between me and Eric Blanc, of France. He leads but I'm running him close. Round Four he hits a big jump, somewhere near 8.30 metres but is red flagged. He's fuming, shaking his finger at the official.

I'm up next to jump. I know he's on the side of the track, watching. I fly through the air. White flag. 8.41 metres. Another new PB.

I force myself to act like it was all in the plan. I look at Eric as I get back to my spot. The fight has drained out of him.

No one jumps further than me.

LEN IS HAPPY. We sit in the breakfast room of the hotel the next morning, sipping orange juice and eating porridge.

'Last night was a huge step forward,' he says. 'You were excellent. Consistent in your run up. The fact you didn't foul highlights that.' There's no laptop now, no stats or spreadsheets. Just Len talking with a gleam in his eye. 'That consistency is something you need to maintain. It's what I've been banging on about all winter. If you red flag, you lose a chance. If you were playing football you wouldn't offer to play with ten or nine men, would you?'

'No,' I say.

'That's what fouling is. It's offering to play your opponent with less. A wasted opportunity.'

'But last night,' I say, trying to drag the conversation back to the positive way it started.

'Last night was better. And not just for the consistency. But for the way you smelt the weak moment in Blanc and seized it. When he fouled and you put in that big PB jump. That broke his spirit. As we carry on with our work over the next few years, you need to remember last night. That control, that seizing your moment. It'll stand you in good stead. Well done. Be pleased with yourself today. Not cocky. But you should be pleased that the work is paying off.'

Lukas Cooke, one of the men I beat last night, moves towards my table. 'Did you hear about Chris Madison?' he asks.

'No,' I say.

'He jumped 8.68 metres in the States last night.'

I put my orange juice down.

'That puts him in the top ten of all time,' Lukas says.

LATE JULY WE go to Crystal Palace for my last competition in the UK before the Worlds. My grandma travels down to watch with my family. She has watched every event I've competed in at this venue.

'It should be a privilege to jump there,' she once told me. 'Like playing football at Old Trafford.'

The line-up is strong, with everyone preparing for Berlin in two weeks.

Round One. I'm jumping in the middle of the pack. I move smoothly down the runway, hit the board, take-off, and land.

White flag. 8.26 metres, which has me leading.

I'm still winning in Round Four when I red flag a big jump that would've increased my lead. The crowd groans. I find Len in the crowd and he makes a small space between his thumb and forefinger, indicating the distance he thinks I was over.

My lead slips. First becomes third in Round Five with Lukas Cooke and George Brown, a Jamaican, overtaking me. I only manage 7.63 metres and I let my frustration show by smacking the sand. I don't look to Len. There's no need.

It's on me now.

One jump left.

I need to hit big to pull something out here.

Chris Madison hits 8.49 metres and takes the competition, forcing me out to fourth. Fucking fourth. The adrenaline drains from me rapidly as a top three finish disappears from my grasp. I shake hands with my fellow competitors, offer congratulations.

'See you in Berlin,' he says.

'Yeah,' I mumble.

BERLIN. BERLIN. Berlin. That is all I think about. I think about the stadium as my sister tells me about the lad she met on her night out the previous weekend.

I think about the blue track as I eat my last meal with my family before I leave for holding camp.

I think about how I can up my performance from Crystal Palace during my last hours with Rachel.

Berlin. Berlin. Berlin.

A long jumper's job is to defy gravity for as long as possible.

11

Berlin, August 2009
The World Athletics Championships

AND THEN IT'S here. My second major final.

Time ticks away. I prepare my bag, pin my number to my vest. Everyone on the bus to the stadium is quiet, hidden in the music from their headphones. I put mine in and lean back in the seat, watching the world pass by, recognising landmarks from the same bus journey on Thursday when I came to the stadium for Qualifying, which I did in one jump.

At the stadium, I register and go to the changing rooms.

The first sight I see as I open the door is Chris Madison, who is dressed in just shorts. He stands tall and solid. 'Big night tonight,' he says.

'Big night,' I repeat.

'You ready?'

'You'll see,' I say.

He laughs. It's a booming laugh that sounds like it's echoing off the walls. 'That's the attitude.'

I make my way to a space in the corner and change.

I warm-up, repeating the same process as always. Everything designed to make me feel like this is just another event, like all the others I've been to since I was twelve.

Waiting to enter the main section of the stadium, I listen to the crowd, let the adrenaline start to take over a bit. I like that there are 70,000 people here because that means 70,000 people are going to see how good I am, how far I can jump. This is what I do. I'm good at it. Tonight is another step forward in becoming great at it.

I look around me at my fellow athletes. *I can beat every one of you*, I think.

I look at him. He looks at me.

Even you.

HE LEADS WITH 8.42 metres as twelve jumpers become eight after three rounds. I'm fifth having jumped a best of 8.18 metres. This is the time to perform. This is the reason for all the winter work, all the time I was sick by the side of the track, when my back creaked like an old staircase as I got out of bed but still put my body through two training sessions in the day. This is the time to use every ounce of strength and speed gained in those dark winter months.

I'm jumping fourth now. I take my place on the runway; focus on the spot over the pit. A rhythmic clap begins from the crowd. I focus on my breathing. In and out. It's just running and jumping. I lean back and start my run up. Faster and faster through the metres, into the board and up. I hang and kick, then hit the sand.

I look for the flag: white.

I stand and let the official measure. 8.42 metres A new PB, with the exact same distance as him. I'm the joint leader.

Two jumps to go.

Round Five. The pressure moves to him. And he handles it perfectly, retaking the lead with 8.48 metres. I see the distance come up on the board, watch him bang his chest and scream 'yeah baby' to the sky. He jumps around and encourages the crowd to chant and clap.

I force the disappointment from my mind and go through my routine. I can't change what he has done. I can only focus on going further than him. Further than I've ever been. Again.

I stand waiting for the runway behind Sergio Rossi, who's fourth. He bounces up from the sand following his jump and holds his hands to his mouth. He waits, the stadium waits. I wait.

8.45 metres.

I'm in the bronze medal position.

I start my run up. I attack the board but feel myself stretching into it. Measured at 8.37 metres. Not good enough. I look at Len, who sits unmoved. It's down to me now. To win, I have to be better. Nothing he can say will change that fact.

The medal positions don't change as the round ends. I go into my final jump knowing a seven-centimetre improvement on my PB will possibly win me the World Championship gold medal.

This is it. This is the moment.

1.00… 0.59… 0.58…

I breathe in and out. Relax.

0.52… 0.51… 0.50…

I focus on the spot over the pit.

0.45… 0.44… 0.43…

I start my run up.

Into the board at speed. Up.

I land in the sand and push forwards. I look at the official: white flag. I look at the measuring board. I stand slowly.

8.39 metres.

It's over.

The competition finishes, and it's confirmed that my first medal at a major Championship is bronze. Rossi and Madison find me and the three of us shake hands and embrace. We will stand on the podium together, listening to the Star-Spangled Banner.

THERE'S A CAMERA on me, my every moment filmed. I smile down the lens. Someone hands me a British flag. I lift it high above me.

Rachel appears at the barrier, and I move across the track to her. We kiss and I pull her into me. She's crying and laughing.

'I love you,' she says. 'You were amazing.'

'I love you too.'

David from the BBC wants to talk. I stand in front of the camera, my medal around my neck.

'Adam,' David says, 'Congratulations. The bronze medal. How does it feel?'

'At first I was disappointed. I didn't jump as well as I'd have liked in the last two rounds. That said, at the beginning of the year I sat in my coach's office and talked about a plan for my career. The plan for this year was to win a medal here, no matter the colour. This,' I say, holding up my bronze medal, 'means I've achieved what we set out to do.'

'Will you share with us the plan for next year?'

'No chance.'

David laughs. 'What now?'

'Sleep probably,' I say. 'The season is over for me now. A few weeks good rest, then it all starts again in the build-up to Barcelona next summer.'

'You certainly deserve your moment in the spotlight, Adam. Well done.'

Before I can thank him, Chris Madison passes behind me. David seizes his moment and says, 'And here is the winner of the men's long jump. Chris, if you could just spare us a minute.'

He stops and smiles. 'Sure thing.'

'Congratulations on your gold medal. You must be delighted,' David says.

'World number one. Man, it feels great. You know we work so hard, everyone is capable of beating anyone at any given time, so it's amazing to walk away with gold.'

'And a word about our own Adam Lowe, standing here with the bronze medal. He ran you close for a while there.'

Chris doesn't look at me when he says, 'The kid jumped well.'

The kid?

'It was a great competition. But, you know, I'm just glad to have won this.' He holds his gold medal up to the camera. 'I'm the World Champion. The World Number One.'

The fucking kid.

The kid.

12

WE'RE TWENTY FLOORS up, overlooking Manchester, in a room in the Hilton Hotel I've booked for us. I checked in early in the afternoon and relaxed, swimming in the pool and lying in the sauna. At about half five, I dressed and walked across town to meet Rachel at her office. She's finished early so we can celebrate my birthday. There is no thought of training, no need to do an abs circuit or a weights session.

She is amazed at the views. We lie on the bed and talk; her telling me about the latest case she's working on and reminding me about the company barbeque I said I'd attend on Saturday.

We shower and change and go for a drink in the bar before going for dinner in a local Greek restaurant Laura recommended. We're back in the room for half-past ten.

The next morning, Rachel wakes early and showers. She dresses again while I lounge in bed. She kisses me on my stale mouth and says, 'I'm sorry this isn't a lazy day in this massive bed.'

'It will be for me.'

She kisses me again and says, 'I'll see you tonight.'

'This is what it will be like when we live together,' I say.

'It won't be anywhere near this fancy.'

She leaves for work, the door softly shutting behind her. I drift in and out of sleep in the comfortable hotel bed, covered in the heavy duvet. In those moments, on the blurred line between being asleep and awake, I see his face and hear his words.

The kid jumped well.

'I HAD A lovely time,' my grandma says. 'What a nice city. I really enjoyed it.'

She's been telling us all about her sightseeing around Berlin, even though my parents and sister, who are also sitting at the dining table in my parents' house along with Rachel, were with her. I listen to stories about the Berlin I didn't see.

My sister passes out plates and my mum serves Sunday dinner.

'Where are you going on holiday?' my dad asks.

'We don't know yet. We'll just book something late.'

'I'm off for a week in a couple of weeks,' Rachel says. 'I just want some sun and a sun bed. I've worked very long hours recently.'

'I liked Rhodes,' my mum says, referencing a holiday they went on a couple of years ago. 'Lovely place, if you avoid the young people bit.'

'Somewhere quiet is all we want,' Rachel says.

My grandma says to Jane, 'Are you going away this year?'

'Thinking about it,' she says.

'Where you thinking?' I ask.

Jane eats her lunch and doesn't look me in the eye.

Confused, I say, 'What's up?'

'Nothing. I'm just thinking about a few places.'

'Why are you being weird?'

'I'm not being weird.'

'You are.'

'Stop it.'

'Stop what?'

'Stop pushing me.'

I sigh and say, 'I'm just asking where you're thinking of going on holiday.'

She puts her knife and fork down. 'Me and Molly from work are thinking of moving to Australia.'

I POUR A glass of red wine and move through the dining room to the open double doors at the back of the house. I step into the garden and walk to where Jane is sitting on a foldout chair. The sun is going down, but the evening remains warm.

I hand her the glass and sit on the grass. 'Peace offering,' I say.

She takes it and sips. We sit quietly for a few seconds. I concentrate on the sound of the birds flapping their wings in the trees.

'I didn't want it to come out like that,' she says.

'Like what?'

'During your special celebratory meal.'

'Don't say it like that. I didn't ask them to make a big deal of it.'

'You never do. But they always do.'

I stay quiet.

She drinks more wine and continues, 'It's only something we are thinking about. We could travel through Asia first, then do six months working in a hospital in Sydney or somewhere. Molly knows a couple of girls who have done it already. They loved it.'

'So, what's the problem with telling Mum and Dad?'

She stops concentrating on the trees and looks at me. 'Because it wasn't just about telling them. It was about telling them in my own time and my own way.'

'And I forced you into saying it when you didn't want to?'

'Not just that. But yes.'

'What else?'

She moves hair behind her ear and looks off into the distance again. It feels colder than when I came out here, but I don't want to leave because it feels like a big deal to her to say something.

'I don't like long jumping,' she says. 'In fact, I hate it.'

'OK.'

'Yet it defines my life. My brother, the Olympian.'

'Where is this coming from?'

'You know that's how it works. Every summer for the next few years is already filled with Mum and Dad planning trips to wherever it is you're competing. I just wanted something that was mine. So, you pushing me into telling them, when I don't even know if I'm going to go, just feels like something else that I want to be about me, being about you.'

I look at her. A lone tear wells in her eye and starts to roll down her cheek. I never considered that what I do has an impact on her life, how my parents treat her. In fact, I've always thought they went out of their way to make things easier for her. They never missed a school play or a graduation. They paid for more holidays for her than they did for me. I got money towards my first car; she got a whole car.

'I think that's unfair,' I say. My voice raises a level. 'What am I supposed to do? Not compete because you don't like it.'

'Don't be stupid.' She pauses, as if her brain is showing her the words she can use and she's deciding which ones fit the moment. 'I know this has come out of the blue. Maybe I'm being unfair. But this feels like the right time to say some things. I love you. You're a good brother. But my life sometimes feels like it's secondary to yours. It's not your fault. It's not Mum and Dad's fault either. I'm sure they'd be devastated if they heard me saying this. But I feel like everything I've done, everything I've achieved is slightly overshadowed.'

'You save lives for a living,' I say.

'Exactly. And yet people I meet want to talk about the fact you jump into a sandpit. The other week, I met a guy in the pub. He was nice and seemed interested in me. We had a laugh, got on well. He asked me out. We went for a drink and he said he'd been watching the start of the Worlds. I told him about you and that was it for the rest of the night. He wanted to know everything. I sat in this pub, with this really nice guy, and all I could think was I wish I hadn't told him about my brother.'

'It sounds like the problem is yours.'

'Maybe it is. Maybe I'm being irrational and stupid. But when you pushed me into telling everyone in there about Australia, it just made me realise how much it all annoys me. Australia was mine. My decision to go and see the world. And you made me talk about it at a meal to celebrate you. There was a bronze medal on the table when you made me talk about it.'

She downs the rest of the wine and we don't say anything for a few minutes.

'I just wanted to sit everyone down and tell them myself. It sounds stupid. But I wanted to have my moment. I don't think that's too much to ask.'

'You have moments. Mum and Dad haven't missed anything of yours. I've never seen them prouder than when you graduated. I'm the son who didn't go to university to concentrate on becoming a professional long jumper. I know what their disappointed faces look like.'

'The year I graduated, you became an Olympian.' She pauses, then says, 'What I'm trying to say is this. I didn't want to bring it up tonight because I didn't want to overshadow your special dinner. You deserve your moment. I don't want to take that away from you. But I didn't want my thing to be an afterthought.'

'I don't think anyone would think that.'

'I did,' she says.

I START TO get the twitchy feeling from not exercising. It's ten days after the Worlds. I've slept late, sat on the couch and watched films and box sets. I've met the lads for drinks and cooked Rachel dinner when she got home from work. But I'm bored.

I start to look online at apartments to rent I make lists of ones worth seeing. At night, Rachel and I discuss the pros and cons of each, whilst looking the photos on the Internet. We narrow the list down and I make calls to the estate agent, arranging viewings for the weekend.

On Saturday, we drive into the city centre and meet several suited estate agents at places in town. The first stop after lunch we go to a place in Castlefield. We take the lift up to the fourth floor and walk into the apartment. We inspect the two bedrooms, the bathroom, and then the main living area, which is split into sections, with a brick pillar in the centre marking the end of the spacious lounge and start of the dining area.

I look at Rachel and she says, 'This is the one.'

I CALL HER at work a few days later.

'I'm trying to get the estate agent to get us the keys by Saturday,' I say. 'Should we set up a joint bank account before or when we've moved in?'

I can hear the tapping of keyboards and the ringing of phones in the background, a layer of chatter.

'Do we have to talk about this now?'

'I'm just trying to get everything sorted.'

'Adam, I'm at work. I'm busy. Can we talk about this tonight?'

'Well, if you let me know now, I can start speaking to the bank.'

She pauses, then says, 'I'll talk to you later.'

The phone goes dead.

I ARRIVE AT her house, unsure of her mood. She opens the door and walks back into the kitchen. No kiss, barely a hello.

'You OK?' I ask.

'Yeah.'

She's dressed in her running kit, and her forehead is red and sweaty. She pours herself a large glass of water from the jug in the fridge.

'How was your run?'

'Good.'

She drinks half the glass in one go.

'Do you want to talk about earlier?'

She drinks the other half without answering.

I start, 'Why did you put the phone down on me?'

'Because the conversation had finished.'

'I hadn't.'

She opens the fridge again and pours more water.

'I'm trying to get the flat sorted as quickly as possible. We're going away next week.'

'I'm aware of that. Which is why I'm working all the hours to get my stuff done. Do you think I can pack up my life and move into a new flat on Saturday? It's only four days away.'

'I just want to get it sorted,' I repeat.

'Why? What's the rush?'

'Because I don't want to be thinking about moving while we are away. I want it to be stress free. For both of us.'

'Rushing around for the next four days and doing a quick job of moving is not going to make for a stress-free holiday. Nothing will be organised, and I'll be thinking about it all while we're away. I want to go on holiday, relax, and then come back and sort it out. We've got the place. We can take our time.'

'I need to be in soon though,' I say.

She shuts the fridge with a thud. 'Why?'

I tell her the truth. I'm desperate to be moved in before training starts again in two weeks. I don't want the distraction and stress of moving while trying to focus on Len's new plans. I need a clear mind to be able to rest. Next year is too important. It needs to start perfectly.

She thinks I'm being dramatic. I can tell from the slight raise of her eyebrows and the way she won't quite look at me.

'You think I'm being stupid, don't you?'

'What do you want me to say?'

'The truth.'

'I think you're being stupid. And selfish. Why is it OK for me to spend the next few days rushing around like an idiot to move into a place on Saturday? Is my job not as important as yours? I'm trying to earn a full-time contract at my work. I need to show my worth. You know all this. So why is it we should work around what you want? I want to go on holiday with a clear mind and a clear desk. Not stressing about a half furnished flat and unpacked boxes, plus a load of work I've not finished.'

First my sister, now Rachel.

I listen and step forward, putting my arms around her. She lets me. 'I'm sorry,' I say. 'You're right. I didn't think about you.'

'Work is hard at the moment. I need you support. I don't want to be arguing.'

'OK. Do you want to talk work?'

'No. I want to eat and talk about our holiday.'

WE FLY TO Greece. For the first time since we met in December, we are going to spend more than a couple of nights together.

We spend a week doing nothing. The first few days we sleep late, sunbath, sleep again in the afternoon, walk into the local town for dinner. We sit on our balcony and talk about our future. A future she says includes promotions for her, medals for me.

A future we can't picture without each other.

By the pool one day, she says, 'We'll have to return the favour to Dan and Michelle when we move and have them over for dinner. And Laura and Pete.'

'I don't want to talk about Dan,' I say.

We're both facing the sky as we speak, enjoying the hot sun on our skin.

'Why not?'

I stay quiet, my eyes closed underneath my sunglasses. I can hear kids splashing in the water and low music playing in the bar across the pool.

Finally, I say, 'He only sent me a text message after Berlin. All the years we trained together, all the advice he gave me, and all he manages is a text message saying *congratulations, mate*. That's it. He was like my mentor. We're friends. Or at least I thought we were. He used to say to me how I was going to win medals, make everybody proud. Then I win one and he couldn't give a shit.'

She moves on to her side to face me, but I continue to lie on my back.

'Do you know why?' she asks.

'Because since he retired, he's been a miserable prick.'

The kid. The kid.

13

LEN FINDS A problem.

He comes to my house, sets up his laptop on my dining table and says, 'I've noticed something.'

I sit across from him and hand him a mug of coffee.

He turns his computer screen towards me and all my competitions from last season are listed in order. There are six columns, each entitled Round One, Round Two, etc. Highlighted in red are the best jumps from each competition. There are no red marks in the final two columns.

'You don't improve your distances after Round Four.'

'I'd not noticed that.'

'It's something we need to work on,' Len says. 'We need to get you to have that big jump in your locker. At the moment the people you're jumping against, if they spot this pattern' – he points to the screen – 'will write you off after Round Four. They'll know if they can jump further than you in Round Five, you'll be out of the chase. If we can get you jumping further in the last couple of rounds, it means you've got the potential to win competitions at the crucial moment. Jumping your furthest in late rounds gives the competition less time to react.'

I look at the screen. 'So, what do we do?'

'I've watched all your performances from last year. You're tired when it gets to the later rounds. Understandably. We're going to put an extra training session in the week. I think the extra work should give you extra when it comes to feeling strong at the later stages of competitions.'

'When in doubt, work harder,' I say.

'Exactly.'

Like last year, we talk about the plan for the year to come. My bronze medal from Berlin means nothing now.

'This year the plan is to win in Barcelona,' Len says. 'Your major challengers for the Worlds next year and the Olympics in 2012 are not European. You need to be showing those guys you're the best in Europe. That carries weight.'

I sit and listen to him. He's thought through every step of my four-year plan. I've followed and, so far, achieved the goals he has set.

Len packs away his things and leaves.

Alone, I think about Barcelona, the end goal of all the training that's about to begin.

Chris Madison won't be there. He won't beat me. He won't call me a kid. Not this time. Barcelona will be about me, not him.

My reflection looks back at me from the mirror. I tell myself that all I can do is focus on me. Focus on me. Focus on me. Control what I can control.

14

I PACK AWAY my life.

I sit in my bedroom with open boxes and fill them with CDs and DVDs. At the bottom of the wardrobe, I find a pile of old local newspapers. I turn the top one over and find a picture of the younger me at a school's event captured in mid-air, legs and arms outstretched, suspended above a sandpit. I look at the picture for a few minutes, recalling exactly how I was feeling in that moment, nine years ago. The strain in my muscles, the grimace on my face, the wide eyes, they all remind me. The photo is of a Personal Best jump, thirty-seven centimetres further than I'd ever gone before. I remember knowing when I was in the air, the moment the photograph was taken, that the jump was big.

Every jump is different. Each jump is changed by the weather, the run up, the take-off. All these things are pieces of the puzzle, and if any of them are off by a fraction, the jump can be affected. But when they all click, when everything is perfect, I can push into the air and everything in life dissolves. In between take-off and landing, the pressures of life, the stress of moving house, or upsetting your sister, the arguments with a girlfriend, all fade away and life is just about flying through the air.

The picture was one of those jumps. I've had others since, but even some of my Personal Bests have not felt like that jump. I know when my hips are too low on the run up or I'm stretching into the board. I, and all my rivals, are working and pushing in the hope that our perfect days will come when we need them most: the Olympics, the Worlds, and the other major events.

I know I need that one jump to take me further than my rivals. Further than him. Further than I've ever been before.

I'M IN FRONT of the bookshelf in the lounge, staring at the thin line between the dictionary and thesaurus. I know the letter I wrote to myself after Beijing is still there. My goal is unmoved. Behind me, Pete and Mike are a carrying a section of my double bed down the stairs.

'A little help wouldn't go a miss,' Pete shouts.

I ignore him and rotate the choice around my brain.

Leave the letter, take the letter?

Take the letter, leave the letter?

I walk away, the letter untouched. It doesn't seem right to move it. I told myself I would go back to it in four years. Now is too soon.

My mum makes us all lunch as we load the contents of my life into the back of a rented van. I eat as I drive, still hungry from my Saturday morning training session.

At my new home, Mike stands on the balcony, taking in the view of the city. 'Great place to come back to after a night out this. If you ever came on any.'

'What you getting at?' I say.

He turns and smiles. 'Only joking, mate. We all know you're only interested in jumping really far. The more serious you are about it, the better.'

'Why's that?'

'I've got a bet on you to win in London.'

'Well, there's a reason to do more training.'

Rachel and I spend the rest of the night and into Sunday organising our lives into one. She decorates the bookshelf in the lounge with pictures of her friends and family as I stack our new plates and bowls in the cupboards. Mid Sunday afternoon we take the short walk into the city centre and sit in a coffee shop and talk about how great it is to be able to make a short walk into the city centre and sit in a coffee shop. Then we walk back to the apartment and cook dinner together.

The next morning, Rachel wakes at half five and gets ready for work. I sleep for another couple of hours, then slowly wake, stretch myself out as I lie under the duvet, feeling the stresses and strains of Saturday's session.

A FEW DAYS later, I arrive at training on my bike. As I lock it up, I hear my phone ringing, then see my sister's number on the screen.

'Adam,' she says. Her voice cracks, even just saying the short word.

'What's wrong?'

'Grandma's had a fall.'

I take the news in. Hundreds of questions fly round my brain, but I can't think of one to ask. I settle on, 'Where is she?'

'She's been taken to Wythenshawe.'

'Where was she when it happened?'

'At home,' she says. 'They found her about an hour ago.'

I look at the entrance to the building I was about to enter, think about the weight session I'm scheduled to do. 'Who's with her?'

'Mum and Dad are on their way.'

'Is she OK?'

'I don't know. Dad said she was conscious.'

'Is there anything I can do right now?'

She is quiet for a few seconds and then says, 'No.' Another pause. 'You're not coming, are you?'

'I'll be there in a couple of hours.'

I WALK ALONG the bland hospital corridor, reading signs above my head. Doctors and nurses pass me, checking their phones as they walk, expertly stepping out of the way of people coming towards them without taking their eyes off the screens.

I ask the receptionist what bed my grandma is in. She points down the corridor and says, 'Four.'

I step onto the ward, rubbing my hands with the cleaning gel. I walk past flowery curtains that are pulled around patients' beds and stop when I see my mum sat on a plastic hospital chair in a private room. My dad and Jane are on the other side of the room, Jane on a hard, plastic chair and my dad leaning on the wall. Their eyes all pointed towards my grandma who lies asleep in bed. She looks peaceful, but years older than the last time I saw her.

'What have they said?' I ask my mum.

'She had a fall in the kitchen. Mrs Thomas next door noticed her on the floor when she was pegging some washing out. She was out for a while. I got there at the same time as the paramedics and she woke up when they started talking to her. We don't know how long she was there, but it must have been a while because she wasn't dressed. She's normally had a walk to the shop by nine o'clock.'

'What has she done?' I ask.

'She's broken her ankle and seems to have sprained her wrist.'

I look at the bruising that runs down the left side of my grandma's face. 'What did she fall on?'

'She dropped the ice tray when taking something out of the freezer. There must have been some cubes on the floor she didn't spot.'

'Seems like a lot of damage.'

'She's not as strong as she used to be,' my dad says. It's the first time he has spoken since I entered the room. He's just been looking at his mum lying in the bed. Her only movement is her chest slowly rising and falling with each breath.

My parents go and get something to eat, and I sit in the chair my mum vacates. My sister doesn't say anything so we listen to the beeps of machines in other rooms, the occasional alarm sounding and nurses discussing another patient in the corridor.

'What took you so long to get here?' Jane asks.

'I had to train.'

She looks back at our grandma.

More beeps.

'Any news on Australia?' I asked.

'You really want to talk about that now?' she says.

'Do you really want to sit in silence?'

She leans back in the chair. Her face still shows stains of the tears cried before I arrived. I think about how this situation must be strange for her. She spends her life in a hospital just like this, caring for people just like our grandma. She is strong and compassionate. She tells us stories at home about learning how to deal with the stressful situations for patients and their families. Now she sits on the other side of the divide. She doesn't have the charts and the numbers of our grandma's progress to review, or the levels of medicine to control. She has memories of fun times and the feelings of sadness as her grandma lies asleep in the metal bed under thin white sheets looking broken.

'We've decided to go,' she says.

'Brilliant,' I say. 'When?'

'Just before Christmas.' She looks at Grandma.

'You need to go and enjoy yourself.'

'I need to apply for jobs, but we want to do a bit of travelling first. Thailand, Malaysia.'

An alarm beeps somewhere on the ward. It seems to signal the end of our conversation.

Later, I take a walk to get us some water. I rub my hands with the gel again, aware of how easily I can pick up an infection in this place.

FOR A FEW days, my life becomes training, hospital, training, bed. Repeat.

I sit by her hospital bed, alone. Grandma wakes up in pain but is fully aware of what happened. Her body broken, but her mind clear.

'I'm glad I got to go to Berlin before I die,' she says.

'Don't say that, Grandma.'

'It's true.'

'You're not dying. You're on the mend.'

'I know that. I'm talking generally. It was a lovely city. But it made me think. When I was growing up, Berlin was a dirty word. That's where the bombs came from. Where the enemy was. I'm glad I went to see it before I go and now have a good feeling about the place. It's given me a small bit of peace. I know it sounds silly.'

She shakes her head and falls silent, as if revealing this inner thought is too much.

'It doesn't sound silly,' I say. 'You went through a lot when you were younger.'

'It was wonderful to watch you win a medal, too. I knew you would win one.'

'You'll see me win more than one in your lifetime, Grandma. You get fit and healthy again and we can dance down Las Ramblas in Barcelona.'

She laughs, which physically hurts her. Holding her side, she says, 'I'd like that.'

The kid. The kid. The kid. The kid. The kid. The kid. The kid.
The kid. The kid. The kid. The kid. The kid. The kid. The kid.
The kid. The kid. The kid. The kid. The kid. The kid. The kid.
The kid. The kid. The kid. The kid. The kid. The kid. The kid.
The kid. The kid. The kid. The kid. The kid. The kid. The kid.
The kid. The kid. The kid. The kid. The kid. The kid. The kid.
The kid. The kid. The kid. The kid. The kid. The kid. The kid.
The kid. The kid. The kid. The kid. The kid. The kid. The kid.
The kid. The kid. The kid. The kid. The kid. The kid. The kid.
The kid. The kid. The kid. The kid. The kid. The kid. The kid.
The kid. The kid. The kid. The kid. The kid. The kid. The kid.
The kid. The kid. The kid. The kid. The kid. The kid. The kid.
The kid. The kid. The kid. The kid. The kid. The kid. The kid.
The kid. The kid. The kid. The kid. The kid. The kid. The kid.
The kid. The kid. The kid. The kid. The kid. The kid. The kid.
The kid. The kid. The kid. The kid. The kid. The kid. The kid.
The kid. The kid. The kid. The kid. The kid. The kid. The kid.
The kid. The kid. The kid. The kid. The kid. The kid. The kid.
The kid. The kid. The kid. The kid. The kid. The kid. The kid.
The kid. The kid. The kid. The kid. The kid. The kid. The kid.
The kid. The kid. The kid. The kid. The kid. The kid. The kid.
The kid. The kid. The kid. The kid. The kid. The kid. The kid.
The kid. The kid. The kid. The kid. The kid. The kid. The kid.
The kid. The kid. The kid. The kid. The kid. The kid. The kid.
The kid. The kid. The kid. The kid. The kid. The kid. The kid.
The kid. The kid. The kid. The kid. The kid. The kid. The kid.
The kid. The kid. The kid. The kid. The kid. The kid. The kid.
The kid. The kid. The kid. The kid. The kid. The kid. The kid.
The kid. The kid. The kid. The kid. The kid. The kid. The kid.
The kid. The kid. The kid. The kid. The kid. The kid. The kid.
The kid. The kid. The kid. The kid. The kid. The kid. The kid.
The kid. The kid. The kid. The kid. The kid. The kid. The kid.
The kid. The kid. The kid. The kid. The kid. The kid. The kid.
The kid. The kid. The kid. The kid. The kid. The kid. The kid.
The kid.

15

DAN WALKS INTO the gym as I'm lifting. I catch a glimpse of him as he walks through the door with a leather bag over one shoulder. He stands silently as I finish my set.

'Looking strong,' he offers as I rise from the bench.

'Remembered where we are then?' I say.

He smiles. It's forced and makes him look uncomfortable.

'This is not my home anymore.'

'What you here for then?'

'I wanted a word.'

'With?'

'You.'

'Maybe you should've just text me.'

He looks at me, then looks around at the other athletes doing their sessions. 'Somewhere a bit more private.'

'When I've finished.'

We meet in the canteen. Dan is halfway down a cup of coffee. I get some food and join him.

'OK?' he asks.

'Yeah.'

He drains his drinks and nods.

'It appears I'm not your favourite person,' he says.

I stab my fork into my food and put it in my mouth. I chew and swallow.

'I was just surprised to see you. Not heard from you for months. Nothing but a text message from you after Berlin.'

'I know,' he says. He looks at his bag on the chair next to him. 'I've had a strange few months. A weird year, actually.'

I put more food into my mouth, letting him continue.

'It's been a harder year than I ever would've imagined. Retiring is the most difficult thing I've ever done. I went into it unprepared for the impact it would have on me. It's caused problems in my relationship. A newly married couple should not argue as much as we do.'

I look at him. He is one of my sporting heroes, one of my best friends, one of the toughest athletes I've ever met in my life. He can't look me in the eye.

'I'm writing a book,' he says. He opens the bag next to him and takes out several sheets of A4 paper, held together by a paper clip. 'I spoke to the publisher who approached me before Beijing and told them I want to write something honest that includes my first year of retirement. They've agreed and I've started writing it. This,' he says, holding up the paper, 'is the first draft of the first few pages.'

He hands the pages to me.

'Don't read it now,' he says. 'Read it at home.'

'What am I? Some kind of book critic?'

'You need to read it.'

AT HOME, I put the kettle on and make a coffee. I take the pages out of my bag, unfold them, and sit in a chair. I look at the first page, the clear black lines of writing printed across it. *Chapter One* is written in bold at the top centre.

I start to read:

A few months after I retired from being an athlete, I went back to my old training group to watch them train. It had been a few months since Beijing and my last competition. I thought I'd be OK. I thought it would be easy to just sit and watch the guys train. I was wrong. Having a coffee with Len, my old coach, in his office, he told me how well Adam Lowe was training. I felt sick with jealously. Adam came into the room and we had a bit of banter. I don't remember the whole conversation, but I know he said to me at one point, 'My star can shine now you've gone.' He was right. He was the main man in the training group now. I was old and gone.

For years, during the build-up to Beijing I'd told Adam that he had the chance to be something special in the sport. That day, sat in the stands as he ran around the track, I noticed how fit and strong he looked. He didn't need me watching over him. It was his time to shine. I was sitting in the stands and felt like a spare part, so I left before the session finished.

Adam Lowe was young. I was old. He had his career ahead of him. My career was over. I went home and laid on my bed and cried.

Adam and his girlfriend came to my house one night a few months later to have a meal with me and my wife, Michelle. Adam asked me if I was going to Berlin to watch the 2009 World Championships. I told him I didn't want to watch people compete in something I wished I was taking part in but couldn't because I'd retired.

I stayed true to my word and didn't travel to Berlin. Instead, I sat on my couch and drank lager from the bottle as Adam won a bronze medal. I sat there, slightly drunk, feeling something very strange. It was happiness. Not happiness because Adam had won a medal, but happiness because he hadn't won gold.

That was the harsh truth of the matter. I didn't want Adam to win because I didn't want him to be better than me. In my career I'd won three medals at major championships: a Commonwealth Gold, World Silver, and Olympic Bronze.

The next morning, I couldn't get out of bed. Not because of my hangover, although that didn't help. I just couldn't move. Michelle tried to get me up to go to work a few times, but I just lay there, hiding under the covers. She told me I was going to be late and left. I shouted at her to leave me alone.

I stayed in bed all day. I thought about the past year of my life. The first year for nearly twenty years where I didn't have athletics, more specifically long jumping, as my focus. I'd got married in the past year, exchanged vows with the woman I loved. I'd started a new job too. But I was miserable. I hated my life. Hated the very thought of getting out of bed. Hated looking at myself in the mirror and seeing the reflection of a failure staring back at me.

I felt like a failure because no matter what I did from that point to the day I died I knew I would never win an Olympic Gold medal.

That day in bed, I faced up to it all. All the arguments with my new wife, ignoring my friends and former colleagues, wanting them to lose just to make me feel better. I thought about the misery of going to work at my new job. My new colleagues were good people who had taken a chance on me when I needed a break, and yet I was bitter and angry all the time and not the most engaged new employee.

When Michelle got home that night, I told her how I was feeling. I cried, and she cried. I told her I was sorry about a hundred times. I told her I would stop being so horrible to live with.

The next day I did two things: I booked some counselling sessions and started writing this book.

I sit stunned. I take a drink of my coffee. It's cold. I realise I've read Dan's words four times. His brutal, honest words. I pick up my phone and go to dial his number before putting it down again. What can I say to him? I knew he wasn't happy about retiring. There had been hints at his wedding. But who would be happy ending a career they loved, a career they sacrificed for?

One line keeps repeating over and over in my mind: I knew I would never win an Olympic Gold medal.

I think about my letter, hidden between two books at my parents' house. The letter with the words: *I, Adam Lowe, will be the 2012 Long Jump Olympic Champion.*

I won't end my career in the same way Dan has ended his. I won't feel his disappointment and bitterness. I won't live the rest of my life with that empty feeling.

I pick up my phone and call him.

'It's just running and jumping.'

16

THE WINTER MONTHS pass in a blur of training. On Wednesdays, I visit my grandma. Although recovered from her fall, she isn't the same person who went into hospital. Crossing the kitchen to make cups of tea takes longer than before, and week on week, she looks to have lost more weight.

My sister is leaving the country in mid-December, meaning my mum is planning a family Christmas dinner for weeks earlier than normal. Jane and I go shopping for presents together.

'How's living with Rachel going?' she asks as we walk through the wave of shoppers.

'Good. It's easier to spend time together than before, even if she's working later. We always try to make sure we spend Sundays together. Sleep late and get breakfast in town.'

'You going to marry this girl?'

'I wouldn't be against the idea.'

Jane spins to look at me, as if not expecting my answer. 'Really?'

'I don't think now is the time to ask,' I say.

'Why not?'

'Because things are so up in the air. The pressure on her at work is incredible. She's so stressed.'

'So, when is the right time?'

'I've not thought about it,' I lie.

In my mind, I know the truth. I will propose after the Olympic Final in 2012, when I've won my gold medal.

TRAINING IS SHIT. Every metre I run is hard; every jump I jump is too forced. Len shouts at me. I shout at him. He says I'm not focusing; I tell him to fuck off. I leave the changing rooms without speaking to anyone. I cycle home and switch on my laptop. I go on *YouTube* and type in *Adam Lowe interview World Championships*. My face appears on screen, being interviewed by David from the BBC. Chris Madison appears behind me, and joins the interview.

'The kid jumped well.'

The kid, the kid, the kid.

I watch it over and over.

Focus, focus, focus.

The kid, the kid, the kid.

The next day is better.

AT OUR EARLY Christmas dinner, I give my sister a Kindle. She seems genuinely touched. I shrug and say, 'I thought it'd be easier than carrying all your books.'

She leans across the table and kisses me on the cheek.

Later, we hug at the front door and she says, 'Are you not coming to the airport tomorrow?'

'No.'

'Let me guess. Training?'

'Exactly.'

'You better win a bloody medal in Barcelona.'

'If I do, will you be there to see it?'

She smiles and says, 'Probably not. I'll be on a beach with my new surfer boyfriend.'

'I'll mention you on the telly.'

'Don't swear again.'

'I'm a grown-up now.' I pause. 'Good luck, sis. Ring me when you're bored.'

We hug again, and then I leave with Rachel.

In the car as we head through the dark December night towards the lights of central Manchester, she says, 'You OK? You've been very quiet.'

'I'm fine,' I respond. 'I was just thinking it's good that Jane has gone away. She needs to do this. To discover what she can achieve.'

'Do you wish you'd gone away and seen the world and discovered yourself?'

'I discover what I'm capable of at work every day.'

We stop at traffic lights near Old Trafford.

'What about you?' I ask.

'There's plenty of time for seeing the world later. When you're a gold medal winning Olympian.'

ON CHRISTMAS EVE, we go back to the pub where we met a year earlier. We sit with the same people and talk about how our lives have changed. We sleep at my parents' and exchange Christmas presents in the morning. Rachel then drives back to her parents' to share the festivities with them and her two brothers. I stay at home and go in the garage, take out an old work out mat that has been rolled up and placed in the corner behind my dad's lawnmower. I do an abs circuit. My grandma comes for dinner, barely eating, content just to sit and listen to stories of Jane's first couple of weeks of travelling. Later, I drive to Rachel's and spend the night with her family, playing Pictionary and arguing over quiz answers.

We wake up together on Boxing Day, our anniversary, and exchange more gifts and spend the day doing what we did on this day last year. We walk through the paths of Dunham and warm up inside the café. We drink coffee and Rachel orders cake.

'Every time I've ordered cake in the last year, I've felt guilty,' she says.

I laugh. 'I'm glad that you've bought so whole-heartedly into my dreams,' I say as she takes a bite of the rich chocolate cake.

With her mouthful she says, 'I really have,' before smiling with chocolate-stained teeth.

RACHEL AND I host the New Year's Eve party. Our friends bring various bottles of wine and crates of beer.

As Johnny walks through the door, he hands me a four pack of Lucozade isotonic drinks and says, 'I saw this and thought of you.'

'You're too kind,' I say.

'We've all got bets on you winning a gold medal in Barcelona. Just doing my bit to help.'

My iPod plays on shuffle. People huddle in small groups, talking and laughing, making promises about their behaviour for the coming year.

The doorbell rings and I make my way through people in my hallway to answer it. My friend Tom Kitson, a 1500 hundred metre runner I've known since we were fourteen, stands with his girlfriend Lucy.

'Finally, another athlete,' I say. Tom and Lucy are introduced to people they don't know and settle into the conversation with Pete and Laura, Rachel and me.

'Do you remember this time last year when we set ourselves those goals?' Laura says. 'I think we all completed them.'

'Only just,' Pete says. 'I only got my car delivered two weeks ago.'

'Are you still banging on about your new car?' Laura says, laughing as Pete sticks the Vs up at her.

'What were the targets?' Tom asks.

'We all said this is the year we will do something,' Rachel says. 'Laura and I ran a half marathon and Pete got a new car.'

'Don't you start,' Laura says.

'Adam's was to medal in Berlin.'

'We should do it again,' Laura says. She takes a big drink of wine. 'Next year I'll qualify as a solicitor.'

'Me too,' says Rachel.

Laura turns to Pete and says, 'What about you? New mats for your car?'

'I think this is the year we should go to New Zealand.'

Laura kisses him and says, 'That is a brilliant idea. There's the adventurous man I love.'

'What about you?' Rachel asks Lucy.

'I like this game,' Lucy replies. 'Next year I'll learn to drive.'

'That's a good one,' Laura says. 'As long as next year you don't stand here and start banging on about getting a new car.'

'What about you guys?' Rachel says to me and Tom.

'Top five in Barcelona,' Tom says.

'Win gold in Barcelona,' I say.

'Bloody athletes, making the rest of us feel bad,' Laura says.

The girls disappear for a tour of the apartment, leaving Pete stood with a beer bottle and me and Tom with our soft drinks.

Pete says, 'I'm going to propose in New Zealand.'

I smile. 'Brilliant, mate.'

'Nice one,' says Tom.

'Will you do the best man honours?' Pete asks.

'Love to,' I say. 'Just remember, early October is the best time for me, wedding wise.'

Pete laughs. I don't. I look at Tom and say, 'He thinks I'm joking.'

Tom smiles.

'Are you not joking?' Pete asks.

'Not really. I'd love to be your best man, mate. Assuming she says yes, of course. The honest answer is, if your wedding is a summer one, the chances are I'm going to have to say I can't do the gig.'

Pete doesn't speak. I watch him, my best friend, who I've known since my first day at secondary school, the first one of my friends to contemplate marriage, as he processes my words. It's clear he doesn't get it. He doesn't understand why I would say what I've just said. Pete can't consider for a second that as much as I love him, as much as his friendship means to me, if the choice is between standing by his side on his wedding day or attending a training session or competition that's going to make me a better athlete, make me jump further, I'm not going to be at his wedding.

'For each individual, sport is a possible source of inner improvement.'

Baron Pierre de Coubertin, The Founder of the Modern Olympics.

17

'IT'S NOT WORKING,' I shout.

'You've not competed since August. You've not jumped indoors for two years. You will improve.'

Len and I are in my hotel room in Sheffield. I'm stood by the window, looking out onto a dark city street. It's mid-February and the people passing under street lights are wrapped in coats and scarves. I turn and look at Len, who is sitting on my bed. It's two hours after my second indoor competition of the season has ended. In Glasgow last week, I didn't improve after the second jump and today I fouled twice in the first three rounds and finished seventh overall.

He continues, 'We are working on something new. It will click.'

The plan this winter was to jump indoors to work on improving my distances after Jump Four. That's why I spent last weekend in a soulless Glasgow hotel while Rachel went out with all my friends to celebrate Pete's birthday. And why last night, I sat in this room watching a pointless action film, trying to distract my mind and body from burning unnecessary energy.

'I get your theory, Len. I'm not an idiot. I understand the need to have this big jump in my locker at the back end of competitions. But I don't feel like myself on the runway. I'm not focusing on the jump in front of me. We've worked all winter on getting me to be stronger at the back end of competitions all I can think about is Jump Five all the time. I won't be qualifying for the later jumps if I carry on like this.'

Len leans back on the wall and stretches his legs out along the bed, folds his arms across his chest. 'All of this can be fixed. You need to relax and not let it affect you. The plan is a long-term one. Moments like this, how you cope with them, they all make up the bigger picture.'

I look at him, with his calm exterior and his smile, and say, 'Fix it how?'

THREE DAYS LATER, I enter Len's office.

Len is sitting with a man I recognise. He's late forties, greying hair, wearing an Institute of Sport polo shirt and tracksuit bottoms.

'Adam,' Len says. 'This is Peter Hedge.'

The name clicks. Peter Hedge, Sports Psychologist.

He stands and offers his hand. I shake it. 'Nice to meet you.'

'You too.'

'Len and I have just been talking about your last couple of meetings. And I think I can help.'

I've never been one for sports psychologists, I've never felt the need.

But there's an assurance in the way he says it, like he added the 'I think' for my benefit. He knows he can help. And I believe him.

'You got a leather couch I can lie on?'

We all laugh, and I can see in Len's eyes that he's glad I've taken to the man he's brought into our circle.

IT'S JUST THE two of us: me and Peter. We're in his plainly decorated office. There's a small bookshelf next to his desk, filled with about twenty books. There are two photographs of his family: one snapped in a studio with his two kids climbing over him and his wife, smiles all round. The other shows the four of them in formal dress at a wedding. His desk houses a laptop and a thin notepad, plus a mug and official Institute of Sport glass.

I'm over assessing everything. A sparsely decorated, de-cluttered room must mean a tidy mind. The bookshelf tells me he's organised and serious, yet family is important.

He catches me looking and says, 'That's Lauren and Thomas. They're nine and seven. A real handful.'

'Looking after athletes must be much the same.'

He laughs and I relax. 'Athletes do have their moments.'

A short silence.

'Can I get you a drink?' he says.

'No, thanks.'

'OK.' Pause. 'Len told me you'd had a couple of bad jumps and thought I might be able to help.'

'It was a couple of bad meetings. Not jumps.'

'What happened?'

'I thought Len told you.'

'Len told me his version. And what you'd told him. I want to hear your version.'

'My view is simple. I had a great year last year. I felt confident and sharp. I improved my PB and won a medal at a major championship. This year I can't focus when I'm on the runway. All I think about is Jump Five.'

'Why Jump Five?'

'Because that's where the problem is.'

He takes a drink. 'The problem?'

'Yeah.' I tell him about Len coming to my house with his laptop and his spreadsheet and telling me I'm shit after Jump Four. 'We feel that having a big jump during those rounds is going to be the difference between winning gold and not.'

Peter hasn't picked up his notepad, hasn't written a single word. We're just talking, stating the issues.

I continue, 'Indoors in Glasgow and Sheffield were my first jumps since we talked about it, and I feel like my routines are off. I'm not focusing on each jump. I just think about the later jumps. It's doing my head in. I thought Glasgow might be a one off, just having that something else to think about. But I didn't sleep properly the few nights leading up to Sheffield, which isn't like me. Then the same thing happened.'

'Last year, when you were jumping in Round Five and Six, how did you feel?'

'Knackered. I jumped a few Personal Bests last year. I was consistently jumping longer distances throughout the year. Jumping that far takes a lot of your body. It takes days to recover properly.'

'So, Len is right about the need for more work to make those later jumps feel better.'

I nod. 'Yeah, he is.'

'How did you feel before the start of this year?'

'At the end of last season, I was flying. I was full of confidence, desperate to keep the improvement going. And then.' I pause, unsure whether to continue, whether to air my views.

'And then,' Peter encourages.

'And then Len comes to my house.' I pause again, this time unclear how to put my thoughts into words.

'And bursts the bubble?' Peter suggests.

'Something like that.'

There's a silence.

I break it. 'Look, I'm not an idiot. This is elite sport. I know what I want to achieve and how hard I need to work. Len's right, being able to jump a long jump in the late rounds will give me a better chance of winning medals. I'm focused on achieving that. I've grafted all winter to make myself have more stamina for competitions. I just wasn't expecting to get on the board and my head goes to shit.'

'When Len pointed out last year's problem, did you lose confidence?'

'Maybe. It did feel a bit like I had such a great year last year, ticked off every goal we set, and then he turned up and said, "All of that was great but there's a massive problem running through the whole year".'

'Do you still think that?'

I shrug.

Silence.

'It's good you recognise Len is right,' he says. 'That means you agree there is a problem to fix. That's the first part of this sorted.'

'What's next? Me lying on a couch and telling you my dad never believed in me?'

'Did your dad believe in you?'

'Yeah. He was very supportive.'

'Mum? Therapy usually brings up problems with the mother.' He laughs and I know he's trying to make me relax about the process.

'Mum was OK too.'

'Good.' He pauses, then says, 'I want you to go home and think about your routine. Especially for major competitions. Every detail, every step. Write it down if you have to. Come see me in a few days and we'll have a chat again. I'll have a think about what you've said to me and we'll start getting all this sorted.'

I stand and offer my hand to shake. He shakes it and taps me on the back.

Then I'm in the corridor alone with my thoughts.

MY ROUTINE CONTROLS my life: what I eat, when I eat, when I train, when I rest. It controls Rachel's life. It controls our evenings and social life. It comes before late nights out drinking and early mornings walking home as the sun comes up. In the winter, Sundays are about recovery. In the summer, they're about travelling back from events and phone conversations about how our respective weekends were. My routine controlled my parents' life and my sister's. It impacts every one of my days.

It comes before anything and anyone. My routine will make me a champion.

I've always known that, always believed it. I'm selfish. Knowing it makes it no less brutal to think about.

I sit in our quiet apartment and go through my competition routine. The packing, the travel, the checking and double checking of my kit.

I write down what I do the night before I jump. I go through the morning and travelling to the venue. I detail my warm-up and preparation to jump, scribbling a couple of sentences about finding the spot past the pit to focus on, about how I look for Len in the crowd.

I read my notes over and over again, adding things, making changes until they're right.

I hear a key turning in the front door. It opens and Rachel shouts, 'Are you home?'

'In the lounge,' I shout back.

I hear her bag drop to the floor and she walks into the room with her coat still on. 'I got invited for coffee today,' she says, the smile across her face unmoved.

'OK?'

'By Caroline Doyle, the head of Employment Law. They want me to start there in September when my training finishes. I've got a bloody job.'

I jump up and give her a tight hug and a long kiss. 'That's amazing,' I say.

'Laura got a job, too. She wants to go out for drinks.'

'When?'

'About an hour.'

It's Wednesday, my night off, meaning I'm free to go.

I DRESS SMARTLY and enter her world. We sit in a central Manchester cocktail bar, around a table filled with trainee solicitors who've all been told they've got jobs.

The drinks are flowing; the atmosphere is relaxed. Everyone is laughing, downing shots, and nipping outside for cigarettes. Someone pours me a glass of champagne that I pass to Rachel.

The conversations are about nothing but work. I sit quietly and watch her enjoy her moment. She looks at me at one point and smiles.

It's the smile of someone who knows all the hours of hard work, all the sacrificed weekends and missed family occasions have been worth it.

I hope in 2012 I'll be smiling the same smile.

'YOU'RE AMAZING,' SHE says, happy-drunk as we walk back to our apartment, my arm around her back to keep her upright.

'Thanks,' I say.

'I'm serious,' she says. 'You're an inspiration to me. When I met you, I thought I'd never meet anyone who would understand my mindset to be so dedicated to my job. It's put a few guys off. But you, you get it. You don't complain when I work late, you don't bitch and moan because I need to stay in or work on a Friday night. I know we're lucky that we're similar in the demands of our jobs. I know you have to sacrifice as well. But I want you to know that I love and appreciate you for your support.'

A day somewhere near the start of our relationship. Driving down a country road, driving for the fun of driving. The joy of being together.

Bruce Springsteen comes on the radio.

I sing along to main line of 'Born to Run', turning to her as she deadpans, 'And jump.'

We laugh.

18

'IMAGINE I'M AN idiot,' Peter Hedge says, after he's finished reading my notes. 'Tell me about a long jump competition.'

'In what way?'

'Generally. The Europeans, for instance. How will that work?'

I explain. 'Thirty-five to forty people will start in the Qualifying Round. The top twelve go through to the final.'

'When's the Qualifying Round?'

'The day before the final. Sometimes two days before. There's a standard qualifying distance, say eight metres, five centimetres. You get three jumps and if you hit that, you're in the final. If only three people hit it, the next nine furthest jumpers will also go through to the final.'

'What if you jump eight twenty on your first attempt?'

'Then you're straight in the final.'

Peter pauses and thinks. 'So potentially, you could jump nine times in the competition, spread over three sections.'

'Technically. Or seven jumps if you hit qualifying distance on the first attempt. Eight if you hit it on the second. But remember, you've got to get through to the last three jumps.'

'Meaning?'

'The twelve people in the final all get three jumps. The top eight jumpers then get the chance to jump the last three. The order changes at this point. If I'm leading, I would jump last. Second jumps second to last and so on.'

He looks at my notes again. I watch his eyes scan down the page. 'Tell me about this thing you do when you look for the spot on the other side of the pit.'

'It's just that. I find a spot to look at on the other side of the pit. Every time I jump, I focus on that point. It's so I don't look at the board. If my run up is right, I don't need to look at the board. When I've found the spot, I search the crowd for Len, so he knows I'm ready. It's my way of snapping into focus, I suppose.'

'When do you do that?'

'Before the first jump.'

'Of Qualifying?'

'And of the final. If there's no Qualifying Round, then just before the first jump.'

More thinking.

'Why don't you do it before every jump?' he asks.

'Because it feels like the start of the event when I do it. Like I know the first jump is coming. The first jump is always awkward because you're desperate just to put in a good jump. By that I mean, not a foul. Once you get something on the board, even if it's a shit jump, you can relax and the next couple of jumps seem easier and less stressful. If you foul the first jump, the pressure increases on the next two. Foul all three, you're gone.'

'So, if you didn't go through the motion of searching for the spot over the pit, your mindset wouldn't feel like it was the first jump, and you wouldn't feel as relaxed?'

'Exactly.'

'If you get a good' – he does the quotations thing – 'jump on the first, how do you feel on the second and third?'

'Pretty relaxed. My best jumps usually come between Two and Four.'

'Four, that's interesting.'

'Why?'

He ignores my question and asks his own.

'Would I be right in saying that relaxed feeling goes away for Jump Five and Six?'

'Yeah.'

'Because your body is tired?'

'Yeah.'

'And the pressure is back on? Especially if you're not winning.'

'That's true.'

He takes a long drink of coffee. I do the same.

'It seems to me that the competition is split into three, but you only treat it as two.'

'What do you mean?'

'Well, you've got the Qualifying, for which you do your routine. And then you've got the final which, at the beginning of, you do the routine again. But then after three rounds there's a break, and it's almost like a second final then. Four people are eliminated, which is a natural reset position for the competition. Especially as the jumping order changes. Different position can mean different mindset. I know the winning jump can come before the elimination point, but everyone who makes the last eight has the opportunity to improve and win. Those last three jumps become, for want of a better word, the final.'

'OK?'

'So, I wonder if it would serve you well to reset your focus at the point by re-establishing your routine and mindset.'

'But Jump Four hasn't been a problem,' I say.

'True. But it might be masking the real issue. You said earlier that your best jumps come between Two and Four. You feel more relaxed then. If you're viewing all six jumps as one block, the natural thing to feel is that Jump One is pressured because you want to start well. Jumps Two to Four are less pressurised because you've still got two left. Five and Six are a different type of pressure because you're running out of attempts, and, therefore, running out of time.'

It feels weird being sat in a room having someone dissect my performances without ever watching me jump. Peter has never seen me move down a runway, push off the board, hang in the air. Yet he sees it all so clearly, so simply.

'We need to work on resetting your mind after Jump Three, before Jump Four to get you back to the focus of Jump One. If you can view the final as two sets of three jumps instead of one set of six, then we can try to work on your Jump Five and Six feeling more like Jump Two and Three.'

'How do we do that?'

Working through run up drills.

Every time I miss the board, every time I'm a fraction over, Len shouts, 'Consistency. Consistency. Consistency. You get six attempts. Don't waste one.'

19

ROME, THE DIAMOND League. My first big event in Europe this season. It's a hot June night with a loud crowd, all good experience for Barcelona. That's what Len tells me. Practise the routines, iron out the mistakes. Prepare, prepare, prepare for Barcelona.

Some of the best in the world are here: Henning Rudman, Eric Blanc, Luka Cooke, and Roberto Lopez, the Olympic Champion. All are jumping well.

Eric Blanc takes the lead, hitting 8.24 metres. I'm in fifth with 8.04 metres from Round Two.

After my third attempt, I walk to my bag and take out a small towel and a new vest. I remove my current vest, unpin my number, and transfer it to my new one. I wipe myself with the towel, quickly and efficiently, removing any sweat. I pull the fresh vest over my head, followed by my tracksuit top, stuffing the old vest in my bag.

When it's time to jump again, I stand on my marker and close my eyes.

I breathe in and count to myself.

One, two, three.

The noise of the crowd reduces slightly.

Four, five, six.

The picture in my mind is of a black space.

Seven, eight, nine.

Ten.

I open my eyes. The view is hazy, but as the seconds pass, everything refocuses. The colours of the stadium, the black and white uniforms of the officials, the athletes warming up on the track, are all sharp and clear. I find my focal point for my run up: an advertising hoarding on the other side of the pit and over the track. It shows the name of a website. I concentrate on one letter: the 'e' of athletics. Then I move my head and look for Len in the crowd again. He nods.

It's time to go to work.

I run and jump.

I'm white flagged and measured at 7.88 metres.

I put my tracksuit on and wait for my next jump. Other guys go through their routines, jump, and return to their own tracksuits. We all sit in our own bubbles, trying not to burn energy.

I stand by my marker ready for Jump Five.

I run, building up good speed. I hit the board and rise through the air, and I know it's good. White flag. The jump is over eight metres.

I stand in the sand and shout, 'Come on!' to no one and everyone. I repeat it three times. My body strained. My fists clenched.

I'm measured at 8.18 metres and move into third.

The crowd reacts to my shout and I wave my hands in the air, encouraging them to keep shouting, keep increasing the volume. To the majority of watchers, my shouts seem like a reaction to moving into third place. I look at Len, the sole person who understands it has nothing to do with third place, nothing to do with this competition, or this jump. Len knows this has everything to do with moving forward as an athlete and breaking the hold Jumps Five and Six had started to have over me.

I DON'T GET back to the hotel until the early hours. I was drug tested, which took ages because I couldn't piss in the pot on demand.

The adrenaline wears off, but I still can't sleep. It's always the same. I just lie on the bed and analyse everything: every jump, every twist and turn of the competition, how my body felt with each run up and take-off.

Rachel has texted me: *You were brilliant. It's strange watching you on the TV. Nice though. Although it does make me miss you. Love you and your jump 5 x x x*

I think about her, alone at home, in our bed. She'll be asleep now, so I don't call. Thinking about her makes me think about the last few months. I've been consumed with my issues, what's going wrong in my world. Distracted is the right word. Distracted and removed. The bad competitions putting me in two-day moods, the constant pressure on me to solve the problem. I acted like a boyfriend, going on nights out with her uni friends, pretending to listen to their old stories, laughing in the right places. Lazy Sundays and lunch at her parents'. But all the time my mind has been drifting to another place. To the track. To the problem.

Until I was seventeen, I'd react badly to defeat. I couldn't shake the feeling of failure. I'd shout and swear after bad jumps, kicking sand. I'd feel like I was letting people down, especially my parents who would drive all over the country to watch me jump. If I had an off day, I'd feel like they resented the time they'd given up to watch me.

And I couldn't shift that feeling. I'd be in a bad mood, train badly the following few days. Len noticed how it impacted my performance and pulled me up on it. He convinced me it wasn't about my parents; it was about me and how I was striving for perfection. Desperate to show the people who thought I was stupid for wanting to be a professional long jumper instead of following a traditional path, that my sacrifice was worth it. I took some convincing, but eventually I agreed with him. Len told me I needed to calm down, to show less emotion following jumps, good and bad. 'It uses too much energy,' he'd say. 'And it makes you look out of control. Show your rivals no weakness. Everything you do on that runway, make it look like you knew it was going to happen, like you can cope with any setback.'

And it worked. I internalised every emotion. I'd run and jump, go back to my tracksuit and wait my turn. I wouldn't clap to get the crowd going. The only person I needed to succeed on the runway was me.

Len said feeling annoyed with bad performances was natural, even acceptable. But I couldn't let the feelings linger. 'A bad jump is a bad jump. But a bad jump followed by a week of bad training is a problem.'

We came up with a system. Being in a mood over a bad competition was allowed until breakfast the next morning. Once I took my first mouthful of cereal, the issue was considered gone. My focus needed to shift to preparing for the next event. Early on, Len would eat with me, or ring me at home, and, as I was eating, he would describe the upcoming sessions to me.

Len taught me that losing was OK, but it was important to lose well, lose professionally.

That control over losing has been slipping. The Jump Five issue had infected my confidence, my routines, my performances. It had seeped into my home life.

Peter Hedge has helped, but it isn't a quick fix. Every competition since I first spoke to Peter – two indoors, three outdoors – has been slightly better than the last. At each one I've focused on Jump Five a bit less. But it has still been there, a dark cloud on the horizon of the competition. Until tonight. Tonight, I thought about Jump Five at the start of Round Five. And I jumped further than I had all night. Not far in terms of my PB, but far enough tonight to move the Olympic Champion from third to fourth. That will plant a seed in his mind for Barcelona. A little niggling doubt that he can't take for granted I'm out of the competition, no longer a threat.

Progress.

ANOTHER DIAMOND LEAGUE meeting, this time in Eugene, America.

He, the World Champion, is supposed to be here but I arrive at the athletes' hotel to the news he's pulled out.

In the breakfast room, I ask Toby Williams why.

'Some kind of virus,' he says.

We talk about our own injuries. Toby says, 'I can't catch a break. Every six weeks I seem to get something. Hurts my rhythm. You?'

I think about Chris Madison dissecting athletes in a Beijing nightclub: Toby Williams. Always injured.

I WIN IN Eugene and then again, a week later, in Gateshead, in front of my family and friends. My grandma couldn't make it, so I go and see her the following day and we watch a recording of the event together.

'Have you spoken to your sister?' she asks.

'Yesterday,' I say. 'Have you?'

'She called me this morning. She's off to New Zealand skiing. A big group of them.'

'I know. Sounds like she's doing well out there. Enjoying herself.'

We both go quiet and concentrate on the screen as I start my run up to Jump Three in Gateshead. The winning jump. Eight metres thirty-nine. No one got within fifteen centimetres of that distance in the rest of the competition.

Later, I make her a cup of tea and leave it on the small side table next to her chair. I kiss her head and say, 'See you when I get back.'

'Make sure you bring me that gold medal.'

'Yes, Grandma.'

She tries to stand, but I tell her not to. I can see the pain it causes her to put pressure on her fragile frame.

Winning: The only thing that matters.
Winners: The only ones who are remembered.

20

Barcelona, July 2010
The European Athletics Championship

DAN REPLACES LINFORD Christie at the front of the room.

Linford read two poems. The first was about his experiences at the Barcelona Olympics in 1992. The words, the atmosphere, and the footage of his 100m races shown to us on a big screen is inspiring stuff. I'm transported back to my grandma's front room where I watched that live as a six-year-old: *I'm going to do that when I'm older.*

'Evening,' Dan says. He stands tall, shoulders back, and looks the athletes in front of him in the eye. A natural. 'I'm Dan Hall and I'm retired. Not retired in the *old person* sense of the word. I've got a job. I help run a company that coaches kids and, in a few days, I'm going to Barcelona to sit in the commentary box and try to add some insight into your races and events.'

Someone coughs a sarcastic remark and there's a ripple of laughter through the room. Dan waits and lets it die, then continues, 'But,' he stresses, 'I used to be sat where you are. I used to be an athlete. And let me tell you, it doesn't get any better than what you're about to go through. Major championships are the reason to be an athlete. It's where the important, career-defining medals are won. You, each one of you, have got the opportunity to make an impact on your career. Make it count.'

No one in the room moves.

'Make it count,' he repeats. 'Because let me tell you, you do not want to look back when you're retired and wish you'd given more, wish you'd pushed harder, left more of yourself on the track. That regret will live with you for longer than the joy of any medal you win. The joy of winning medals only lasts as long as the bus ride back to the team hotel. Then you focus on winning the next medal, feeling that high again. But regret' – he pauses and looks at me – 'regret will stay with you every day of your life. So, I'm giving you this advice now, as someone who has been where you are and wishes every day I could go back and re-do some of my performances, some of my career-defining moments. Give everything. Not nearly everything. Every single thing you have. Fight to the line. Run hard, jump far, jump high. Leave the arena feeling like you've got nothing left. More importantly, have no regrets. Only then, when you're retired, can you look in the mirror and feel at ease.'

Silence as we digest his words.

'Thanks for listening.'

BEING A MEDAL contender means additional media work. I sit in the afternoon sun and do a face to camera interview for the BBC. It's a simple piece with questions about goals: 'I'm no different to anyone else. I want to win a gold medal.'

We finish and I stand, unclipping the small microphone from my Team GB polo shirt. I pull the wire out and hand it back to the cameraman.

'Thanks for that,' he says.

Before I can respond, my phone rings in my pocket.

'Hello,' I answer.

There's a small pause on the line. 'Adam.'

I hold my hand up in apology to the cameraman and turn away from our conversation. 'Hi, Mum.'

'I've got some bad news, I'm afraid. I'm really sorry to be calling you now.'

'What is it?'

'Grandma is in hospital again. Looks like she's going to be in a few days. I'm not sure whether me and your dad are going to be able to come to Barcelona.'

I process the information quickly. 'Is she OK?'

'She will be. I just wanted you to know.'

This doesn't change anything. There's nothing I can do. Whether my parents are sat in the stand or not won't change how far or how well I jump.

Only I can do that.

'I'VE MADE YOU something,' Len says.

We are in the athlete's Village in Barcelona. Tomorrow is my Qualifying event. We've just gone over some final preparations; practical things like the time we're leaving for the warm-up track and what time I'll eat.

'Is it a mix tape?' I say as he hands me a DVD case.

'Sort of.' He laughs.

'All that 80s rubbish you like?'

'Good music.'

'I'll be the judge of that.'

I go back to my room and open my laptop and insert the DVD into my computer. An image of the fifteen-year-old me appears. The shaky footage starts to move as I run down the track and jump into the pit. The screen goes black and white words flash up. A quote from Muhammed Ali, '*Champions are made from something they have deep inside them… a dream.*'

More footage of me appears, still photos mixed with old jumping competitions. Quotes flash up. More Ali, '*What keeps me going is goals.*'

I'm in the gym now, mobile phone footage taken by Len. He zooms in as my face strains with effort to lift the weights. Another quote: '*The harder you work, the harder it is to surrender.*' Vince Lombardi.

The pictures change, a montage of old images of successful jumps and celebrations with family. The pictures fade away and my dad appears on the screen, sat facing the camera in his front room. 'Hello, son,' he says. 'Barcelona is everything you've worked for. You told me when you were fourteen years old that you wanted to win gold medals. Now is your time. Make it happen.'

My mum is next, in their kitchen. 'Good luck, Adam. We love you.'

My grandma appears, sat in her chair at home. She looks uncomfortable. 'Is it on?' she asks. A pause. 'Do yourself proud, Adam. I love you.'

In my room I think of her, for half a second, in hospital. Weak and unwell, not the woman who smiles from my screen. I force the thoughts from my mind. They won't help me win. I can't fix my grandma. Distractions from home won't help me focus.

On screen, Rachel appears. She smiles too, then says, 'I don't see why we need to make this stupid video. It's only running and jumping. Some of us work for a living.'

We laugh together. Her weeks ago, when this was filmed, and me now, in my room, the night before the event I've worked since October for. It's only running and jumping. The first words she ever said to me.

The screen fades to black, followed by the words: 'Gold medals aren't really made of gold. They're made of sweat, determination, and a hard-to-find alloy called guts.'

A picture of me as a fifteen-year-old appears. Smiling, covered in sand, a small gold medal from a national junior championship in my hand. A gold medal. Always the goal. Always the dream.

THE PEACOCKING IS going on in the tunnel. My competitors stand, shoulders back, chests out. Everyone playing the big man, trying to psyche out everyone else. I see little hints of their emotions showing behind the act. There are twitches of nerves in their mouths, dry lips, too much energy to burn as they bounce on their toes.

I feel removed from it all. I feel nothing. No nerves, no butterflies.

I'm calm.
Relaxed.
Ready.

Lopez takes the lead in the First Round with 8.29 metres; the Olympic Champion in his last championship, laying down a marker.

I follow him, jumping 8.25 metres.

Eric Blanc hits 8.28 metres to put himself second.

We are the top three and stay that way for the Second Round, none of us improving on our distances.

I step to the line for my third jump, breathing in and out. Rachel's words appear in my mind: *It's only running and jumping.*

I run and jump, knowing it's big as I hit the sand. I push forward and move out of the pit. White flag.

I wait for the measurement and it comes in at 8.38 metres, a nine-centimetre lead.

Twelve jumpers become eight. I'll jump last because I'm leading. Lopez second to last. Blanc third to last.

Blanc fouls on his fourth jump. Lopez hits 7.77 metres and lets his frustration show in the pit, screaming to the floodlit sky. Another round gone; another opportunity missed. Another jump down in a career that now has only two remaining.

I step to my marker in my new vest. I close my eyes and count to ten. I open them and allow myself to refocus. I search for the spot beyond the pit. I push myself down the runway, take-off well, and fly through the air. Another white flag. The measurement shows I've increased my lead to 8.40 metres. One centimetre less than my PB, two centimetres further than the previous round.

More importantly, I've extended my lead to eleven centimetres. It takes every fibre of my being to not celebrate the distance and the jump's importance. I keep my face neutral, offer no emotion. I look at Lopez as I walk back from the pit. He's deflated. In the last two rounds, I've jumped into the lead and then extended it, taking control of this final.

He fouls his fifth jump.

I white flag mine but only manage 8.12 metres.

The Final Round.

One round away from my first gold medal at a major championship. Every word Len has ever said to me about the importance of staying focused, of being ready to put in a big jump in the later rounds, of the competition not being over until everybody has jumped, race through my mind. One by one, the other seven guys take their final attempt. One by one they jump too short to take the lead. One by one, I get closer to winning.

Three jumps to go.

Blanc moves down the track at speed. I don't want to watch, but I can't help it. I try to concentrate on my routine, but I see him hit the board and move through the air. I see the red flag before he does. He's out. Finished.

Only one man can beat me now. Only one man in the whole of Europe can take my medal away from me.

Lopez.

The current Olympic Champion. Words that mean something. A position not to be dismissed.

His run up feels like it's moving in slow motion. He hangs in the air for an age. He hits the sand, stands, and waits.

I'm stood on the runway over fifty metres away from him. I don't think he's jumped further than me, but I can't tell for certain. I wait for the officials to make an announcement. They measure the distance and Lopez's shoulders slump. His disappointment laid bare.

I drop to my knees and lift my hands to the sky, clenching my fists.

I won.

I won, I won, I won.

I am Adam Lowe.

I am a gold medallist.

I am the European Champion.

I RUN ACROSS the track to where I see a British flag. I get to the advertising barrier and take the flag from a young girl who smiles as she passes it to me. I give her a high five and hold the flag above my head, swinging it round and round. Flashes appear in front of me, cameras capturing my smiling face.

I see Pete appear at the barrier further down the track. I start jogging towards him, soaking in the crowd's applause and shaking people's hands along the way. Rachel is next to him. I move through the photographers on the track who have positioned themselves between us and pull her into a long kiss.

We part and I say, 'Love you.'

She laughs and kisses me again. I can feel the salt of her tears on my lips.

I turn to the cameras and raise the flag behind my back and smile. Photographers shout instruction. I move and reposition the flag, giving them their shot.

Adam Lowe.

Gold medallist.

The European Champion.

AFTER THE MEDAL ceremony, I stand in front of the television cameras; my smile being transmitted around the world.

I answer the questions, talk about how that was the best performance of my life, how I've worked so hard to achieve this victory.

Then I hold the medal up to the camera and say, 'I'd like to dedicate this medal to my grandma who couldn't fly out to see me win it because she's in hospital.'

'Thanks, Adam,' the interviewer says. 'And I hope your grandma gets well soon.'

LEN AND I get a quiet moment in an empty corridor.

He is smiling more than I am. 'Perfect,' he says. 'Controlled. Increased the lead at the right time. I'm proud of you. Well done.'

'I need to be jumping further,' I say.

He puts his hand up. 'Don't. Don't worry about anything. Enjoy the next couple of days. Go out tonight and celebrate. Plenty of time to talk about improving.'

I nod.

He smiles again. The man who designed the plan is seeing it come together. 'Perfect.'

I CALL MY mum, who says, 'I'm so happy for you.'

'Where are you?'

'Just got home from the hospital.'

'Oh,' I say. 'I was hoping to speak to Grandma.'

'Well done, Adam,' my mum adds. 'I'll put you onto your dad.'

There's a mumbling of words between them I can't make out. Seconds tick to nearly a minute before my dad's voice appears. 'Well done, son. We love you.'

IT'S LATE, BUT everywhere is busy. Bars are overflowing with people, and there is a constant layer of noise wherever we go. I walk hand in hand with Rachel. Pete and Johnny are behind us, waiting for Mike who is at the cash machine.

'Do you still think it's just running and jumping?'

'I'm starting to understand a bit more now,' she says. 'I felt like I'd won gold. I can't imagine how you felt.'

'Like I was going to explode.'

We stop and turn to see where the lads are. The three of them are slowly moving down the road, not a rush in them.

I kiss her. 'Thank you for all your support.'

We find a quiet place still serving food. I pay for all the drinks. I stick to water as my body is desperate to rehydrate. We raise our glasses in the middle of the table and they toast me.

'So, how did you two end up here?' I ask Mike and Johnny. 'I thought you couldn't get tickets.'

'We used your parents'.'

'You should've been at the front when I won. You'd have been on tele.'

'I can't. I've phoned in sick,' Johnny says.

'Really?'

'Yeah. I'm supposed to be back at work in the morning.' He turns to Mike and says, 'Make sure I get up for eight to call in.'

Mike holds his hands up. 'It's on you, mate.'

'Friends,' Johnny says. He downs his lager and stands. 'Who wants another? Adam? Beer?'

'No thanks.'

'Come on. Let me buy the gold medallist a beer.'

'Honestly, no thanks.'

We order food and devour it when it arrives. We move on to a couple of bars, meet up with other athletes, and dance through the night. Everyone wants to talk to me, shake my hand, congratulate me on my gold medal.

I finally leave them at their hotel at about 6 a.m.

I get back to my room.

I lie on the bed, looking at my medal. I start to drift off to sleep, but force myself to get up and shower.

My media commitments start at 8 a.m.

RACHEL FLIES HOME first but waits at Manchester Airport to collect me and drive me to my parents' house. My mum opens the door, and a smile appears across her face. It doesn't spread to her tired eyes. She hugs me tight, kisses my cheek.

We move through to the kitchen. My dad is sitting at the dining table, his laptop open in front of him. He stands and comes over to me and hugs me as well.

'Congratulations, son. You were fantastic.'

'Thanks.'

He positions himself next to my mum, slips his arms around her back.

'We've got something to tell you.'

I know immediately what it is. I can tell by the sombre atmosphere.

'Grandma died,' my dad says.

'When?' I ask.

'Yesterday.'

The day of my final.

'Did she see me win?'

A pause, followed by a shared look between them.

'Don't lie to me,' I say.

'No,' my dad says. 'She died about an hour before the final.'

I am a gold medallist. I am the European Champion. I know he was watching. I know he'll have taken note.

21

WE STAND GRAVESIDE. All four of us. My sister holds my mum's hand. Her flight from Australia only landed this morning. She showered and changed straight into the black dress she wears now. She started crying in the funeral car when she said, 'I can't believe I didn't get a chance to say goodbye.' Those tears still roll down her face. They are slower and her body has stopped jerking up and down with every release of emotion.

The coffin is lowered slowly. The men from the funeral home take care with every inch of its descent. It comes to rest and the men step away, placing their hands together in a gesture of respect. My dad steps forward and throws some soil onto the wood. The noise is loud in the silent graveyard. Others step forward and hold their hands above the grave, let flowers and soil fall into the hole.

People move away and embrace or share a word of remembrance or comfort.

Rachel stands beside me, her hand clamped to mine. 'Are you OK?' she asks.

I nod and say, 'Just give me a minute.'

I stand alone at the side of the grave. I put my hand deep into my pocket and pull out my medal. I bend my knees and kiss the gold before holding the ribbon over the hole.

'I told you I'd win,' I say to her.

I let the ribbon slip through my fingers.

The medal thuds against the coffin and rests with her.

Thud.
My heart breaks.

22

ME, THE EUROPEAN Champion, versus Him, the World Champion. That's how everyone is building our meeting up at the press conference before the London Diamond League.

'There are six other people jumping on Sunday,' I say. 'To win, we have to beat all of them, not just each other.'

I sit on a raised floor behind a table filled with recording devices and microphones. Every word captured. Another question from the floor about him and me.

'Chris Madison is a fantastic long jumper,' I say with slightly more force. 'He's the World Champion. The man to beat in every competition he is in. I need to keep improving and put myself in a position to challenge him at the World's next year and here at the Olympics. I've never beaten him, so I need to change that at some point to challenge for the big medals.'

The kid. The kid.

'Adam, will you be going to Delhi?'

'No,' I answer. 'It doesn't fit with my plan for the year. I've set up my year to compete in major competitions in July or August. October is too late. My coach and I made the decision at the start of the season. British Athletics have known for some time that I didn't want to be selected.'

I take a sip of water. I hear a couple of clicks of cameras.

I say, 'Look, I don't mean to be rude about this, but I'm not here to talk about the Commonwealth Games. I'm here to concentrate on winning on Sunday and improving as a long jumper.'

I'm here to beat Chris Madison.

AND I DO beat him.

Him and everyone else. I've never felt so unbeatable in my life. Every run up is fast and smooth, every jump a white flag. The crowd's reaction makes it feel like every one of them is there for me. I'm a Champion.

Their Champion.

And I milk it. I encourage them. I stand in the pit and use my arms to push them louder and louder, like a front man of a rock 'n' roll band.

They're my crowd. My people.

This is my day. Not his.

He offers a challenge, but even he, with his top ten of all-time Personal Bests, can't dislodge the confidence of my performance. He trails me from Round Two and stays there all day. But he can't beat me. Not today.

Jump Five. The problem jump at the beginning of the year. The cause of all the stresses and sleepless nights, and confessions to Peter Hedge. Today, all that fades away. He jumps first, pushing me, landing within two centimetres of my lead. I relax, I breathe. I'm winning. I just need to hold on to the lead, and I'll have beaten him for the first time in my life.

I power down the runway and push off in front of the board. I fly. And fly. Hanging and hanging. And I know, I just know, that it's further than I've ever gone before.

A new PB. 8.54 metres.

I stand with my arms at maximum wingspan and listen to my crowd roar.

I see Len across the track. He shakes his tightly clenched fist before turning it into a thumbs up. I resist the temptation to race across the track and hug him. Instead, I think about how this competition is not over, about how I have not won. About how he has one jump left and is capable of 8.68 metres. Of beating me.

I go back to my stuff and wait.

His final jump offers no threat.

I win.

LATER, I'M IN the hotel reception with my friend, Tom Kitson, the 1500 metre runner. We're sitting at a small table, trying to unwind and allow our minds to adjust after the high of competition. Tom put in a good third place in his race, which is positive because he's had two disappointing championships recently. In Berlin he was ill. In Barcelona he raced badly, not getting out of the heat.

Now, he says, 'I'm worried about my funding.'

'Why?'

'Because they keep spending money on me going to major championships and I keep letting people down.'

'You're not letting anyone down. Don't be daft.'

'I'm letting myself down.'

'There's always Delhi.'

He shrugs.

'What will you do if they do cut your funding?' I ask.

'I don't know. Not sure I can afford this life on my own.'

I look at my friend. The friend I've known since I was fourteen. Whose dream has always been to race in an Olympic Final. That goal is worth all the hours of pain and suffering on the road and on the track. Like every one of us, he relies on other people's budgeting decisions to allow him to live this life and keep that dream going.

'Stay focused, mate.' I council. 'Control what you can control. Everything else will sort itself out.'

We finish our drinks and stand up. As we walk back through the reception, Chris Madison walks towards me. He's in step with another athlete, talking. He looks at me. I nod. Nothing too friendly. No smile or hello. But a small acknowledgement.

He offers nothing and looks away from me.

As he passes, I slam my shoulder into his.

He stumbles to the side, then regains his balances. 'What the hell, man?'

'I didn't jump too badly for a fucking kid,' I say.

He moves closer, eyeballing me. 'What did you say?'

'You heard.'

We step towards each other.

The athlete with him pulls him backwards. Tom does the same to me. 'What's this about?'

'He knows,' I say.

Madison just stares.

'Me and you,' I say. 'Me and you. Your words.'

'You're fucking crazy, man.' He turns and walks away, waving his hand in the air as if to dismiss me.

I look around the reception and people are staring, wondering what just happened.

'Let's go.'

We head to the lift with all eyes on us. The doors open and we step in. I say nothing, just stare at the line where the two closing doors meet.

'Where did that come from?' Tom asks.

I don't answer.

BACK IN MY room, I lie on the bed. My heart beats in my chest.

Thud.

Thud.

Thud.

Each beat sounds like my gold medal hitting my grandma's coffin.

Time passes and the adrenaline wears off. My mind drifts and somewhere in a mash of thoughts about my grandma, and Pete preparing to propose to Laura in New Zealand, and how worried Tom looked about his funding, and Chris Madison, and how I need to sort out my birthday night out, somewhere as the dark of night passes the baton to the light of morning, I fall asleep.

I jolt awake a couple of hours later and go down for breakfast.

I SIT WITH Len, who sips coffee. Before he can say anything, Madison walks over. He drops a tabloid newspaper in front of me.

'Eyes everywhere.'

I scan the small article, which is accompanied by a photograph of me collecting my gold medal in Barcelona. It reads: *European Long Jump Champion, Adam Lowe, squared off against his World Champion rival Chris Madison in a London hotel last night. Shocked bystanders watched as the two athletes had to be pulled apart by teammates after a heated exchange. Lowe and Madison had competed against each other just hours earlier in the London Diamond League meeting, which saw Lowe win with a new Personal Best jump.*

Lowe has suffered a personal tragedy recently…

I stop reading, wondering who told them about my grandma.

'I guess this makes us official rivals now,' I say.

'Guess so.'

'Last night. You OK?'

'Yep.'

'Good to know.'

'You can keep the paper,' he says, leaving.

Len looks at me from over his coffee cup. 'At least one good thing comes out of this whole thing.'

'What's that?'

'He knows you're a fighter now.'

Is it all worth it just to be better than someone else – everyone else – at jumping in sand?

23

THE SEASON ENDS.

A few days later, Rachel surprises me with a short trip to Paris to celebrate my birthday. On our first night in the city, I get a text from Pete simply saying: *She said yes.*

Rachel and I wander around Paris hand in hand, taking endless tourist photos. We pose in front of the Eiffel Tower and use school-learnt French to order in restaurants. I see the city as a tourist for the first time, having only been here previously to compete.

We don't talk about work.

We talk about Pete and Laura's engagement, about the party they're going to have to celebrate, about stag dos and hen dos. We talk about our future, about how long we should rent for, which area we should look to buy a house in.

We stop at cafés and sit at street facing tables watching the world rush by as we relax.

On our last afternoon at one of these cafés, Rachel says, 'I'm sorry this was just a quick break. I really wanted to do something a bit mad, like book to go to Mauritius or something, so we could just lie on a beach for a couple of weeks. It's just needing to be back for work.'

'Don't be daft. This is amazing.'

Then I ask, 'Why do you say Mauritius?'

'I've always wanted to go.'

'That's what we should do after London.'

My own proposal plan continues to form.

Mornings spent watching video footage of myself doing run ups as I shovel cereal into my mouth, taking notes of where I've gone wrong, what can be done to improve.

Afternoons spent researching upcoming competition venues. The changing facilities, the layout, the expected and previous years' weather.

Speaking to people who have jumped there before, grilling them for details.

No stone unturned, nothing left to chance.

No surprises.

24

'BARCELONA IS GONE,' Len says. 'Gold means nothing here. A new season means you're just another athlete chasing medals again.'

Day one. Always looking forward. Always looking to improve.

'This year is going to be strange,' he continues. 'For us, the focus is to improve again. The goal is to win in Daegu. But I've had all kinds of meetings already about London and Olympic preparation. You're going to be asked about it in every interview, there's going to be corporate sponsorship events, people wanting things from you in a way we've not experienced before. We, as a team, need to handle that.'

'I just want to win medals.'

'Good. The other stuff can be fun, and it might help you switch off from the stresses of this life but focus on the end goal.'

'Haven't I always?'

'I can't deny that,' Len says. 'But you're entering a different phase of your career now.'

My life becomes a cycle of warm-ups, running sessions, abs circuits, weight training, step work, standing jumps, technique.

Work, work, work.

Repeat.

LATE NOVEMBER, RACHEL comes home from work and throws her bag down in the hallway. I hear a loud thump as it hits the wooden floor.

She walks into the room to find that I've set up the table for dinner.

'How was your day?' I ask.

'Busy. Yours?'

'Just training.' I check on the chicken breasts in the oven. 'Oh, and I got nominated for Sports Personality of the Year.'

I allow myself a smile.

'Are you going?'

'We are,' I say.

'Us? Me?'

'Yeah.'

'I didn't think that would be your thing.'

'This year feels the right one to go to,' I say.

THE BBC EVENT is all glitz and glamour. We, me in my suit and skinny tie, Rachel in her new dress, are surrounded by athletes I'm used to seeing in tracksuits or shorts and vests. The lads have got their hair styled and the girls have faces full of make-up. Everyone is smiling for the cameras and happily doing interviews on the red carpet.

Rachel pulls me close at one point and says, 'If even one newspaper calls me a WAG tomorrow, we are over.'

A radio station asks me about my nomination. 'I'm guessing I'm the person on the list no one has heard of,' I say. 'There's one every year that people go "Who?" That'll be me this year.'

'Are you a fan of the event?'

'Yeah. When I was a kid, I used to watch it with my grandma so it's good to actually be here.'

I move down the line. Another camera, another microphone.

'What do you think of your chances of winning?'

'Zero. It's just good to be on the list.'

And it is. Because it would've made my grandma proud.

We take our seats, and the event starts.

A young BBC runner with a headset comes to my seat and leads me away, leaving Rachel alone. I'm taken backstage to wait to be introduced. I wait, suddenly feeling extremely sick. I try to imagine being on a runway at the start of a run up. I go through the motions of breathing and search around me for something to focus on. My eyes are drawn to the small TV screen which shows the host on stage saying, 'Our first nominee is a long jumper from Manchester who this year followed up his bronze medal in last year's World Championships with a gold medal at the European Championships in Barcelona.'

The screen in front of me changes. Moving images of my winning jump in Barcelona appear, followed by me on the podium, gold medal around my neck, a smile across my face. The commentator says, 'Adam Lowe is the Champion.'

Dan Hall appears, a pre-recorded talking head interview. He's at home; I recognise the bookshelf behind him. 'Something's changed in Adam in the last couple of years, maybe since Beijing 2008, when he finished fourth. He seems to have become more focused, and his work rate has improved. He understands what's expected of him now. When you talk to him, he talks about wanting to improve and win medals. That's the annoying thing about Adam. You get the impression he doesn't actually know how good he can be. He's talking about winning medals and jumping further. And I look at him and think, *You can dominate the sport for years to come.* He's a brilliant athlete, one who will only get better and better.'

More footage of me jumping appears on screen.

Then Dan comes back again. 'He is very professional in the way he goes about his work. He's not one for announcing his life on social media or chasing fame. He wants to be a great long jumper, and he doesn't really let much get in the way of that. He's a funny guy, good to be around and train with. And he has a will to win that's up there with anyone I've ever met.'

The young runner whispers in my ear, 'You ready?'

I nod as the host says, 'Ladies and gentlemen, Adam Lowe.'

I walk through a small opening and onto the stage in front of a room full of the greatest sports people in the country. There's applause and blinding lights and I just smile and hope I don't look too stupid.

The interview lasts about a minute. I say all the right things about winning and thank Dan for his video message, before adding, 'Although, I'll admit to being a bit surprised as when we trained together, he used to spend all day insulting me.'

There's laughter from the audience, and I leave the stage feeling more relaxed.

I return to my seat and Rachel squeezes my hand.

We watch the rest of the ceremony. My fellow nominees go through their interviews, telling stories of their year.

The awards are handed out: unsung hero, young sports personality. David Beckham collects a lifetime achievement award. He lists the great clubs he's played for, and I think about all he's won. All those important goals. People use the word legend to describe him. Him and so many others in the room.

Finally, after all the interviews and video footage, after all the praise and applause, the main event is here. Votes in, lines closed.

And the winner is: Tony McCoy. The greatest jockey of all time; the man who has ridden more winners than anyone else. Tony McCoy who says, 'I want to keep going now. I want to be at the top of my sport.' I look from him to the man who stands just to the side, Phil Taylor, the darts player who finished second. The man who has won fifteen world titles.

Domination. That's what comes to mind as I see both of these men in front of me. Total domination of their respective sports. To be a winner is one thing. To be a great is something else. That's the challenge for me.

To dominate my sport.

Dominate him.

Wake.
Eat.
Train.
Eat.
Rest.
Eat.
Train.
Eat.
Sleep.
Repeat...

25

PETE AND LAURA book their wedding for October 2012, post Olympics.

'I can't have my best man not at the wedding,' Pete says.

Johnny wants to talk about the stag do so one Saturday night in early March, just before I'm due to fly to America for warm weather training, we meet in a bar in the Northern Quarter. It's a trendy place with deep leather couches and a jukebox playing Manchester classics. The Smiths are on when I order three pints and an orange juice. The barman is singing along as he pours the drinks, tapping a beat out on the pump with his fingers as the glasses fill.

'This meeting is important,' Johnny says. 'Pete, as the first one of us to get married, your stag do will set the standard for everything to follow. We have to start as we mean to go on.'

'Meaning?'

'This needs to be big.'

We discuss every potential option. Vegas, Berlin, staying local. Go karting, paint balling, handcuffing Pete to a Smurf dwarf. We talk about dates and if dads should be invited. After going around and around, Mike finally says to Pete, 'What do you actually want to do?'

Pete hesitates and looks at me.

'What?' I say.

'Nothing.'

'No, go on.'

He sips his drink. 'I wouldn't mind going to Poland for the Euros. Base ourselves in Krakow or Warsaw and try to get to a couple of games. If we plan it early enough, we should be OK sorting tickets.'

I know why he looked hesitant before he spoke.

'That's a brilliant idea,' Mike says.

Pete looks at me again.

I say, 'It's OK, mate. Don't worry.'

Johnny's eyes go from me to Pete, Pete to me. 'What's going on?'

'If you do the Euros,' I say, 'I won't be able to come. Pete was just worried about bringing it up.'

'Why not?' Johnny asks. 'You're the best man.'

'Because the Euros is weeks before the Olympics,' I say. 'I'll be preparing for that.'

A blanket of silence suffocates the table.

'The best man has to be on the stag,' Johnny says.

I say nothing.

'What kind of stag is it without the best man? You could fly out for a couple of days. It's not like you'll be drinking.'

I look at Pete. He knows I have no intention of trying to make it happen. He knows London comes first and that nothing Johnny says will make any difference.

'I think it's a great idea for a stag,' I say. 'It's like you planned a wedding in a year with a European Championship, just to get an excuse to go.'

'Would I do that?' Pete says.

We laugh.

'Is it worth it?' Johnny asks.

'What?'

'The missing out.'

Missing out. There's that question again. Johnny means missing out on nights out, on stag dos, and friendships. He means missing out on the in jokes that Pete, Mike, and he have. I used to punctuate my training with nights with them, but since Beijing things have changed. And it's me who misses out, me who's separate from the group. They carry on as they were, having the same experiences we all would have had if I'd decided to give up on athletics and go to university and get a normal job. I'm sat facing my three best friends, lads I've known since the first day of secondary school, and I can't lie.

'Yes, it's worth it. I'll only ever get one chance to win an Olympic Gold medal at a home Games. I don't see it as missing out.'

I ache. I drift on the couch. Sleep visiting and leaving every few minutes.

My alarm beeps. I switch it off and stand. I ride to training for the second time today.

I push my body over and over for a couple of hours.

I get back on my bike and ride home.

I eat and get back on the couch.

I drift.

26

I GO TO America for warm weather training.

At the end of the three weeks, I compete at a local event again. Chris Madison sits in the crowd, just as he did a couple of years ago. This time I don't ignore him. This time I walk over, look him in the eye, and shake his hand. Then I jump 8.48 metres in the Second Round and win by forty centimetres. I search the stand for him at the end of the competition, but he's gone.

I return to England and prepare for the summer outdoor season.

And when that starts, I keep winning.

I win in the first Diamond League of the season in Shanghai. I then fly back to America and win in Eugene, beating him in his own country.

He shakes my hand and says, 'Well done' but he doesn't look me in the eye. Five days later, he sits in the press conference for the Oslo meet and says, 'I'm not worried about my form. I've jumped one of the top ten jumps of all time. I know I can go long.'

He's telling a room full of journalists. But he's talking to me.

At the event, he jumps 8.35 metres and finishes second.

I win again.

I'M IN THE kind of winning form athletes dream about, and all Peter Hedge wants to talk about is losing.

He says, 'Winning is easy. Losing can be hard to recover from. How are you going to cope?'

We talk about this over and over in sessions. What if I'm losing with two rounds to go, with one to go? What if I lose in the Diamond League to someone unexpected? How does that differ to losing to Chris Madison?'

'Why do you bring his name up?' I ask.

'He's your rival. The World Champion. His PB is further than yours. If you lose to him in the last competition before the World Championships, will that create a fear factor for you?'

Even when I'm winning, when I'm top of the World rankings, Chris Madison is there, in the background, the question mark over my whole career.

The kid.

'No fear factor,' I say.

The fucking kid.

I tell him about my routine after a defeat. About how Len lets me be angry until my next breakfast.

'That's good,' Peter says. 'But it's harder to shake the feeling of defeat when the stakes are higher.'

I sit back in my chair and stretch out my arms. 'Peter, you can be so negative. Don't worry, I'm going to win.'

I smile, and he laughs.

MY MUM CALLS on a Saturday night and tells me they're having a barbeque the following day that we can't miss. I try to argue about needing to rest but, harshly, she says, 'Adam. You will be there. For me.'

The following afternoon, we drive to my parents' house and park outside. I carry flowers for my mum, that Rachel made us stop for, and a bottle of wine.

'Hello,' I say as I push the door open.

'Come through, come through,' my mum shouts.

We walk down the hall and into the kitchen.

'All right, bro?'

Jane, my sister, stands in front of me, a wide smile across her face. 'Surprise.'

I quickly hand the flowers and wine to my mum and give my sister a tight hug. 'What are you doing here?'

'I'm home.'

'For good?'

Jane explains she applied for a job at a North Manchester hospital a few months ago and got it but didn't want to tell anyone until coming home was confirmed. She only told my parents a week ago.

She looks different from the last time I saw her. Not just because she is tanned but something about her is more confident, like being out in the world on her own has really changed her.

Later, we sit in the back garden with Rachel. My parents inside preparing all the food that will be eaten by Jane's friends who are due to arrive soon.

'Why have you come back?' I ask. 'I thought you loved it out there.'

'I did,' she says. 'I wanted to go and live abroad to see if I could face the challenge. I feel like I've got it out of my system. Plus, I missed people.'

'Ah, thanks,' I say, joking.

'She means me,' says Rachel.

The pair laugh and I feel really happy they're getting along before a strange sadness creeps over me as I think about how this is a moment my grandma would've loved.

Jane snaps me out of it by asking about Pete and Laura's wedding plans. Then she says to me, 'No pressure on you.' Before looking at Rachel and laughing.

Rachel slips her hand through mine and says, 'We're all right. I don't need a shiny ring.'

'Good to know,' I reply.

Rachel spends the day quizzing Jane about all aspects of travelling life, then later turns to me and says, 'When are you retiring?'

'I don't know. Hadn't really given it much thought. Why?'

'I think we should quit everything and do a massive trip around the world when you do.'

'After Rio?' I say.

'When's that?' Jane asks.

I don't think in actual calendar years. I think in events. This year is 2011 to normal people, to me it's Daegu. 2012: London. 2013: Moscow. 2014: Glasgow and Zurich. 2015: Beijing for the Worlds, not to be confused with Beijing 2008 for the Olympics. Finally, Rio, or as most people know it: 2016. There will be another European Championships in 2016, but the destination hasn't been announced. Each one of my years starts in October and finishes the following August or early September.

'2016,' Rachel says. She turns to me again. 'What do you think?'

'Sounds like a plan.'

PARIS, EARLY JULY. Another Diamond League meeting:
Round One. Him: 8.09 metres. Me: 8.01 metres.
Round Two. Him: Foul. Me: 8.17 metres.
Round Three. Him: 8.34 metres. Me: 8.30 metres.
Round Four. Him: 8.50 metres. Me: Foul.
Round Five. Him: 8.16 metres. Me: 8.69 metres.
Round Six. Him: Foul. Me: No jump.

I STAND IN front of David from the BBC in the Mix Zone. He's smiling, saying, 'Adam, that was a fantastic night for you. A new Personal Best.'

'It's amazing,' I say. 'A perfect night, really. I said to my coach earlier today that I felt good. Sometimes you wake up and can tell by the way the body feels that you're going to jump well. But even I wasn't expecting a jump of that length.'

'Eight point six-nine metres. That puts you in the top ten jumpers of all time.'

I smile.

I also know that 8.69 metres puts my Personal Best ahead of *his* by one centimetre.

'You are on quite the run at the moment. You've not lost since before the European Championships last year. You must be full of confidence going into the Worlds in Daegu.'

'Daegu is everything I've worked for this year. None of this good run will mean anything if I don't perform there.'

I move away and another journalist signals he wants to speak to me. To get to him, I have to pass Chris Madison. We are in cramped quarters, with cameras and cameramen, journalists and press officers. He steps backwards; I pass in front.

One centimetre apart.

MY EUROPEAN GOLD, my potential as a medal winner, my unbeaten streak – which continues in Stockholm and London– makes me someone Team GB want to promote. A journalist is sent from one of the broadsheet papers to spend some time with me. The idea is for him to watch me train a few times in the build-up to the Worlds, speak to me in the holding camp, and then after the championships. There will then be a large piece written and printed for the Sunday edition following the final.

'You'd better hope I qualify,' I say to him on the day I meet him for the first time at the track. 'Or else your story is going to be fucked.'

Len laughs. The journalist, Richard, doesn't.

After training, I invite him back to the apartment so I can feel like I'm relaxing before the evening session.

'Thanks for allowing me access,' Richard says as I fill the kettle with water.

I shrug. 'No problem.'

'I've noticed when doing my background that you don't do a lot of these things. You don't have a Twitter account or an official Facebook page. Seems like you're one of the few athletes to do that. Any reason?'

'Not really. Just not my thing. I've got a personal Facebook. I'm not big into sharing my feelings with anyone outside my inner circle. Coach, girlfriend, people like that. I'm pretty convinced the world doesn't need to see pictures of my breakfast. I could probably get away with one tweet. Just *eat, sleep, train.* That's my life, really. Plus, I did swear on live TV once. Makes you think twice about what you're saying.'

He laughs. 'A lot of sponsors expect it now.'

'I do my fair share when asked,' I say.

The kettle boils and I make the drinks. As I put the milk back in the fridge, I carry on. 'Honestly, I've always thought talking a lot before events and stuff can make you end up looking stupid. I'd rather just concentrate on my own work and preparation. I'm not going to say to a journalist or on Twitter I'm going to jump X distance and then come competition day jump Y distance and look daft. Same with my competitors. To me it's obvious. I'm not going to stand around before the jump saying I want to win gold. That's the job. Same for Eric Blanc or Chris Madison, or any of the other guys I compete against. All the talk is just theatre.'

'Is that the case privately? Say on the warm-up track or in the call room.'

I pass him his cup of tea and he blows it.

'Don't get me wrong, there's a lot of peacocking goes on. Everyone wants an advantage. But I don't think Chris Madison is going to be too worried if I put on Twitter I want to jump far.'

I sip my tea. I remain standing in the kitchen, leaning on the side. Richard sits at the breakfast bar, tape recorder next to him, red light indicating it's recording.

'My granddad told me once,' I say, 'that there are two types of people. People who say they're going to hit you and people who just hit you. It's the ones that just hit you that you need to watch out for. I'd rather be someone who performs well than someone who talks about how well I'm going to perform. Does that make sense?'

'Your current winning streak must be helping that. People fearing your record.'

'To a degree. But I've only won one medal since I started winning consistently.'

Our conversation continues for the next couple of hours. He asks about my childhood, my athletics career and history, my family. My grandma comes up a lot. I answer the questions, make more tea, and eventually see him out. He thanks me for my time, and we arrange to talk again at the holding camp before the Worlds.

There are days when I'm in my office; normal days that involve meetings and spreadsheets, and I think about the fact that no matter how long I live, I'll never achieve my dream of winning a World Championship or Olympic Gold medal.

From Dan Hall's autobiography.

27

Daegu, August 2011
The World Athletics Championships

THE JUMP IS shit.

I stretch into the board and I don't get enough height. I land and push away, knowing it's under the 8.15 metres needed to qualify. I don't wait for the measurement. I move back to my bag, ignoring Len, ignoring everyone.

I sit on a plastic chair and try to focus. I go through my small warm-up routine and wait for jumper after jumper to jump their jumps. My name is called. Again, I step to the line. Again, I go through my routine. I start to run, moving quickly down the track. I hit the board and push off into the air. There is more height, more distance on this jump. I land and get out of the sand quickly.

I look at the official sat on his stool by the board. He holds his red flag in the air. Foul.

My eyes drop to the sand. My imprint starts at about 8.20 metres, over the qualifying distance.

Fuck.

I approach Len.

'This isn't in the plan.'

'Just relax. You get three attempts for a reason.'

'That your big plan, coach?'

'I can't do it for you.'

I sit again. I hear Peter Hedge's voice in my head telling me to treat this like any other jump. To follow the same routine as normal. The same routine that has won me every single competition since last June. Guys come and go around me. The qualifiers pack away their bags and leave, safely through to tomorrow's final.

Where I want to be, need to be.

I strip, down to my T-shirt and shorts, again. I get the blood flowing and the legs moving. Ready to work.

I remove my T-shirt and reveal my Team GB vest for the third time.

I stand on the line for the last time today.

My body is tense.

I breathe. My breath is short, sticking midway through the rising of my chest.

Tension is natural, I tell myself. Stress is expected.

The clock ticks, numbers disappearing: 52... 51... 50... 49...

I focus on the spot I've picked across the pit. For the third time.

43... 42... 41...

One good jump.

38... 37...

One good jump over 8.15 metres and all this stress goes away.

33...

I start my run up. I fly down the track and hit the board well. I kick through the air and land... sand flying in front of me. I'm up and out of the pit.

I look at the official on the stool by the board. He holds his flag in the air, above his head. His white flag.

I wait for the measurement. Just to be sure. Just to be safe.

8.23 metres.

I live to jump tomorrow.

Tomorrow is another day. A freshly swept pit of sand and medals to be won.

28

'YOU GAVE ME a scare there,' Len says, smiling. 'Don't do that again.'

'I don't know what happened,' I say.

'It's gone,' he says. 'You're in the final. That's all we can ask.' He reaches into his bag and says, 'I made you something.' He hands me a DVD case, just as he did in Barcelona last year.

'This is becoming embarrassing. I never get you anything.'

I go into my room and switch on my laptop, inserting the DVD. I expect my family and friends to appear. I expect a montage of my last year in long jumping: win after win after win. Al Pacino appears, stood in an American football changing room, surrounded by his players. *Any Given Sunday*. I've seen this film many times. I know what's coming, the words he is about to deliver. I feel a tingle in my neck.

Pacino addresses his players, telling them how they need to fight for every inch, how he can't do it for them – echoing the exact words Len said to me earlier.

I know instantly what message Len is trying to get across to me. Inches. Small margins that, in sport, are the difference between winning and losing. American football games, tennis matches, long jump competitions. Inches, centimetres, millimetres. Each one the difference between champions and losers. Gold and everyone else.

Len is questioning me. Are you willing to give everything?

I am.

Do you want it enough?

I do.

Will you fight for the smallest margin of victory?

I will.

An inch: 2.54 centimetres.

Two and a half times the distance between my Personal Best and his.

29

I STEP TO the line for my fourth jump. I'm third, as twelve jumpers become eight. Eric Blanc leads with 8.27 metres, Madison is second with 8.21 metres.

The clock starts and I go through the routine. I lean back and push forwards into the run up. I raise my head, and my body straightens. Tall and fast. My hips are high. I push into the board and jump.

I kick and hang. And hang.

I land and push forward.

I look at the board. It's big.

I look at the flag: White.

I stand and wait while the officials measure.

It's announced: 8.57 metres.

I am leading the World Championships.

There's a roar from the crowd behind me. I don't smile, don't react how my body wants to, jumping around and smashing my fists into the air. I act as if everything has gone according to my plan.

I don't watch other people's jumps. I can tell from the crowd that they don't go as far as me. I pull my top over my head and sit on my plastic chair for a few minutes, composing myself.

I'm leading the World Championship.

I know the next jump is crucial. My last jump really put them under pressure. I need to go further. He's here and capable of jumping 8.68 metres, at least. I know it'll be burning inside him that I'm in the gold medal position. That I'm winning. That if he doesn't go further than me, the kid will be crowned the World's Best Long Jumper.

I'm called to the line. There is a red cone on the runway, telling me not to start my run up. The clock is still at 1.00.

I wait.

The red cone is removed by an official, and the runway becomes mine. 0.59... 0.58... 0.57...

Breathe in, breathe out.

I speed down the runway and hit the board, push off.

Sand explodes around me. The flag is white, and the jump is good. Not as big as Jump Four, but another solid effort. It's measured at 8.42 metres.

I look back down at the top of the runway. Chris Madison stands ready to jump, ready to put every fibre of his body into beating me. He jumps 8.21 metres. He lets his frustration show. A scream to the skies and a fist slammed into the sand.

The pressure moves to Eric Blanc, who red flags.

I put my tracksuit back on and stay relaxed. I don't walk over to Len because nothing he can say will change the situation. Seven athletes have one jump each to jump further than 8.57 metres. If they don't, I'm the World Champion.

The first five don't. They don't get within thirty centimetres of it.

I step forward to jump. My body is suddenly tired. Everything aches. I want to curl up and sleep. I force myself into one last run, one last jump. I move down the runway, tired legs turning over, pushing me forward.

I jump 8.06 metres.

Utter shit.

I stand on the empty blue track and clap the crowd. I stop and stand alone, watch him jump. Watch him try to beat me.

My world stops when he's in the air.

He hangs and hangs.

When he lands, he's going to be the gold medallist or nothing.

Sand flies from the pit.

He has failed.

He hit 8.44 metres, landing in the silver medal position, pushing Eric into third. Eric now has one chance to become a World Champion, to take it away from me.

I can't look. Instead, I look at Madison. I study his face, wait on his reaction. There's a steady rhythm of clapping from the crowd. My eyes stay on him. I watch him watch Eric.

Madison puts his arms in the air. A celebration, fake and forced. He didn't come for silver.

I turn to the pit. The judge is holding his red flag in the air.

It hits me:

I am the World Champion.

MY HEAD IS fuzzy. A TV camera is in my face and I step towards it, throw my hands in the air, and shout, 'Come on.' Emotion rushes through me. I feel no pain of competition, no aches or pulls, just joy running through every vein in my body.

I turn to the crowd and find Len. He's leaning over the advertising barrier. A grin spread across his face. I run to him and we hug. He pulls me close and says, 'I'm proud of you.'

'Thank you, thank you, thank you,' I say.

I turn and find Eric Blanc stood behind me. I shake his hand. 'I thought you were going to take the silver,' I say.

'He is very strong. He gives everything to the end,' he says of Chris Madison.

I walk across the track to where my competitors are packing away their kits. They offer their congratulations, a round of handshakes, and smiles.

And then it's him.

We stand and face each other.

The runner-up and the Champion.

'Great jump,' he says, his voice betraying his words.

The silver and the gold.

'Thanks.'

We shake hands, but there is no embrace.

I step back onto the track, wrap the flag around me, and acknowledge the crowd. I inch my way around the exterior of the blue lanes. I sign autographs for kids who push pens and programmes through the mass of hands that stretch towards me. Cameras click. Flashes flash. I'm followed continuously by a TV crew, every moment of celebration sent around the world, back home to Rachel, who decided not to come so she could use her limited holidays somewhere she could actually see me. I think of her watching me in our lounge, and for a few seconds, I just want to disappear under the stand and call her to share this moment.

My smiling parents' tear-filled eyes appear in front of me. My mum is shouting my name and I run to her. She kisses me and tells me she loves me. My dad is laughing, completely overtaken by the moment.

'Thank you for everything,' I say.

I continue my lap of honour until I reach David from the BBC.

'Adam,' he says. 'Try to sum up how you're feeling.'

'It's pretty incredible. You dream of moments like this as an athlete. Gold medals at major championships. There were a lot of good jumpers in the competition tonight, so to finish as the winner is a great feeling.'

'It's been a spectacular year for you. Unbeaten. A second successive gold medal at a major championship.'

'It's down to hard work. Not just by me, but from my team. My coach Len, Peter Hedge, the physios, and masseurs. My girlfriend Rachel, my parents, my mates. Everyone has been pulling in the right direction, giving me the best chance to win.'

'So, a World Champion, number one ranked long jumper in the world, a Personal Best in the top ten of all time, where do you go from here?'

'On holiday,' I joke.

David laughs and then says, 'Thanks, Adam.'

I go back to collect my bag. It's the last one remaining. The crowd has shifted their focus to other events that have started on the track. I look down the runway to the pit. The officials have swept it and the sand looks untouched, unbroken. No sign of my winning jump remains. I smile: my World Championship winning jump.

THE THREE OF us wait to receive our medals. We are in our tracksuits, our team colours brightly advertised. Eric steps onto the podium first, the bronze medal placed over his head by the official.

He is next. He steps forward, waving and smiling. I know he's hurting. He wants to be stood where I'm stood, watching and waiting to be presented with the gold medal. The winner's medal. He looks at the silver medal, holds it aloft, convincing the world that he's comfortable with the outcome.

I know he's lying.

I know, because I would be the same.

Now it's my turn. I step up onto the podium, raised higher than them. I wave to the crowd. I lean down and the official shakes my hand and offers me his congratulations. He hangs the gold medal around my neck. I stand tall and hold the medal up towards the section of the stand where my parents are sitting. For a moment, I think of my grandma.

I'm snapped out of it by the Union Jack being raised up the pole. The national anthem begins, and I stand on top of the world, him just below me, and think about that moment in Club Bud, when he told me it would just be me and him. It is just the two of us now.

One and two in the world.

Me, number one.

A photographer asks us to step together. Madison and Eric step up onto my podium.

I put my arms around their backs and pull them towards me.

I look at him. He turns to me.

Eye to eye.

Silver to gold.

'I'm not a fucking kid anymore.'

Carl Lewis.
Mike Powell.
Ivan Pedroso.
Dwight Phillips.
Him.
Me.
The Long Jump World Champions.

30

I'VE BEEN BACK for two days. We walk through Manchester to our favourite Italian restaurant that Rachel has booked for the two of us to spend some time together and celebrate.

A bell pings above the door as we enter, and a waiter approaches us.

'It's under Thornton,' Rachel says of the reservation. The waiter smiles and dramatically leads us towards the back of the place, past empty tables for two, towards the stairs at the back and, confused, I climb them, Rachel behind me.

I click when I see my mum.

I step into the room to be greeted by smiling faces. Everyone stands and starts clapping. I laugh, but I'm embarrassed by the attention. I move my eyes around the room, taking in the faces that have surprised me. My mum and dad, my sister. Pete and Laura, Mike and Emma, Johnny. Dan and Michelle. I turn to Rachel, who is laughing.

I do the rounds of the large table, shaking hands and kissing cheeks. My mum gives me a long hug.

As I get to my seat, Johnny says, 'I thought you'd be wearing the medal.'

'If I'd have known you lot were coming, I would have brought it.'

Rachel leans into her bag and says, 'I did.'

Everyone cheers.

I catch Dan's eye. He smiles and says, 'Pleased for you, mate.'

'You sure? Your book tells me otherwise.'

He laughs at the reference to his recently released memoir.

'Don't let Dan have that medal,' I say to Laura, who's holding it. 'I might not get it back.'

Dan pretends to throw a knife at me.

The evening passes in a blur of laughter and stories. Johnny, at one point, says, 'It would've been amazing if you'd stood on the podium and shouted, *I'm the king of the world* like DiCaprio did in *Titanic.*'

I'm not a fucking kid anymore.

'I can't believe you don't swear on TV anymore,' says Pete. 'I miss those days.'

My medal gets passed around and I have it placed back over my head a few times for photographs.

Later, outside the restaurant, we say goodbye in a blur of hugs and handshakes. I hear the phrase 'we are proud of you' repeated over and over.

Dan approaches, a big smile on his face. 'So, it turns out you're better than me at long jumping.'

'We always knew that.'

RACHEL AND I are alone again, walking through the streets of Manchester back home. I slip my hand into hers.

'So, all that stuff about wanting to spend an evening just the two of us wasn't quite what you had in mind,' I say.

'Sorry about that. Were you genuinely surprised?'

'Definitely.'

We pass Deansgate Locks, the bars quiet.

'You're amazing,' I say.

She squeezes my hand. 'You're not too bad yourself.'

I SPEND THURSDAY morning with Richard the journalist; following up our two earlier conversations with an interview about my feelings now I've won the World title. The chat doesn't last long. Then we head outside the Institute of Sport to my training track to do a series of photographs of me and my medal, posing by the pit. I sit in the stand for a couple of minutes while the photographer is changing a lens and I look down on the track where all the hours of work have been put in and allow myself a brief moment of pleasure at my achievements.

I leave Richard and make my way into the city centre. This is the first free time I've had since my return.

I find a coffee shop and order. As I wait, the lad behind the counter congratulates me on my medal. I take my coffee, grab a newspaper from the mounted wall stand, and sit at the back. I touch the medal and then zip up my jacket pocket, so it doesn't fall out. The year's achievements flash through my mind again. All of this was part of Len's plan when we spoke before the 2009 season started. Medal in Berlin. Win gold in Barcelona. Win gold in Daegu. The plan that takes us all the way to London.

Plans.

My life is run by plans. Training plans for winter, training plans for summer. For micro phases and macro phases. Every session mapped out. Career plans. Retirement plans. Plans to travel, to buy a house. Plans for one boy and one girl. For driveways and good schools. Plans for our future together.

I think about Rachel's influence on me. The successful period in my career has been linked with the successful relationship we've got. She inspires me with her own work ethic, understands the sacrifice needed to achieve my goals.

I think of my secret plan for after London and make a decision.

I leave the coffee shop and walk across town, cutting through a busy Market Street, avoiding the charity collectors and buskers, walking quicker than the average shopper who is browsing in windows. I move onto a quieter side street, maintaining my pace. I stop outside a jeweller on the corner of St Anne's Square. A bell pings above the door as I step inside. Waist height glass cabinets run down three sides of the room. A man appears from a small room at the back and smiles.

'How can I help?' he asks.

'I'm looking to buy an engagement ring.'

I view ring after ring: big, small, with one diamond, two diamonds. This carat, that carat. I want something to reflect her. Something graceful and elegant. Something amazing.

And then I see it.

'That one,' I say, pointing to a simple white gold band that holds a single bright diamond.

The man behind the counter says, 'Excellent choice.'

He takes the ring out and places it carefully in a small box. I pay and place the bag and box in my pocket. I leave the shop and begin to walk home. Halfway down Deansgate, I laugh at myself. I'm carrying my engagement ring in one pocket and my World Championship gold medal in the other. The strange thought of what if I get run over by a bus and this is how I'm remembered, passes through my mind. The guy who carried his winner's medal around on his day off. No one would know it was for an earlier photo shoot.

At home, I go straight into our bedroom. I open the drawer below my side of the bed and place the ring inside a spare kit bag, closing the zip and hiding it away.

SUNDAY MORNING. WE lie in bed, the light from the mid-morning sun creeping through the curtains and lighting the room. Rachel moves over and kisses me, then wraps herself into the crook of my arm. We lie there looking at the ceiling. Her phone beeps with a text message. She leans over and reads it.

'It's from my mum,' she says. 'We've been invited for dinner. My brothers are going to be there.'

'We should go over early and have a walk at Dunham first.'

I think back to the walk we took together on Boxing Day 2008, a couple of days after we first met, and how so much has changed since then. Yet, nearly three years later, the simple act of going for a walk and talking to each other is still appealing, still something to look forward to. I look at her and feel a strong surge of love race through my body. I feel grateful that she came to that pub that night with Laura. Happy she agreed to be mine. I think about the ring, forty centimetres beneath me, zipped in a kit bag. I get an urge to roll over and take out the ring, to turn to this girl, who I love more than I've ever loved anyone before, and ask her to become my wife. I fast forward to this afternoon and how nice dinner would be with her whole family, telling them, Rachel showing off the ring, talking about wedding plans and bridesmaids and possible honeymoon destinations. Lying here in our bed, on a standard Sunday morning, seems like the right time to show her how I feel about her and take our relationship forward.

I move onto my left side and start to lean down towards the drawer.

I stop.

The plan is to propose on a beach in Mauritius.

I stare at the wooden floor; torn between the spontaneous romance of this moment and the planned gesture I've been thinking about for months.

My whole life is run by plans.

'You OK?' she asks.

'Yeah,' I say, reaching out to my mobile phone. 'Just checking the time.'

I roll back over and kiss her. She kisses me back and moves on top of me.

The ring sits in the kit bag, forty centimetres below us.

The medal is suspended in the air.
It hangs for hours, days.
Falls.
Down.
Down.
Down.
Into the black.
Thud.

31

A HOLIDAY TO Portugal disappears in a haze of relaxation, and then we're back home to work. The day after we return, I film a video presentation talking about my experiences as a first time Olympian in Beijing, that will be made available to every Team GB athlete. Not just track and field but water polo players, horse riders, archers. Everyone.

I stand in front of the camera and truthfully say, 'When I was six, I told my grandma that I was going to win an Olympic Gold medal. But it wasn't until I actually went to Beijing that I understood what being an Olympian meant. Being there, competing there, seeing all the other sports and people, how much it means to them, something changed in me. My Beijing experience changed my outlook on myself as an athlete and what I wanted from my career. Before then, I was a twenty-two-year-old kid who went to the Olympics and thought, well obviously I'll go, because I can. I came back changed from the experience.'

AUTUMN BECOMES WINTER, but nothing really changes. Train. Rest. Repeat. The mornings are dark, the nights darker. If I'm not training for London, I'm in meetings about it.

One meeting is in a room that has been decorated by one of our managers, Chris, in images taken from personal social media accounts of everyone in the room who didn't have privacy setting activated properly. At the front of the room a former tabloid journalist explains to us how current tabloid journalists go about seeking their stories.

'If a water polo player plays well on national telly and the next day, some girl wants to talk about how she shagged him for a couple of weeks, the papers want a picture of the two of them.

The papers already have people trawling through your Internet profiles, downloading photos just like the ones Chris has done to cover the walls here today, just in case they should ever need them.' He pushes the point further. 'If you put something on Facebook when you're pissed off or drunk or after a row with your husband or wife, you can't take those words back once they've been logged and stored by the papers. If you don't want it to happen, protect yourselves.'

The message is clear to all of us. Even if we don't want it to be, London is different.

IN EARLY DECEMBER, Rachel's university friends come to stay for the weekend. I've had the date marked as important in my mental diary for months. The group arrives on Friday afternoon, our hallway filling up with wheelie cases, handbags, and slush covered boots. Their plan is to visit the Christmas Markets and have a night out on Saturday. The apartment can't hold us all, so I move to my parents' house for the weekend.

I train on Saturday morning and then go back to my parents'. I go into the garage and open my dad's golf bag, sliding a driver and a wedge out from the collection of clubs.

Half an hour later, I'm at the driving range with Rachel's dad, Derek.

We are sharing a tee on the top level. Derek places his ball down first and concentrates. He is quiet. The clinking sound of club on ball can be heard from different sections of the range, balls flying through the air onto the mass of green in front of us, which is peppered with white dots.

I'm quiet as he practises a swing and then hits the ball.

I compliment his shot and then take my turn.

He takes his. Again, he's the picture of concentration. I stay silent.

'What's Rachel doing today again?' he asks, before rotating through a practice swing.

'The uni girls are here. They're going out.'

'Oh.'

'I wanted to talk to you about Rachel,' I say.

He swings for real, the ball flying at an angle off to the right. 'Shit,' he says.

We switch places. He's still focused on where his ball ended up, so I don't continue the conversation. Instead, I line up my shot, swing, and watch the ball fly straight, landing near a flag that blows in the wind.

I step to the side and he moves forward to place his ball down.

Before he has a chance to get comfortable, I say, 'As I was saying, I wanted to talk to you about Rachel.'

'What about?'

He brings his club backwards. 'I was wondering if you'd be OK with me asking her to marry me.'

He drops the club, turns to face me. Every fibre of my being freezes. His face is stone.

'I bloody would be OK with it.'

I breathe for what feels like the first time in hours.

He smiles a wide, genuine smile.

'You little romantic. When are you thinking of asking? Christmas?'

'After London.'

'That's bloody August. You're prepared, aren't you?'

He's right, I am thinking ahead. Part of my thinking is in the build-up to London, when I'm ticking things off my to-do list: pack for holding camp, check spikes, check kit, check everything once, twice, three times, I don't want to have to try to fit in catching up with Rachel's dad, in private, to ask him for his daughter's hand in marriage. It's better to ask him nine months in advance, when I know she is elsewhere, distracted by university friends, mulled wine, and Christmas Markets.

'Preparation is key,' I say.

LATER THAT NIGHT, I watch *Match of the Day* with my dad.

I look around the lounge and notice my mum has changed a few of the photos on the fireplace. Newly framed images of my mum and dad on holiday, of Jane from her time in Australia, of Rachel and I dressed smartly the night of my surprise meal for winning the World Championships. On the far left is one of the four of us: Mum, Dad, Jane, and me from when I was at primary school. It's a holiday photo taken by the pool at a Spanish resort. This photo has been here for years, unchanged. Smiling, happy family.

I think about Rachel. There'll be a photo of our wedding day added to this collection at some point.

My eyes are drawn from the pictures to the bookshelf. I find the dictionary and the thesaurus, knowing the letter I wrote just over three years ago is still there.

I, Adam Lowe, will be the 2012 Olympic Long Jump Champion.

It's getting closer.

WE HAVE OUR Christmas Eve night out. The conversations have changed over the years. Now they're about weddings and stag dos, savings accounts and invitation prices.

The next day I train in my parents' garage. I do my usual set, not thinking about the dinner I'm about to eat, the presents we exchanged, the look on my dad's face when he opened the new golf club I'd bought. None of that stuff is relevant, even on this day.

I only think about him.

RACHEL AND I walk through Dunham Massey, hand in hand. Our Boxing Day anniversary.

'Do you remember when we came here that first time?' she asks.

'Yeah. Of course, I do.'

'You said you wanted to be the best long jumper in the world.'

'I did.'

'And now you are.'

And now I am.
Me, not him.

WE STAND IN Pete's back garden, watching fireworks race into the sky and explode colourfully. The sky is filled with bangs and fizzes. Reds, greens, blues, oranges, yellows. Dancing colours and cheering people.

Someone starts a countdown. 'Ten, nine, eight…'

I turn to Rachel.

'Seven, six, five.'

She kisses me.

'Four, three, two.'

I pull her closer.

'One.'

'Happy New Year.'

2012: The year I'll become the Olympic Champion.

2012: The year I'll ask this woman to marry me.

I heave by the side of the track, my body telling me to stop.

'Let's go again,' shouts Len.

My body begs.

I stand, walk back to the start line.

My body knows I'm not listening. It goes quiet, preparing itself for more pain.

32

'WE'VE GOT SOME news,' says Dan.

We are sitting around their dining room table, the starters cooking in the oven.

'We're having a baby,' says Michelle.

Rachel nearly spills her wine. She jumps up and races round the table to hug her.

I shake Dan's hand. 'Nice one. How long?'

'Due just before London.'

'Does everything have to be referenced in Olympics?' Michelle says, laughing. 'We're due in June,' she adds.

They show us the scan picture: a blurry black-and-white image of a growing baby. Rachel holds it, studies it. 'Amazing.'

Dan smiles, the happiest I've seen him in years.

Later, over dessert, Michelle admits, 'We weren't sure we'd ever get to this point. When he retired, I didn't think we were going to survive. The moods, the rows, the depression.' She looks at Dan. 'Can I use that word?'

'Yeah, sure. It's true.'

'And it's in his book,' I say.

Dan laughs. Michelle doesn't. She takes his hand from the table and squeezes it. 'But I'm glad we got through it.'

Rachel toasts them. 'To happy futures.'

All of us: 'Happy futures.'

'The book still selling well?' I ask.

Dan smiles cautiously. His book is a hit; sales higher than his publishers expected, the public fascinated by his honest account of his early retirement, his dark days. It led to a more prominent media role and a newspaper column. 'Ticking over,' he says.

HE APPEARS ON my television screen. I switch the channel over to watch *Inside Lane*, a weekly athletics magazine show, and there he is, smiling and laughing with the interviewer at his American training centre. The sun is shining; the sky is blue. He's sat in the small section of grass on the inside of the track, relaxed and strong.

The words: *Chris Madison, Long Jumper* appear on the screen.

'*The plan for the year is to stay fit and healthy. That's first and foremost. Anything after that's a bonus,*' he says, a standard answer.

'*London?*'

He smiles. '*That's what every athlete is building towards.*'

'*Can you win?*'

'*If I stay fit and healthy, I'm in with a good chance. There are a lot of good jumpers out there.*' He lists some of our competitors. Not my name.

'*Adam Lowe?*' the interviewer prompts.

Another smile. '*Obviously. Adam Lowe is the man to beat.*'

I see through the smiles.

I see through the laughter.

I see through the *nice guy* routine.

I press a button on the remote. His face disappears from my screen.

Black.

He's still there, in my mind.

I still see the man who stood in a Beijing nightclub three years ago and dismissed the chances of the good jumpers he's just listed. Guys he didn't think were good enough to compete with him.

The man who called me a kid.

RACHEL AND I are walking through Dunham Massey hand in hand, on a clear, cold Sunday at the end of January. She is telling me about her work plans for the next few weeks: clients in London one day, Southampton the next. She's got hours of work to do when we get home.

'I can't wait,' she says, 'to be on that beach in Mauritius. I can't wait to relax.'

I say nothing.

'I can't wait,' she continues, 'to drink that first glass of wine, to read something that isn't a briefing or legalisation. To read a book just for the fun of reading a book.'

I watch a dog belonging to a family walking in front of us as it runs ahead, chasing the stick a young girl has just thrown.

'I can't wait to just be with you.'

The dog returns. The girl takes the stick from his mouth and throws it again.

'Am I talking to myself?'

I say, 'I can't have this conversation. I feel like I can't let my mind think about relaxing after the Games. It'll feel like I'm not focused.'

'That's ridiculous. We are just talking about our holiday.'

'I don't feel like I can.'

'We've talked about it before,' she argues.

'I know. I just don't feel like I can talk about it now. This year.'

'This is stupid.'

She lets go of my hand.

LATER, I LIE in bed thinking, thinking, thinking.

Are my chances of winning Olympic Gold really going to be reduced because I talk about the beach in Mauritius? Is it worth the fight to not discuss something I'm actually looking forward to just in case I don't win Olympic Gold? Will I really blame that one conversation if I don't win? Are the hours I've spent lying in bed thinking about all of this worth the hassle? Wouldn't it have just been easier to talk about it, to allow myself the few seconds of escape from the constant Olympic pounding in my head?

The problem is mindset.

If I relax, if I allow myself the briefest moment of thought beyond the Olympics, I'll feel like I'm not giving everything.

That's one of the reasons I planned the proposal before 2011 rolled into 2012. What else will start to slip? If I don't win, will I blame Rachel for diverting my focus? The truth is, I need to feel like the total relaxation in Mauritius is to be earned through winning. Dreaming about it; imagining the sun on my face, cold drink in my hand, feels like cheating.

None of this is Rachel's fault. Her life is consumed with London, with my desperation to win, as much as mine is. Our schedules are built around my training programmes far more than her cases. She works hard too. She should be allowed to dream about holidays, the beach, and a cocktail glass with an umbrella sticking out of it, as much as every other person with a so-called normal job.

She stirs in her sleep and turns over. Her eyes open and she notices I'm awake. 'You OK?' she croaks.

'Yeah,' I lie.

The problem with flying through the air for a living is you always come crashing down.

From Dan Hall's autobiography.

33

COUNTDOWNS ARE EVERYWHERE: Three hundred days to go. Two hundred days to go...

Another airport goodbye before I fly to America for warm weather training. Three weeks of being able to eat, sleep, and train. Three weeks to solely focus on the final winter preparation before the season starts.

I shut my eyes and rest my head against the chair as the plane powers down the runway and lifts into the Manchester skies.

Three weeks until competition starts.

Until I can get back to winning.

I RECOGNISE THE running style from across the track. He moves down a lane at pace, long strides, tall, straight body. He looks fit and fast.

'What the hell is he doing here?' I ask.

'Who?' says Len. We walk off the track and onto the grass in the middle. All around us athletes are warming up, starting training sessions.

'Him,' I say, pointing to Chris Madison. He has finished his sprint and is walking back to the blocks he started from.

'Madison? Don't worry about him.'

'He's everywhere. He's like a virus.'

'He's probably here to learn your secrets. You're the World Champion. He's here to steal from you.'

I put my arm on Len's shoulder. 'You're a good man, Len.'

Len laughs. 'Let's get started.'

I find a space and put down my water bottle. I jog a couple of loops of the track. On the second loop, I pass him.

He nods.

I nod.

I go through my session, glancing over at him a couple of times. We catch each other's eye once. We say nothing. Do nothing. Just turn our heads away.

'Focus on what you're doing,' Len says. 'Not on him.'

TWO DAYS LATER, I leave my small, basic room, put the key in the door and lock it. I turn to walk down the long, thin corridor. The door at the far end opens, and he walks through. It's just the two of us, step by step, walking closer together.

We stop less than a metre apart.

'Hey, man. How are you?' he asks.

'Good. You?'

'Had a good solid winter.'

He laughs.

'How was your Christmas?'

'Good.'

'I got engaged,' he says. His face breaks into a big smile. 'Christmas morning. Wrapped the ring in a big box. Last present she opened.'

He got engaged before me.

'That's great,' I say. 'I'm pleased for you,' I add.

Beat me to it.

He sticks his hand out and I know I'm expected to shake it. 'Thanks. Appreciate it,' he says. 'I'll leave you to…' He doesn't finish the sentence, instead points to the door I was walking towards.

Chris Madison walks one way. I walk the other.

'HOW'S MICHELLE?'

I sit with Dan in a coffee shop, sipping free refills from oversized cups.

He has flown out to watch me train for three days and interview me.

'Good,' he answers. 'Sickness has passed. She seems to be enjoying it. She's tired a lot though.'

'Must make a change, her lying around complaining about aches and pains and not you.'

He laughs. 'My life has changed.'

He drinks and then says, 'How's training going?'

'Really good. I feel sharp.'

'I notice Madison is here.'

'Yeah. He's putting it in each session. He looks fit.'

He drinks, then leans down into his bag and pulls out a digital recorder.

'Do you mind?' he asks.

'Are we starting the interview properly now?'

'I'd like to.'

'Sure.'

He clicks the Record button and says, 'Interview one with Adam Lowe for pre-Olympic 2012 piece.'

'Professional.'

'Thanks.'

We continue our chat, with Dan asking more pre-planned questions. He talks about winter training, lifestyle, my continuing winning streak. He punctuates the conversation with some of his own experiences and his impressions of how he feels I've changed over the years he's known me. I agree with most of them.

Then he says, 'Would you rather win Olympic Gold or break the World Record?'

A memory is stirred from Dan's wedding, when his friend, Gareth, asked me the same question. It's clear from Dan's question that Gareth has never revealed the conversation to him.

I pause, unsure how much to reveal.

He continues. 'I'm asking because I read something recently about World Records and how Olympic Champions can change every four years, but World Records can stay for years and years. Take Paula Radcliffe, for example. Her World Record for the London Marathon has stood for nearly nine years now. She's had issues at the Olympics and the gold medal has always eluded her. Yet no one in the world, Olympic Champion or not, is getting near what she did on that day in London.'

I sip coffee and watch as the traffic lights outside change from red to green.

'Legacy is the word of the moment,' he continues. 'I'm just wondering how you'd like yours to be viewed.'

'I'm fully focused on winning Olympic Gold. It means everything to me. If I break the World Record in my career but don't win an Olympic Gold, in London or Rio, the way I feel today, I won't think of my career as a success. Olympic Champion. Those are the words I crave, the title that validates us all as athletes. I know you still regret not winning.'

'I do,' he says.

'But if I broke the World Record, especially in our sport, where the record tends not to get broken too often. Mike Powell broke it in 1991. So, his record has stood for twenty-one years. Before that, the last time the record was broken was Bob Beaman in 1968?'

Dan nods.

'So, yeah, if I broke the World Record at some point in my career, the chances are that record might outlive an Olympic cycle, maybe even two. It would be something to be proud of. But this year, I can't see further than trying to win in London.'

He consults his small notebook. Before he says anything, I add, 'My Personal Best is currently 8.69 metres I need to add a few centimetres before thinking about the World Record.'

BEFORE FLYING HOME from training camp, I win again, at a small meet in New York. I jump 8.59 metres in the Third Round and tell Len I feel like I can go further.

'Save it,' he says.

We fly home.

It's night-time. We fly in a high arch above the dark earth, the cabin quiet. Passengers sleep or watch films on small screens, sound delivered through headphones. Len and I are awake.

'This year is going to be special for you,' he says.

'I hope so.'

'Believe it. Injury free. Fitter than I've ever seen you. Special. I mean it. Just stay focused and the prizes are yours for the taking.'

I look out of the window in the black.

On top of the world.

APRIL ROLLS INTO May. Pete, Johnny, and the boys are having meetings about the stag do details. I attend because a best man should, but when they mention flight times and hotel details for Poland, I think about my own flights to Doha, Rome, and New York. Madison will be at each one, desperate to beat me before the Olympics.

Everyone wants to beat me.

To knock me off my unbeaten perch.

To show the world I'm nothing to fear.

To break my winning streak.

To break my spirit.

Break me.

'What do you reckon, best man?'

'To what?'

'Are you listening?' Johnny asks.

'Yeah. I just got distracted.'

'By what?'

'That massive cock on your head,' I say.

The lads laugh. Johnny throws a beer mat at me.

'To having another stag,' Mike says. 'After London. In Manchester. So, the dads can come.'

'And the best man,' Johnny says.

'Sounds good,' I say.

They won't break me.

I STAND AT my marker in the dry Doha heat, focus on a spot over the pit. The seconds tick down. I start my run up, moving smoothly through the phases, into the board. I push up, hanging and kicking. I land in the sand and push forwards.

The flag is white.

It's measured: 8.49 metres.

No one beats me.

ROME. ANOTHER KISS goodbye to Rachel, another airport lounge, another athlete's hotel, another set of press interviews, another stadium, another runway, another pit.

Another win.

NEW YORK. ON the warm-up track, Madison is louder than normal, talking to himself, making sure we can all hear him.

'I'm the man. This is my house. My town.'

He continues through his warm-up with the ongoing commentary.

'Chest out. Head high. Ready to fly.'

He looks at me and I show no emotion, no crack of a smile.

He taps a closed fist against his chest. 'Ready to fly.'

And he does fly. The night is perfect for it, dry conditions, a small, legal tailwind pushing us down the runway. In Round One, he hits 8.57 metres and takes the lead. Two guys go next but don't get near him. I take the lane, speed down it, hit the board well. I get up high, hang for ages. It's good, well over 8.60 metres. I land and look: red flag. I make my way back to the plastic chairs, knowing I was close on the board.

He's about twelve metres away from me, going through the motions. Pumping his legs, flexing and stretching. 'Ready to fly,' he repeats.

He jumps again, improving his lead: 8.62 metres.

I go through my routine, ignoring everyone. On the runway, I adjust my marker slightly. I start to run and jump. This time the flag is white, but the jump is only 8.19 metres. Solid, not special.

I sit in my seat. My mind is starting to race a bit quicker than normal. Four attempts left. He is winning. Focus on what you can control. He is *winning*. Focus on getting your own jumps right. *He is winning.*

He strips off again and approaches the runway. The other guys stop what they're doing and watch him. Something is happening tonight; they can feel it. There's a potential they'll witness a man jump further than he ever has done.

I turn away. I don't need to see where he lands.

I just need to jump further.

The roar of the crowd; the New York crowd, his crowd, tells me his jump is big. I turn, see him on the track bouncing, banging his chest. 'Chest out. Head high. Ready to fly.' People are on their feet, waving fists, cheering, and clapping.

The distance appears on the screen: 8.77 metres.

It is further than he's ever jumped before.

It's further than I've ever jumped before.

He walks back to his chair, eyes wide, head up. Buzzing. A couple of other guys shake his hand or fist bump him. He's the man. The fucking man.

This is his time.

He is winning.

Stripped and ready, I take a deep breath.

A red cone tells me I can't jump.

Another deep breath. Long and slow. In and out.

The cone is removed, the clock starts, and I begin my run up.

I jump.

8.59 metres.

A big jump. Not big enough.

I cross the track to Len, waiting at the advertising board. I lean over and listen. He says, 'This is it now. This is the test we've been waiting for. You want to keep this winning streak going you've got to perform. Now. You've got three jumps. This is his hometown. His crowd. He's just jumped one of the top five of all time. You are capable of going further. You do that now; he won't know how to react. Everything we've learnt, trained for, over the last four years is for days like today. Every session.

Every jump. Everything I asked of you and you asked of yourself. It was all to prove you're the best around. You go over there now and show you can't be beaten by an 8.77 metre jump and people will take you more seriously than they've ever done.'

I absorb his words.

'Focus on you,' he says. 'Smooth and fast.'

I wait for a race to pass and jog across the track back to my chair. I change my jumping vest for a fresh one, and wait, alone with my thoughts and Len's words. 'The test we've been waiting for.'

He jumps again but doesn't improve his lead.

I step to the line, ready.

I start my run up and move fast down the runway. My legs and arms are pumping, pushing me forward. I hit the board and fly. I'm in the air for what feels like an age. I desperately try to hold my position, stay high for as long as possible.

I hit the sand hard.

The flag is white.

I look at the board and know I'm close. I wait for the measurement, my focus on the imprint in the broken sand. The official calls it: 8.80 metres.

I throw my hands in the air and look back to the communal athlete area and watch his head drop, like he's been hit with an invisible hammer. I don't run off down the track. I don't acknowledge the cheering crowd. I want to convince them I expected it, that winning is what I do.

A few of the guys greet me as I get back to my seat, just as they did him: handshakes and fist bumps.

He doesn't look at me.

We go through our processes again in preparation for Round Five. Neither of us gets near our night's best distances.

He red flags his final round.

I walk across the track to Len. He shakes my hand, pulls me towards him awkwardly over the advertising board.

'Eight fucking eighty,' I say.

'Absolutely amazing,' he says.

I applaud the crowd. His crowd, who screamed and bounced when he jumped 8.77 metres, who were so desperate for their local hero to win. They applaud me now. They reach out to touch my hands. It's me their cameras take photos of.

I return to my chair to collect my bag. Some of my competitors are waiting for me. I accept their praise, content I've fired a warning to all of them.

Even if you jumped one of the top five distances of all time, I'm still not beaten.

I'M CHAPERONED THROUGH the bowels of the stadium to be drug tested. A door is opened, and I'm led through it into a makeshift waiting room with uncomfortable chairs and low florescent lighting. And him.

He's not alone either. He has someone with him while he waits to piss in a pot.

Since I've entered the room, his posture has changed. He is more upright in his chair; his head not leant against the wall.

I sit, the scraping of my chair on the floor sounds like a needle across vinyl. I look at the wall opposite me.

After a few minutes, he offers, 'Some night.'

We finally assess each other, hold each other's eyes.

'Two of the top five of all time,' I say.

He looks how I feel: tired, hungry, physically drained.

The only difference is his eyes show the hollow glow of defeat.

SOMEWHERE BETWEEN THE end of night and start of morning, I lie on my bed in the athlete's hotel, looking out into the dark of New York. My phone is calling Rachel, the dial tone repeating over and over. There's a click and then, 'Hello.'

'Did you see it?'

'Yes. You were amazing.'

'He didn't beat me,' I say.

As always in our long-distance phone calls, there's a brief moment of silence before she answers, 'You mean you won.'

'That's what I said.'

'You said he didn't beat me.'

I know what I mean.

I SWITCH MY phone on as the plane sits on the Manchester runway. It updates, adjusting back to local networks. It beeps several times with picture messages from Johnny. Photos of Pete asleep in a Polish town square, obviously drunk. Another arrives, this time of him posing with a few of the lads. The last one is of a strip club, taken from a low angle to avoid detection. It's blurry, but I can see a naked dancer clear enough. This one has a caption attached: *Wish you were here?*

No.

I wish I was in London. It's so close now and New York has proven to me I'm ready.

Him and me.
Me and him.

34

I'M BACK AT school. Mr Francis, a proud guide, has nearly finished showing me around the building. It's the same as I remember from my tour four years ago, only fresher in colour and with more modern equipment in the classrooms.

Mr Francis leads me through a door that opens out onto the corridor where the staff room is. Kids pass us, moving in tight packs, glancing at me from behind long fringes or mobile screens.

'The children really respond to former pupils coming in and talking to them about life after finishing here. Your last visit here helped us shape things in that area. A young man done good if you like. It shows them what can be achieved if you put talent and hard work together.'

'Happy to be able to help,' I say.

Mr Francis holds open the door of the staff room. As I enter, the first person I see is Abbie, who is in conversation with another teacher. Their conversation stops as she looks at me. I smile, hoping the time that has passed between us has healed her wounds. She smiles too and walks over to me.

'Hi,' she says.

'Hi.'

I notice the subtle differences in her appearance. Her hair is shorter, slightly darker. She wears glasses too. She doesn't look as tired or stressed as she used to be on the nights I'd go round to see her.

'Long time.'

'Yeah.'

I think about that night after Beijing: the argument in the street, the end of our relationship, just as it was beginning.

'You OK?'

'Yeah. Great. You?'

'Getting there. Just preparing for London.'

'How's it going?'

I remember the words that ended us. 'If you're asking me to choose between you and the Olympics, I'm going to choose the Olympics every time.'

My brutal, honest words.

'Really well.'

She lifts her hands up to adjust the files she's holding. I notice engagement and wedding rings.

'Congratulations,' I say, pointing at them.

She looks at them. 'Thank you.'

'How long?'

'We got married last summer. His name is Craig.'

'What does he do?'

'English teacher. We met here.' She pauses. 'I see you're with someone now.'

I must look confused as she explains, 'I watched Sports Personality of the Year. I saw your girlfriend sat next to you.'

A short silence.

'I voted for you,' she adds.

'Thanks.'

'I watched the video thing they made of your year. It was nice to see you winning medals. I know that's what you always wanted.'

Medals, not her.

THE KIDS LOOK up, amazed. One of them, a girl of about thirteen, who asked about how far I've jumped, stands nervously across the stage, 8.80 metres away, a thin white tape measure between us.

'In New York,' I say. 'I jumped this far.'

I roll the tape measure up and thank the kid. She climbs carefully down off stage, quickly making her way back to the safety of the group.

I look up as the door clicks open. Abbie slips through it and stands at the back.

The next question is asked, 'Have you ever met the queen?'

'No. I turned down the opportunity to go to Buckingham Palace after the last Olympics because I had to train.'

The kids look at me, not really grasping how the two things would be connected. I continue, 'I've dedicated my life to winning,' I say. 'Sometimes that means I've missed out on fun things I've wanted to do. My family and friends have to fit in around my life, which can be very frustrating for them and me. But I work very hard to try to be the best at what I do. And when you work hard at something, really put everything you've got into it, it can hurt. It sometimes doesn't feel like it's all worth it. But when you win, the reward of all that hard work feels so much sweeter. It makes it easier to understand why you made choices that some people in your life, even people who are important to you, might not like or understand.'

I look at the back. She is still stood there, her eyes looking at the file in her hand.

'My mum was very upset when I said I didn't want to go to the palace to meet the queen. I think she felt I was letting down my country.'

The kids laugh.

As their laughter dies, I hear the door at the back of the room click.

WE'VE NAMED IT Swag Day.

I drive to Loughborough University ready to collect all the kit I'll need to get me through the next few weeks as an Olympian. The day is planned out: video presentation from Sir Clive Woodward about what the team is trying to achieve, followed by kitting out and interviews. A press walk-though area has been put together to mimic what it will be like after our events at the actual Games. It's not just a case of collecting a tracksuit and a couple of pairs of shorts.

This is what we've been waiting for. The Games are nearly here. The camera phones are out, capturing all the details. There are iconic images on the wall of former Olympians: Sally Gunnell hurdling, face full of concentration, Sir Steve Redgrave rowing, every muscle working to the extreme. I stop and look at the pictures, focusing on Denise Lewis, arms spread, mouth open in a smile as she crossed the finish line to win gold.

We're split into groups. My group attends an anti-doping talk before heading to the kit stations.

'This is like Christmas,' someone says as we walk into the first room.

I move through the rooms with a smiling volunteer who's been assigned to me. They write down all the sizes I need on a clipboard with my picture attached to it, as I try on the formal wear for the closing ceremony. I explain to the volunteer that I don't need the opening ceremony stuff as I'll be in Portugal for holding camp when it's going on. I'm then kitted out with all my Village, training, and competition kit. I get a rush of excitement as I slip the vest I'll use for competition over my head. The Olympics are close.

Laughter is erupting from photo booths across the room. Pairs of athletes are falling out, wearing stupid oversized sunglasses and Team GB head bands. Pictures are printed to be kept as souvenirs of this strange, exciting day.

My phone rings in my pocket. Dan's name flashing on the screen. I answer and he says, 'Isla Elizabeth Hall was born at nine fifteen this morning.'

'Brilliant,' I say. 'Everything all right?'

'Absolutely perfect.'

More laughter from the photo booths.

'Where are you?'

'Swag Day.'

'How much random stuff have you got?'

'Loads. There's an MP3 player. Bermuda shorts with Team GB on them.'

We speak for a few more minutes about Isla and Michelle and then agree to catch-up in a few days when his family life has settled down.

I move through to the mocked-up media section. There are microphones and small silver recorders with small red lights on constantly. Every word is recorded. I try to keep my answers simple and standard. Boring.

'Given your rivalry with Chris Madison and your recent competition in New York, can we expect something similar in London?'

Chris Madison is everywhere. Every question, every training session.

'I'm just trying to focus on winning.'

In the moments before I fall asleep.

'Focusing on preparing properly.'

In the moments just after I wake.

I collect my bags at the end of the day, checking them and all the kit inside twice. They are loaded onto an airport style trolley and I push them out to the car park. I load the red holdall, the gym bag, the two dark-blue Next suit bags, the suitcase with wheels, into the car. All are embossed with the Union Jack, the Olympic rings, and the words Team GB. The back of my car is stuffed. I get in and plug my new MP3 player in, and drive listening to pre-recorded voices of inspiration.

WEEKS LATER, THE same bags are packed and waiting by the door. Team GB kit stacked and ready to go. Tomorrow is holding camp, when I enter the bubble of the Games. When I return, I'll have my medal in my hands.

My gold medal.

Tonight, though, is about Rachel.

We sit at our small dining table, eating the meal she has come home early from work to cook.

'I'm proud of you,' she says.

'Thank you for everything. All your support. All the sacrifice.'

She smiles, slightly embarrassed by my words.

'It's what we do,' she says. 'We are a team. We support each other. You've done it for me through my time at work. All my training.'

We share a smile across the table.

'I love you,' she says. 'Now just win that bloody gold medal.'

LATER, IN OUR bed, she sleeps, and I stare at the ceiling. Sleep feels like hours away. Instead of fighting it, I quietly get out of bed and go to the hallway. I dig through one of my new Team GB bags and pull out one of my training diaries. I go back to bed and switch on the small lamp on my bedside table. Light shines across the pages of my diary and I flick randomly through, the words reminding my body of sessions it has done, of days when it felt broken, of nights when it felt stronger than ever. I try to use the facts in front of me to calm that small voice of doubt that says I haven't done enough. It works, and after half an hour I put the diary back in my bag and go back to bed.

I lie down and feel my body relax and my mind drift away.

In the half a second before sleep comes, I think, *I bet he's done more.*

Ever since I was a kid, all I ever wanted to be was the Olympic Champion.
From Dan Hall's autobiography.

35

London, August 2012
The Olympic Games

I ENTER THE Village.

My bags are taken to be delivered to the apartment that will be my home for the next ten days. I'm given a laminated accreditation that has my picture and my information on it. I have to wear it at all times, the security person tells me. There's a barcode at the bottom that I'm informed will give me access to all the vending machines around the Village. I just need to swipe it, select the energy drink of my choice, and it'll fall out, no charge.

We are given a tour of the Village. It's greener than I was expecting, with groups of athletes sat on the grass areas, dressed in their team colours. Those that have been here for a few days look calm and comfortable. Some people pose in front of the enormous Olympic rings. There are food stalls dotted around that serve tea and coffee, nuts and fruit. We are informed that we can just go up and take whatever we want. It's all free.

The apartment blocks are all uniform, with rows and rows of doors on either side of a central concrete section. Different blocks have flags of the nation who are staying in that block: the green and gold of Jamaica, the bright orange of Holland, his Stars and Stripes.

We are shown to our apartments. One of the benefits of home advantage is that Team GB are in the quietest section, at the furthest point away from the noise of the basketball venue, close to our own, purpose-built medical centre.

We walk up the stairs, along the corridors, passing door after door. I stop at my allocated one. There is a sheet of paper stuck on the door, informing me of what the day's colour is. Today is a White day, meaning I'm expected to wear my white Team GB issued Village kit. Tomorrow will be Blue. The sheet will be updated every day.

I go inside. The apartment is decorated simply, all plain walls, wooden flooring, and standard furniture. The lounge has a couch, chair, and TV. There is a set of sliding doors that lead onto the balcony. I step outside and take it all in. The stadium dominates the view, the white beams of its exterior shining brightly in the sunshine. Back inside, I notice the kettle, toaster, and the fridge. There's no kitchen as the Food Hall will take care of all of our meals.

I've been lucky enough to have drawn a single room. No sharing my space with someone else. I open the door and take in the room. The white walls continue, but there is an injection of colour from the blue duvet that's neatly covering the single bed. There are forty squares on it showing white outlined figures doing different Olympic sports: weightlifting, boxing, tennis. The square backgrounds are different colours such as red and orange. There is a rolled-up Team GB towel on the bed and a Team GB teddy leaning on the white pillow. On the bedside table is more free stuff, all embossed with Olympic rings and Team GB logo. I pick each item up and look at them. There's a new toothbrush, a mug, shower gel, and shaving foam, factor 30 sun cream, and a map of the Village. I take a couple of photos of the room and send them to Rachel.

Arrived. Love you.

I unpack my bags, setting my laptop up. I pile the DVDs I've brought with me on the bedside table. Action films and comedies to distract my mind in the next few days as I tick away the hours in between my final training sessions.

Today is Tuesday. Qualifying is on Friday at 7:50 p.m.

I WAKE UP under my Team GB duvet. I lie for a few minutes, enjoying the peace. No Rachel rushing round getting ready for work, no team bus or flight to catch. I get up and dress in my blue kit as instructed, and leave the apartment to get breakfast.

The Food Hall is the size of nineteen football pitches and offers every type of food you could wish for at any time of night or day. McDonald's has a place here, which gets more popular once competitions finish. I sit with a few other track athletes, eating sensibly and trying to relax. There's a lot of banter flying round. A lot of star spotting. Everyone looking for a distraction.

My eyes move around the Hall and lock on someone.

He is stood in a queue, laughing with a teammate.

He glances across the room and sees me.

Our stares hold for a second. No smiles. No nods of acknowledgement.

Just a long, hard stare.

It's Wednesday. Two days to go.

THURSDAY PASSES IN much the same way as Wednesday. Killing time and trying to relax, lying on the bed imagining what tomorrow will bring.

IT'S FRIDAY. I'M stood on the London 2012 runway, watching the Olympic official move the small red cone from in front of the board, informing me I'm free to jump. The clock ticks down. 1.00… 0.59… 0.58…

This is what the last four years have all been about. Every step I've walked, every run I've run, has all been about arriving at this spot. Ready, prepared, focused.

0.47.

I start my run up.

I run onto the board and jump. In the air, I know it's not the best I've ever jumped. It's flat, and I stretched into the take-off. I land, sand popping up around me.

The flag is white.

I stand and wait for the measurement, already knowing.

It's confirmed at 8.19 metres, nine centimetres over the qualifying distance.

I walk back calmly to my stuff. No celebration, no emotion. I've qualified for tomorrow night. Job done.

As I collect my stuff, I take in the enormous bowl that is the Olympic stadium. Peter Hedge advised me to do this. To take it all in, enjoy the wonder and the spectacle of it. Allow myself the moment of enjoyment. To comprehend the size. So that, tomorrow in the final, I don't look up and see the stands rising up towards the London night sky and get taken by surprise. So, now, I stand in the long jump section and let my eyes take in the view: the flame burning, the mass crowd, the athletes working their way around the track, their faces strained.

This is London.

The Olympics.

This is why I've put myself through everything. Why I haven't seen my friends, why I've missed birthday celebrations, why I walked out of a relationship with Abbie before it had the chance to start.

I pack up and leave my competitors to their attempts.

I look up at the family section of the stands and see Rachel there. She blows me a kiss and I pretend to catch it.

This event, this moment in my life, is why her last four years have been harder than they needed to be. I've limited our lives to a series of routines that are built strictly for my needs.

I hope that now, stood in this place watching me jump, she'll fully understand why.

Five rings: Blue. Yellow. Black. Green. Red.
Three medals: Bronze. Silver. Gold.
One Champion: Him or me?

36

THE CALL ROOM, Olympic Final Day.

This is it. This is the moment I've built towards.

No one in this final, in this tightly packed call room, has ever jumped further than me. Not even him. Only four men in the history of the sport have ever jumped further than me. I'm ready.

We are called.

I leave the room, head high, shoulders back. Confident, assured, ready to work.

We step out into the stadium, all colour and noise. I walk across the track and find a position in the small seating area. I put my bag down and get my bearings. I look for Len in the crowd. I see him, dressed in his Team GB tracksuit, cap on his head. He nods. *You're ready.*

I'm down to jump seventh.

I strip my tracksuit off and stand in my vest and shorts. The Olympic official calls me forwards and I step to the runway as Henning Rudman starts his run up. I stand at my run up marker as he lands in the sand. The red cone appears.

I go through my routine.

The clock ticks. I close my eyes and breathe slowly in and out. I open my eyes and focus again on my spot beyond the pit. Everything is quieter, sharper. I take a final breath as her words appear in my mind: 'It's just running and jumping.'

I power down the runway, hitting the board at speed. I push into the air and kick and hang, land in the sand.

The flag is white.

The official measures. 8.41 metres.

Long and good. A perfect start.

I return to my seat. Among the guys, it feels like any other competition. A track is a track, a pit is a pit. Everyone is in their own routine. Some talk, some watch the other jumps. Some sit, wrapped in an invisible blanket of protection from the outside world, waiting only for their time to jump.

I sit and wait.

He hits 8.29 metres. Good, but not good enough.

I lead at the end of the First Round.

I step to my mark for my second jump. None of the first six guys got anywhere near me. I can feel all the tension in my body has gone. Everything I've worked for, grafted for, in the last four years has prepared me for these jumps. I've got one on the board, the leading jump after the Opening Round. I can afford to really go for this, really push myself. I fly down the runway, pushing my body forwards. I push from the board and kick and hang. In the air, I know this jump is further than before. I land and look at the board. It's around 8.60 metres and the flag is white. I've increased my lead.

The official measures again and confirms 8.61 metres I've gone twenty centimetres further, added pressure to all eleven guys. To him.

I go back to my seat and wait, ignoring Len. Nothing he can say to me now is going to improve my position. My technique is good, my speed is great. Everything we've worked towards, planned for, on all those cold winter mornings and all those long summer afternoons is coming together.

Madison red flags.

I sense his desperation as he comes back to the seating area. He paces up and down, talking to himself, pumping his body up. That conversation in a Beijing nightclub seems so far away, yet feels like yesterday. His words, 'My plan is to dominate. Way I see it, only you can stop me.'

I'm four jumps away from becoming the Olympic Champion.

Round Three: 8.48 metres

I've jumped the longest three jumps of the day in the first three rounds. I'm dominating. The crowd is responding, cheering, and clapping. I'm desperate to acknowledge them, to show them I appreciate their efforts, but I can't let one small glimmer of weakness into my mind.

I cross the track and walk towards Len. He leans over the barrier and cautions, 'Now is not the time to let your focus slip. Every guy left is after what have you now. Follow your routine. And let everything fly. This is where we fight. Leave everything you've got in that pit. No regrets.'

I change my vest for a fresh one, like always. Twelve have become eight. The order has changed. I earned the right to jump eighth. Madison hit 8.40 metres when I was talking to Len. He is in second place. He will go seventh, one before me.

Three jumps left.

None of the first six jump further than me.

I stand next to the runway as Madison starts his run up. The moment his feet start to move I stand on the track. I watch him jump, seeing the motion of his take-off from behind. He hangs in the air for a long time, and for a moment I worry. He has just jumped a big jump. Everything pauses. The digital countdown clock is reset to 1.00 and freezes there. The single red cone is in front of the pit, informing me I can't jump. He stands by the pit waiting and waiting for the result.

It's announced: 8.59 metres.

He holds his head and screams, 'fuck!' to the London night sky. He was three centimetres away from leading. He tries to get the crowd going, clapping and waving his arms. He's trying to get them onside for his next attempt. He's running out of chances and he knows he'll need every single bit of their energy.

Instinctively, I do something I've not done in years. I clap. Slowly and rhythmically, hands above my head, encouraging the crowd to do the same. They do, building the atmosphere with every beat. I go through my routine with this soundtrack pounding from the stands.

This is London. These are my fans.

I start my run up and push myself off the board, every inch of my body straining to get the maximum power and height. I land in the sand, knowing I've extended my lead.

8.68 metres.

I stand by the pit and raise my hands to the cheering crowd. My crowd.

I walk back to my seat, my eyes fixed on him. He stands his ground, eyes locked on mine. My mind races back to that Beijing nightclub. His prediction is coming true. This final is about me and him. No one else is getting near our distances. His words: '*Only you can stop me.*' I am stopping him. Beating him. Dominating him.

I sit and let out a long breath. My body aches. I've jumped close to or over eight and a half metres four times. My body is telling me it can't take much more. All the training, all the strength building, the conditioning, every session I've done in the last four years, in my life, have prepared me for this moment. But it doesn't mean that it's easy, that the pressure on my joints when I push off from the ground is any less. I can feel every ache, every twinge, every pain. I know the fight is in my mind now. I know I need to push through the pain, to push myself to the limit for two more jumps.

Round Five. The top three positions haven't changed as he steps on to the runway. I focus on me, on my well-practised routine. Focus on what I can do, what I can control.

I don't watch his jump. I lift my head when he's hit the sand and can tell from his body language as he slowly pushes himself up that his jump is not good enough, not far enough to challenge my leading distance. It is measured at 8.35 metres. He has one jump remaining. One jump to beat me.

I stand ready for Jump Five. The jump that caused all the problems a couple of years ago. The jump that Len wanted me to go further with, that Peter Hedge designed an entire routine around. That all the work has been about. If I can go further now, I can break him, break all of them, for the final Round. We're all tired, we all ache. All our bodies hurt. If I can be the one to push myself harder and further, I can end this competition now.

I don't clap this time, but the crowd, my crowd, start anyway. 1.00… 0.59… 0.58…

I focus on the spot beyond the pit.

I breathe in and breathe out. Slow and controlled.

0.51… 0.50… 0.49…

I lean back slightly.

I push myself forwards.

0.46…

Her face appears in my mind: It's only running and jumping.

0.45…

I'm running. It's fast and smooth, my feet moving perfectly into each step. My back is straight, my head high. I hit the board and push into the air. I'm high, climbing higher. I kick and hang. And hang.

I land and immediately look at the board. It's big. Bigger than anything I've ever jumped.

I look at the official's flag, desperate to see white. And the small white square hangs in the air, above the official's head. I turn my attention to the measurement. It seems to take forever. The world is silent. I look at the marker, at the officials, at the marks of distance along the board. And I wait, desperate to know, to confirm what I think might be true. I've jumped thousands of times, into hundreds of pits. I've been through this routine, this moment of waiting for a distance to be measured, more than I've done almost every other thing in my life. None of the other times have ever felt like this. This is different. I can sense it. This is London. This is the Olympics. This is everything.

The official calls it: 8.96 metres.

There's an enormous eruption of noise from the stands behind me.

I've broken the World Record.

EIGHT METRES AND ninety-six centimetres.

One centimetre further than anyone has ever jumped before.

I've broken the World Record…

I take-off like a shot across the track towards Len. My arms are in the air and the crowd is a blur of smiling faces and applauding hands. I reach Len, who stands on the other side of the advertising board, arms out wide.

'One centimetre. One fucking centimetre.'

Len pulls me into him and says, 'Perfect.'

I stand in front of the crowd, spread my arms wide and clench my fists. 'Come on!' I shout.

I walk back to my seat. A couple of my competitors shake my hand or fist bump me. He does nothing. He stares into the distance, showing no emotion, no hint of recognition for what I've just done.

I look at the digital board with our distances on. I read the numbers again. 8.96 metres, followed by New WR. I allow myself a smile.

Round Six has started, and I pull myself together. I go through my routine again, keeping my legs loose, my mind clear of distraction. Adrenaline flows through me at a rate I've never experienced before. Since we became eight competitors after Round Three, each round has taken about twenty-five minutes. The minutes tick by in slow motion. Every time someone steps to the line to jump, I feel sick.

I don't watch.

I can't watch.

They all have one jump to beat me. The first four fail. I strip down to my shorts and vest. I take my body through a short warm-up to get the blood pumping. I know if no one beats me, I won't jump again. But there is comfort in the routine, in controlling what I can control. I can't step onto the track and stop the others from jumping. We don't touch in this sport. We stand side by side, perform in front of each other, sit and wait next to each other. We try to impact their performances through our actions. We eyeball each other, project a cool or a pumped-up exterior. We peacock. We fake. We lie. We do everything we can to convince the other guys we are better, to apply pressure to make him fail. But we can't control what another man is going to do, what he is going to jump. We can only control ourselves.

'Come on,' he screams. 'You fucking got this.'

I look at him. Chris Madison, my rival, beating his chest, talking to himself, shouting to anyone and no one, 'You got one shot.'

I watch him walk to his marker.

I place myself in his eyeline.

He's in a trance like focus. He starts clapping, trying to get the crowd to going.

The only man who can beat me starts his run up and I step onto the runway. I stare at my feet. I can't watch. A strange noise erupts around me as he lands. It's part cheer, part groan.

I look up. There's a white flag in the air. He's stood by the side of the pit, staring intensely at the measuring official. Suddenly his face widens, and his eyes look like they're going to pop out of his head. He throws his arms in the air and runs wildly across the track.

The noise and colour drain from my senses. My legs feel like they're in cement and my head feels light and dizzy.

The electronic scoreboard flashes: 8.97 metres New WR.

One centimetre.

MY MIND RACES. Random images flash like a strobe light in a darkened room. A Beijing nightclub, my grandma dying, random training sessions, Rachel laughing, my sister leaving for Australia, me and him being pulled apart in the reception of a hotel, the kid, the kid, the fucking kid, the podium in Daegu, arguing with Abbie in the Manchester night, my grandma's funeral, the loud thud of my European gold medal hitting the coffin.

The images swirl together, then disappear like dirty water down a plughole.

Black.

THE PIT HAS been swept and the red cone is removed. It's my turn to jump. I try to get a grip of the situation, try to refocus my eyes.

1.00... 0.59... 0.58...

This is the Olympic Final. The last jump. To win, I need to break the World Record. Again. I desperately try to slow my mind down. The pulse in my head beats like a boxer smashing punches against the inside of my temple.

0.51... 0.50... 0.49...

I look beyond the pit. I focus.

I think of Peter Hedge.

A jump is a jump. A pit is a pit.

Routine is key.

0.43... 0.42... 0.41...

I breathe in.

0.38... 0.37... 0.36...

Out.

0.29... 0.28... 0.27...

It's only running and jumping.

0.22... 0.21... 0.20...

I lean back.

Hold my position, breathe again.

0.13... 0.12... 0.11...

I start my run up.

My speed is good, but I overstep in the middle and desperately try to adjust my feet to find my rhythm again, but I stretch into the board. My jump is flat. I land in the sand and roll out. I'm somewhere around 8.20 metres. Nothing. Nowhere. Miles away from his World Record.

I look up and see a red flag.

This is how it ends, a foul and a silver medal.

I stand by the pit unsure of what to do, of where to go, of how to move.

He beat me.

He beat me.

I stare at the sand, my imprint untouched.

He beat me by one centimetre.

He appears in front of me and pulls me into a hug. 'We've just been part of history,' he says. I'm dazed, stunned into silence. My mind throws up the word 'Congratulations' but my mouth won't form it, won't put it out into the world.

He lets me go and a couple of the other guys come over and shake my hand and tap my back, knowing how they'd feel in my position. Broken, destroyed.

He's started his lap of honour, wrapped in his Stars and Stripes. He's playing the game; posing for photos, smiling for the kids, signing autographs on the programmes that are shoved in front of him.

I look at the crowd – my crowd – and know, as a medal winner, I'm expected to do the same. I need to thank them for their support, for the encouragement, despite the fact I want to bury myself underneath the sand and hide forever. I want sand to pour into me and suffocate me, so I don't have to feel what I feel right now.

I start to walk, waving, and forcing myself to smile at the blur of faces. All these thousands of faces and I've never felt so alone. No one in this stadium, in these Games, in the world, can understand what I'm going through.

I broke the World Record and still lost.

Her face appears stained with fallen tears. I move to her, the only person in the world I want to see at this moment. She holds her arms out and I collapse into her.

'I love you,' she says.

'One centimetre,' I say.

'I know.'

She lets me go and I step backwards. My parents and my sister are behind her. They share their words of encouragement, of pride, and support. I smile and move on, in front of more faces and requests for photographs, through words of condolence.

I make it to the press section. David from the BBC is waiting, microphone in hand. He places his hand on my back and pulls me towards the camera.

'Adam,' he says. 'That was one of the greatest Olympic finals there has ever been. Can you sum up your feelings at this moment? I realise this can't be easy.'

'I'm just in shock. I thought I'd done enough to win on Jump Five, but Chris came back in the final Round and beat me.'

'No World Record in long jumping for twenty-one years.'

'I know. It's amazing, really. People have talked about mine and Chris's rivalry, but the last couple of times we've faced each other it's really gone up a level. We obviously push each other to jump further. I knew I had a massive jump in me, I just didn't expect that tonight.'

'A silver medal in the Olympic Final is a fantastic achievement.'

The interview ends. I walk across the track to collect my bag. I can't look at the pit. I quietly pick up my stuff and walk back across the lanes, under the stand, past two stewards, and into a toilet. I lock the door and sit on the floor.

Finally, alone.

I lost.
I broke the World Record and still lost.

37

THE KNOCKING GETS louder.

'Adam, it's me. Open up.'

'Go away.'

'Adam, you need to let me in.'

'Fuck off.'

'You've been in there for thirty-five minutes. We need to get you drug tested.'

I stand, my numb legs nearly giving way. I'm light-headed. My body needs food to refuel after the exertion of the last few hours. I splash water on my face, pick up my bag, and open the door. We just look at each other. No hug or handshake, no pat on the back.

'I'm incredibly proud of you,' Len says.

He leads me down corridors and through doors until we arrive at the drug testing area.

'Has he been tested yet?'

'Not yet. He's still doing press.'

I drink cup after cup of water, desperately trying to get things moving before he arrives. I don't want to be trapped in such close quarters with him. I don't want to talk to him about what a final we've just been involved in. Because no matter how amazing it was, how much of a spectacle it was for the watching world, I know the ending will never change. He beat me. I hadn't lost in nearly two years. I was leading for the entire final until the Final Round. He was never ahead, never winning. Until the end. Until it mattered.

I give a sample and leave. He's somewhere in the stadium, still doing press, still talking about breaking the World Record, and winning his gold medal.

I GO BACK to the Village on the bus, dump my stuff on the bed, shower quickly, and dress in more Team GB kit.

I leave the Village through the secure streets that lead to Team GB house. The route is quiet and private, cut off from the busy world outside our private, temporary home. I enter the building and get into the lift. The doors slide open at the floor Team GB have redesigned from its original office state to be a relaxing place for British team members. I walk across the carpet that's been designed to look like a running track and keep my head down.

I don't want to be here.

I move to the corner where Rachel, my parents, and my sister are. They are talking quietly, waiting for me, waiting to assess my mood.

'Hello, son,' my dad says. He pulls me to him and gives me a hug. Something he's not done for years.

I kiss my mum and Jane. I hug and hold Rachel.

I don't want to be here.

There's nothing I can say. No explanation for what happened. I look at them all, the people who have sacrificed huge parts of their lives for my dream, and realise I've failed them. I wanted to walk back in here tonight as the Olympic Champion. I wanted them to smile and cheer and feel like everything they've given up was worth it.

'What happens now?' Jane asks.

'We stay here for a bit. I go to bed and in about six hours I've got to go on the BBC and face questions about how I feel about my silver medal.'

'And how do you feel?'

'Numb.'

I try for them.

I force a smile and ask about their experience. I drag out being here, in this Team GB only place, knowing he can't gain access to it. Knowing I won't turn around and see the man who went on television and called me a kid, who purposely tried to embarrass me and belittle me. Knowing he can't infect this place with his smile and his medal and his World fucking Record.

Rachel holds my hand throughout. At one point she says, 'I wish I could stay with you tonight.'

'Me too,' I say.

But she can't, because to decision makers she's not part of the team. She doesn't have the right access or laminate or the right job title. She's just my girlfriend and that isn't enough to allow her to be with me on the night I need her most.

The night I lost.

I LIE UNDER the Team GB duvet, thinking about the final. I analyse every jump. Every run up and take-off, every second in the air. I'm searching for answers, for a different outcome. Searching for the moment when the red flag raises on his sixth jump.

It never comes.

The hours disappear, but the result never changes. This is my life now. I'm the guy who lost. All the years of work have not been enough. The plain beige walls of my bedroom feel like they're closing in and sleep never comes.

I get up and go outside.

I walk aimlessly around the Village, my hood up, head down, trying not to be seen. It's just gone five and I know the food court will be quiet. I pile my plate high and find a corner to sit in, my back to the room so no one will disturb me.

I struggle to eat. My body is reacting to every move, reminding me each time I lift my arm about the aches and pains that come with pushing your body through the air for 8.96 metres. I force some down, knowing I've got to be on television soon. My day is planned out. Contracted interviews and photographs.

Back in my room, I lie on my bed again and think about turning my phone on. I don't, not wanting to read messages from people who watched last night and want to try to make me feel better with an awkwardly crafted sentence or three little *x* marks.

I shower and change into the Team GB kit I have to wear despite the badge making me feel sick and the material feeling unnatural against my skin. I'm still a team member, still a representative. I've still got a job to do.

I want to curl up and hide.

IN THE EVENING, I sit on the bus back to the Olympic stadium.

The three of us stand together, slightly away from the crowd and the track. Henning, the bronze medal. Me, the silver. Him, the gold. We are waiting for the official to call us to the ceremony.

I don't want to go out there.

The official calls us.

I can't go out there.

We step forward.

I don't want to go out there and stand on a podium and smile and wave and kiss the flower girl and shake his hand and listen to his national anthem.

We enter the stadium.

I don't acknowledge the crowd, don't look at long jump pit.

We stand behind our podiums.

I want to run, but my legs feel like they're trapped in cement.

I stare forward as Henning stands on his podium and smiles to the crowd as he receives his bronze medal.

I'm next.

I don't want to be next.

Henning waves to the crowd. The official steps to the side, in front of my podium.

I force my legs to step up.

I look at the official. I see the medal in his hand. My silver medal.

I didn't come here for silver. I came here for gold.

And I failed.

This is not a dream. This is not a nightmare. This is life. My life.

38

THERE IS NOWHERE to hide.

All I can do is watch as the official presents him with the medal. He shakes the official's hand, accepts his praise. He stands tall, holding the medal closer to his eyes. He studies it, adores it.

Gold.

First.

Everything.

My silver medal hangs like a dead weight.

My dream is dead.

One centimetre.

39

I FACE A TV camera. David from the BBC is opposite me, microphone in hand. 'I'm here with long jumper and Olympic silver medallist, Adam Lowe.'

Medallist, not Champion.

Silver, not gold.

I LIE ON the bed, staring into nothing. The medal is next to me. I can't look at it. When I do, it reminds me that all the hours of pain and sacrifice weren't enough.

I stand and make my way out of the apartment, across the Village to the Food Hall. It's busy; a mass of conversation and languages. I queue with my head down.

'I bet you're feeling pretty shit today,' a voice says.

I turn and see Simon Lewis, the swimmer, behind me. A welcome, friendly face. 'What are you doing tonight?' he asks.

'Nothing.'

'In that case, eat your dinner, go upstairs, put your glad rags on, bit of gel in your hair and come out with us.' He nods behind him to a couple of other swimmers.

We move two steps forward in the queue.

'OK,' I say.

IT'S BEEN NEARLY four years since my last drink, but now I'm stood leaning on the bar in a nightclub, drunk. My medal means the booze is free and I take full advantage.

Strangers, Joe Public, come over and say hello, tell me how they've never really watched long jumping before, but they were fully engrossed last night. They describe how they felt with every twist and turn, as if they felt the pain. The drink helps me play nice.

Some guy introduces himself as the brother of an Australian athlete, whose sport I don't catch in the conversation. He starts banging on about what happened, and I can't tell through the alcohol haze if he's being friendly or not. 'You cost me money. I had a bet on you to win gold six months ago.'

Unsure what I'm supposed to say, I just shrug. He carries on talking, but I can't make out what he's saying over the loud music.

Simon's hand lands in the middle of the guy's chest. The guy swipes it, but it's unmoved. Simon clenches the guy's shirt and pulls him forward. 'Why don't you just fuck off?'

The guy is trying to protest, saying he wants to talk, that he's just being friendly.

'Would you want to talk? I don't think so. Now fuck off.'

The guy does the maths and doesn't fancy his chances against three swimmers and me. He backs away through the crowd, offering a waved apology.

'Thanks,' I say. 'I'm too drunk for this shit.'

I walk through the dancing crowd to the toilet. The room is small, dark, and quiet, apart from a dull throb of bass pounding through the wall from the main club. I splash water on my face in the hope it'll sober me up. It doesn't. There's a burst of music as the door opens and a man walks in. We both look at my drunken face in the mirror. I dry my face on a roll of towel and leave.

I stand by the dance floor trying to get my bearings. A woman looks at me from the crowd and smiles. I smile back and place her: Mia Sonner, the German triathlete. She moves around people to me and kisses my cheek.

'How are you?' she asks.

'I've been better. You?'

As she answers, I'm transported back to Beijing. In a club like this, both relaxed following our finals, full of Olympic fever. She's flirting again, now; a slight touch of my arm, leaning too close to make herself heard, she tells me she was in the stadium for my final. I notice an engagement ring on her finger. Not that it matters. There are no rules here. What goes on in the Village, stays in the Village.

I ask her how her race went. She shrugs and says, 'Top twenty.'

'Rio?'

'I don't know. I'm tired. I need a holiday.'

'We all do.'

She laughs. Another touch of the arm.

'I need to go,' I say.

'Oh.' She pauses. Then, 'I could come with you.'

Just like Beijing.

It would be easy go back to one of our rooms. To fuck and forget. Forget about defeat and pain, about the real world.

To forget about him.

I look at her.

She at me. She smiles, waiting.

'No. I don't want that.'

THE NEXT NIGHT. Drunk again. People dancing all around me. Girls laugh with their friends as they make eyes at a couple of sprinters, who soak up the attention. It feels like every other person is an athlete. Athletes who have earned these moments of release. Everyone is smiling. Everyone is laughing. Happy.

Everyone but me.

I leave and go back to the Village. In my room, I stumble about, almost falling backwards as I reach down into my kitbag and pull out my medal.

I look at it properly for the first time. It is my reward.

Silver, not gold.

History will show gold was won by someone else.

Gold will always belong to him.

MY ACCREDITATION ALLOWS me into the stadium at all times.

If Saturday had ended with gold, I would've spent hours here. Instead, I hid in the security of the Village, away from the public and requests for autographs, away from the looks of recognition and pity. A couple of nights of drinking helped numb the pain and made sleep a dreamless black.

I SIT HIGH in the stand, alone. It's between sessions, so the seats are empty. I put my feet up on the white chair in front of me and take in the view: the deep red track, the mass of green field in the middle. My focus moves around the huge bowl of the stadium. It settles, inevitably, on the long jump runway. My eyes move down the empty runway to the pit. It's covered now. There's no hint of the drama of Saturday night. No evidence of our battle. No sign of the raw emotion we went through. I went through. For every moment of pain I feel, he feels joy. For every tear, he smiles.

I know I can stare at the pit forever and the result will never change. There will be no second chance. No one will peel the cover back and reveal perfectly raked sand. The officials won't reposition themselves. The timer won't be reset. We won't power down the runway in perfectly timed run ups, won't launch ourselves from perfectly executed take offs, we won't land in the perfectly raked sand. Not again. Not in this stadium. Not in 2012.

He will always be the winner.

I will always be nothing.

TOM'S FACE OVERLOOKS the stadium. He's relaxed as he's introduced to the crowd, giving a little wave. My friend living his dream of running in an Olympic Final. The athletes line up and the gun goes. They start running, quickly into the rhythm, twenty-four legs a mass blur as they circle the track in a bunch. Tom sits in the middle, boxed in on the inside. For two laps, the pack stays together. I watch Tom, not the other runners. A couple of times he tries to get out but can't. He glances around him, trying to gauge other people's movements. They hit the bell and I look to the front as the race picks up speed. The pack stretches and Tom doesn't have enough to go with them. He grits his teeth and pushes his body. He's running for pride, which is a hard thing to do, Olympic Final or not. At the front, a runner breaks free, creating a gap between himself and the rest of the field, claiming his title. Seconds later, I watch Tom cross the line and collapse on the track.

TOM'S DREAM IS over. It becomes his personal mission to make me make the most of this once in a lifetime position. He drags me to see all the Games. He's like a tourist, endlessly snapping photos on his phone. Last night, he signed up for tickets for an event away from the stadium.

'I know it hurts, but you can't sit around being miserable all day,' he says as we eat lunch. 'We dreamed of being Olympians when we were kids. Try to get something out of it.'

I dreamed of winning.

But Tom is insistent.

So, we take an official bus from inside the Village to the Copper Box to spend the day watching the quarterfinals of the men's handball. In the evening we watch women throw themselves fearlessly off the 10-metre board at the diving centre. It's good to get lost in the competition of other sports.

Thursday afternoon. We leave the Village and walk into a mob of people hanging around the Village looking for photo opportunities and autographs. Some of them don't care who you are as long as you're wearing official team kit, they assume you must be someone important.

I go back to lying. People are friendly, telling me they couldn't believe Saturday and it's clear I've become *The Long Jump Guy*. I pose for photos and sign pieces of paper. I thank them for their support; tell them it makes the whole experience worth it. I lie. And lie. And lie.

I FAKE A smile and force myself to enjoy the night. As the night of drinking and arms in the air and no-one-is-watching dancing, ticks on, I start to feel like Tom's infectiousness, and Simon's determination to snap me out of my darkness, are starting to work. We waste no minutes, no seconds. We will never get these moments again and we cling to them, swear we'll never let them go. Performances and results don't matter at this second. Sacrifice and commitment are for another day. All that's important is music, laughter, and youth. We are Olympians. That means something here.

I smile at Tom and he drunkenly hugs me, singing along to 'Mr Brightside' as it blasts through the speakers.

My eyes look through the crowd and fix on the bar.

I see him.

He sees me.

I freeze.

He lifts his glass, tilts it in my direction.

I stare.

Chris Madison smiles.

Champion, not medallist.

I'M OUTSIDE BY the bins in a cobbled alley filled with kebab wrappers and polystyrene takeaway cartons. I pull my phone out of my pocket and dial. It rings and rings and then her voice appears.

'Adam? What's wrong?'

'I'm sorry,' I say. 'Really, really sorry. I let you down. I let everybody down. You supported me through all of it. You must feel like you've given up a life for nothing. I'm so sorry.'

'Adam, stop. You didn't let me down.'

But it's too late. I'm already slumped against the wall, crying uncontrollably.

HIS SMILING FACE lives in every sleeping second, so I get up early and shower. The apartment is quiet. Everyone else sleeps off the previous night's excesses. In my room I start to pack ready for leaving tomorrow. My medal lies at the bottom of my red kit bag. I slowly cover it with Team GB stuff and think about tonight's closing ceremony.

I don't want to go and stand in the stadium and celebrate the wonder of the Olympics. I don't care about handing over to Rio, don't give a shit about Madness singing 'Baggy fucking Trousers'.

I don't want to get dressed into my Team GB issued suit and walk to that stadium because I'm afraid that I'll see one man among thousands. One man, who jumped further into a sandpit than I did. One man, who is capable of sending my mood into a downward spiral by raising a glass and smiling.

WHEN THE CEREMONY has finished, we, Team GB, gather at the outdoor barbeque area of the Village. For the first time in the Games, alcohol is allowed inside. At the vending machines we scan our accreditations and beer or wine is dispensed in place of water and energy drink. This night is the first time I've realised the size of the team I was part of. It's a mix of everyone: athletes, physios, and support staff.

In the queue for food, I turn to the woman behind me and say, 'It's going to feel strange tomorrow when all this is over and we have to start paying for food again.'

She laughs. 'It's not over for me yet.' I look at her accreditation. *Name: Joanna Wray. Sport: Water Polo.* She continues, 'I've still got to make sure twenty-six athletes get up, packed, out of here on buses by eleven o'clock in the morning.'

I look at the scene in front of me, the final party playing out. Athletes and staff drinking freely, no one looking like their night will end soon.

'I don't envy you.' I pause. 'How are you going to get everyone up? Banging on doors?'

'If that's what it takes.'

'Like a teacher on a school trip.'

'That's the job.' She smiles. 'Performance Director. Part boss, part schoolteacher. The person who says no.'

I arrive at the front of the queue and order my food, then turn back to Joanna. 'You don't seem stressed about it.'

'I'm too tired to feel anything.'

I'm handed a full plate from behind the barbeque. 'Good luck tomorrow,' I say.

I walk away, thinking about how for people like Joanna, the Olympics don't stop because the athletes have competed, or the medals have been placed around people's necks.

I SIT WITH Tom on top of a picnic table. Two childhood friends at the last night of the Olympics. The air around us is filled with talk and laughter. There's a lot of flirting going on. People grabbing their last chance with the ones they've had their eye on for the last few weeks, hoping for one last opportunity to act in the privacy of the Village before returning to normality tomorrow.

He turns to me at one point and says, 'When you win in Rio…'

'Tom don't.'

'I'm serious,' he says. 'All the pain you've been feeling this week. Save it all. Use it all. Then, when you win in Rio, you'll know it was all worth it.'

AND THEN IT'S over. There's not another closing ceremony in the Village, just athletes saying final goodbyes to friends made. I think of Joanna from last night and her task of getting athletes and staff home. There's organised chaos all around me as hundreds of Joannas try to get thousands of people, many hung-over or still drunk, on to buses, trains, and aeroplanes. Cadburys have left piles of chocolate around the Village and people grab what they can to aid their recovery. Bottles of energy drink are stuffed inside kit bags for the journeys to wherever home is.

I spend a few minutes watching the activity swirl around me, knowing these are the last moments of my life where I can hide from the real world.

And then, with the simple act of walking out of the Village, my 2012 Olympics are finished.

My dream has died. My nightmare is alive and kicking.

40

MY PARENTS' HOUSE is full. Family, friends, and neighbours all gathered around the *bit of a buffet* my mum has put in the dining room. Everyone wants to share where they were, how they suffered on that Saturday. I smile and lie.

My medal is being passed across the breakfast bar that separates the kitchen and dining room. People pose with it, wear it, do the joke where they pretend to bite it.

Someone shouts, 'Speech,' and I'm pushed towards an open part of the room, and the medal is handed to me. I wave away the call for words, but most of my parents' friends have other ideas.

'Well, I haven't prepared anything.' I pause and suppress the lump in my throat. I look at Rachel, then to my parents and sister. 'Being an Olympian,' I say, unsure what will follow. A few seconds later I add, 'isn't easy. It's not just about walking out in a stadium and trying to win. It's about years of graft. Of hard, hard work. Sacrifice. Not just of the athlete, but of his family and friends. I wouldn't have had the experiences of the last few years, especially the last few weeks, without so many of you.'

I stop again and take another deep breath. 'Without Rachel, I wouldn't have been able to live this life. She's supported me every day, through every high and every low.' There's a small tear welling in Rachel's eye. 'I just wanted to say thank you for everything.'

Someone starts clapping and Rachel smiles as she wipes her eyes.

'Jane,' I say. 'I know it's not always been easy for you. Especially when we were younger. All those weekends that were built around me competing. If it was the other way around, I would've hated you. Instead, you just sat in the car and read book after bloody book. No wonder you're the smart one.'

My sister laughs.

'Again, thank you.' I turn to my parents and say, 'Dad, Mum. This medal is not really mine. All the hours you spent encouraging me, sacrificing for me. The money you spent supporting me. I don't even want to think about how much I owe you.'

'A lot,' my dad says, and everyone laughs.

'Driving miles and miles to meets all over the country so I could try to get better at something that, let's face it, is not that impressive. Well, like I said, this medal isn't really mine. It's yours.'

I step forward and place the medal around my mum's neck. 'I'm just sorry it wasn't gold.'

My family embrace and people clap again.

LATER, WHEN THE guests have gone, my dad says, 'We are proud of you, you know.'

'For what?'

'The way you handled last week. And for winning a silver medal.'

'I didn't win a silver medal, Dad. I lost a gold one. That's different.'

WE STAY OVER, sleeping in my old bedroom. We talk in whispers, wrapped in each other. Rachel eventually falls asleep resting on my chest. I lie awake, knowing sleep won't come. I know what will happen. I try to stop myself, try to convince myself it's a bad idea but at half-past two I get dressed and go downstairs into the front room, running my fingers across the bookshelf until I find the small gap between the dictionary and thesaurus. I pull out the envelope and stuff it into my pocket before unlocking the front door and stepping out into the night.

Head down, I walk for about ten minutes, stopping at a bench that's illuminated by street light. I sit and pull out the envelope. My hands shake as I open it. The orange glow from above me highlights the words.

I stare at them, knowing they won't change.

I read them.

They are further evidence that I've failed.

SIX DAYS AFTER the Olympics ends, Rachel and I fly to Mauritius. We spend two days lying in the sun and sleeping. My body begins to recharge, and a fog begins to lift.

At sunset on the third night, we walk on the beach.

I stop and face her. I tell her I love her more than anything.

She says she loves me too.

I drop to one knee.

She smiles.

I take the box out of my pocket.

'Rachel Thornton, will you marry me?'

I open the box.

'Yes.'

I take the ring on put it on her finger.

It's white gold.

All I see is silver.

PART TWO

41

AT LEAST ONE plan went right this summer. Rachel looks at the ring, assessing every angle and smiling uncontrollably.

'I'm so happy.'

We're sat at a small, candle-lit table. Champagne bottle in an ice bucket, bubbles floating in our glasses. The staff fuss over us, as excited as we are.

'Were you expecting it?' I ask.

'Not at all. When did you buy it?'

I think back to the day I walked the streets of Manchester, World Championship gold – gold, not silver – medal in one pocket, the engagement ring in another. I tell her the story and, as her laughter fades, says, 'Imagine if you'd have got run over. You'd have looked pretty weird with that medal in your pocket.'

'That's what I thought,' I say, laughing. 'I asked your dad just before Christmas.'

'So, they already know?'

'Your dad knows. He said he'd let you tell your mum. Plus, he only knows I was asking. He didn't know you'd say yes.'

'Of course, I was going to say yes.'

I lift my champagne glass. 'To happy futures.'

She raises her own glass, and we clink.

The night flies by in a series of kisses and conversations about weddings, bridesmaids, and honeymoons. I ask when she thinks we should plan it for.

'After Moscow next year?' she asks.

'Perfect,' I say.

We walk back to our room, hand in hand. Our future one step closer.

FOR DAYS I don't have to force happiness. She has agreed to be my wife. She didn't need me to have a gold medal around my neck to say I'm the best. She simply said *yes*.

Yet, occasionally, in the quiet moments on the beach, when she's nipped back to our room to get a new book, or gone to the pool bar to order drinks, I look out and realise I'm surrounded by sand. I can feel every tiny grain stuck between my toes, irritating my skin, rubbing at me, reminding me of all the hours and days and weeks I've spent jumping into it. When I step out of the clear sea and walk along the beach, the wet sand forms around my feet, clinging to me, unmoveable. Every step flashing my memory back to the shower I had following the Olympic Final when I scrubbed the sand from me, desperately trying to rid myself of any part of the event, my skin red raw when I'd finished.

There are hours where I don't think about it. I get lost in my football magazine or in drafting my best man's speech for Pete's wedding, running lines by my new fiancée. Then, I lie on the sun lounger, eyes open, staring at the perfect, cloudless blue sky, and I'll see his face. His face, changing from nothing to Olympic Champion, from long jumper to The Greatest Long Jumper of All Time. The reaction as his face couldn't hold back the emotion of realising his dreams, and of destroying mine.

Three days before we're due to fly home, I wake at half five. Light creeps into the room by the side of the heavy blinds. Rachel is in a deep sleep. She won't wake for another five hours.

I slip out of bed, move through the lounge area, and open the sliding doors that lead onto our private terrace. I sit on one of our sun loungers and look out at the quiet world in front of me. The sun is just above the ocean and a low orange glow hovers above the rolling waves. I step onto the empty beach. I know this is where I'm supposed to let it all go. To take all the memories and all the pain and cast them off into the middle of the deep sea and return to England more focused and determined to win than ever.

Instead, I stand on the sand – the fucking sand – and think. What if that was my one chance to win? What if that was my one chance to be a World Record holder? What if London was the peak of my career?

What do I do next?

Defeat: *vb* **1** to win a victory over. **2** to thwart or frustrate: this accident has defeated all his hopes of winning. *n* **3** the act of defeating or state of being defeated. [Old French desfaire to undo, ruin]

Source: Collins Essential English Dictionary.

42

I'M DRUNK, HAMMERED in fact, in the bar of a hotel, the night before Pete and Laura's wedding. The girls are staying at the venue, a few miles up the country roads that surround us. This was supposed to be a few quiet beers before the big day, but it's turned messy. Pete is avoiding the shots that are doing the rounds.

Laura's dad comes up to me at one point and says, 'We were all rooting for you in London.'

'Cheers.'

'I couldn't believe it when that American,' he virtually spits the words out, 'won. Horrible.'

'I'm not being funny,' I say. 'But I'm here to celebrate Pete and Laura. I really don't want to talk about London.'

'Of course, of course,' he says. I've offended the man; I can see it in his eyes.

'Let me buy you a drink,' I say.

Later, I wander outside, holding a bottle of lager, the song from the jukebox continuing loudly inside my head. I stand on the grass and drink, no real focus.

'Ready for your speech, lad?' I hear from behind.

Mike and Johnny stand behind me, cigarettes in hand. They share a light and inhale deeply.

'Preparation is key,' I say.

They smoke, I drink.

'I need a piss,' Mike says. He heads off to a wall at the end of the car park and jumps it. The drop on the other side is longer than he expected, and he disappears from view. Johnny and I laugh as Mike's head appears from the other side. 'I'm all right,' he shouts.

Then there's no sound other than the low baseline of the music inside.

'This what you wanted?' I ask Johnny.

'What do you mean?'

'Me, hammered. This what you wanted for the last four years? How am I doing? Am I a better friend now I'm drunk?'

Johnny looks at me, clueless. 'What?'

'This.' I lift my bottle. 'The drink. Isn't that what you've been banging on about since I quit. "Have a drink". "Let me buy the Champion a drink". "The best man has to be on the stag do". Am I not a good friend unless I'm pissed?'

Johnny stares at me and I can tell he has no idea where my words are coming from.

'What the fuck are you on about?'

'You know,' I say.

'I fucking don't.'

'It's all I've heard from you for four years. "Why you not drinking?" "You're letting your mates down by not going on the stag do".'

'I never said that.'

'Might as well have.'

'Don't put your Olympic shit on me, mate.'

I step towards him.

'Olympic shit?'

He holds his ground. 'Yeah. You lost. It's shit. Don't start having a pop at me because you feel bad. You want to drink, drink. You don't, don't. I don't care. Think all that training has gone to your head.'

'Fuck you.'

'Fuck off, Adam.'

I look at him. He's about five foot ten, solid, but built like a runner. I stand over him, my six-foot three frame, strong and powerful. He holds his ground.

'This the game now, is it? You lost, so now you look for someone to blame.'

His words, our words, are booze-soaked and loose. It's unclear who means what, who intends to hurt the other. I'm struggling to even remember how the conversation started.

'What's going on?' Mike shouts as he runs across the grass.

Then Johnny says, 'It's pretty simple, mate. You jumped in a sandpit and then some American bloke did it further. You lost. Get over it.'

I punch him.

THE THUDDING IN my head emerges from the blackness to become a knocking on the door. I wake in my clothes on top of the bed. I'm not a hundred per cent sure where I am, but I know I'm rough.

Thud.

Thud, thud, thud.

'Adam, open the door.'

Mike.

'Adam, mate. Time to get up.'

'One minute,' I croak.

I slowly get up and cross the room. The door opens and Mike is stood in front of me dressed fully in his usher's suit.

'What the hell were you playing at?'

'What?'

'With Johnny?'

The flashbacks begin. The argument, the punch, the rolling around on the grass. I look down at last night's clothes and see stained jeans and a ripped shirt.

'Is he all right?'

'He's pissed off. But his face hasn't bruised. Pete is fuming.' He steps inside and walks over to the small fridge and takes out a bottle of water and hands it to me. 'Drink.'

I gulp down half a bottle and nearly throw it back up.

'Why did you hit him?'

'Something he said.'

'Well, whatever it was, it's not acceptable. It's Pete's wedding day. You're the fucking best man. Pete's dad had to help me carry you to bed.'

I don't know what to say.

'You need to apologise to Pete and Johnny. And you need to be dressed and ready to leave in half an hour.'

I spend fifteen minutes in the shower, willing the heat and steam to rid me of last night. I play it over and over. It's not going away. Like everything else that has passed, it cannot be changed. Like London and World Records and Olympic fucking Final results.

I dress quickly, then walk to Pete's room and knock. Johnny answers.

'Can I have a word?'

He steps into the corridor and shuts the door.

'I have no valid explanation,' I say. 'Nothing that will make sense to you or anyone. I was drunk, something you said touched a nerve, and I reacted terribly. No excuses. You can hate me forever and I'll understand, but please don't let me have fucked up Pete's day.'

He looks at me and assesses my apology.

'You'll be paying for all my drinks tonight.'

We step inside and I repeat my apology. No excuses. No blaming anyone else.

Pete is harsher in his tone. 'I shouldn't have to be dealing with this shit today. Not from you.'

I hold my hand up. 'I know.'

'Your speech better be funny,' Mike says.

The four of us laugh, and I hope years of friendship will count when it comes to letting this situation heal.

I eat a sausage sandwich someone has brought me from the breakfast I was supposed to attend but slept through. My phone rings and I see Rachel's name on the screen.

'Dare I ask what the hell went on last night?' she says.

'I'm sorry.'

'Is it sorted out?'

'I think so. I feel terrible.'

'So, you should.'

I STAND AT the front of the venue waiting with Pete. His eyes are on the door where his new bride will appear through an oak beamed archway.

'I'm sorry, mate,' I say.

'I'm guessing this has got something to do with London.'

'Probably.'

Orchestral music starts.

'We can't really discuss it now though can we,' he says.

'Guess not.'

My wife-to-be enters, looking stunning in a dark-blue dress. Her hair is perfect, her face smiling. She moves slowly in the role of bridesmaid, edging her way down the aisle. She looks at me and I smile. She smiles back, not fully, but part of the tension I've been carrying on my shoulders disappears.

Two more bridesmaids follow Rachel.

Laura and her dad appear. The beautiful bride and the proud father. Everyone turns to face her, to take in the picture of her moving towards Pete.

The ceremony flies by. I do my bit with the rings and sit alone in the front row.

OUTSIDE THE VENUE, away from staring guests, I try, through tears, to explain to Rachel what I did and why. The words don't flow, and my explanation doesn't get anywhere near the level of detail I know she needs.

'You really embarrassed me,' she says.

'I know.'

'People are going to talk about London. You can't go around punching them all.'

WE, THE GROOMSMEN, pose for photographs. Johnny at one end of the line, me at the other.

'Smile,' Pete says. 'Or Adam will batter you.'

Laughter. Full and genuine.

Johnny moves down the line and pretends to punch me. The photographer clicks away, unsure what we are doing.

LATER, I STAND in the bathroom, feeling something I've not felt in a long time: fear. There are eighty people in the room where we've just eaten, and I've got to give my speech. I try to control my nerves by controlling my breathing, like before a jump. I adjust my hair in the mirror and return to my seat at the top table.

When it's my turn to speak, I stand. Last night's excesses remain in my head, a dull thud continuing. I sip some water and focus on a spot at the back of the room.

'Hello,' I say. 'I'm Adam. I'm Pete's best man.'

I look at Johnny.

'Before I start, I'd like to just say sorry to the bride and groom and my mate, Johnny. I was a bit worse for wear last night and I made a fool of myself. I thought the best man was covered by some kind of right-to-do-what-you-like rule, but turns out that's not the case, so I'm sorry for not acting as I should have done at such a special and important occasion.'

Johnny nods. I look to Laura, whose face softens into a smile.

I breathe again.

'Hello, everyone,' I say. 'Welcome to Pete and Laura's special day. I'm Adam Lowe, Pete's friend and best man. I'm also an Olympic medal winner, just as a point of reference.' People laugh. I look at my notes, the words I've prepared in black on the crisp white page: *It's a funny phrase, 'the best man'. It points to being the best and most important man in this room. In the entire wedding. Yet, despite the name, that's simply not true. Being the best man does not make you the best. The groom is far more important than the best man. Being a best man is kind of like breaking a World Record in a long jump competition and still not winning. You're important, but you're not the one people really want to take photos of.*

This was my joke, my moment to let it all go. To show I can handle what happened. When I wrote the words in Mauritius, it was in the hope I'd be ready to say them when I stood here now. I'm not. I can't pretend. So, I stand in front of all the guests in a strange, awkward silence as I try to gather my composure and move on to my next section.

My eyes jump down the page and I say something nice about Laura, followed by something funny about Pete. My rhythm picks up and I continue with more praise for Laura, through the paragraphs I've written about my friendship with Pete. I make jokes about him, tell stories about him from our school days.

'I don't know if I've mentioned this previously, but I was in the Olympics.' More laughter. 'Being in the Olympics meant unfortunately I wasn't able to attend Pete's stag do. At this point, I'd like to invite Johnny up here to give you a small presentation of the weekend.'

Johnny walks from his table, through the crowd, pumping his arms and getting people to cheer. He taps a couple of keys on a laptop and Pete's face appears on a pull-down screen across the room. Pete is drunk in the photo, wearing a hat that looks like a nipple.

Into the microphone I've just handed him, Johnny says, 'I'm Johnny, and things are about to getting interesting.'

Music starts: soft and classical. It plays as the photos change every few seconds. The stag dressed as a Smurf, the stag asleep in a bar in the early hours of the morning. Johnny makes jokes about the photos, giving little bits of information to accompany the images on the screen and add to the laughter in the room. The photos are embarrassing, but the presentation is harmless. Laura laughs as Pete slips further and further into his chair.

When the final photo freezes and the music stops, Johnny hands me back the microphone and shakes my hand.

'Ladies and gentlemen,' I say. 'Pete's stag do best man, Johnny. Please give it up for him.'

Applause and whistles lead Johnny back to his seat.

I end my speech with nice words about the future for the bride and groom and return to my seat.

The wedding day merges into the wedding reception.

More guests arrive, more drinks flow.

Music gets turned up, and a band starts to set up.

I drink, and dance, I smile for photos.

I spin the bride around the dance floor and buy Johnny drink after drink after drink. I slow dance with my bride-to-be. I tell her I can't wait until our wedding.

'You're drunk,' she says.

'I know. No more after tonight. I've only got a week until training starts.'

I do everything I've not done for years with my friends. I down shots and play air guitar in front of the band. I throw my arms around Johnny and Pete and Mike and tell them that I love them.

I smile and relax. I have fun.

I spend one night lost in the haze of other people's happiness.

I don't think about gold or silver or winning and losing or World Records broken and beaten.

For the first night since that night, I don't think about him.

The fucking kid.

43

WE BEGIN AGAIN, where we always do. Len's office, facing each other.

'I've not had a day go by when I haven't thought about that final,' he says. 'Not one day where it hasn't popped into my head. I've been through every piece of preparation we did. There's nothing we could've done differently. The moment he broke your record, I've never felt so empty in my life. The world should not have been that cruel. I've been angry, hurt. I've spent nights sat at home in disbelief. And I didn't jump. So, I cannot imagine how you've been feeling. What I want you to do is remember exactly how you felt when you stepped onto that podium, when he had that gold medal put round his neck. Remember that hurt, that disappointment.'

That hate.

'Use those feelings as fuel to make sure it never happens again. London has gone. We can't change what happened. We can only move forward and win again.'

It's like he has reached into my brain and picked the exact words I wanted him to say.

Len stands. 'Let's go to work.'

RACHEL AND I book our wedding for the second weekend in October, after the Moscow World Championship. The wedding allows me to distract my mind at home. If I'm alone in the apartment, I spend my free time looking at suits for me and my groomsmen to wear or thinking about stag do destinations. When Rachel is home, we plan and plan. 'Preparation is key,' I say over and over.

Sometimes, when we're sat watching TV before bed, I catch her out of the corner of my eye, her index finger and thumb of her right hand playing with her engagement ring as her eyes concentrate on the screen. I'm not sure she knows she's doing it. I realise that she has done it since she agreed to wear it. In the restaurant on holiday, she would sit and spin it round the finger it sits on. At that time, I still didn't really see the ring, only its colour. I didn't see what the ring represented to us as a couple, our decision to become a family. I saw silver, the colour of the medal that now lives at my mum and dad's house. The medal I hate. Now, as the days are filled with training for Moscow and planning for a future that includes a new wife and new dreams, I see the ring for what it is. A sign of hope.

TRAINING GOES WELL through December. As we finish for Christmas, Len shakes my hand, tells me to enjoy my few days off. 'I'm pleased with you,' he says. 'Have a nice break.'

As I'm leaving the car park on my bike, I see Peter Hedge getting into his car. I put my head down, cycle quickly past him. He waves at me, but I pretend not to notice. I ignore him, as I've ignored every phone call from him since that night in London.

I don't want to talk to him.

I don't want to talk about what happened.

I don't want to look back.

I want to get through Christmas and New Year and let 2012 end. I want to stop looking at my phone each day and seeing the date on my home screen first. I want to stop living in the year when London happened.

I don't want to face up to how it has affected me.

CHRISTMAS IS A standard family affair. Just before dinner I stand in the lounge, in front of the bookshelf, focused on the space between the dictionary and thesaurus. The empty space where my letter used to be. I haven't written another one for the next four years. A couple of times after training, alone at the back of a coffee shop, I've sat with a freshly bought pen and pad and tried to put in words what I want from the next Olympic cycle. I've actually written things, put my hopes and dreams in ink. But each time, I've ripped the paper off the pad and screwed it into a tight ball in my fist. Every word I've written has the potential to break my heart. Every word of hope is a potential reminder of failure. The space on this bookshelf, where I've hidden my goals for years, remains empty.

Her hand touches my back, making me jump.

'You OK?' she asks.

'Yeah,' I lie. Always a lie. 'Just wondering whether to start reading something. My dad is always banging on about Ian Rankin.'

'Good idea,' she says.

She sits down.

I take one last look at the empty space where my dreams used to be.

ON OUR BOXING Day anniversary walk she says, 'Next year this won't be our anniversary anymore.'

'Why?'

'Our wedding date will take over.'

We walk in silence through the trees.

'Are you OK?'

'Yeah,' I say. 'Fine.'

'You've gone quiet, that's all.'

'Just enjoying the walk.'

'You've been doing it a lot in the last few months,' she says. 'Little moments of silence where you look a bit dazed.'

I shrug. 'I'm OK.'

'I know you're not.'

'What do you want me to say?'

'Nothing,' she says. 'I just want you to know if you want to say something, to get something off your chest, I'm OK with that.'

I stay silent.

'Four years ago, to this day, you told me you wanted to be the best long jumper in the world. I know how important that goal is to you.'

'I was the best ever for twenty minutes,' I say.

'And I know that hurts you,' she says. 'I want you to know I understand.' She corrects herself, 'OK, not understand, but I know it hurts. You don't have to hide that hurt from me.'

I know this is the time to release every feeling since the moment he beat me. I know this is one of the reasons I've chosen to spend my life with this woman. She understands me. She wants to share everything. The pain as well as the glory. In sickness and in health.

'I'm OK.'

Always a lie.

Is he holding the medal now? Admiring it, showing it to friends, allowing himself to reflect on the greatest of achievements.

44

IT'S THE END of January and Glasgow is wrapped in darkness. I lie in a nondescript hotel room, staring at the ceiling, trying to focus on tomorrow when I'll jump in a competition again.

It's easy to fake to the world that London is gone. It was easy to sit behind the table during the press conference this afternoon, microphones and tape recorders lined up in front of me, capturing my every word, holding it forever, and lie.

When a journalist asked, 'How, as an athlete, do you start to rebuild following a defeat like the Olympic Final?' I found it natural to say, 'London was very hard to take. I won't sit here and say I shrugged it off. I'm the guy who broke the World Record and still didn't win. I know how that sounds. But I took the only option available to me. I went back to work and trained harder. I've taken confidence from the fact I showed the world how far I can jump.' I shrug. 'I can only come to competitions like this one and try to win. Well, that and hope some journalist decides to cut me a break and not ask me about bloody London.'

The room laughed. I smiled. I told part of a lie, part of the truth. Showed them part of me, kept some of it hidden, covered it with a joke. This is my life now.

'How do you feel about tomorrow?' another asked.

'I just want to jump well.'

Questions, questions.

Truth and lies.

Now, hours later, in this hotel room, lying on a single bed that's too short for my long frame, London is the only thing I see. When I imagine jumping a long, strong jump tomorrow, the thoughts of London come rushing back. Will jumping far ever be enough? Will any jump ever be enough to win?

I think about him. Always him. No one else beat me. Only him. And he's not here tomorrow, so if I jump to my best, I win. That's the attitude I need, the attitude I push to the front of my thoughts. The attitude I'll put across in every movement tomorrow. At breakfast, when the other jumpers are checking each other out from across tables, I want them to see a man unaffected by his experience. A man with a renewed fire of determination, ready to fight. A man who won't be beaten again, who will jump further than them, beat them, never break because of them.

I drift, knowing as I finally cross the line from waking to sleeping, his face, like most nights, will be the last face I see.

IN THE CALL room, some competitors chat to each other, others are lost in their thoughts or focused on the ground beneath their feet. I walk around like I own the place. Head high, shoulders back. Fuck you stare. My body language tells them it won't be happening again.

We leave the call room and walk out to the pit. A tingle of excitement rushes down my spine. London is gone. There's a fresh pit of sand, raked flat and ready for the event. No one has laid a marker down yet. No one is leading, no one is losing. A fresh pit for a fresh start.

Within no time, I'm back on the runway, stood waiting to jump. Not a training jump. My first proper jump since August. I take in every detail: the crowd packed in tight to the track, the digital clock set to 1.00, the deep red cone in front of the pit. The long blue runway stretches in front of me, awaiting my feet. An official removes the cone, and the clock starts ticking backwards. A rhythmic clap from the crowd soundtracks me.

I breathe. This is it. Here I go.

I move into my run up. My speed increases as my leg turnover quickens. I'm into the board, up and in the air, down into the sand, almost popping back out. I do my checks: the flag is white. The jump's not massive, but my imprint is clearly over eight metres. I don't wait for the measurement but move back down past the runway towards my stuff. My distance is announced: 8.05 metres.

I lead.

I look at the other guys who are waiting to jump. I can see it in their eyes. They don't think I've jumped far enough. They know I can jump further, and it still won't matter. They will always have a chance against me. One, a young lad from Sweden I've not jumped against before, smiles. Straight at me. I see his thoughts in the small curl of his lip. He's thinking I'm the guy that lost. I look at them. All of them warming up or watching other sports going on in the stadium. They all think I lost, therefore I'm nothing.

I want to take a walk but there's no place to go as the runway and pit are tucked tight in the centre of the arena, surrounded by track and pole vaulting and cameras. Lenses everywhere. I hadn't noticed until now. Each one is pointed in my direction. I hold people's looks, showing them my eyes, showing them my heart. I'm here to win. I'm here to beat you. All of you. Every single one of you fuckers who doubt me. Just watch. I'll give you something to stare at.

My name is called. I step up, knowing I need to jump further. To push myself.

I hit 8.19 metres. Improvement. A bigger lead. More pressure on them. More proof I'm here to win. When it's called, I don't clap or cheer or let any snippet of emotion seep out into the arena. I knew that was going to happen, my walk says. I'm in control.

Len calls me over. I jog across the sloping track and stand in front of him while he delivers his instruction.

'No one has got anywhere near eight metres yet. Don't chase a big jump,' he says. 'Today is a day for controlling the field.'

I nod.

I return to the small bench we share between jumps and prepare myself again.

I'm called.

I stand on the runway and breathe, listening to my body, every muscle ready to work. I know I can go further. I need to go further. To put more distance between me and second place. To add more pressure on them. Just one more big jump and I'll ease off. I can jump 8.35 metres here.

The red cone is removed.

I start running.

My speed increases. I'm moving faster than my previous jumps. I know my whole body is with me, willing to push itself through the barriers of pain to get higher, to go longer.

Four steps out.

Three steps out, my turnover increasing into the board, preparing to push myself into the air.

Two steps out, I tear my hamstring.

Him and me.
Me and him.
Every dream.
Every nightmare.

45

A PAIN SHOOTS through my right leg. I grab the back of it. Instead of jumping through air, I hobble across sand, out to the side where I scream to everyone and no one. The pain defeats me, and I sit on the floor.

My hamstring has gone.

Torn.

Fucked.

An official runs to me, concern on his face.

'Are you OK?'

'No.'

He waves his hand at someone in the crowd.

A medic appears, and I give her the information she needs. She helps me to my feet and offers to take my weight and escort me from the arena.

'I'll walk,' I say. I limp heavily across the blue track, underneath the stands. The crowd applauds me, but I can't even bring myself to offer half a smile.

My spikes make a high-pitched tap against the hard medical-room floor. I ease myself onto the bed, my leg stretched out as far as it will go without disabling pain going through me. There's a knock then Len enters the room. He looks at me strangely, with a mix of concern and anger. He knows I wasn't following instructions, knows I was pushing too hard. He wants to bollock me, put me in my place, stress to me the importance of listening to him. But he can't because I'm laid out in agony on a medical bed in an artificially lit room. So, he just nods at me and turns to the medic.

'What do we think, doc?'

The medic looks at me.

'It's OK, he's my coach,' I say.

'Hamstring. Probably a grade two tear. It'll need a scan tomorrow.'

Len nods. He's already planning where to get me booked in, thinking of who he needs to speak to. Recovery plans form in his mind.

'Recovery time?' I ask.

'I can't diagnose that, Adam. Get a scan and speak to your people.'

'What can I do now?'

'Nothing. Back to the hotel, rest up, take painkillers. Ice it, keep it strapped.'

I stay silent.

'Thanks,' Len says.

'I'll be back in a minute,' the medic says, before leaving.

It's just me and Len.

'You want me to call anyone?'

'No.' I say.

'Not even Rachel?'

I think of Rachel in her office, pouring over work, tapping away on her laptop, one of many in her firm working on a Saturday. There's nothing she can do for me but worry.

'I'll do it later,' I say, my tone harsh.

Silence. The unsaid hanging between us.

'I was just feeling good,' I say.

Len looks at the wall.

I'M ON THE bed, flicking through the channels, too tired to watch, in too much pain to sleep. My phone rings next to me on the bed, vibrating and glowing in the near dark room, Rachel's name on the screen. She's calling me after reading the text message I've just sent her. I let the phone ring through to voicemail.

On the television, *Match of the Day* is starting, but the theme tune barely registers. I'm stare at it, numb.

Rachel is in Manchester, thinking about me. Worrying about my state of mind, my feelings.

I'm in Glasgow, thinking about Moscow, annoyed that this setback is giving *him* an advantage.

THE HOTEL RECEPTION. Nods of sympathy from passing athletes. I sip my coffee and will time to pass faster.

Len appears at my side.

'The scan is booked for tomorrow. The Alex. Eleven o'clock.'

'Nothing sooner?'

'It's Sunday. Eleven on Monday is sooner.'

'I want to get started on treatment.'

Len looks at me with a cold stare. 'I know. And you will. At eleven in the morning.'

My phone rings. Rachel. Again.

I get up and slowly move away from Len.

'How are you doing?' she asks.

'Shitty.'

'Are you coming back today?'

'Yeah. As normal.'

'I thought you might be going for a scan.'

'Eleven in the morning, at the Alex.'

'That's fast. Which is good.'

I make a sound. Not a word. Barely audible.

'Right?' she says, encouraging conversation from me.

'Yeah. I suppose.'

I stare around at the hive of activity in the reception. Athletes everywhere, huge bags stuffed full of kit next to them on the floor. They're all talking and laughing, fit and healthy.

'I called you last night,' she says.

'I know. I was asleep. I got your voicemail this morning.' My words stumble out, like a hurdler hitting all the hurdles. 'I've been busy this morning, getting my leg strapped again and stuff.'

A lie. A small, insignificant lie. An excuse because I didn't want to talk to her. To anyone.

'We can talk later,' she offers. 'If you want.'

'Yeah. OK.'

'At least you won,' she says.

I put the phone down.

ON THE PLANE, I think about wedding lists. That's what we were supposed to do tonight. Sit at our tiny dining room table, eat a meal Rachel's probably cooking already, and write a list of people we'd like to come and watch us get married. She promised to clear all her work so we could concentrate on it.

The plane starts its descent through rainy Manchester skies. I look out of the window and think of my jump again, question why I didn't listen to Len.

The plane hits the runway at speed and immediately breaks hard, going from speed to stop as fast as possible. Like me yesterday.

'WE DON'T HAVE to do the list tonight,' she says.

'Thanks.'

We're on the couch, her head leaning on my shoulder.

'I missed you,' she says.

The oven beeps, and she gets up to attend to it. I pick up the remote and switch the TV on, flicking through to our recorded programmes.

Yesterday's competition is there, sitting in the list along with the unwatched *Olympic Final* programme, episodes of a BBC cop drama, and *The X Factor* that Rachel has watched but not deleted.

'What are you doing?' she asks.

'I was just going to watch my jumps from yesterday.'

'Why?'

'I just wanted to see it.'

'It's not going to be easy to watch.'

'How do you know?'

'Because I watched it this morning,' she says, voice strained slightly. 'It wasn't nice to see you in pain.'

'I just want to see what went wrong.'

'Dinner's ready.'

'I'll be there in a minute.'

I press play and forward to my jumps.

I watch them all, including the last one. My hamstring still tears, I still leave the pit in pain and agony. I'm still now sat at home, feeling shit, annoyed at Rachel for no reason other than she is here, and I'm injured, and I need someone to be annoyed at.

We eat slowly, quietly. Sitting at the dining table is uncomfortable. I want to be on the couch with my leg up.

'I'm sorry you're hurt,' she says.

'It's my own fault,' I answer.

EARLY THE NEXT morning, the pain returns before I open my eyes.

Rachel lies next to me, looking at the ceiling.

'Morning,' I say.

'Morning.'

'Has the alarm gone off?'

'Not yet.'

I move, trying to prop myself up. It's awkward, painful.

'Were you really asleep when I called you the other night?' she asks.

A brief pause. 'Why?'

'Because I'm asking.'

I breathe out. 'I was awake.'

Silence. Me facing her, her facing the ceiling.

'I didn't want to talk to anyone,' I say. 'I was in pain and pissed off for letting myself get injured.'

'Why did you lie?'

No answer.

She stands and her T-shirt rides up. She yanks it back down, covering her underwear, and walks to the bathroom.

'Rach.'

'Don't.'

She disappears through the en suite door. It slams, its vibrations ringing around the apartment.

I shout, 'Don't be like that.'

I hear the toilet flush. Water burst into the sink. There are a few seconds where I imagine she's drying her hands on the green towel that hangs on the rail radiator that runs up the wall.

The door opens again and she half steps out. 'Don't even dare tell me not to be like anything.'

'Rach, come on.'

'No. Absolutely not. You want to sit in a hotel room being pissed off, fine. I don't care. You want to spend the night crying in your pillow. No problem. But you don't get to lie to me about it. You can tell me you don't feel like talking. You can be honest with me. You do not get to lie to me about being asleep.'

'I just didn't want to upset you.'

'Well, you did a fucking fantastic job of that, didn't you?'

I say nothing.

'Have you any idea what it was like for me? I was sat in my office when my dad called and tells me he's been watching you on TV and you'd been hurt. I can't talk to you. I can't do anything. I'm on the Internet trying to find any thread of information to find out you're all right. I finally get a fucking text message *three hours* later. And when I do call, you pretend to be asleep. And then you lie to me about it the next day. No. That is not OK.'

Her face is red with anger. She has a toothbrush pointed at me, toothpaste clinging to it, about to fall on the wooden floor.

'Lies are not what our relationship is built on,' she adds.

Before I can answer, the buzzer of our apartment screams through the air. It surprises us both. She turns and goes back into the bathroom. I get up, slowly, and carefully walk to the front door. I push the intercom. 'Hello?'

Two drug testers identify themselves.

'Are you lot taking the piss?' I say. 'I was at a competition two days ago.'

'Please let us in, Mr Lowe.'

I buzz them up.

Rachel appears, half dressed. 'Who is it?'

'Drug guys.'

'Well, obviously. Would be too much to ask to have some privacy to have an argument, wouldn't it?'

'It's not my fault.'

From the bedroom she shouts, 'I didn't say it was, did I?'

THE MRI SCAN confirms a Grade 2 hamstring tear. The whole thing doesn't take long and then we are back in the car, Len talking and planning as he drives.

The buzz words are floating round the car: rest, mental strength, treatment.

'Routine,' Len says. That word again. 'I want you to keep a good routine. Come into work, be around the sessions, make sure you don't just sit on the couch and think about being injured. Being injured is part of this job. Like travelling to competitions or press conferences. It's just something you've got to deal with. Let's deal with it well and get back to jumping.'

Pep talk over.

I FOLLOW HIS advice and try to be a good patient. I go into work as normal. I watch the sessions, see the physio, get rubbed and massaged, listen to the banter of the other athletes as they work out.

But when I get home, I feel different. My body hasn't earned an afternoon sleep or an hour on the couch watching Spanish football highlights. I'm not recovering from hard work. My aches are not from pushing myself to the limit.

I sit on the couch and force myself to rest, force myself to recover properly.

This goes on for over a week. I hate every minute.

I do all the cooking, eating alone most nights because Rachel works late. She returns home, dumps her jacket over a dining chair, heats up whatever I've made, and eats it sat on the couch next to me. We talk about our days. Me weary, her tired.

We get up the next day and the cycle repeats.

Day eleven of recovery. I point the remote control at the TV and flick through the channels. Nothing stands out. It's all guests shouting on talk shows and home improvement stuff. I go into our recorded shows and pick out one programme I've been avoiding. *The Olympic Final*. The recording has been on the TV since August, untouched.

I'm one press away from opening it. One press away from re-living the entire thing.

I pause. I know I want to watch, to see it. To watch myself break the World Record.

I don't want to watch. I can't re-live it.

My finger rests on the button. One push and it'll be there on the screen.

I think about deleting it. I could press two buttons and it would be gone, no longer on the TV haunting me, daring me to watch it. My worst moment vanished. But it won't be gone in my mind. It will still be there, ingrained in my brain, prowling through my memory.

London has gone for everyone else. I can tell by the way they act towards me. London is no longer the elephant in the room. Those first few months after the Games, people were more aware of what they said, which questions they asked. Rachel, my family and hers, my friends, all edged around the subject. They talked about future plans, our upcoming wedding, the stag do, honeymoon destinations. The future is positive, was the general message. I don't know if they got together and planned how to deal with me, but they were all united. Once I started training again, things changed. It was like people were trying to get me through to a new season, with new goals. Moscow, not London.

The only person who didn't treat me differently was Johnny. Johnny got drunk and told me to get over it, and anger sped through me so fast I don't think I understand it even now. His words hit me so hard I needed to fight back. So, I punched him.

Len is, and has been since we left London, focused on the new season. Every word he says, every session he puts on, is about Moscow. Focus on future goals. The last year is gone.

Over. Finished. It won't change. It can't be undone. Move forward.

I desperately wanted to get on-board with his programme. After I hit Johnny, after the hangover of Pete and Laura's wedding had faded, I pledged to myself I would focus on defending my World title.

And after one competition, I sit injured. I'm already behind in my preparations. I've not cleared the first hurdle in the race to Moscow. And I feel like I can see Chris Madison pulling away from me.

I put the remote down and leave the recording where it is.

I ease out of my seated position and go to the bathroom to get something to wipe my eyes.

IN DAN AND Michelle's dining room, Rachel and I are sat next to each other. Michelle is in the kitchen adding the final touches to our meal. Dan is upstairs trying to settle Isla.

'Do you think we've arrived too early?'

'No,' I say. 'It's just one of those things with kids.'

Michelle comes through from the archway that leads to the kitchen, a glass of wine in her hand. She sits opposite us and says, 'Sorry about this. She never settles on the nights we need her to. Dan'll be down soon.'

'It's OK.'

Michelle asks how the wedding planning is going and Rachel fills her in.

'Any thoughts on a honeymoon?'

'We've not had time to properly talk about it,' I say.

'Oh.' Michelle sips from her glass.

'I've spent the last couple of weeks working late. All wedding stuff has gone a bit quiet.'

Dan appears after slowly creeping down the stairs. He's buttoning a shirt as he turns into the dining room. 'Sorry,' he says. 'She was being a bit clingy.'

Michelle turns in her chair to face him. 'Everything OK?'

'Yeah.' He reaches out and touches her shoulder. 'She just needed cuddling. It's always the nights when we've got plans.' He turns to us at the table and says, 'Drinks?'

'Not for me,' I say.

Rachel holds up her glass. 'Please.'

Dan looks at Michelle, who shakes her head. He then disappears to the kitchen, arriving back at the table with a bottle of lager for himself and more wine for Rachel.

'How's the hamstring?' he asks me.

'Really?' Michelle says before I can answer.

'What?'

'You've been sat down for three seconds and we're already talking about long jumping.'

'No,' he says. 'I'm asking after the man's health. When he answered, I was going to ask if Rachel's, erm, earlobes were OK.'

Michelle smiles and shakes her head. 'Idiot.'

'What's wrong with my earlobes?' Rachel asks.

'Nothing. Perfectly lovely,' Dan says.

'Why've you been looking at my wife-to-be's earlobes, you weirdo?' I ask.

Everyone laughs, apart from Dan, who hides behind his bottle of lager.

'My hamstring is getting better. I should start some proper stationary bike sessions on Monday. Hopefully build-up to running again soon.'

Michelle turns to Rachel and says, 'They are horrible when they're injured, aren't they? Lots of moods, lots of silences.'

'I've been at work so much I've missed a lot of the recovery period.'

'Yes, I've been sat at home, crying on my own,' I say.

Michelle goes to the kitchen and returns with our starters and we eat.

'How are the stag do plans coming?' Dan asks.

'Not in my hands, I'm afraid. Mike, Pete, and Johnny have been given that role. I've asked for something local-ish. Maybe a race day or something. I've given them your email address so you'll be getting something soon I would imagine.'

'Post Worlds?'

'That's what I've told them.'

'That reminds me,' Rachel says to Michelle. 'Laura, one of my bridesmaids, was doing some group email planning today. I need to give you the date of my hen do.'

'When is it?'

'The weekend of the sixteenth of August. The Friday night until Sunday. We're getting a big house in York. It's got a pool and a hot tub.'

'The sixteenth is the World Final in Moscow,' I say.

'I know,' Rachel responds. 'I've asked for that weekend specifically because I knew you'd be away. We've already talked about me not coming to Moscow so I can save holidays for the wedding stuff.'

'Won't you be watching the final though?'

'Yes. Don't worry. On the Friday night we are having a big party in the house and I can make sure the final is on as the main event.' She touches my leg under the table and says, 'Don't worry, I'm not going to miss you defending your World Title.'

Michelle puts up her hand and says, 'I'm no longer the wife of a long jumper, so I'll probably just be getting drunk in the kitchen. It'll be my first weekend away from Isla, so I'll make the most of it. Please don't wake me up in the morning. I'll be enjoying my lie in.'

'I'll be in Moscow with work,' Dan says.

'My mum will have Isla,' Michelle says. Then she turns to Rachel and says, 'Or she can go to Moscow. I'm coming on your hen do.'

The evening passes in a flow of conversation that's mainly about babies and wedding seating plans. Michelle tells us about family politics during the build-up to her wedding, how Uncle John couldn't sit next to Uncle Dave because of something that happened in 1989.

'I didn't want to invite most of them,' Dan says.

Michelle leads Rachel upstairs at one point to check on Isla and Dan turns to me and says, 'I bumped into Peter Hedge the other day.'

'Oh right. Where?'

'We were having a work's dinner with some new clients in town. He was in the same restaurant with his wife.'

'Is he all right?'

'Seemed it. He asked after you though, which I thought was strange.'

'Why?'

'Because I thought he was part of the team.'

'I've not spoken to him for a while.'

'Oh. How long?'

'Just after London.'

'Really?' Dan seems genuinely shocked, and I realise Peter Hedge didn't share this information with him.

'Is that a problem?'

'No. Course not. Just thought he'd be the person you'd have spoken to the most.'

'Why?'

'Frankly, because if I'd have broken the World Record one jump before the end of the Olympic Final and someone else had beaten me, Peter Hedge is the sort of guy I'd want to talk to. Help me build myself back up for jumping again. Clear all that shit out of my head.'

'What's to talk about? I jumped one distance, Chris Madison jumped further. He won, I lost. It's happened before. It'll probably happen again.'

'It's just the manner of the defeat,' he says as the girls walk back in the room.

'I know the manner of the defeat, Dan. I was there. I just don't want to sit in a room going over and over it. I don't see the point.'

'What are we talking about?' Michelle asks, as she sits down.

'London,' Dan says.

'Oh, Adam,' Michelle says, a sympathetic smile across her face, slightly lopsided due to the wine she's had. 'I know we've seen you since then and said this before, but what happened to you in London was bloody awful. Absolutely shit. When that American lad, what's his name, Marathon?'

'Chris Madison,' I say, not wanting to. Not wanting to feed this conversation, to fuel it so it turns into an evening of re-living every single detail.

'Madison. That's it. When he jumped further than you, I just sat heartbroken. It was horrible for you to lose in that way. I cried for you.'

I say nothing.

'I mean I'd not slept for a few weeks at that point, and I was breastfeeding a baby eight hundred times a day, so I might have been a bit on the edge, but still, my tears were genuine.'

Rachel and Dan laugh. I laugh too, but it's fake.

As always lately, I'm smiling with dead eyes.

I STAND IN the shop, laughing. The red tie is around my head like a child playing a game in the playground, the suit hanging too big, white shirt untucked.

'Well?'

'You're an idiot,' she says, laughing too.

I spin, giving her the full view. She's sat on a small square stool in the waiting area. My ordinary clothes are hung in the dressing room behind me.

'So, just for clarification, I won't be wearing this to our wedding?'

'No.' She smiles a beautiful smile. The type I've not seen for weeks as she's been coming home late. Even when she's got home before eight, she's been tired, stressed. 'You won't be wearing that at our wedding. It's not quite silly enough for me.'

The joke over, I go back into the dressing room and put on the actual suit I've picked to get married in. It's a dark grey three-piece with a crisp white shirt. I step out from behind the curtain. Her face lights up.

'Wow,' she says.

'I know there's no tie, but I thought a skinny one, to match the colour scheme.'

'The to-be-decided colour scheme.'

'Exactly. I thought the lads could have one colour tie and me another. Then we could all have matching pocket squares sticking out of this little pocket thing.' I point to a small slit in the breast of my jacket. 'I'll be the only one wearing a waistcoat. You know, to set me apart as the groom.'

'In case I get everyone mixed up?'

'Yeah. Don't want you marrying Johnny.'

She stands and places herself next to me, slipping her arm through mine. We take a second to look in the mirror, her picturing a dress she's not chosen yet, me picturing a dress that will live in my imagination until our wedding day. We smile, the future looking good.

I talk to the shop manager, arranging an appointment to come back with my groomsmen to try on their suits.

Then we walk out of the shop and into the main section of the Trafford Centre. It's Sunday, the place is hammered. Hundreds of people moving from shop to shop under the strong artificial lights. We find peace in the corner of a coffee shop.

I queue and order, then carry our drinks carefully to the table. We blow some heat from coffees. I look at her, her at me.

'We've needed today,' she says.

I nod.

'Not just to get wedding stuff done. To spend some time together. Especially before you go to America. I feel like we've been missing each other a lot at the moment.'

'You've been busy.'

'I know. But I feel like I've sort of left you to be injured on your own.'

I shrug. 'It's my job.'

'Being injured?'

'Sort of. Recovery is part of it.'

'Work has been so stressful for me. I've hardly had time to think. I'm so tired.'

'Let's not worry about it today. Let's just sort out wedding stuff.'

She leans down into her bag and pulls out her phone and a black moleskin notebook, a pen attached to the string that wraps around the cover. She unclips the pen and opens the book. She finds a blank page and writes Wedding To-Do in neat, precise handwriting.

'So, what do we need to do?'

We sit and discuss our next few months. The list grows: book a band, bridesmaids' dresses, cake, book honeymoon, flowers, save the dates, invitations, food and drink, and centre pieces.

'Do we need presents for parents?'

'I don't know,' I say. 'Do we?'

'People do.'

'Oh, people do. I see. Therefore, we should.'

She laughs. 'Stupid people.'

'What about just flowers for the mums?'

'Good idea.' She writes the job in her book.

We list more things to do. Forming plans.

What is it like to be the man who won?

46

WINNING IS A habit, and I can't get a fix.

My rehab went well. Despite the frustration of sitting on the couch for what felt like forever, my desperation to stop going to physio every day and get back on the track meant I listened to all the advice and recovered properly. I rested when I was told, did every exercise and stretch I was given. A model patient. I went to America for warm weather training and felt like I was back to normal.

Now, in the middle of May, at the Diamond League in Shanghai, I manage third.

Then I fly to Eugene, in America. He's here, the Olympic fucking Champion. He beats me by twenty centimetres. Len calls me over after every jump, pounds it into me that I'm dropping my knee when I'm running. 'Pick it up,' he says. 'Higher, higher.'

'I'm trying,' I say, feeling frustration rise inside me.

I fly home and get off the plane to a text message and a voicemail from Rachel. She's ill with a virus and can't meet me at the airport. I get a taxi home, drop my bags in the hallway, and walk into the lounge.

'Hi,' she manages through her sickness. She looks terrible, huddled under a duvet on the couch, her face pale, her voice strained.

I move towards her, stopping short of the couch. 'How've you caught this?'

'I've missed you too.'

'How have you caught it?'

'I just have. People get ill. I work seventy hours a week in a shitty air-conditioned office, and at some point, it was going to take its toll, no matter how many times I washed my hands like I'm in *Grey's Anatomy*.'

I'm silent, unsure of my own feelings and not understanding why I can't just walk over to her and give her a comforting hug. All I can think is, *I can't get ill. I've got too much training to do.*

I take my bags through to the bedroom and put them on the bed. I catch a glimpse of my reflection in the mirror, and I wonder if he treats his partner like this.

AT AN EVENT in Birmingham, my knees are higher, and my approach is improved. But I still don't win. Rachel's in the crowd, but I can't put in a performance worthy of her sacrificed Sunday. I finish second, but I'm chasing the winner from Jump Two and I don't feel like I've got enough to get ahead of him.

The journey back to Manchester is soundtracked by Rachel's small talk and my silences.

THE FOLLOWING WEEKEND I sit in a conference room in a Paris hotel, facing the press.

'How are you feeling?' one asks.

'Fine,' I say. 'Ready to jump well. To hopefully get back to winning ways.'

'Does it make a difference to you that Chris Madison isn't here?'

'No.'

A British journalist says, 'Just a question about the Anniversary Games that are coming up in a few weeks.'

The Anniversary Games, the Diamond League meeting at the London Olympic stadium. A chance for everyone to celebrate the previous year's successes. The anniversary of my silver fucking medal.

'How important to you is it to win in that stadium, after what happened last year?'

'What happened last year?' I ask, smiling.

The room laughs.

'I must have been asleep,' I say. 'Or on holiday. I don't remember last year.'

The next day, in the Stade De France, I finally win. 8.36 metres. My biggest jump of the season. I smile in interviews, wave to the crowd, accept Len's handshake. 'Better,' he says. 'Much better. Coming together for Moscow now. I can see it.'

It takes me ages to piss in a pot for the drug testers and, while I'm waiting, I feel light-headed, shaky and sick. I get back to the hotel late, crawl into bed, and pull the covers over me. I start to shake uncontrollably. I can't find the energy to move. At some point sleep comes, but it's broken, and I regularly wake, fixed in the same position, unable to move for fear of being sick. I know my temperature is high. I manage to flick the covers away, but the cold air makes no difference.

Somewhere in dark hours, I think of Rachel and how she'll treat me better than I treated her.

I MAKE IT home, but the journey is a blur of hell. Every movement of the plane, the ascents and descents, my body feels like it's going to break. She meets me at the airport, carries my bag, and takes me home.

I crawl into bed, and she kisses my head.

'I'm sorry,' I say as I drift into darkness.

THE DOCTOR ADVISES me to ride it out. Plenty of fluid, plenty of rest. Len says, 'We don't need to push you. We need to think about the whole season.'

I miss a week of training, another week in a season where I've already missed so many.

There are just under six weeks until the World Championship in Moscow.

WE PULL ONTO the driveway of her parents' house and get out. Rachel carefully removes the flowers we've just stopped to buy from the back seat. Her mum greets us at the door with tight hugs, then goes to the kitchen to put the flowers in water. The others are already here: Rachel's parents, both her brothers, and their partners. They are stood in the dining room, drinking wine and beer.

'You looking forward to jumping in the Olympic stadium again next week?' Rachel's younger brother asks.

No, I think. No, I don't want to stand on that track and jump against him. I don't want to feel my body moving down that runway, feeling the same feelings as last time I was there. In my mind, I can still see every step of my last approach. I can hear the air of the stadium being sucked out as he hit 8.97 metres and stole my medal. I can still hear my heart break.

'I'm just glad I'm fit enough to go,' I answer.

'Oh yeah, Rachel was saying you've been unwell.'

'It was just a virus. Hit me hard though.'

After half an hour of catching up, Rachel's mum gathers us all to eat the full Sunday roast she's prepared. Conversation, as normal in this setting, turns to the wedding. Rachel says, 'There's so much to do. I keep thinking Vegas would've been a good idea.'

Her mum looks horrified. 'Oh, Rachel, don't say that.'

'I'm only joking. I'm just sick of trying to make a decision about table names. Why do we need to name our tables?'

Her older brother laughs. 'It's true. It all gets a bit silly, doesn't it?'

'What did you do?'

He looks at his wife. She says, 'It was places we'd been on holiday. The top table was our honeymoon destination.'

'We've not been on that many holidays together,' I say.

'What about places you've jumped?' Rachel's dad asks. 'The top table could be Moscow, as you'll have just won gold there.'

I don't get a chance to put my answer to the room.

Her brother says, 'Or you could have like a first, second, third podium thing. Top table raised higher than the second one, which is higher than the third. It'd be awesome just to see the waitresses trying to serve your food.'

Rachel is laughing but her mum says, 'Don't be daft.'

'Oh, sorry, Mum. I thought their wedding was allowed to be a happy thing.'

Her mum ignores him and says, 'What about colours? The top table could be gold. Another silver and another on bronze. Maybe blue, red, and white for the Team GB colours. Incorporate Adam's success into the wedding. Celebrate his achievements.'

Anger swells inside me as I say, 'We're not having gold and silver.' My tone is harsh, and a silence covers the table like a thick fog, suffocating the previously light atmosphere.

'Mum was only suggesting,' Rachel says before I cut her off.

'I know. I'm not being funny. But I'm not having gold as a colour. Or silver. I'm just not, so I'm sorry, but no.'

'Why are you being like that?' Rachel asks.

'I'm not being like anything. I'm just not having any themes of gold and silver or anything to do with long jumping. Simple.'

WE ARE IN the car heading home a couple of hours later, and there's an argument brewing. I can sense it; the way animals can sense a storm coming. There are hints in Rachel's body language, her focus being forward through the windscreen and the way she adjusts her leg slightly when I place my hand on it when I'm driving.

'Everything OK?' I ask.

'Yep.'

The sounds of XFM fill the silence, covering the tension slightly. In the breaks between songs, I try to start a conversation. I mention something her brother said about his work, something her dad said about his new gym membership. I get little back.

Manchester city centre appears through the windscreen, Beethem Tower looming over us. I turn left off the main road into our car park and whip the car into our space.

'If you've got something to say,' I say, switching the engine off.

'Not here.'

She opens her door and gets out. I sit in the car and breathe in, release the air slowly.

I get out and follow her into our building as the silver doors of the lift slide open. We get in. She presses the button.

'This is daft,' I say.

'I don't want to have this conversation in the corridor, or in the lift.'

I shut up, my mind racing back through the scenes of dinner and knowing she wants to talk about the way I spoke to her mum. I feel myself growing angrier as I follow her out of the lift and through our front door.

'Go on,' I say.

'Why did you speak to my mum like that?' she snaps.

'I didn't speak to her like anything. I just gave an honest opinion about not wanting those stupid colours as table names.'

'Stupid colours?'

'Yeah. Stupid colours.'

She throws her bag down on the floor and walks into the lounge where she stops in the middle of the room, arms folded across her chest. 'She was just saying how nice it might be to celebrate your achievements as part of the wedding. Why is that stupid? My parents are proud of you. She was just expressing that.'

'What achievements?' I'm halfway to shouting.

'Your achievements. Your gold medals.'

'My gold medal from two years ago?'

'And the one you're going to win in Moscow.' She pauses and then says, 'I'm angry with you because you embarrassed me in front of my family.'

'I might not win in Moscow.'

'Don't say that,' she says.

'It's true.' Anger is pumping through me now. 'And what do we do then? What if I finish second again? Do we sit at the silver table? Does that celebrate my achievements? Who would then get to sit at the gold table? Do we invite whoever wins in Moscow?'

'You're being ridiculous.'

'How am I being ridiculous?' I shout the words and her face changes, like the words have slapped her.

She doesn't respond, and I push her for an answer. 'Well?'

Nothing.

I say, 'I just want one day where it's about us and not about me being a fucking long jumper. Is that too much to ask? I just want one day in my life, one day where I don't have to think about it. I want to have a day to celebrate you and me.'

She moves to the kitchen area and fills the kettle. 'And what difference would having gold as a top table name make to that? Really? I think it would be nice to celebrate that part of your life.'

'Then you don't get it.'

Her shoulders fall in a weary movement and I hear her breath release as she huffs towards the wall. She turns to face me, the kettle starting to hum.

'We need to arrange all this stuff before I go to Moscow, right?' I say. 'So, what if I don't win? And don't say it won't happen because it could. I know it could. Because it's happened before. What if I go to Moscow and I jump 8.98 metres? A new World Record. And he jumps 8.99 metres.'

Her face shows the strain of my onslaught of words. They have flowed out of me like an erupting volcano. 'That won't—'

'You can't say it won't happen,' I explode. 'Because it happened. It happened in London in front of the whole bloody world. And it can happen again.'

The heat of the kettle rises, coming to the boil.

'Let's say I don't win. Just for argument's sake. Let's say I agree to have a gold fucking table name and I don't win. Do you know how my day is going to go? I'm going to spend the day looking at that name in the centre of our top table, at our wedding, and I'm going to think about London. And Moscow. And Chris fucking Madison. I'm going to be thinking about how I'm not good enough, how I failed at the only goal I've ever set myself. How I'm forever going be the guy who finished second after breaking the World Record. I can never change that.'

LATER, I LIE on the bed watching the evening sun disappear in the sky. We've not spoken in over an hour. I've just lay here, waiting and thinking. Thinking about the last few hours, the next week, the next few months.

Next weekend is the Anniversary Games. One year since London. Everyone getting together and celebrating what an all-round rousing success London twenty-twelve was.

Everyone but me.

The sound of her tapping her laptop keys has filled the air for the last forty-five minutes. It stops and I hear her chair slide across the wooden floor. She appears at the door and looks at me. Without speaking, she comes and lies next to me, her head resting in the nook of my arm.

'I'm sorry about the way I shouted,' I say.

We lie for a few minutes, saying nothing, just enjoying the silence.

'Do you want to talk about London?' she asks.

Yes. I want to reveal everything. I want to sit here for hours and explain how I can't grasp my own feelings, can't understand my anger, the speed of my temper. To talk about how I've got to spend a week answering question after question about World Records and broken dreams. Questions, questions, questions I don't have the answers to. Answers I'm not willing to share. And then, when the questions stop, I've got to go back there. Back into that stadium and stand at the end of that runway and look down at that pit: the pit where my life changed, the pit where he beat me, and try to put it all out of my mind and focus on jumping in the moment. To focus on winning in 2013, not repeating the lasting defeat of 2012.

I want to tell her how what happened at the Olympics is the first thing I think about in the morning, the last thing I think about at night. That it lives like a fog in my mind, shifting and thinning from time to time, but always there, day after day after day.

I don't. Because I can't open my mouth and let the words come out. I can't admit the hurt I feel because I want it inside me. I need it for when I step to the line in Moscow. I need to look at him and use my pain to fuel my performance, to use my hate to beat him.

'No,' I lie.

FRIDAY NIGHT. ANOTHER hotel bed, another window to stare out of. My phone is in my hand, my thumb over the dial button. I press it and lie in the dark, listening to five, six, seven rings. I wait for it to click to voicemail, knowing I won't leave a message.

'Hello,' the voice says.

Surprised that there's an answer, I say nothing.

'Adam. Are you there?'

'Yeah.'

'Is everything OK?'

'I'm sorry it's so late,' I say.

'Are you all right?'

'Not really.'

'Just… please, hang on a minute. I'll just go to my office.'

There's noise in the background: the creaking of a door, footsteps moving downstairs, the shutting of another door.

'I'm sorry if I woke you. I couldn't sleep. I've not really slept properly since London if I'm honest.'

'OK.'

'I got all your voicemails,' I say. 'I'm sorry I never called back.'

'I understand,' Peter Hedge says.

There's a silence between us and I think about how I've dragged this man out of bed at 11.58 p.m. on a Friday night and my mind seems incapable of selecting words to form conversation.

'How can I help you now, Adam?' he asks.

'I can't focus properly on going back there.'

'To the stadium?'

'The stadium, the runway, the pit. All of it.'

Peter pauses and I look out of the window again, into the black. I can hear the sound of my own breathing.

'Can I offer a suggestion?'

'That's why I'm calling,' I say. 'That, and to apologise for ignoring your calls.'

He moves past my apology, straight to the heart of the problem I've called about. 'We don't have a lot of time, so I suggest this. When you put the phone down, try to remember how you felt just before the fifth jump last year, when you broke the World Record. Try to remember every little detail, the confidence you had. Take those feelings with you tomorrow. Focus solely on the positive experience you had in the stadium last year.'

AND I TRY. I desperately try to conjure up the memories of the few brief moments before my fifth Olympic Final jump, when the World Record was still twenty-one years old, and I was about to become the one person in history to go further than 8.95 metres. But for every moment of confidence I remember, there's an image of him celebrating, for every piece of joy, there's a clear picture in my mind of his flag being raised, his national anthem playing, him receiving his gold medal.

Now, back in the stadium, everything gets worse as I step to the line for my first jump. Nothing feels right. Not my legs, my arms, my eyes. I try to find a spot across the pit to focus on during my run up, but everything looks blurry. I see an image of him, emerging from the pit, the look of raw shock and amazement as he realises he has broken the World Record. And I'm stood now, right where I was stood then, unable to change the situation. This is the exact spot my world fell apart.

The clock ticks and I breathe in and out for what feels like the first time in an hour.

I start my run up, move into the board and jump.

In the air I know I've fouled. I could feel the board underneath my heel, and I know I'm a mile over the line.

The red flag confirms it.

A foul. Just like my last jump at this stadium. This fucking stadium.

My next jump is closer to the line but another foul. I look back at the line like that will change something. It doesn't. The stone-faced official sits on his stool and raises his red flag again.

I look to Len. His face reveals nothing, but his hand calls me over.

'I know,' I say, before he's had a chance to speak.

'Relax,' he says. 'Breathe. You're better than this.'

I nod.

'Move your run up back and focus.'

I nod again.

I go back to my stuff and wait. I look around the stadium and try to remember some positive memory, a small moment of happiness I experienced here a year ago. It looks the same: the white and black seats, the huge triangle structure of floodlights angled down into the enormous bowl of the stadium, the track wrapped around the deep green field in the centre. The atmosphere is good, although the emotion and electricity of that night are missing. I stand and take a walk around. I repeat to myself: relax and breathe, relax and breathe.

My name is called again, and I strip off my tracksuit and move to the line. The jumper in front of me is watching as their jump is measured. I say to myself, I'm here to win. I'm here to win. I'm here to win. I'm trying to convince myself, to get myself going, to stop the run of foul after foul.

The red cone is removed, and I start my run up. It's a better approach than my last two. There's more speed, more purpose. My feet quicken as I move into the board and as I push off, I feel something: a twinge. The speed of everything means I continue to move into the air, going through my jump, up and down, into my landing. I get up slowly, worried about my leg, but there is no negative response.

The flag is white.

'Better,' Len says as I lean on the barrier between the track and the crowd. He's leaning forward so I can hear every word. 'Are you OK?' he asks.

I think about the twinge. My leg seems OK, so I don't say anything. I just nod and say, 'I'm going to win this.'

'Good answer,' he says, actually smiling.

I'm called again.

I step to the line. The red cone is removed and I'm powering down the runway. I am motoring, the fastest approach of the day. My body is straight, my knees are high, my arms driving me towards the board. My foot turnover increases for the last few steps into the line, just before I lift off the twinge becomes a snap.

I'm in the sand, hand clamped to the back of my burning leg. I know my hamstring has gone. The feeling is the same as Glasgow. I hobble out of the pit and plant myself on the floor. There's a buzz of activity around me as the medics and officials rush over to check on me. I can feel the eyes of the crowd staring at me. A camera shoved in my face, recording every wince of pain, every second of concern. If it could record my thoughts, it would reveal one thing: I'm not going to Moscow.

Silver. The medal will always be silver.

47

MY SEASON IS over.

A scan reveals another grade two tear.

Instead of spending three weeks training to improve my sharpness, and getting mentally prepared to defend my World Title, I spend three weeks in a dark haze. The experts tell me I won't make Moscow. The time between the injury and the competition is not enough to heal properly, to give myself a fighting chance of even jumping, let alone winning. I spend miserable hours between physio appointments sat on the couch watching mindless daytime TV. I don't go to the track, as Len wants, as I did earlier in the year. I have no routine. No motivation.

There is no point in fighting.

I spend three weeks knowing he'll win and there is nothing I can do about it.

Rachel tries to distract me, but she has hours of work to do so she can have time off for her hen do. Work she would've been able to do without distraction if I'd flown out to holding camp. She cooks dinner every night, smiles every morning. She tries and tries. I give nothing back.

My phone rings on the Monday before Rachel's hen do. My dad's number flashing on the screen. I answer it and move outside onto the balcony and look out over Manchester city centre.

'Hello.'

'How you doing?'

'I've been better.'

I look out at the buildings in front of me: offices filled with real people with real jobs.

'What are you doing on Friday night?'

'I'm going out with Pete, Mike, and Johnny.'

'Are you watching the final before you go out?' he asks.

The question hangs. I stare at a plane rising in the clear blue sky, a white trail behind it. All those people above the world, escaping.

'I don't know. Why?'

'I thought you might want to watch it here.'

'I don't think so, Dad. If I watch it, it'll be alone.'

The long jump final is four days away. The day my wife-to-be goes away to celebrate our upcoming marriage with all her closest friends. I'll be home, alone.

I repeat, 'If I watch.'

THE BED DIVIDES us. Her stuff is laid out across it; dresses and shoes, two bikinis, underwear, all placed into different piles. An open, empty suitcase is next to my pillow. Rachel is on the window side, half dressed in jeans and a bra. She was wrestling with a T-shirt that was inside out, but now she holds it in one hand as she looks at me and sighs.

'Why is this so difficult?'

'It's not.'

'And yet we're shouting at each other.'

My feet are planted, unmoved; my arms are folded across my chest.

She continues, 'All I'm asking is that you sort a few things out for our wedding.'

'I'm not even supposed to be here this weekend.'

Another sigh: long and slow. 'I really wish you were in Moscow. I do. I wish I'd spent the last two weeks on my own, getting in bed' – she throws her T-shirt on it – 'alone every night. I wish tomorrow, on my hen do, I was having a long jumping party so I could watch you compete. It's not exactly the hen do every girl dreams of, is it? But there is nothing I wanted more than to have a massive party celebrating you. The man I'm going to marry. I'm sorry that you got injured again. I know it's awful. But you are here. It's shit but you are. That's the end of it. And all I'm asking is you send a few emails and tick a few things off the to-do list for our wedding.'

I say nothing. I'm thinking about Moscow: about the runway and the pit, about the podium and the medals. About him. Always about him.

'Do you even want to get married?'

The question shocks me back into the room.

'Is it even worth me packing this case to go on this hen do? Or do you want to call it all off?'

'Of course I want to get married,' I say.

'Well, at least act like it. You've hardly shown any interest in months. You've just walked around here in a fog.'

'I've been injured.'

'I know,' she shouts. 'And I've been here for you and worried about you and trying to get you to open up. And I've got nothing back. You're like a wall.'

'No, I'm not.'

'Yes, you are.'

We pause and I think about how stupid this conversation is.

She says, 'Don't get me wrong, we've had our good moments, but the majority of the time I feel like there is something going on with you I can't understand or get to. So, I'm standing here worried that you're regretting your decision to ask me to marry you.'

I look across the mess on the bed at my wife-to-be. She looks tired and on the edge of tears.

'I'm struggling with having a bad year,' I say. 'Struggling with the injuries and not going to Moscow. But please don't ever think I don't want to marry you. Because I do. More than anything.' I beg her to understand, to hear the truth in my words. I want her to understand that the fog she talks about is more than just my injuries. It's about London, about that silver medal, about Chris Madison winning tomorrow, and taking my World Championship title without me even being able to put a jump up against him. I pause and try to calm my thoughts. My tone more measured, I say, 'This weekend is just difficult.'

She softens her tone too. 'I understand that. And if you want me to tell all the girls that I'll drive down to my hen do on Saturday so I can be here with you tomorrow, I will do that. We can watch the final together.'

'You don't need to do that.'

'I want you to know I'm willing to do it. I love you. I want you to be happy and I know this is a difficult time for you, but our lives are about more than just our jobs. We have other things, other responsibilities. We have each other.'

She picks up her T-shirt again and slips it over her head, pushes her arms through the holes, adjusts it in the mirror.

'I'm sorry,' I say.

I WATCH THE coverage from Moscow on the BBC while Rachel carries on packing and getting sorted for tomorrow. I struggle to watch as a fan, and every time the camera pans across the stadium I focus on the pit and think about what tomorrow could've been like.

Rachel joins me about an hour later. She places herself underneath my arm, leans her head on my chest. We watch a panel show, laugh in the right places, and go to bed. Our goodnight kiss is a little too fast, a little too forced, the frost of the argument from a couple of hours ago not yet fully thawed.

The next morning, the atmosphere is slightly better as we eat the breakfast I've cooked. I try hard to be positive, encouraging her to have a fun, relaxed time. When it's time for her to leave, I carry her bag to the car, kiss her goodbye and return to the apartment, alone.

AND JUST LIKE that, I'm no longer the World Champion. Nothing in my physical world changes. The TV still plays, my feet are still stretched out across the couch, my phone still sits on the coffee table next to my empty coffee cup. And yet, when the competition is over, everything has changed.

He has won.

Chris Madison jumped 8.59 metres in the Second Round, and I knew when I looked in the close-up camera shots of the other jumpers' eyes that no one was capable of beating him. They all looked like they were fighting for second. No one believed they could win.

Two minutes ago, I was the reigning World Champion.

Now I'm the *former* World Champion.

And there is nothing I can do about it.

My phone rings, Rachel's name coming up on the screen.

'Are you OK?'

'Yeah. It's what I expected.'

MANCHESTER IS BUSY. After work drinkers, dressed in suits and loose ties, congregate in packs outside bars and sip wine or lager and share lighters and cigarettes. Outdoor tables are full of people enjoying the late evening sunshine, surrounded by increasing numbers of empty glasses. I work my way through the city, down Deansgate, and over to the Northern Quarter. I step into a busy bar and scan the crowd. I spot Johnny and Mike at the bar.

'Drink?'

'Yeah.'

Johnny turns and tries to get the barman's attention.

Mike says, 'You OK, mate?'

'Not a lot I can do. I've known since I got injured that someone else would win.'

Someone else: Him. It was always going to be him.

Mike downs the remainder of his bottle. He tips it to Johnny, indicating he wants a new one.

I look around the bar. There's a buzz about the place, a hum of conversation heard over the riff of the Stone Roses. The door opens and I see Pete step inside, then work his way to us.

'Johnny, sort him out.'

Johnny's being served and adds to his order. Pete stretches out his hand and shakes mine. He pulls me towards him and taps my back. He doesn't say anything, but it's clear his gesture is a reference to Moscow.

Johnny provides us all with bottles and we tap them together. 'To girls on a hen do.'

'Are you just thinking of all our girlfriends and wives in bikinis in a hot tub?' Mike asks Johnny.

'Obviously. Are you not?'

More laughter.

'And happy birthday for Sunday,' Pete says to me.

'Cheers.'

We move away from the bar, letting a couple of girls into our space. We stand in a tight circle. We move through the usual conversation: how my injury is healing, David Moyes' upcoming first league game as the United manager.

Then Johnny says, 'So, I'm moving to Australia.'

'What?'

'I'm moving to Australia.'

'Yeah, we heard your words. We're just looking for some background information,' Mike says.

'Work are opening an office in Sydney and they want me to go and head it up.'

'Nice one,' I say. 'My sister loved it when she lived there. When do you go?'

'I leave in January to live, but I'm flying out in November for a couple of weeks to get a few things sorted. I wanted to wait until it was all sorted before I said anything. Got the sign off today.'

We click bottles again. I take a long drink, the cold lager sliding easily down my throat. Too easily. I go to the bar and order. I hook my fingers round the neck of the four bottles and work my way back to the group. The conversation has turned to my wedding. The lads stand in front of me, my best man and two of my ushers. My oldest friends. The best people I can be with tonight to stop my mind from wandering a few thousand miles towards Moscow.

'You've only got one job,' Johnny says to Pete.

'I'm the best man. I've got loads to do. Organising you two, making sure he doesn't do a runner, ordering strippers for the morning of the wedding, making sure everyone is fed, the speech, looking cool. It's a big day for me.'

'One job,' Johnny repeats.

'And what's that?' Mike asks.

'Not punching me.'

Johnny looks at me and laughs, the laughter spreading around the group.

We move out into the now dark street, stepping into the road to avoid a group of high-heeled girls who are spread across the full width of the pavement. They're laughing about something, loud and full, one of them nearly stumbling off the pavement. My mind flashes back to a memory and I realise I'm in the exact spot I ended my brief relationship with Abbie, five years earlier.

Johnny leads us down some steps at the side of an old warehouse, and we enter another bar I've never been in. Manchester is full of these now. Places my friends know and have memories from and in-jokes about. My eyes adjust to the low light and I take in the place. Booths line one side, the bar the other. There's a pool table in a small side room with a group of lads stood around. A bright jukebox stands next to the bar, currently playing the Arctic Monkeys' 'Mardy Bum'. Above one corner of the bar, a small TV is fixed to the wall with the sports news playing on mute.

It's my round and I lean on the bar and wait.

A barman appears, tapping a bottle opener to the beat of the music. I place my order and look at the TV while he opens fridges and pulls out bottles. The TV is previewing the opening day of the football season, tomorrow. Talking heads of ex-players giving opinions based on preseason games and money spent in the transfer market. I can tell what's being said even without the sound on.

'Eighteen pounds please.'

I hand over a twenty and carry the drinks to the lads. Conversation floats back to Johnny moving to Australia, only it's louder this time, to be heard over the jukebox and the noise of the bar. I glance up at the TV and it's playing highlights from Moscow. His face appears on the screen, being interviewed.

'Oh, for fuck's sake,' I say.

'What's up?'

I point my lager bottle to the TV. 'This. I came out to get away from this shit.'

Mike says, 'Is that Madison?'

'Yeah.'

'I fucking hate that guy. He's a right smug prick.'

I laugh and say, 'Thanks, Mike. You don't have to.'

'I'm not just saying it because of him beating you in London and the World Record thing and all that.'

'And that he's taken the World Champion title off you,' Johnny adds.

'Yeah, we shouldn't forget that,' I say.

'I'm serious,' Mike says. 'Look at him. I hate his face. He looks like an arrogant prick. Is he an arrogant prick?'

I shrug. 'He's the best long jumper of all time, he's allowed to be.'

Johnny turns to the barman and says, 'Mate,' then louder, 'Turn that tele off, will you? That long jumper is offending me. He's bringing the vibe of this place down.'

The barman looks a bit unsure of what he's hearing and heads off down the other end of the bar to serve someone else.

'All right, lads, you can stop now,' I say, laughing at their efforts.

Pete says, 'That is your medal. Yours.' Pete turns to the TV, where Chris Madison's smiling face beams out across the bar. 'That medal is just on loan you fucking World Record stealing twat. My boy' – he throws his arm around me as he says – 'is coming for you.'

We all laugh, a moment of pain for me averted for another few minutes.

'Let's get shots,' Johnny says.

Minutes or hours later, I'm dancing in a dark and sweaty room, throwing my hands around and drinking and trying to focus on my friends and the girl Johnny is talking to and trying to type a text message to Rachel that will never send because we are so far underground the signal is shit and every tune that comes on is amazing and Mike looks as drunk as I feel and everything, just for those brief seconds of our daft dancing or us laughing at Pete bending down in the middle of the dance floor to tie his shoelace, everything is all right.

I CONVINCE THE lads I'll be OK as they pile into their taxis. I move through town at a fast pace, head down. I check my phone in the lift of my building and it's nearly half-past four. I get my key in the door on the second attempt and kick my shoes off in the hallway. I fill a training bottle with water and, instead of heading to bed, I find myself being pulled towards the couch. I find the remote and search through my recorded history and select the event from yesterday. In the dark of my apartment at nearly five o'clock in the morning, I watch him win again and again and again. Tears stream down my face and at one point my body gives up the fight and I break. I sit huddled on the couch, unable to pull myself back. I grab my own hair, pulling it, desperately trying to focus on something other than the pain of his victory and the pain of my hamstring, which is throbbing from all the dancing. It flashes through my mind that I've probably put my recovery back by weeks. Then the rush of tears takes over again.

I stumble around the lounge, opening drawers, searching for a pen and paper. I fall on the couch and focus enough to write two words.

I'm not sure how much later I go to the bathroom, piss and undress, leaning on the wall for balance.

I get myself into bed and sleep for hours.

THERE'S A LOUD, repetitive sound forcing its way into my head. The darkness of sleep slowly fades, but the sound increases, becoming clearer. The door buzzer, being pressed every couple of seconds, over and over. I move out of bed, the hangover immediately kicking in.

In the hallway, I press the intercom. 'Hello?' My voice barely works.

'Let me in.'

I press the button and there's a loud click as the main door downstairs releases.

I quickly go to the bathroom, stepping over my clothes from the last night. I use the toilet and then throw cold water on my face: once, twice, five times in the hope of clearing my head. The view in the mirror is a pale imitation of me.

There's a knock on the front door.

'One minute,' I shout.

In the bedroom, I grab a pair of shorts and a T-shirt.

I open the door and Len stands there. His mouth curls into a small, soft smile. 'Are you OK?'

I flick my hand and signal for him to come in. He does and I follow him into the main room. I stand across from him.

'I wanted to check on you,' he says. 'You missed physio.'

'I was in bed.'

'Drunk?' It's a question, but not a question. He knows. He can see the state of me.

'Yeah.'

The look between us lasts an age. I've made this man angry hundreds of times in our years together, but I've never seen such disappointment in his eyes.

'Last night must have been tough,' he says quietly. 'But I thought you'd be in this morning for treatment.'

I snap. 'What good would it do me today, Len? Having physio this morning still means I didn't win a medal yesterday. I still sat on my couch watching everyone else jump.'

'I understand last night was difficult.'

I turn away and fill the kettle, anger rising inside me as the water hits the metal bottom. I turn back to face Len and say, 'When I got injured in Glasgow, I gave every day to get back as quick as possible. I came in and watched everybody else training, went to every session, kept every routine. And what good has it done me? It's not helped me win in Moscow, has it? So maybe I was unprofessional last night, but at least for one night I got to forget about being injured and not being the World Champion. And guess what? I missed physio today, and he still has that gold medal.'

'Adam,' he says, still not shouting, still not dropping to my ever-falling level. 'I'm tempted to say just take all the time you need and get yourself sorted. But I don't think that's what you want. Sitting around getting drunk, moping about. We need to get you stronger so you can compete.'

I shout, 'Exactly. It's me that competes. Not you. You don't lose. You don't win the medals. It wasn't you who jumped a World Record distance only to have him take it from you. It was me. It's my body that hurts, my leg that's fucked. This is my pain.'

'Adam,' he says. His eyes are pleading with me. 'Don't do this.'

'Don't, Len.' I'm still shouting. 'Don't stand there and pretend it hurts you too. Because you'll never know what it feels like to go through what I've been through.'

I expect him to shout back, to get in my face and tell me to snap out of it, to get back on the runway and fight. To tell me he's been by my side since I was a teenager and that means something to him. To force me out of this darkness. To pull me back into a world where I can see a future.

Instead, he walks out.

I PICK MY jeans up off the bathroom floor and dig my phone out of the pocket. There are twenty-seven missed calls: Rachel, my sister, my mum and dad, Rachel's dad. There are seventeen texts from the same people, all getting more and more urgent in their wording. *Am I OK? Can I call them? Why am I not answering?*

I phone Rachel. She picks up in two rings.

'Where have you been?'

'Asleep.'

'Until now?'

'I got a bit drunk last night.'

'We've all been worried.'

I pause, then say, 'What did you think I might do?'

'I don't know,' Rachel says, her voice a bit shaky. 'I just didn't like that I couldn't get hold of you and no one had seen you since last night.'

'I'm fine,' I say, trying to reassure her. 'How's the hen do?'

'Good. Better now I know you're OK. How are you feeling about Moscow?'

I don't tell her about the tears when I got in, about watching him win over and over, about my argument with Len.

I just lie. 'I'm fine.'

8.96 metres
8.97 metres
Nothing
Everything

48

IT FEELS LIKE I'm moving on autopilot. I park in the empty car park and walk down the path next to well-kept grass verges. Headstones rise out of the ground, varying in size and height, brief histories of the dead carved into stone. I don't take them in. I'm too numb.

I arrive at my grandma's grave. Someone must have been here recently as fresh flowers decorate the ground above where she rests. Where my European gold medal rests. I look at her headstone for a few minutes before I realise I'm crying.

Without understanding why, I start to talk out loud. 'I'm glad you weren't alive to witness it, Grandma. It would've broken your heart. It's broken mine. I don't know what to do, how to act. I'm don't even know who I am anymore. I treat Rachel like shit. Sorry, like dirt. I'm not honest with her, I can't bring myself to say the things that I feel because I feel like it will make me less of a competitor. But I don't even know if I can compete anymore. It's like London broke me and there are all these pieces of my shattered body across the floor, but I don't know how to put them back together. I'm ashamed of myself. You'd be ashamed of me. But I don't know how to fix it.'

Tears pour from me. Loud, uncontrollable sobs that sound like eruptions of thunder in the silent cemetery.

'It's like I'm,' I pause, the words not coming, the one word that will sum up how I'm feeling. It's like my brain knows the answer, but it can't say it because that might mean there is no going back. So, I stare at my grandma's grave. I love her. I miss her, and I wish that I could hug her, and she could tell me everything will be OK.

And then the word rises through me and leaves my lips. 'Grieving.'

My heart is broken.

49

'I'M NOT FINE,' I say.

Rachel's just walked through the door, her hen do ending as she steps across the threshold. The hen do she's been on because we are getting married after I proposed with a ring I couldn't look at because it reminded me of my silver medal.

I can't take this anymore.

I feel sick at the thought of my own actions.

I need to fix it.

She puts her bag down and rushes towards me, throwing her arms around me and it's only as my face squashes against her shoulder that I realise I'm crying again.

'I'm sorry,' I say, pulling back from her. 'I'm so sorry.'

She ushers me to the couch and says, 'Tell me what's happened.'

I can't speak.

'Talk to me,' she says. Her voice packed with worry, filled with nerves about what might come out of me when I do speak. The worry that I'm about to call off our wedding or tell her I've cheated or had some kind of diagnosis. All the worst fears of any normal relationship. The things I'd fear if our roles were reversed.

Images run through my brain. London, the podium, silver. Madison posing for the cameras in front of the World Record board. That conversation in that Beijing nightclub. Him, the Olympic Champion. Him, the World Champion. Him, him, him. Who I see in my dreams, my nightmares, in the hours I lie awake at night when sleep is a million miles away.

Her hand is on my back, rubbing up and down. 'Adam. Tell me what's going on.' Her voice is calmer, comforting. 'Talk to me.'

Talk to me. Let it out.

Stop fighting the pain, the secrets, the lies.

'I can't cope with what happened in London.'

NOW THE WORDS are out there, floating around in the atmosphere. They sound so flimsy. So weak. I feel stupid.

Yet her reaction is to pull me close and hold me.

We sit on the couch, me in an awkward lean into her, half twisted.

'What do you mean?'

I sit up, face her, and tell her everything: London to the visit to my grandma's grave yesterday via my injuries, the build-up of emotion before punching Johnny, the shame at nearly ruining Pete's wedding, the sleepless nights, a life haunted by Chris Madison, my fight with Len. The words pour out of me. Over a year's worth of pain and hurt.

'No matter what I do, how hard I try, I can't shake the feeling of failure.'

'You're not a failure,' she says. The first words she's said in about ten minutes.

'Do you remember when we went on our first walk through Dunham? That first Boxing Day, when we'd just met?'

'Of course.'

'I told you then I wanted to be the best long jumper in the world.'

'I remember.'

'When I was at Dan and Michelle's wedding, one of Dan's mates asked if I'd rather have a gold medal or a World Record. I said both. And I had a World Record and was in the gold medal position with one jump to go in the Olympic Final. I had everything I've worked for. For twenty minutes. Now I feel like I'm always going to be the guy who broke the World Record and lost. That feeling of failure haunts me every day. Because the truth is, I'll never be that good again. The weather will never be right, the competition won't push me as far. I had one chance, and I came away with nothing. Nothing but funny looks in coffee shops and people's pity and sympathy. And I hate it.'

She looks at me. She's crying now, hurting because I'm hurting.

'People don't look at you funny,' she says.

'They do.'

She stays quiet.

'I feel like I've let everyone down. My sister spoke to me years ago about how my life was more important than hers, or at least that's how she felt. I wanted to win gold to show her that all my work was worth it. That I was grateful for her sacrifice, and my parents', and look what I achieved. I wanted her to be able to tell people her brother was the best in the world.'

'Why have you not said anything before?'

'I've been trying to deal with it.'

We look at each other. Stained cheeks and red eyes.

'Happy birthday to me,' I say.

I GO INTO work early the next morning. Len's in his office, reading emails.

'Morning.'

'Morning.'

'I'm struggling. London, injuries, everything. What I said was out of order. It won't happen again.'

'Tell me and let's get it sorted.'

It would've broken your heart.

50

I SIP MY water and stand. As the master of ceremonies hands me a microphone, I catch a glimpse of my wedding ring: shiny and new. It makes my hand feel different, but not strange or uncomfortable.

I look at the sea of friendly, smiling faces. My whole world in one room, all happy and together.

Before I start talking, I look at Dan and remember sitting in a room like this and listening to him speak. Honesty pouring from him as he started his marriage and ended his career.

'My wife and I…'

Cheering, clapping, knives tapping against champagne glasses.

'… would like to thank you for coming.'

I look to my left at Rachel. Smiling, beautiful Rachel.

'Thank you to everyone who has helped put today together. Thank you to the bridesmaids for making sure Rachel turned up and went through with it. Both sets of parents for making today easier than if it had been left to Rachel, who works more than fifty hours a week, and me, who is trained for nothing more than jumping in sand.'

Laughter.

'Thanks to everyone who attended my stag do, for understanding when I said I wasn't going to drink alcohol, although most of you quite happily drank my share.'

More laughter.

'To be a bit more specific on some of the boys, I'd like to thank Mike, Dan, and Johnny for being my ushers. I've known Mike and Johnny since I was a kid and it would've been easy for us to grow apart over the years as they lived what some people would call normal lives, and I became an athlete.'

'Have you been to the Olympics?' Johnny shouts. 'You've never mentioned it.'

I let the room finish laughing.

'I'm trying to be nice here,' I say, and Johnny raises his lager in apology.

I continue. 'But it says something that we are still friends, still the four lads who used to kick a ball about after school, chasing the same girls at secondary school.' I turn to Rachel and say, 'I probably shouldn't mention that today.' She smiles. 'I say four lads because Pete, my best man, is also included in that group. Pete is a great friend, one of my fiercest supporters, not just in a sporting sense, but in life too. He's also not someone to embarrass me in a room full of my closest friends and family by giving a speech about me that might make me look less than brilliant.'

'Well, you say that,' Pete says.

'And Dan,' I say. 'He was someone I looked up to growing up. A fantastic athlete and turns out he is a great man. His book is good too, if you're looking for something to read over the coming weeks.'

Dan, nodding and smiling, gives me a thumbs up.

'I'd like to thank Derek and Helen for taking me into their family and continually making me feel welcome.'

I raise my glass of water to them.

'To my own parents for all their help and encouragement over the years and for making Rachel feel part of the family. The same can be said for my sister, Jane, who, as a bridesmaid, shows how close she and Rachel have become.'

Another raise of the glass.

'I'd like to mention my grandma at this point as well. She's so missed and would've loved today.'

People clap and I think of standing over the grave, dropping my European medal on her coffin. Thud. And my confession at her grave that led me back to a happier path. I push the thoughts from my mind. Today is a happy day. No sadness. That's the promise I made myself. Only laughter and love.

'Before I talk about my amazing new wife,' more cheers, 'I'd like to raise a glass of water to Len, my coach. A huge influence on my life. My biggest critic. Well, my biggest critic in the athletics world. I think Rachel wins the overall award for that otherwise.'

She pretends to hit me, and I do a little hip swivel.

'And now, to the new Mrs Lowe.'

Applause, whistles, cheering.

I wait until they stop, shuffle my notes, try to find my place. I've written the whole speech, every word thought over, but now I'm going off script and I've lost my flow. The words are a blur.

'I'm more nervous than I'm letting on,' I say into the microphone as I scan the pages. Then I see the words, the start of the section about her. I stand up straight. Focus on one person at the back of the room, breathe in and out, just like on the runway.

'It's just running and jumping,' I say. 'They were essentially the first words Rachel ever said to me. We were in a pub on Christmas Eve. She had been invited along by Laura.' I point to Laura who gives a little wave to the other guests. 'Thank you, Laura.'

I turn and face Rachel. 'And when she said that about my entire life's work, I thought, who the hell is this newcomer, having a pop at my job? Then I looked again, and she was the most beautiful woman I'd ever seen. She then made a joke about me playing with a bucket and spade in the sand, and I thought I've got to get to know her more. We swapped numbers that night and two days later we went for a massive walk at Dunham, and I fell in love. Rachel is amazing, as you all know, in your own ways. She's a great friend, incredibly driven, smart, very funny, fully understanding of what my life requires to achieve what I want to achieve. She has her own goals, and we support each other through working towards what we want in life.'

Rachel is crying. The tears are slow, and they fall to her smiling lips.

'I love her more than she'll ever know. Marrying her today is the greatest thing I've ever done. Being Rachel's husband is like winning the Olympics, the World Championships and breaking the World Record all in one.'

I raise my glass of water and say, 'To the new Mrs Lowe.'

'To the new Mrs Lowe,' our guests repeat as I bend down and kiss Rachel.

Pete stands and accepts the microphone.

'Hi. I'm Pete, the best man.'

Pete does more thank yous, running through a list of people he's been asked to mention. He hands out bouquets of flowers to our mothers, gifts for the bridesmaids, then pulls his speech out of the inside pocket of his suit jacket and says, 'Right, let's get on with taking the piss out of Adam, shall we?'

Applause and whistles.

'Adam hasn't given me an easy job here, has he?' Pete starts. 'I mean, how do you write a speech full of jokes about a guy who has numerous gold medals and has competed at the Olympic Games? Well, all I can say to Rachel is I hope for your sake his wedding night performance lasts longer than his World Record did.'

Laughter fills the room, including from me.

He carries on: telling stories of our youth, praising Rachel, passing around pictures of a younger, skinnier me, with a stupid haircut, playing the role of Jesus in a school play. 'He always thought he was some kind of God,' he says.

'Obviously, Adam has a lot to thank me for,' he says. 'It was my wife Laura who brought Rachel out that fateful Christmas Eve. My choice of wife has basically changed Adam's life for the better.'

He pauses and flips the page of his notes over.

'That said, the boy who outran me in nearly every football match we ever played has grown into an Olympic medal winning long jumping legend. His achievements have been written about and discussed by more important sporting legends than me. But they don't get to understand the feelings of watching your mate' – he turns to me – 'your very best mate, standing on a podium and knowing he's a World Champion at something. That feeling makes me, and the rest of us, incredibly proud. So,' he says to the room. 'Ladies and gentlemen, please raise your glasses to the new Mr and Mrs Lowe.'

Rachel and I smile and kiss, the applause getting louder as we hold our lips together.

The evening starts. People relax with post meal drinks. Hand in hand, Rachel and I go to all the tables, making sure we see everyone in the room, stopping to kiss aunties and shake hands with people from Rachel's work.

'How are you?'

'Did you enjoy the ceremony?'

'Thanks for coming.'

Table to table, guest to guest. Handshakes and hugs. Kisses and smiles.

We stop at the table with Johnny, Mike and Emma, and Pete and Laura.

'Nice speech,' I say to Pete.

'Yours wasn't bad either.'

'You look beautiful,' Emma says.

'Thanks,' I say.

'I meant Rachel.'

Rachel does a small, dipped bow and says, 'Why thank you.'

Pete stands up and says, 'Have you lot got a minute?'

We all look at each other.

'Not here.'

He takes Laura's hand and leads her through the gaps between the tables.

We're outside now, in a corridor. The buzz of the main room lost behind the heavy door that Mike closes. We stand and look at each other, confused.

Laura looks straight at Rachel, and with tears filling her eyes says, 'I really hope you don't mind us doing this now. But we can't wait.'

Rachel and I share a look. 'What's the matter?' Rachel asks.

'I'm pregnant,' Laura says.

There's a gasp from the girls, followed by an immediate and tight hug.

'How far gone are you?' Rachel asks.

'It's only a few weeks,' Pete says. 'No scan or anything. Very early. But as today is going to be filled with alcohol and Laura won't be drinking so we wanted to tell you guys so it wasn't weird.'

I shake Pete's hand. 'Brilliant news.'

'I think it happened the night we got back from your hen do. So only a few weeks. I've not felt right, and I took a test yesterday.'

I listen to Laura's words then flashback on our own experience after Rachel's hen do. Tears and confessions, sitting on the couch pouring out my soul. The end of a terrible year. The pain of London. The pain of silver.

Not today. Today is a new future.

'Stick with me, Laura. No one gives me grief if I don't drink,' I say.

I give her a kiss on the cheek. 'Congratulations.'

'It's early days,' she says. 'But thanks.'

'Didn't you drink the champagne when we were getting ready this morning?' Rachel asks her.

Laura smiles. 'There's a glass in your spare bedroom, not touched. I also poured one down the sink in the bathroom.'

Pete points his finger to all of us in one fluid motion. 'Remember, this is a secret.'

WE DANCE THE first dance, slowly, as everyone takes photos and videos. The lights are down, and we are greeted by camera phone flashes and guests who stare at us as we move.

'I feel like I'm being papped,' she says.

I wave my hand and encourage the watchers onto the dance floor and then we are surrounded by our friends and family, all dancing along to our wedding song.

'I love you, Mrs Lowe,' I say.

'I love you too.'

I glance over at Pete, who has Laura's head rested on his shoulder. No longer just two, their lives about to change forever. He catches my eye and smiles. My best mate, my best man.

Happy.

I make a cup of tea, he's there. I brush my teeth, he's there. There when I eat, there when I shower. There when I hang up the washing. He's always smiling. Always wearing that fucking medal.

51

WE LIE ON hammocks, side by side, shaded from the hot afternoon sun by a palm tree. Our panoramic view is of white sands and clear water. Rachel's eyes are hidden behind aviator sunglasses. We just lie, two newlyweds enjoying the peace of a Caribbean paradise.

'I could get used to this,' she says.

'Me too.'

'Really?'

'Yeah.'

'No training, no competition?'

I'm silent for a minute, the slow sway of the hammock beneath me.

'It's going to have to change at some point,' I say.

She pushes her sunglasses up and looks at me. 'What are you getting at?'

'I don't know really,' I say, looking back at her. 'Retirement needs to be thought about. Rio isn't that far away. I won't have another Olympics in me after that.'

'What would you like to do?'

'I honestly don't know.'

I shut my eyes, enjoy the quiet.

Back to our room to shower away the sun cream and sand. Rachel does her hair and make-up while I sit on the double balcony in a pair of shorts, overlooking the sea.

Thinking.

When Rachel is ready, I put on a shirt and we leave the room and walk to the bar. We sit on the outside terrace and take in the orange sky, the sun lazily reflecting on the calm water.

'That's amazing,' she says.

'I know,' I say. 'Makes a change to enjoy the view.'

'What do you mean?'

'I've been to a lot of places to compete, but I don't always feel like I've been to the country. Just the manufactured Village or the hotel. I've been to Beijing, but I couldn't tell you what Beijing was like. I've seen Olympic Beijing. Do you know what I mean?'

'I think so.' She takes a slow drink of wine. 'Would you like to see more of it?'

'Yeah, I would. At some point. Definitely before we have kids.'

'You've been thinking about having kids?'

'I think it's because Laura is pregnant. And getting married obviously.'

'I still can't believe she's pregnant,' she says.

'I know. And Johnny moving.'

'Everyone is growing up.'

We finish our drinks, and walk to one of the resort's restaurants where we get shown to a small table in the corner. Happy, relaxed people all around us, sun kissed faces and holiday smiles.

We consult the menu and order.

'So, these kids you've been thinking about.'

'We've talked about it before.'

'I know, but never timescales.'

'Well, you get a say as well, obviously.' She laughs. 'But not before I've retired.'

'Do you know when that will be?'

'I've got a choice to make.'

'The choice being?'

'Rio or London.'

Rio: The Olympics. London: The Worlds in 2017. Back there, in that city, in that stadium.

'What is involved in the decision?'

'Simply whether I want to carry on to London. My body won't take the work of another Olympic cycle. The honest truth is, if I don't win in Rio, I'll never win an Olympic Gold medal. The dream will be over. The decision really is do I want to do another year, either having won in Rio or face another year having not won.'

'Does the fact it's London play a part?'

Yes: I don't want to jump there. I don't want to lose there again. I don't want to stand on the podium and look up at him again. Him with his gold medal. Not in that stadium. Not ever.

'Yes and no. I don't want to lose there again. But winning there and retiring might be a nice way to finish.'

'How do you feel about retiring?'

'I don't want to end up in the same position as Dan.'

'Which is?'

'Lost.'

A waiter places drinks in front of us, smiles and leaves. We clink our glasses together.

'How do you mean, lost?'

'There was something about the way he spoke at his wedding,' I say. 'I didn't notice it at the time; it was only after reading his book I realised that I'd seen him starting to struggle even as far back as then. He just looked lost, unsure what to do with himself. He just couldn't believe it was over. I still don't think he's really over it. He went from being a top athlete to a married man with a job he's not that into, just like everyone else. I'm not sure he was expecting how hard that transition was.'

'Are you prepared?'

'No. But that's why I need to think about it now. Maybe start planning for afterwards so it doesn't hit me so hard. Not necessarily about what I want to do work wise or anything, just the fact that I can't do this forever. My mind needs to be right for after being an athlete, so it's not hard on me. Or you. I don't want to go through the problems Dan and Michelle went through.'

She reaches out across the table and squeezes my hand. 'I love you.'

'I love you too.'

'When it comes to having kids, I think you're right about waiting until you've retired,' Rachel says. 'That makes sense. I'd like to do a few more years in work before having them. I also want to get a house. I don't want to have a child in our apartment.'

'Should we be looking?' I ask.

'For a house?'

'Yeah. Why not? We're doing all right money wise. We can afford it.'

'I'd not really thought about it. Maybe now would be a good time. Before the Olympic stuff starts.'

'And I'm never at home?'

'Basically. If London is anything to go by.'

'It won't be as bad as London,' I say. Then, 'What kind of house were you thinking?'

Rachel says, 'I've always liked the idea of buying somewhere that needs gutting and doing the whole thing up.'

'Really?'

'Yeah. It might be fun.'

I shrug. 'Let's do that then.'

She looks at me, me at her. Another shared smile.

Just like that, we're planning the future. Our family's future.

Plans, plans, always plans.

RACHEL IS SAT up in bed when I wake.

'Morning,' she says.

'Morning,' I say, eyes adjusting to the room.

'I've got an idea.'

Smile on her face, glint in her eye.

'What if, when you retire, I leave work and we go around the world?'

I blink the sleep out of my eyes, then prop myself up against the pillows.

'Go on.'

'I couldn't sleep thinking about it. I want to see more of the world too. With you. We talked about travelling once before at your parents'. I liked the idea then. Let's do it. We're in a good position. Let's buy somewhere, do it up, and rent it out while we are away, and then we can go around the world for a year and you can get your head straight over retiring. When we get back, we can do the whole kids thing.'

'What about your job?'

'I'll ask if I can take a year unpaid.'

'And if not?'

'I'll find something else.'

'Really? I thought you're doing what you wanted to do.'

'I am. But it doesn't have to be forever.' She smiles and says, 'I'm a highly skilled, highly trained individual. I can do anything.'

'I can't.'

'What do you think?' she asks.

'It sounds like a plan.'

Plans, plans, new plans.

THE AFTERNOON SUN beats down as we lie on sunbeds by the pool. The water is still, free of people who are either sheltered from the heat at the poolside bar or lay on identical beds, letting the sun coat their bodies.

It starts creeping back into my thoughts.

Glasgow and Zurich.

Beijing and Amsterdam.

Rio.

London?

I stand and take off my sunglasses, walk across the hot poolside and dive in, swimming for a few strokes under the water, my body temperature reducing with each movement.

I come up for air.

Glasgow.

I push off the side of the pool and dive under the water again. Deeper, touching the bottom.

Zurich.

I flip in the water, rotating and kicking my feet off the tiled bottom.

Beijing. Amsterdam. Rio.

Above the water I take in air and lie back, my eyes focus on the clear blue nothing above me.

I float, almost still. Abs tense, holding me in place.

London?

Ending by winning there. Ending by losing there. Exorcising the pain. Piling on more. Questions. Questions.

No answers.

I swim to the side, put my hands flat on the tiles and push myself up, arms tensing. I turn and sit, legs in the water, the sun drying me.

Rachel's legs appear, tanned and smooth. She sits next to me and slips her legs into the water. 'All right, husband?'

'Yes, wife.'

'What are you thinking about?'

Kitbags and medals. Weight sessions. Macro and micro training cycles. Spikes and vests. Chris fucking Madison. Red flags. White flags. The bounce of the track, the feel of the sand. The expectant silence just before a jump.

'Winning.'

A GATHERING OF friends at Pete and Laura's. It's more reserved than previous New Year Eves. Pete and Laura, Mike and Emma, Johnny, Rachel and me. We eat a meal of chilli, rice, wraps, nachos, and dips. Rachel and Emma share bottles of red wine. Pete, Mike, and Johnny work their way through the crate of lager Johnny carried on his shoulder as he arrived. Laura and I sit in the sober corner with our soft drinks.

'How are you feeling?' Emma asks Laura.

'Tired.' she says.

'And pissed off,' Pete says.

'And pissed off,' Laura agrees.

'At me,' Pete says.

Laughter all round.

A Beatles album we've been listening to comes to an end and Johnny wanders over to Pete's CD collection and starts running his fingers along the albums. He picks out The Smith's *The Queen is Dead* and switches the CDs.

'What's this?' Laura asks as the music kicks in.

'The Smiths.'

'Happy New Year to us,' she says. 'Now let me go kill myself.'

'Don't be like that,' Johnny says. 'I'm moving in a week. You've got to be nice to me. Let me have things my way.'

'Go on then.'

I help clear up the plates, piling them high and moving them into the kitchen. Pete is tipping uneaten rice into the food bin and putting plates on the side next to the sink.

'How's training going?' he asks. He moves around me to the fridge and pulls out three bottles of lager.

'Really well,' I answer.

And it is. I went back to work straight after the honeymoon, my mind focused and ready. Len and I sat down on that first morning back and I told him, 'My goal is to win everything before I finish. All five medals. I want to hold all the major Championship medals at the same time.'

Glasgow, the Commonwealth Games.

Zurich, the European Championships.

Beijing, the World Championships.

Amsterdam, the European Championships again.

Rio, the Olympic Games.

'Let's get to work then.'

Now, in Pete's kitchen, I say, 'I feel really strong. And I feel like my focus is where it needs to be.'

'This year has been a tough year for you, hasn't it? Injuries and all that.'

'Professionally, yes. Personally, no.'

We hear a noise from the dining room, something crashing to the floor. We make our way back into the room and Johnny is surrounded by Jenga bricks, the tower reduced to a pile.

'We're playing Jenga,' he says.

'Looks like you're losing.'

The tower is rebuilt, and we all join in, carefully removing bricks and placing them back on the top, not wanting to be the one who knocks the whole thing over. There are lots of jokes, attempts at putting people off, a lot of shouting about only using one hand.

The tower wobbles as I pull out a brick and place it carefully on the top. I live to fight again as the bricks hold. I sit down and Rachel stands for her go. Mike is on the arm of the chair next to me. He's quiet, more so than normal.

'You OK?' I ask.

'Fine,' he offers.

Crash.

Rachel stands, brick in hand, the floor covered in the remains of the tower.

'Drink, drink, drink,' Johnny shouts and a couple of others join in. Johnny pours a shot from a bottle and Rachel necks it.

'I didn't realise it was a drinking game,' Laura says.

'Olympians and pregnant people are exempt,' I say.

Rachel rebuilds the tower, and we play again.

'New Year will be a bit different next year,' Laura says. 'We'll have this little thing to contend with,' she says, pointing to her stomach. 'You'll be in Australia,' she says to Johnny.

Mike stands and heads for the kitchen, quietly saying, 'I'm just getting a drink.'

'What about you?' Laura says to Rachel. 'What do you want to do next year?'

'I wondered when you were going to get around to this,' Rachel says. 'Every year you ask this.'

'I just like to keep you focused.'

Rachel sips some wine and says, 'Well given his competing schedule this year,' she says, pointing at me, '2014 will be the year I try to enjoy all the time we get to spend together. We don't always get that many days.'

Laura turns to Johnny. 'Working on my tan,' he says.

Pete, '2014 is the year I'll become a dad,' he says, a massive smile across his face.

Emma, '2014 is the year I think I'll change my job.'

'Really?' Laura asks. 'That's a big one.'

'Yeah. I'm really bored doing what I'm doing at the moment.'

'Adam? Let me guess? Winning a gold medal.'

'No,' I say.

'Really?'

'Two gold medals.'

Laura laughs.

Mike comes in from the kitchen.

'What about you, Michael?' Laura says. 'What do you want from 2014?'

'Hopefully 2014 will be the year we plan our wedding,' he says.

There's a moment of pause, a confused silence across the room. Emma looks at him as he walks towards her. He drops to one knee, pulls a ring from his pocket and says, 'I was just wondering if you wouldn't mind marrying me?'

She jumps at him, throwing her arms around him and says, 'Yes. Yes. Yes.'

The group breaks into a smile.

'Amazing,' Laura says.

The ring is on Emma's finger. She's showing it off to the girls, tears in her eyes. We shake Mike's hand, give him hugs.

I look at my friends. Pete and Laura; married, with a kid on the way. Mike and Emma; newly engaged. Johnny; a move to Australia days away. All moving forward. All changing their lives in different ways. All happy.

I look at Rachel, my wife. We've moved forward, we committed to each other. But we are stuck. Well, she's stuck. Stuck waiting for me to finish with my career. Waiting for me to achieve a dream I've had since I was six years old, watching Linford Christie winning in Barcelona.

Rachel smiles at me and says, 'How brilliant to be here when he did it.'

No matter how much I want the things we talked about on our honeymoon: the house, the travel, the kids, I know my need to win medals – gold medals – is stronger. Life will move for everyone else, but I still need to compete, still need to be an athlete.

I still need to be the best.

To beat him.

I look at Rachel and know she is happy to wait. Happy for our lives to revolve around my world, my goals. Around Glasgow and Zurich. Around Beijing, Amsterdam and Rio.

I've got three years, five major championships.

They are what is important. The competitions, the medals available. Everything else can wait.

Standing in this room, seeing my future through the lives of my friends, I realise that the pain of London has eased. It has been moulded into a burning desire to not be beaten again. To stand on the gold podium, looking down on him, down on everyone else. Not looking up, so close, but so far away.

I've got one chance left. One chance to be what I've always wanted.

We raise our glasses, toast the happy couple.

Emma approaches me and shows me her new ring. It's gold. Gold. The only colour that matters.

In Glasgow and Zurich. In Beijing and Amsterdam.

In Rio.

I've got one chance left to achieve my dream.

PART THREE

52

Glasgow, July 2014
The Commonwealth Games

THE RUNWAY STRETCHES out in front of me. Perfect, freshly scraped sand lies beyond the red cone.

I go through my routine.

I look beyond the pit, finding a stairwell in the Hampden Park stand to focus on.

It's time to bring together all the training I've done since October and win another medal. Time to continue on the unbeaten season I'm having. To execute Len's plan of hitting a big jump in an early round.

The official removes the red cone.

The clock starts.

I breathe in, then slowly out.

0.52... 0.51... 0.50...

I lean back and then push forward.

I'm into my running, moving quickly down the runway. I'm through the phases, head up, back straight, legs and arms pumping. My step quickens into the board and I'm up and over the sand.

I'M BY THE side of the Hampden Park track with a red and white cross of Saint George flag draped over my shoulders. A TV camera is aimed at me, a wall of press photographers to my side, flashes flashing, capturing my image.

'Adam Lowe joins us,' says David from the BBC. 'Adam, the new Commonwealth Champion. Congratulations.'

'Thanks.'

'You led from the First Round, increasing your lead in the second. How comfortable were you that you'd done enough early on?'

'Given what happened in London a couple of years ago, I know more than anyone, you can never feel a competition is over until the last jump. Someone is always capable of pulling out a big jump and winning. That said, today the plan was to go out early and try to get a good lead and see what happened. Fortunately, everything went to plan. Today was about winning.'

Every day is about winning.

Gold is everything. Silver is nothing.

'You've now won three of the four major competitions. Rio must be the overall goal.'

'Yes. But it's a long way off. I need to go home, recover from today and get focused for Zurich in two weeks' time and defending my European title.'

'How important is this year, and the chance of two gold medals, after missing the Worlds last year?'

Last year. Moscow. The black weekend where he won, and the dam holding back my pain finally broke.

Every session I've done with Peter Hedge since I started training again in October appears in my mind. Every bit of preparation, every conversation about rebuilding my confidence, about working towards strong mental focus for moving forward. They will ask you questions about London, he said. They will talk about injuries and Chris Madison and World Records and Rio. Being mentally ready for them is key. Understanding it's their job. Knowing the answers to give which mean you don't dwell on the negative experiences for too long.

I've faced hours of his questions:

What do you want from your career?

To win.

Why?

Because winning is everything.

And what if you don't win?

That's what I need to deal with.

And we've worked towards doing that. I've experienced one of the worst defeats ever. Coming back strong is vital. Peter probes and pushes me. What did it feel like when you broke the World Record? What did it feel like when he broke it? What happened mentally when you were standing on the line waiting for your last London jump? If you could do it again, what would you do differently? What is success? What happens if you don't win another medal? Will your family and friends see you differently? Do they care if you win gold or silver? Do they care if you're a long jumper? Did they treat you differently after London? Over and over and over. Getting me ready for competing, for winning. And for life after it.

I look at David from the BBC and say, 'Last year was a difficult year. I struggled with the injury setbacks. I'm stronger now. Ready for the challenges ahead. Ready to work hard and, hopefully, win again in Zurich.'

I step away from the camera and hold the flag above my head. I continue to walk the edge of the track, soaking up the cheers and the applause, enjoying the few minutes of feeling untouchable. The few minutes of being number one. Smile for the cameras, pose with the fans. Let the feeling of winning run through me.

I see Rachel. She's at the front of the stand, leaning over an advertising board, camera phone in hand, pointing it at me.

I run over and kiss her.

'One down, one to go,' she says.

It is hours before I see her again following the standard winner's interviews and drugs test. We, the two of us and my parents, eat at a restaurant in Glasgow, near where they're staying.

It's late by the time we finish eating, me shovelling down portion after portion in a desperate attempt to refuel.

In the lobby of their hotel, I ask Rachel, 'What time's your train back tomorrow?'

'Seven-ish,' she says.

'Will you be going to the house?'

'Yeah. The builder will be there.'

'I'll be home in the afternoon.'

I make my way back across the city and go to bed, knowing sleep won't come and the early morning TV interviews are not far away. I check the messages on my phone, including one from Johnny in Australia saying: *Well worth getting up at stupid o'clock this morning for you, you gold medal winning legend. I'm going to spend the day bragging to these Aussie twats that my mate beat all of them.*

I text him back saying: *No Australian jumpers made the Final.*

He responds quickly: *You've got long jumping mate. My sport is taking the piss out of my host country. Don't spoil the fun.*

JACOB IS ASLEEP in my arms, his tiny hands tightly curled into a fist. Little snoring noises escape from his nose. The coffee I've been poured is going cold on the side table next to my chair. My Commonwealth gold medal has been placed on his chest, emphasising how small he is. Laura has got her camera out, snapping hundreds of pictures.

'How's the house coming on?' Pete asks.

'Really well. The builders have been great. They've finished the rewire now. The kitchen diner has been knocked through.'

'It's such a brilliant project,' Laura says as she focuses the lens on Jacob.

'It's mainly her doing,' I say, referring to Rachel. 'I've been jumping in sand.'

'That jumping in sand has helped pay for it,' Rachel says.

'When will it be ready?'

'Not sure.'

'Are you still going to rent it out?'

'We might move into it for a couple of years, then rent it out when we go away,' I say.

'I think we should buy another one,' Rachel says.

I look at her. 'What?'

'Something smaller with less work to do. Rent it out.'

'Fucking Sarah Beaney here.'

'I'm serious.'

I shrug. 'Let's finish this one first. See if we're still together.'

I look down at the sleeping baby. 'See this gold medal, Jacob? I'm going to Zurich in a few days and I'm going to win another one. I'll bring it back and show you.'

I look up and Rachel is smiling.

My aches ache.
My sweat sweats.
My lungs burn.
Another day of training over.
Another day of the plan done.
Another step closer.

53

Zurich, August 2014
The European Athletics Championships

I'M IN A dark hole, light above me fading rapidly. Nothing feels right. I don't look like the defending Champion, a former World Champion, an Olympic silver medallist. I barely look like a long jumper.

I stand at the edge of the pit, staring at the official's red flag. It's the second time he's raised it. One for each of my first two jumps in the final, ruling my distances null and void. Two jumps, two fouls. One more and I'm gone. No last eight. No defending my title. No gold medal.

Anger erupts in me. I don't need the red flag to tell me it was a foul. I felt my foot slam over the board. Just like the first jump. The adjustments I made to my run up didn't work. I try to push the anger back, to show no emotion, to give the air of being fully in control of any situation. Two fouls, no problem. No one will believe me. I don't believe me.

I go to Len. He's ready and waiting at the front of the coaches' area, his identity badge hanging from the lanyard around his neck, a serious photo of his face swinging from side to side. His actual face doesn't look so serious. 'Making hard work of this, aren't you?' he says.

I say nothing. I'm trying to control my breathing, calm myself down, not panic about the next jump being all or nothing.

Len says, 'You're overstretching into the board because your run up is off in the middle. Aim for smooth steps. You've got the quality to do this. Just relax. Trust your ability.' No stress in his voice, calm and relaxed. Trusting me to get the job done.

I nod.

'All the work with Peter you've done. It's for moments like this.'

I go back to my seat and try to block out the world. All I have to do is concentrate on one good jump. This is what Peter Hedge has tried to drill into me. Not to worry about the outcomes. We actually talked about this scenario in his office months ago, on a cold January day. What do you do if you foul the first jump? And the second one? We've focused on the importance of controlling emotions, fears, and the next jump.

The situation is now simple. At the current standings, I need to jump over 7.91 metres to make the last eight. There are still five other jumpers to follow me, two not in the top eight so far. I could hit 7.91 metres and still go out if they go further. Those two have never gone over 7.95 metres, so the scenario changes again. Eight metres should put me in the top eight. Ninety-six centimetres below my Personal Best. Simple enough. If I don't foul.

My name is called, and I go through my preparations. Preparations I've done hundreds of times, for hundreds of good, white-flagged jumps.

Thomas Svensson, the twenty-three-year-old Swedish jumper who is leading with a Personal Best of 8.27 metres goes before me. He hits the pit and bounces out, quickly looking to the officials. A white flag is raised. He waits and waits for the next bit. The measurement is called at 8.32 metres. Svensson jumps along the side of the pit, throwing his fists in the air, waving his arms around to the cheering crowd.

I stand on my marker, waiting. A red cone placed in front of the board while they prepare the pit again.

I try to relax, to slow the world down, to block out Svensson's celebration. I breathe in.

This is my last chance.

Breathe out.

One jump.

Breathe in.

One good jump.

Breathe out.

The officials move the cone. The clock starts.

I lean forward and then rock back, pushing myself forward down the runway.

My take-off is close to the board. Too close.

I land and push out of the pit, my head spinning towards the official with the flags.

White or red?

Red or white?

He raises it…

White.

Relief rushes through every fibre of my being.

The jump is measured at 8.09 metres and I move up to fourth.

I go to Len, who says, 'Right, no more scares. There's a gold medal to be won.'

THE FOUR FAILED jumpers pack up their stuff and head to the changing rooms. I take a towel and wipe myself down, removing the sweat that clings to my skin. I change my vest and do a small warm-up. Resetting my body and mind, hoping to feel something close to fresh.

We are down to eight. Three more attempts each. Twenty-four jumps to decide on a Champion. Thomas Svensson, desperate to hold onto his lead position and win his first ever medal. He's improved his Personal Best twice in his first three jumps at a major competition. If he can hold out, today will be the greatest day of his life.

The remaining seven of us want to break his heart.

There are four jumpers before me, but the lead doesn't change.

I stand on my marker and stare down the runway, focused over the pit. I move forward, power down the runway, the best I've felt all day.

I hit the board and rise. Up and up. Over the sand. Hanging and kicking. I come down hard.

White flag.

I wait on the measurement, knowing it's very close to the lead.

8.30 metres. Two centimetres short of Svensson. I'm into second.

Svensson catches my eye as I move back towards to the waiting area. He looks at me for half a second too long. I hold his gaze.

He breaks the eye contact first.

Arms folded across my chest, feet planted firmly on the ground, I watch him jump. Let's see what you've got, Thomas. Can you handle the pressure? I've been here before. I've won these competitions. I've got the medals at home, tucked away. Can you hold a lead with a target on your back? Now's the time to show the world what you've got.

He fouls.

I'm coming for you, Thomas.

Round Five. Everything feels right: the smoothness of my run up, the speed, the take-off. One of those when you just know. I strain in the air, desperate to hold shape. Tension as my arms and legs reach forward for the extra centimetres.

A white flag and 8.58 metres measurement. The lead is mine.

It's my third biggest jump of the season, but I don't react. I walk away, showing calm on the outside. Internally it's like fireworks have gone off. I'm the defending Champion. This is my medal. If you want it, Thomas, you need to jump better than 8.32 metres. You're playing in the big leagues now, pal. Medals are earned. Not given away.

I look at him. He looks at me.

Your move, Thomas.

What have you got?

The last jump of the Fifth Round: 8.35 metres. His third Personal Best of the day. He falls to the floor, probably pulled somewhere between being elated at another PB and broken at the knowledge that he's still twenty-three centimetres behind me. He lies there, begging his body for more. Asking his body to give him one more jump. One more improvement. Thirty more centimetres. Twenty-five more centimetres. Twenty-four more centimetres.

Round Six. No one beats me. No one has enough to go to 8.59 metres. The medal positions don't change. I jump 8.38 metres and Svensson fouls.

I've defended my European title.

I accept the congratulations from the other guys, but I'm moving them along quickly to get to Svensson. He looks broken. The last couple of hours of effort have sapped everything from him.

I put my arm out and pull him off floor where his head is slumped between his knees. I wrap my arm around him and say, 'You were fantastic today. Three Personal Bests in a one day is something to be proud of.'

He nods because he can't speak.

'Keep jumping like that, your silver medal will become gold very soon.'

'Thank you,' he whispers.

I head off to Len, to Rachel, my parents, and sister, to wrap myself in a Union Jack and do a lap of honour.

A Champion.

Again.

LEN AND I walk through the streets of Zurich, taking in the place.

I think of my wish to see more of the places I've competed in than just the inside of hotel rooms and athletic venues. Rachel would like it here. She flew home this morning with my parents and sister. Back to the office this afternoon. Saturday, catching up on Friday's missed work.

We end up in a park by the lake. Len wanders towards a small stand selling drinks and orders two coffees. While he waits, I look at the people in the park. There's a couple lay on the grass, the girl's head on the guy's stomach, both reading: her, a book, him, his phone. An old man sits alone on a bench just taking in the view. Cyclists pass through the scene, a blur of wheels and coloured jackets.

Len pays and hands me coffee in a takeaway cup.

'Thanks.'

'To gold medals,' he says, and we tap our cups together.

We stand on the grass and watch the boats on the water, moving slowly across the scene.

'I need to talk to you,' Len says. 'About retiring.'

'I've not decided yet,' I say. 'Rio or London, that's the choice.'

'Not you,' he says. 'Me.'

Winner: *n* **1** a person or thing that wins. **2** Informal a person or thing that seems sure to be successful.

Loser: *n* **1** a person or thing that loses. **2** Informal a person or thing that seems destined to fail: he's a bit of a loser.

Source: Collins Essential English Dictionary

54

Beijing, August 2015
The World Athletics Championships

I'M ON A plane going back to where it all began between us.

It's been seven years since he beat me to Olympic bronze by two centimetres. Since we stood in Club Bud and he predicted the future and said the following years would be dominated by the two of us. Seven years since the start of something that has been woven into the fabric of my life.

Me and him.

Him and me.

Rivals.

A TECH GUY is wiring me for sound. He's checking levels, making sure everything is connected. Dan stands in front of me going through the same process.

'How's Michelle feeling?'

'Sick.'

'That'll pass though, right?'

'Yeah. Then there's a few weeks of loving me again. Then she'll get heavy, fat, swollen ankles, and then I'll be back in the spare room being told to never touch her again. Then the baby will come and who knows how she'll feel.'

'Still, it's good news.'

'Yeah. Really good.'

'All good,' the tech says.

'Camera?' Dan asks.

'Ready.'

Dan turns to me. 'You ready?'

'Yeah.'

Dan starts his interview, introducing me, giving a rundown of my medal history.

'Adam, thanks for taking the time to sit down with me.'

'No problem.'

'How's your preparation gone?'

'Really well. I feel fast and strong. I've jumped well all year.'

'You're coming off the back of an excellent 2014. Unbeaten, two major medals. Your only loss this year was to Chris Madison in New York. You've beaten him in Oslo. This feels like it's building to you versus him again. Given what happened at the London Olympics, does it feel like your long jumping careers will always be linked?'

In the past, this is where I would lie. This is where I would say that anyone in the finals can win on their day. That everyone wants to beat me, and I want to beat everyone. That I can only control my jumps and not care about anyone else. In the past.

Now I say, 'Chris wants to beat me, and I want to beat him. When we jump together, we push each other further. Ask him. If I'm there, his will to win is increased.'

Dan smiles off camera.

'Winning is everything to both of us,' I say.

But only one of us can.

I LEAD AFTER the first two rounds with 8.35 metres. He is second. He fouled in the First Round but jumped 8.28 metres in the Second.

Round Three:

Me: 8.51 metres.

Him: 8.46 metres.

Chasing me. Getting close, but not close enough.

Twelve become eight.

Round Four:

Him: 8.54 metres – Seen.

Me: 8.61 metres – Raised.

It won't be enough. I know I'll have to improve, to go further. The defending World Champion, the Olympic Champion, the World Record holder, won't rest. He is not beaten. London taught me this. I still bear the scars of his previous comeback.

I try to stay relaxed while everyone jumps. I keep my limbs loose, covered in tracksuit bottoms and a zip-up top. I watch a couple of attempts. None trouble me, none get close to the medal positions.

I strip again and move to the runway. He's in front of me, preparing for Jump Five. His powerful frame is by his marker, swinging his arms by his sides, trying to purge some of the tension out of his shoulders. He's only got two chances left to beat me. It's come down to this. Me and him again, fighting it out, jump after jump, for the main medal. For the right to be called the Champion of the World.

For gold.

His body changes in front of me, rising up on to his toes, then rocking backwards towards me. Then he's gone, pushing off down the runway. The small white square of his event number gets smaller and smaller with every step. He's sprinting at close to top speed and I fear this jump. Fear if he hits the board right, if his technique is close to perfect, that I'm going to be chasing him with two jumps to go.

The take-off never comes.

Where the push off should be, he runs through into the sand, clutching the back of his leg. He falls and a scream, or a shout, or a swear word, or some strange feral mix of all three are released from him and sent high into the Beijing sky.

I stand at the end of the long runway, viewing the scene. I feel like I'm looking into someone's most private moment, through a dirty window. A moment they, he, wouldn't want me to witness. A moment of utter pain and devastation. Of weakness. His hamstring has gone, that's obvious. I've been there, feeling what he's feeling right at this very second. Disappointment, anger, the brutal reality of knowing you won't jump again. He looks distraught, his face hollow. He hobbles to the side of the track and leans on an advertising board. His night over, his fight lost.

I have won.

I STAND BEHIND the top podium. Him to my left. Thomas Svensson to my right.

First. Second. Third.

Gold. Silver. Bronze.

Svensson collects his bronze medal, accepts the applause of the host nation. He waves and smiles, stares at his medal.

Then it's his turn. No one went further than his 8.54 metres, so he won the silver medal that the official is placing over his head. And here he is, leg strapped and limping, fallen hero: injured, beaten but still a medal winner.

Now it's my turn.

I step onto the podium and view the stadium from my raised position. Above him, above everyone. Cameras click, flashes of light exploding in front of my eyes. I lean down to shake the official's hand and accept my medal.

I am the World Champion.

A title I earned in Daegu and didn't get a chance to defend in Moscow. A title he took from me while I sat at home alone in my apartment, feeling empty and deflated. Two years of work has brought me back to this elevated place. Two years spent climbing out of the darkest hole I've ever been in. A climb that started two days after he won in Moscow, when I finally admitted out loud that London had broken me. Now, I stand with pieces of me glued back together. I hold up my gold medal and show it to the section of crowd I know my family are in.

There's a brief moment where the sounds that surround me: the applause, the cheering, the announcements in the arena fade away in my mind and I think of my grandma. I kiss the medal, close my eyes, and picture her smile.

Instructed by a photographer, Svensson and he step onto my podium. We pose, each holding our medals in front of us. Each of us smiling. Mine genuine, his fake.

AND THEN, WE find ourselves alone in a corridor underneath the stand, below the thousands of people who are watching the remainder of the events.

Me and him.

Him and me.

Six feet apart, hidden away from the world.

'I was coming for you,' he says.

'What?'

'Those last two rounds. I was coming for you.'

'I improved on everything you offered,' I say.

'Still, you know I'm never beaten.' He smiles, big and wide, showing too many teeth. Like he's joking. I can read his eyes though.

'London was three years ago,' I say. 'You were beaten today.'

'I guess we'll never know,' he says. 'Anything could've happened in those last two rounds.'

'You had your fifth,' I say. 'You fell apart.'

Another smile. Dead eyes.

A door opens behind me, then shuts again a couple of seconds later, shifting his attention to beyond me for a second.

'We'll see in Rio,' he says.

He walks away before I can respond.

'That is massive. I think that might be a new World Record.' Pause. 'It is. It's a new World Record. Adam Lowe has broken the long jump World Record in the Olympic Final. This is incredible. The man from Manchester has gone further than anyone has ever gone before. Adam Lowe, World Record holder. Brilliant. Simply brilliant.'

'So, here's Chris Madison on the runway. One jump remaining. He's got to break the World Record to win. What pressure. What must he be feeling right now? He starts his approach and...' Silence. 'I think he's done it. He has done it. Chris Madison has jumped further than Adam Lowe. Incredible. Absolutely incredible. What a finish to the long jumping Olympic Final. I've never seen a night like this. One centimetre is the difference between the gold and silver medal positions. Both jumps are longer than we've ever seen before. Poor Adam Lowe. What must he be feeling?'

From the television commentary of the London 2012 Olympic Final.

55

Rio de Janeiro, August 2016
The Olympic Games

I'M BACK ON my old school stage, playing along as Mr Francis continues our long running theme of these days: former pupil-done-good.

I answer all the students' questions:

'Are you worried about the Zika virus?'

'No. That's down to the authorities.'

'What do you think to the Russian doping ban?'

'Again, that's down to the authorities.'

'What's your greatest ever performance?'

'The World Championships in Beijing last year. I improved in the first four rounds to a winning position and didn't foul once.'

Afterwards, I see Abbie in the staffroom.

She's friendly, filling me in on the details of her life. She's married now, with a young daughter, and has been recently promoted to deputy head of the school.

When it's time to leave, she says, 'I'll see you out.'

We walk down several corridors, Abbie leading the way through a newly built science block. We reach an exit that leads onto the car park and she holds the door for me, then follows me into the car park.

'Are you making sure I don't sneak back in and nick some Bunsen burners?' I ask.

'No,' she says. 'I, erm, I just wanted to say something. Something I didn't want to say in there.'

We take a few steps towards my car and I suddenly pick up on her nervous body language.

We stop.

She takes a deep breath. 'I don't want to come across as weird. But I need to say something for my own peace of mind.'

She pushes a stray hair away from her face. 'I've been thinking about this a lot.'

'Go on,' I say, unsure what will follow.

'I know we weren't together long. And I know we might not have lasted, anyway. But the last few years have been really weird for me, with you coming to the school and talking about how brilliant your life is, doing what you love. It always felt like the life I could've had, if I'd understood more, or made different choices, was just being paraded in front of me.'

'That was never my intention.'

'I know that. But you don't understand how strange it is to have an ex-boyfriend constantly turning up at your work talking about the very thing that made you split up in the first place. It made me really bitter. Whenever I knew you were competing, I wanted you to lose. I thought that would make me feel better.' She looks at me and says, 'Don't worry, when you lost in London, it didn't make me feel any better. Anyway, the point I'm rambling towards is, I don't feel like that anymore. I love my life. My husband, my daughter. Everything that has happened in my life, including us, led me to them. And I wouldn't change anything because of that.'

I nod, not really sure what to add to the conversation.

'The last couple of times you've been here,' she continues, 'I've seen you differently. Someone who dedicated themselves to a dream. I respect that. I really hope you win that gold medal in Rio.'

'Thank you,' I say.

IT'S OVER. ALL the preparation, the interviews, the countdowns, holding camp. Each one completed.

The only thing left to do is win.

My last chance.

THE PATTERN ON arrival follows Beijing and London. Bus from the airport to the Village, full security check and settle in our new Olympic home.

In my room, I unpack.

A dull tap on the door gets my attention. Tap, tap. Pause. Repeat.

'Come in.'

Dan's now brother-in-law, Simon Lewis appears. The former Olympic swimmer is now a coach. The man who dragged me out of my dark hole in London four years ago, forcing me out of the Village, standing up for me in a nightclub when I wasn't capable of standing.

'How are you?' he asks.

'Very good. You?'

I step towards him and shake his hand. I've not seen him for a couple of years, since a meal we had at Dan's following my Commonwealth and European double.

'Have you eaten?'

'No.'

We cross the Village to the Food Hall. It's busy and my senses adjust to the noise, the smells. Athletes walking around create a huge movement of colour. Deep reds, bright yellows, dark and light greens. A blur of blue. Orange and gold. Colours swirling into one. The whole world can be traced through this room, country by country, dish by dish. Chicken sizzles on the enormous circular frying pans at one side of the room, fresh salad chopped and served on another.

We get our food and sit.

'How's the coaching life?' I ask him.

He shrugs. 'I'm not sure it's for me.'

'Really?'

'Yeah. I just miss swimming. I thought coaching would help me feel close to it, but it's just made me realise how much I miss competing. You know what it's like. There's an enjoyment in competition that you don't get anywhere else in life. Going up against the best. Challenging yourself. Pushing yourself. You're one of the best long jumpers of all time. The enjoyment you must get out of that, the buzz when you hit a good jump must be incredible.'

I chew my food. 'I don't always think about it. It's about focus. Focus on getting everything right.'

'You should think about it.'

'Are you looking around thinking you could still compete here?'

'Fuck no. Some of the kids, and I mean kids, fifteen, sixteen years old, coming out of China and America, I can't compete with that. It's a young man's game now. I'm too old. But coaching, I'm not sure it's for me.'

'What about the people you're coaching?'

'Good swimmers. Not going to medal individually, but good, hard-working swimmers. I'm knocking it on the head after this Games.' He looks at me. 'Not for public knowledge until after though.'

I nod. 'What you going to do?'

'I've started a business which is going OK.'

'Dan was telling me about this. Is this Simon's Swimming or something?'

'Swim with Simon.' He loads his fork with pasta, holds it in the air, and says, 'We run these swimming courses in Spain. Five days a month at this hotel we've found with a fifty-metre pool. Quiet town, near the beach. We get a lot of people training for Ironman and other triathlon stuff. They want to improve in the water, but their technique isn't right. Five days with me, two sessions a day, intense stuff, sorts it out. Full board, flights, and everything, all included. There are a lot of high-powered people, lawyers and all that. Think they enjoy the peace away from their jobs for a few days too. We run follow-up sessions in England once a month and there's online coaching too.'

'That sounds brilliant.'

'It's started small, but it's building. We've done four trips now.'

He pauses and eats.

'I'm also,' he says cautiously, then stops.

I give him a couple of seconds to restart, but he looks around the room and continues to eat.

'Go on.'

'I'm going on that dancing show.'

'Really?'

'Yeah.'

I laugh loud. Too loud.

'Is it that daft?'

'No. Don't you remember?'

'Remember what?'

'Dan's wedding, you said when you finally retire, you're going to go on reality TV. Like any self-respecting athlete.'

Simon laughs.

'They asked me a couple of years ago and I said no but this time I thought it would be a good way to promote the business, get my name out there. Plus, the money is very good. Too good to turn down.'

'Really?'

'Better than lottery funding.'

'Nice one. Glad things are going well.'

I sip some water, take in the scene around me. The Olympics in full flow. Every country represented sitting together, sharing food.

'What about you?' Simon asks.

'What about me?'

'Is this your last competition?'

'I don't want to talk about retirement, Si.'

'I understand. Focus on the medals, right?'

'On gold.'

'Dan says you're building quite the property empire.'

'Getting there,' I answer. 'We've bought one to live in, which we've done up and we've bought, done up, and sold two more since. Last one went through about six weeks ago.'

'That's good.' Another mouthful, his plate showing the last scraps of food. 'How's your coach?'

'Good.'

Pause.

'You ready for this?'

I point and turn my finger, taking in the room but meaning the whole thing: the Olympics, the experience. 'The Olympics?'

'Yeah. After last time.'

Last time. London. Breaking the World Record and not winning.

'Only one way to find out,' I say.

EVERYTHING BECOMES THE last something. The last time I'll qualify for an Olympic Final, which I did comfortably earlier, the last time I'll go through my pre-competition evening routine: shower, prepare my bag for the final, watch a film to let my mind escape for a couple of hours. Everything, every detail, has the prefix of the last.

Dan told me it would be like this. Peter Hedge had suggested speaking to former Olympians about their final Games. How they felt, how it changed performance or routine. I called Dan, and he took me through all his build-up for the few months before Beijing. I could hear how difficult he still finds not being an athlete. I was expecting the feelings I have as I lie on the bed, waiting for my last sleep before my last Olympic Final: a feeling of emptiness, mixed with colourful thoughts about what life will be like on Sunday morning if I'm the Olympic Champion, or how I'll act if I face the darkness of being second again.

I think about the last everything tomorrow will bring:

My last Olympic Final.

My last warm-up.

My last time in a call room.

My last first jump, second jump, third jump.

My last jump Four, Five, and Six.

My last chance to win Olympic Gold.

IT'S BEEN FOUR years since London.

Four years since the lowest point of my life.

Four years since he won, and I lost.

Four years of walking the long road back. The road that missed Moscow, but went via Glasgow, Zurich, Amsterdam - where I defended my European title - and Beijing. Every step leading me to this line. The line between a good jump and a foul. The line at the end of the runway, on the board, just before the pit.

I hit the board just before the line, fly through the air, land in the sand. I'm measured at 8.28 metres.

Jump One of the Rio Olympic long jump final has gone.

I've got five remaining.

Five jumps to win gold.

EIGHT POINT TWO-eight metres has me leading for a few minutes then Madison, jumping three behind me, hits 8.52 metres. He's pumped, fists going, animal like screams leaving his wide-open mouth at the side of the pit. The defending Olympic Champion, playing to the crowd.

Five jumps to beat him.

I sit and wait, processing all the information from my first jump: what the track felt like under my feet, how my body reacted as I moved through the phases, how the wind impacted my run up. I make mental adjustments, preparing for the next attempt. I focus on the ground between my feet, the small piece of red flooring. I can hear the sounds of the stadium from all around me: the cheers of the crowd, applause, the rapid pounding of feet on the runway, a grunt and thud as a jumper takes off.

JUMP TWO: I lean back and then push forward into my run up. It's not as quick as I'd like. I'm forcing myself to run faster and it's knocking off my steps slightly. I hit the board and jump. I'm white flagged but only measured at 8.19 metres.

He hits 8.31 metres.

He still leads.

BACK ON THE runway for Jump Three, I wait for the red cone to be removed. The officials are raking the sand. The clock is reset to 1.00.

I look down the runway and for some reason I get a flashback to my grandma's garden when I was a kid. The long stretch of grass I used to run down, using a towel as my board, is there at the front of my mind. The memory is clear: the red baseball cap marking my previous jump, the glass of water my grandma had placed next to the tree, her stood at the kitchen window washing dishes and smiling at me as I focused on my run up. I would run and jump, my feet digging into the grass as I landed, leaving two imprints from the heels of my trainers. If I'd jumped further than the cap, I'd pick it up with pride and move it in line with my latest landing spot. My grandma would tap on the window and clap. And I'd smile.

Now, stood at the top of the runway, facing an Olympic long jump pit, four jumps to go, I smile again. *It's just running and jumping.*

I start running. I'm moving faster and sharper than I have all day. The board is approaching, my foot turnover increases, and I'm up. And up. And I hang and kick and I land.

I bounce out of the side and look at the board. It's big. I'm leading if the flag is white. I turn to the official who is holding up the white flag. I wait for it to be measured, but the numbers are just technical.

The official distance is 8.73 metres.

I'm leading the Olympics. Again.

I look to the coaching section and smile. The smile is returned with a clenched fist.

He jumps 8.57 metres, which, on another day might be enough to become the Olympic Champion. Not today though.

Today I'm going to make him earn it, like he did four years ago.

I SENSE A chance to increase the pressure. He is stood by the side of the pit, shocked expression on his face, staring at the official's red flag. He's pleading his case to them. His hands clapped together as if in prayer. But the flag remains unmoved. He's wasted his fourth jump. I ignore him as I stare down the runway. Now is the time to perform, to go further.

I breathe in, slowly release the air. In, out. In, out.

Focus.

Focus.

Focus.

Every single fibre of my being is concentrated on powering down the runway and jumping further than 8.73 metres. Increasing my lead, increasing the pressure on him.

The sounds of the stadium fade away. I can only hear my own heart beating a strong, steady rhythm in my chest.

To win Olympic Gold, these are the moments to perform. Everything I've experienced in the last four years; the loss, the anger, the pain, the highs of winning, all of it needs to be finally put to rest with a jump worthy of winning an Olympic Gold medal.

0.51… 0.50… 0.49…

In, out. In, out.

0.42… 0.41… 0.40…

In, out. In, out.

I lean back and then push forward. I'm quickly up straight, in my running position. The track disappears in front of me, every step pushing me towards the pit. I quicken my step into the board, and I push off…

Every inch of me is in the jump. The speed, the tension, the power, all combine as I hit the sand, and the force vibrates through me.

It's white flagged and I stand and wait by the pit, watching the officials performing the measurement. They call it: 8.79 metres.

DOUBT ARRIVES, THE unwelcome guest. A hooded figure, slipping in through a slightly open window at the back of my mind, creeping around corners, whispering:

That jump isn't good enough.

This'll end like London.

No matter how far you jump, he will always jump further.

London will haunt you forever.

As long as he is around, you will always be second.

Four years on, nothing has changed. Two jumps to go in an Olympic Final: I'm winning. He is second.

I've prepared for doubt. I've told myself over and over that each competition is different, to focus on each round, on the here and now, not on four years ago.

We are back on our feet, stripped down to our vests and shorts, bouncing on our toes, waiting for our turn to jump. Three people to jump before him, two people, one more person. And then he's at his marker, talking to himself, willing himself to jump close to his existing World Record. To take the lead at this late stage and break my heart. Again. 'I'm ready to fly.'

He starts his run up. I watch his back move away from me. He's up and over the pit and then landing, pushing up and out.

I see the flag before he does: White.

I can't read his face. The jump is long and I feel sick as I watch them measure it. Doubt is laughing at me, telling me I'm beaten. Telling me it told me so.

The officials call it: 8.68 metres.

I feel my body relax. It's an incredible effort. But it's not even the second longest of the day.

He's now only got one jump to win. The sixth jump. The one he beat me with last time.

I start my run up, desperate to improve on 8.79 metres I call on every session I've ever done, every weight I've ever lifted, every ounce of pain I've ever felt to see me through the next two jumps, to push myself to my very limit. Again.

I land somewhere around 8.40 metres.

I turn and look at the official and he sits there, face blank, emotionless, holding his red flag in the air. Foul.

Laughter swells inside me, then spills out. I'm stood at the edge of the pit, now one jump away from the end of the Olympics, laughing. Like someone has just told me a joke that no one else in the stadium heard. An official looks at me, unsure of my reaction. I turn to the coaches' section and shrug my shoulders. I don't question the decision, don't go and check the board. I just walk back to my seat still laughing.

THE FINAL ROUND starts. I'm winning, just like in London. He is second, just like in London. This time he doesn't have to beat the World Record to win, but he's got to jump one of the longest jumps of all time. Fear has pulled up a chair in my mind. Fear has got its feet on the table.

I force myself to concentrate on my usual routine: my short warm-up, keeping the blood flowing through my legs. But I feel sick. I watch each jump. One doesn't beat me, then another, and another. Three to go until he jumps. I see a red flag and another jumper misses their chance. Then another. The Olympic Final is down to three. Another red flag.

It's just the two of us.

Me and him.

Him and me.

Always.

We are here; four years further down this road of rivalry but nothing has changed. I'm stood behind him at the top of the runway, waiting for him to jump, waiting to see if he can beat my leading jump in an Olympic Final.

Sick.

My legs are weak, and it's an effort to stand.

He's taking forever to start his run up, composing himself, knowing he's got one chance. 'You've done this before,' I hear him shout. 'One more time. Eight eighty, baby. Let's go. Let's fly.'

And he's away.

The next few seconds feel like I'm drowning. Air can't get to my lungs, and everything I see in front of me is a blur. The noise from the crowd is muffled, my brain distorted. The only thing that's clear is the words that are beating against the inside of my head:

He's going to beat me.

He's going to beat me.

He's going to beat me.

He jumps and I feel like my heart has stopped.

He's going to beat me.

Again.

EVERYTHING IS THE same.

I'm stood at the top of the runway, looking down to the pit. He is at the side, looking down at the imprint his body has left. He offers no reaction.

Everything is different.

MY MIND FLASHES back to my grandma's front room. 1992: Linford Christie on the TV, crossing the line in Barcelona. I turn to my grandma. 'I'm going to do that one day.'

And I have.

I am the Olympic Champion.

Everything is different.

I DROP TO my knees, let out a roar of celebration. Everything comes out in that one moment, merged together as it releases from my body: London, the aftermath of losing, punching Johnny, the horrible feeling of nearly ruining Pete's wedding, the injuries, Moscow, the tears on my couch as I sat drunk and alone, arguing with Rachel, letting down family, friends, myself. It is all purged from me, twisted and wrapped together and sent towards the Rio skies.

Everything is different.

I am the Olympic Champion.

THE PIT HAS been prepared; the clock reset. I don't have to do this. I want to do this.

I cut out all the noise, all the celebration from the stands, the other athletes who have wandered over to shake my hand. I make it clear by my movements that I want to jump again.

0.56… 0.55… 0.54…

I lean back and then push off into my run up.

My speed is good, every bit of my body feels relaxed. There is no pressure.

I push off the board and up.

My last jump.

My first as the Olympic Champion.

I hit the sand.

The flag is white.

The distance doesn't matter.

I RACE OFF to the coaching area. Len has managed to scramble his way over the advertising board. He pulls me to him, hugs me tight.

'You've done it. You've done it,' he repeats over and over.

'We've done it,' I say.

Len smiles.

'I guess you're not fuming,' I add.

He laughs. We both think about the same conversation.

Zurich: two years before. The pair of us stood at the edge of a lake, coffees in hand. The European Champion and his coach, talking about the future. 'Judith and I have been talking about retirement more and more,' he said, his eyes on the water.

'And?'

'I'm finishing after Rio.'

'OK.'

'I wanted to give you plenty of notice.'

'Thanks.'

'Now you better win that gold medal or I'm going to be fuming.'

I paused and said, 'Len, I want to thank you for everything you've done for me.'

'Don't get soft on me,' he said. 'Just win in Beijing, Amsterdam, and Rio so I don't spend my days wondering what might have been.'

He stands in front of me now, at the end of our third Olympics together, at the end of our journey, and says, 'I can retire a happy man.'

I blink and feel the wet of tears beneath my eyelids.

'YOU'RE THE OLYMPIC Champion,' Rachel says.

Those words, the words, out of her mouth.

A smile spreads across my face. A smile I hope never fades.

I step back onto the track, extend my arms out wide, the Union Jack stretching across my back. Fans are clapping and cheering. A wall of cameras facing me, capturing this moment. Click, flash, click, flash. Each one a slightly different image of me: The Commonwealth, European, World, and Olympic Champion.

I DO A lap of honour, trying to soak in every detail. All the colours and the faces, the banners, and the flags. I sign autographs and pose for photographs. My smile remains, a constant companion.

I bend down to remove my spikes, with the intention of giving them to a kid from England who has just asked me for an autograph, told me I'm his hero. I stop. Freeze. I can't do it, not yet. I'm not ready. I look up at the kid, he's smiling and laughing with his mum at the picture I've just taken with him. I remove the flag from my shoulders and hand it to him. His eyes light up.

I jog on.

I catch-up with the other medal winners. Jermaine Morgan, a Jamaican who finished third, and Madison, are moving slowly around the track together. I speed up and position myself to Morgan's side as some press photographers take pictures.

Morgan shakes my hand, smiles. 'Here he is. The King.'

I laugh.

Madison looks at me, pauses, assesses, waits, then offers his hand.

I accept.

DAVID FROM THE BBC: 'Adam Lowe, the new Olympic Long Jump Champion, is with me.'

My smile beams back across the ocean from Brazil to Britain, via the BBC camera.

'Adam, how good does it feel to hear those words?'

'Amazing,' I say. 'It's everything I've worked for. Everything I've ever wanted.'

'How hard was it for you to come back after London?'

'It was very difficult. Personally, I was very down after London. I struggled to get to grips with being so close to the Olympic title and not winning it. I know it was hard for a lot of people close to me. It wasn't always easy being me in those months that followed that final, and I think worse than that, it was harder to actually be around me. Luckily, I've got a good set of friends and family, an incredible wife and a great coach who helped me through. After missing Moscow through injury, I realised I might not have many competitions left to achieve my goals.'

David from the BBC says, 'Was there any reason you jumped the last jump, even though you'd already won the gold medal?'

'Yes. That was the last jump of my career, so I wanted to savour every last second of competition.'

'Of your Olympic career?'

'No. My career.'

'You're retiring?'

'Yes.'

There's a pause from the interviewer.

'An exclusive for you,' I say.

David from the BBC puts out his hand and says, 'Adam, it's been a pleasure watching you jump all these years. What a way to retire, as the Olympic Champion.'

I'M FILMED, PHOTOGRAPHED, and drug tested. I sign hundreds of autographs, shake what feels like thousands of hands. And somewhere, at the end of it all, I'm in a room with Rachel and my family.

'So,' I say. 'That went well.'

Laughter fills the room. My mum is in tears, my dad is fighting them back. My sister pulls me to one side and says, 'Grandma would've been very proud tonight.'

I pull Jane into me and hug her tightly.

'Thank you.'

I DON'T SLEEP.

I lie on the bed and replay every moment; each beautiful second.

I am the Olympic Champion.

The words dance around my head, spinning and flipping, leaving golden trails. I read the messages on my phone. There's nearly a hundred. Friends, family, other athletes. Even one from a number I don't recognise saying,

Congratulations on achieving your dreams. Abbie x

Mike, Johnny, Pete, and Dan have all left voicemails. Dan says, '*I'm very proud and very jealous. Holding all four is some achievement.*'

And I think about his words and think through what he means:

I am the Commonwealth Champion.

I am the European Champion.

I am the World Champion.

I am the Olympic Champion.

This is what it must feel like to be high.

I get up and make my way out into the Village. The early morning sun is warm, and the brightness blinds me for a second. My eyes adjust and I see a few other athletes walking around. It's that funny time of the day, when some people are preparing for their events as others are stumbling home from nights out, free from training schedules and strict routine.

I walk for a few minutes, taking in my surroundings, actually enjoying the views for the first time. I sit down on a bench and shut my eyes for half a second. When I open them, he's standing over me.

'Morning.'

'Morning.'

'What you doing out?'

'Couldn't sleep,' I say.

'Same.'

'Coffee?' I ask.

'Yeah.'

I stand and we walk to one of the purpose-built coffee places inside the Village.

The place is quiet. He goes to the counter and I go to the back corner and sink into a comfortable armchair. As the minutes pass, sleep flirts with me.

Chris Madison presents me with a large cup of coffee and sits down opposite me.

Me and him.

Him and me.

'Congratulations,' he says.

'Thank you.'

A silence.

Sips of coffee.

'So.'

'So.'

I laugh, not loudly.

'What are you laughing at?'

'This. Us.'

'What do you mean?'

'Sharing coffee. Sitting down to talk. We're like a bad first date.'

He laughs too.

'Some kind of rom-com thing.'

'A shit one.'

'Aren't they all?'

'True.'

He blows the heat from the top of his coffee.

'You're retiring.'

'I am.'

He doesn't respond, but there's a small look, a glance away, a roll of the eyes, something I don't quite catch that makes me say, 'What?'

'What?'

'That little look.'

'No look.'

I study this man in front of me. The man who has been shackled to me for the last eight years. The man who has been in every corner of my world. In every dream, every nightmare.

'Can we knock this on the head now?' I say.

'What?'

'The mind games.'

The man who my Olympic Gold medal has freed me from.

'Mind games?'

I laugh. 'Yeah. The mind games.'

'I'm just here to have coffee,' he says.

I drink from my cup and smile.

I lean back in my chair. Tiredness is shooting through twitching legs, encouraging me to stand up and walk out. Go back across the Village to my room and fall into my bed and sleep for a week, safe in the knowledge that when I wake, I'll still be the Olympic Champion. Then I remember all the interviews the morning has got planned for me.

'Look,' I say. 'I'm not being funny, I'm really not. But I'm shattered. I've got loads of press to do this morning. I'm happy to sit here and drink coffee with you and talk about our lives and the last few years and this journey we've shared as rivals and all that stuff, but let's do each other a favour. Let's just be honest with each other. OK? Cut out all the mind games. I'm retired now. I don't need it anyone more.'

He goes quiet, processes my words.

'OK.'

Pause.

He says, 'How does it feel to be retired?'

'I don't feel like I am yet. I think it'll hit me when I leave here.'

'The bubble of the Games.'

'Yep.'

'Why do you hate me?'

Despite my appeal for honesty, I'm taken aback by the directness of the question. His body language demands a serious answer. I think, *because you embarrassed me on television in front of the world; you belittled me, called me a kid, broke my heart, changed my life for the worse, you pushed me and poked me and baited me and made me hate you. Because I needed to hate you to push myself to the level required to win.*

'I don't hate you,' I say. 'I just wanted to beat you. Every time.'

Laughter explodes from him; loud and booming, echoing across the room. The other people in the place look over. He claps four times and points at me. 'That is the right answer, Adam. The right answer.'

'Why do you hate me?' I ask.

It's his turn to think.

'I don't,' he says.

The door opens and a few athletes come in and find a table. The noise level increases around us. Chairs scrape across the floor, laughter at some joke I didn't catch, in a language I don't speak.

He says, 'You lit a fire in me, though. That night in London for the Diamond League, couple years before the Olympics. In the hotel lobby, when you wanted to fight me. You said something in my ear. I don't know what it was, but I thought you've just beaten me and now you want to fight me, in front of all these people. I thought that was disrespectful. And I walked out of there and thought I'll never let him beat me again. I'm going to win in Daegu and London, on his home turf, and in Moscow. I'm going to beat him and beat him and beat him. You know, I hated the fact you were injured for Moscow. I didn't just want to win the medal. I wanted you there, watching me, standing close to me, when I beat you.'

I laugh.

'Something funny?'

'You really have no idea what I said in that hotel that day?'

'Nope.'

I lean forward. 'I thought we were stopping the mind games.'

He holds his hands up. 'I swear to God.'

'I said, "I didn't jump too badly for a fucking kid".'

I leave a gap between us, a silent space, as he flicks through the shelves of his mind looking for the memory. He comes up blank.

'In Berlin,' I say. 'You hijacked my interview. Called me a kid.' I push my finger into the table, the anger of that night in 2009 rising up in me. '"The kid jumped well", you said. The kid. You belittled me live on TV.' I hit the table again. 'And we are the same age. Do you know how many days there are between our birthdays? Three hundred and four. I know because I checked.'

I pause and breathe, then continue, 'But you made everyone think I was this lucky little kid who managed to land himself a bronze. You were the big man, though. No one should forget that. Before that, I thought the conversation we'd had in Beijing was just a bit of mind games between us. In Club Bud, when you wrote off all the other jumpers, I thought you were just trying to get in my head. The same when you came to watch me jump in America. Can I handle it? But then you called me a kid, and something changed. I wanted to prove to you, and everyone, I was a man in this world.'

'I call everyone kid.'

His words don't sink in at first. I'm still wound up from him not remembering what he said to me, still angry the moment in our rivalry that changed everything for me was nothing to him.

Then, slowly, my head comes out of the fuzz of annoyance and I hear him talking.

'It's just a throwaway term. Like *Man*. Or *Dude*. Like in the seventies when people called people *Cat*. I didn't mean any disrespect.' He shrugs. 'You know. It's natural when they ask, "how did he jump", that I would say, "The kid jumped well".'

I hide behind my coffee cup, draining the last of the liquid but holding the cup in front of my face for a couple of extra seconds.

The kid.

The kid.

'Do you want another drink?' I ask.

'Sure.'

I stand. My legs feel like they're walking through water. Less than a day ago I jumped 8.79 metres and I've not slept. The twinges of tiredness are getting worse, becoming tides washing over me.

I order our drinks and wait.

The kid.

The kid.

He calls everyone kid.

I place the cups on the table and sit.

'What was London like?' I ask. The words surprise me. They jump from my mouth like robbers from a moving train, tumbling and rolling towards him, gone before I realise.

'Greatest night of my life, kid.'

He says the words with his American accent exaggerated and I laugh, just as I'm trying to drink more coffee. The liquid spills out of my mouth and onto the table. He's laughing too now.

'It's not that funny,' he says.

'London wasn't funny at all,' I say, as I use a napkin to wipe up the coffee. I stand and get another handful, dry the table and my eyes.

I continue. 'London changed me as a person. I did things after losing in London I can never take back.'

'Like what?'

'I punched a friend at another friend's wedding.'

His turn to laugh. 'Really?'

'Yeah. I was the best man.'

'Damn. That's dark.'

'Yep. The twelve months after London were the worst of my life. I couldn't rewatch the final for nearly a year. My wife was on her hen do, bachelorette party, or whatever you guys call it, during Moscow. Obviously, I was supposed to be out of the country. Anyway, I was home, injured. I got absolutely hammered one night and broke down. She came home the next day, and I let it all out: how much London had impacted me, broken me. The next day, she sat and watched the Olympic Final with me, as some kind of attempt to give me closure on the whole thing.'

'Did it work?'

'Not really. I don't think anything will erase what happened. But last night, winning,' I see the hurt pass across his face and realise this is what my face must have done automatically for the last four years every time someone mentioned him winning in London, 'has made things a bit easier.'

'For me,' he says, 'London started in that hotel lobby after the Diamond League. Two years out. That night I spoke to my coach, and I was angry. I had no idea why we were suddenly face to face like that, but I felt disrespected. I said to my coach "No way that mother fucker is gonna beat me in London. No fucking way." Every single minute of every day I thought about London. Every training session was about beating you. I was worse after you took my World title in Daegu.'

I feel like I'm stood in front of a mirror, like I'm listening to myself.

'I didn't expect the whole thing to end like it did though.'

Me neither.

'You must have thought breaking the World Record was enough.'

'Obviously.'

'I would have.'

He pauses, drinks.

'When you broke Mike Powell's record, I thought, no way he's doing that to me. I watched you running away, celebrating, and I wanted you to suffer. Especially after taking my World Championship title from me the year before. I thought I want this guy to feel pain.'

He sits across from me, eye to eye. His words brutal.

'And I don't know how, but I made it happen.'

We say nothing for a few seconds. The weight of that night coming back to us, the realisation of what we were part of sinking in again.

'I broke the World Record, won the Olympics, and beat you in one jump. Life was perfect that night. I put everything I had, all the hate, all the anger at you beating me in Daegu, every fight I'd ever had with every girlfriend, all of it, and it worked. One centimetre was all it took to break you. At the top of the runway, I thought I was beaten but something special happened and I'll never forget your face when you realised I'd won.'

Anger boils in him, just under the surface. He's re-living his greatest moment, and it's tainted because he's sat across from me, the morning after I took his Olympic title.

'What's the real reason you're retiring?'

'I'm done. Finished.'

'I don't believe you.'

'You don't have to.'

'I think you're scared,' he says.

There he is, my rival of eight years, still trying to pick away at my skin and crawl underneath it.

'I thought we were stopping these mind games.'

'You keep saying this. Mind games, mind games.'

Our tones are harsher with each other, the mask of friendliness starting to slip.

I sigh. 'OK. I'll play along. What am I scared of?'

'London.'

Always London.

'I think you're scared of going back to London and the same thing happening. Of me stepping onto the runway and breaking your heart in front of your home crowd. You're thirty-one years old and you're telling me you're done with being an athlete. Bullshit, man. No way.'

'Have you read Dan Hall's book?'

'Yeah.'

'You know all that stuff he says about feeling shit when he retired? All the stuff about not achieving his dreams and how that made him depressed. Like he was some kind of failure?'

He nods.

'I don't want that to be me.'

'How can it be? You're the Olympic Champion.'

'And that's how I want to stay. My age, my fitness levels, I could do another a couple of years, maybe even win more medals. But even if I kept going and made it to the next Olympics, at thirty-five years old, I'm not winning. I'm doing what Dan did. Finishing sixth and retiring feeling like I shouldn't have bothered. Dan is a very good friend of mine. Some of the stuff we've talked about over the years, stuff that he didn't put in the book, it'll break your heart. He will never get over Beijing. Never. I don't want that.'

'You're not Dan Hall.'

'I know. I'm better. But it's not lasting forever. I've got another friend, Tom. He was actually with me in London that night we had our little pushing match in the hotel. He dragged me away.'

'I know who you mean.'

'Well, Tom had some hard years leading up to London. Illness, running badly. He worried about funding and sponsorship. In London he made it to an Olympic Final. Finished nowhere. But his life's dream was complete. All he ever wanted since he was six years old was to race an Olympic Final. But he got the bug. He thought, if I can make the final in London, I can make the final in Moscow. But he didn't. He got injured again, and he lost his funding. And he got a shitty job doing shitty office work, and he paid for himself to train and compete, and he tried and tried and for whatever reason life didn't deal him the right cards and his injuries flared up again and he called it a day. Retired. Never competed for his country again. And when things were bad for me, when I was struggling, I used to think; well at least I'm not Tom.'

'What's your point?'

'I don't want to turn into Tom. I don't want to spend the next few years going from being the best, to being an also ran. And I don't have to.'

'What about me?' he asks.

'What about you?'

'What am I supposed to do now?'

'I don't get your point.'

He takes a deep breath. 'For eight years we've made each other better. Most of my longest jumps have come when I've been competing against you. How am I supposed to carry on? Who's going to push me and make me better? I'm not done yet. I've still got jumps in my legs. I still want to get on that runway and face up to you and beat you.'

I feel a strange sensation pass through me. I've never seen this in him before: showing weakness.

Everything I felt about him, he feels about me.

I hated him. He hated me.

I needed him to make me better. He needed me.

'Come on, go to London.'

Pushing me.

'Let's go toe to toe, one more time.'

Goading me.

For half a second, I want to. I want to agree to his plan, to break myself over and over. Run and jump and lift, repeat. To get stronger, faster. To be an athlete again.

'Come on.'

I think of my Olympic Gold medal.

'One more time.'

I don't need him anymore.

'You'll love it.'

'No.' I snap. 'What happened in London, with you winning, taking that World Record, I'm never getting that back. That pain will be with me forever. Now I want you to remember, that when I retired, I was the World and Olympic Champion. You might go to London next year and win, but you won't ever take the World Championship from me. What you said before, about being disappointed because I was injured in Moscow, and I wasn't there to watch you beat me. I get that. But guess what? You were there in Beijing when I won last year. You watched me beat you. You looked in my eyes as I got that medal.'

He stares at me.

'And you could compete for another hundred years and you'll never take my Olympic title. You might win another fifty Olympic medals, but you'll never take mine. I'm walking away with all four.' I count them on my fingers in front of his face. 'Commonwealth, European, World, and Olympic Champion. I'm ending on my terms.'

There's a silence between us. It lasts for a second, a minute, an hour. The truth, the honesty of what I just said, is enough for both of us.

'I can never change what happened in London,' I say. 'Never un-feel that pain. But at least now I can make you feel something like it. For the rest of your life, you will experience some of that hurt. Because, you know, no matter how many medals you win between now and the end, you will never take another medal from me. And I know you. I know us. I know this rivalry.'

He can't speak. My words have pinned him to his chair.

'I know it will hurt you,' I say.

We look at each other.

Him and me.

Me and him.

'Because it would hurt me.'

Different.

The same.

Finally, he says, 'So it's over? This thing of ours. All these years, all those competitions, all those nights under the lights. Over?'

'It's over,' I say.

Another pause, another silence.

I say, 'Let me tell you something. Something no one else knows. When I was nineteen and starting to think about seriously competing in Beijing, I wrote a letter to myself. It was just a few words about what I wanted to achieve in the Games. No one knew about it, I never told anyone the contents. I sealed the envelope and hid it between the dictionary and thesaurus on the bookshelf in my front room.'

I sip some coffee. It's cold. 'We went to Beijing, and it went really well. I broke the British Record and finished fourth, to you, by two centimetres. Two fucking centimetres. A preview of London, it turns out. Everyone said it was amazing how I'd competed. But I knew when I got home, that I'd open that letter between the dictionary and the thesaurus, and I'd know that I hadn't done what I set out to do.'

'Which was?'

'Win a medal.'

'Because I beat you by two centimetres.'

'Exactly. So, we had our little chat in Club Bud, and I came home with a renewed determination. I sat down and I wrote another letter. This time about London. I sealed the envelope and placed it back between the dictionary and the thesaurus. Again, no one knew about it. Can you guess what it said?'

'Win gold in London?'

'Pretty much.'

'And I beat you by one centimetre.'

'You beat me by one centimetre.'

He drinks from his cup. I know he's suppressing a smile.

'I didn't write another letter after London. Not straight away. It took me a year. I wrote it after you won in Moscow. I got drunk that night, out of my mind. At some point, I wrote two words on a piece of paper and stuffed it in the drawer under my bed. I didn't remember it until a few weeks later, but when I took it out and read it, those two simple words became a code that I've lived my life by for the last three years. The code which has brought me to this point.'

He guesses the two words. 'Olympic Gold?'

'No.'

'All four?'

'No.'

'Are you going to tell me?'

I think about his question, wonder if I should leave him hanging. Then I realise that this man who sits across from me is probably the only person in the whole world who will understand.

And I say, 'No regrets.'

ACKNOWLEDGEMENTS

Matt Hulyer, who spent hours telling me the story of his life in long jumping. He provided an honest, sometimes difficult, insight into not only what being an athlete entails but also what it means. I'd like to thank him for believing that I wanted to tell the story of a long jumper in a real and honest way.

Jo Cook. Despite Jo and I being friends for over a decade, it was with some nerves that I asked if she'd mind reliving 'the boring stuff' from the four years of her life when she was an integral part of the senior management team for the British Water Polo teams who competed at London 2012.

It turns out one of Jo's favourite things to do is talk about the journey to London 2012. The hours we spent discussing the behind the scenes of the Olympics, along with the people who make it possible for athletes to achieve their goals and dreams, made *Running and Jumping* a better novel. I never thought looking at hundreds of photos of Olympic themed duvets and apartment blocks in the Village would be fascinating, but Jo's passion for that world made it so.

Matt Cook, for allowing me to interrupt his precious evenings with his wife, Jo, and for being a fantastic source of knowledge for all things coaching related.

Firm handshakes to Toby Turner, Justin Scholes, Paul Garner, Susan Lindon-Hall, Rene Levesley and Mark Barry for being readers of early drafts who provided helpful feedback.

Chris McDonald, Jonathan Whitelaw and Rob Parker for the support they provide in this writing life.

And finally, to my wife, Gemma, for her love and support. Dreams are easier to achieve when you've got someone in your corner encouraging you. I'm very lucky to have Gemma in mine.

There's always a fear when creating a list of people who have given up time and energy to be interviewed, help with research, or provide advice and encouragement, that I will have missed someone. Anyone who deserves their name in print but doesn't find themselves listed above, this is purely an error on my part, but it doesn't mean I'm not grateful.

Thanks,
Steven

ABOUT THE AUTHOR

Steven Kedie lives in Manchester with his wife and two sons. He is the author of the novel *Suburb*.

Details of his writing can be found at www.stevenkedie.com

Steven is also the co-founder of the music website, www.eightalbums.co.uk, where people share the reasons and stories behind why certain albums are important to them.